# The Fashion Orphans

# Also from Randy Susan Meyers

Waisted
The Widow of Wall Street
Accidents of Marriage
The Comfort of Lies
The Murderer's Daughters
Women Under Scrutiny
19 Myths About Cheating: A Novella

**Randy Susan Meyers and M.J. Rose**
The Fashion Orphans

# Also from M.J. Rose

The Last Tiara
Cartier's Hope
Tiffany Blues
The Library of Light and Shadow
The Secret Language of Stones
The Witch of Painted Sorrows
The Collector of Dying Breaths
The Seduction of Victor H.
The Book of Lost Fragrances
The Hypnotist
The Memoirist
The Reincarnationist
Lip Service
In Fidelity
Flesh Tones
Sheet Music
The Halo Effect
The Delilah Complex
The Venus Fix
Lying in Bed

**M.J. Rose and Steve Berry**
The Museum of Mysteries
The Lake of Learning
The House of Long Ago
The End of Forever

**M.J. Rose and C. W. Gortner**
The Steal
The Bait

**M.J. Rose and Randy Susan Meyers**
The Fashion Orphans

# The Fashion Orphans

RANDY SUSAN
MEYERS
AND
M.J. ROSE

BLUE
BOX
PRESS

The Fashion Orphans
By Randy Susan Meyers and M.J. Rose

Copyright 2022 Randy Susan Meyers and M.J. Rose
ISBN: 978-1-952457-70-8

Illustrations by Carol Gillott

Published by Blue Box Press, an imprint of Evil Eye
Concepts, Incorporated

# Dedication

*From M.J.*
To Liz Berry & Jillian Stein, who only see possibilities when others see problems.

*From Randy*
For Jeff,
Always

"To achieve great things, we must first dream."

— **Coco Chanel**

# Preface

## 1976

Sad little girls in New York City were not an unusual sight. Put those girls alone on a subway platform, however, and people paid attention. Strangers approached Gabrielle and Lulu when they traveled, asking questions in concerned voices: "Are you lost? Do you need help?"

Kindly police officers often knelt before them with sympathetic eyes and asked about their mother's whereabouts.

On the weekends, fewer people crowded the subway platform, giving the sisters far more breathing room as they waited for the train to Grand Central. Only one man paid much attention that Saturday; he stared at them with the sort of interest of which Gabrielle had learned to be wary. Thankfully, Grandpa had recently taught her how to scream her lungs out in dangerous situations.

With luck, the girls would arrive at their grandparents'

house in Poughkeepsie by noon. Then, finally—thankfully—Gabrielle would be off older-sister duty until their return trip on Sunday evening.

Gabrielle was twelve, and Lulu five. Though the girls appeared much younger, both possessed the wary antennae of experienced subway riders. Gabrielle, being older, one hundred percent took charge, and her rules were law. Under her guidance, Lulu stood with her back against the subway wall until the train came to a full and complete stop. They needed to hold hands—whether the thermometer read ninety-five degrees and they longed to unlock their sweaty palms, or a deep February freeze iced the city, and their hands, mittened or not, screamed to be jammed into pockets.

Today, with the weather holding a kiss of spring, their clasped hands comforted both girls.

Once the train pulled into the station, they ran, squeezing through crowds to get on before the doors slammed shut. Gabrielle always sussed out the best seats in seconds. Corners meant danger; a man could press so close you wanted to throw up. Hanging on the middle pole left you open on all sides. Both girls preferred sitting next to a mother-aged woman—grandmother-aged was better. Older seatmates were far more likely to stick up for the girls.

Flashers lurked everywhere. Even at five, Lulu understood the menace, keeping her eyes focused on people only at neck-level and above.

Once settled in the safest seats, Lulu studied her sister with a grave expression. "Who took you on the train when you were little?"

Answering Lulu's question required finesse. Before her sister's birth, Gabrielle rode only in town cars and always in the company of her mother. Gabrielle's handsome, rich father had provided every possible protection, but he'd died when she was five.

The next father—Lulu's dad—was perfectly okay, but their mother didn't care much for him. At least, that's how Grandma had explained it. He'd moved out when Lulu was three.

"I only remember one thing from when I was little," Gabrielle fibbed.

"What?" Lulu wiggled closer on the two-person seat.

"You weren't born yet, and being without you was really lonely."

Little girls riding the subway without a parent in New York might be sad, but those traveling with sisters looking out for each other were luckier than those who rode alone. Even at twelve and five, Gabrielle and Lulu knew that particular truth.

# Chapter One

## Lulu

Lulu was sick to death of death.

As she dressed for her trip into New York City, she didn't know what made her more anxious—anticipating seeing her sister or hearing her mother's will read.

No.

She knew.

Seeing Gabrielle.

Her mother's will didn't portend any surprises—Bette had made it clear for years that both of her daughters would equally share her estate. But facing Gabrielle terrified her. Lulu had seen her sister just three times in the past two and a half years—twice for funerals and once at a wedding.

The meeting at the lawyer's office wasn't till ten o'clock, but Lulu was already worried about being late. A normal person wouldn't be stopping off at work on such a stressful day, except today was the massive goodbye party for Ditmas

Junior High's beloved principal. Lulu couldn't trust Victoria, her sister-in-law and assistant, to manage both baking and decorating the gigantic cake in the shape of the principal's talismanic basketball.

And so here she was on a cold November day, at barely five-thirty a.m., rushing to dress and get to Quattros', hoping she could bake the cake, get it decorated, and make it to her mother's lawyer's office on time.

Ten minutes later, Lulu raced down Cortelyou Road toward the bakery, trying to avoid the ice patches from the previous night's freezing rain. Overstuffed ninety-nine-cent stores, windows crammed with dust mops, batteries, and cans of Spam, were wedged next to restaurants with glowing oak tables visible through immaculate smudge-free glass doors. Despite living in Brooklyn for her entire marriage, she still noticed the difference between the streets here and those of Manhattan, where she'd grown up with her mother and Gabrielle. No matter how much Brooklyn gentrified, there would always be mops positioned next to upscale coffee.

Quattros' echoed as Lulu closed the door behind her and hurried into the kitchen. After putting on her apron, she began pulling out ingredients. For the next two and a half hours, she measured, poured, mixed, rolled, and then cut fondant to create the basketball's shell.

Lulu's anxiety and sadness fought for first place as she worked, with sadness winning. She and her mother might have been oil and water, but Bette had still been her mom. Her death had made Lulu an orphan. That realization made her think about how much she still missed her father, who'd died four years ago.

And that thought almost made Lulu collapse, sure as she was that she would forever miss her husband.

The tears started to roll. But cake batter wasn't improved by saltwater, so Lulu forced her focus back to her mother's will. She had no idea how large Bette's estate might be, but based on how her mother had lived, Lulu assumed there'd be plenty to help lessen her financial woes. What would she do first? Pay off her kids' college loans? Get rid of her second mortgage? Her fiscal grocery list could unfurl from here to the cash register in the front of the store.

Lulu checked the time. Ten after nine. Now, she had to rush like hell. She cleaned up and ran out. When she reached the nearby cottage-like subway station house, she took the stairs as fast as possible, praying she wouldn't miss the train as she heard it screeching to a stop.

She barely made it aboard when the doors closed behind her. Panting and sweating, she looked around. Of course, there was no place to sit. The best the packed train offered was a spot Lulu could grab hold of on the crowded metal pole.

When she was little, only Gabrielle stood between Lulu and the looming terrors of a subway ride. Now, everything was different. She had to navigate the trains fearlessly on her own, and her relationship with Gabrielle was all but nonexistent.

Their ties had begun fraying two and a half years ago when Lulu had lost Matt to a heart attack and became a widow at forty-five. And then the remnants of their connection altogether unraveled six months later at Lulu's son's wedding. She had barely held herself together through the ceremony—there was no sturdy Matt to lean on, no beaming Matt with whom she could share her parental pride. Nobody's hand to squeeze as they took pictures in Prospect Park, across from the Brooklyn Society for Ethical Culture, the wedding site.

If Matt were there, he'd have made a snarky joke about the bride's uber-serious parents, who knelt before the altar of cultural respect as though convening directly with Jesus. If

Matt were there, Lulu would have whispered how thrilled the mother-of-the-bride seemed by the diversity the Quattro family offered Bridget's purely Lutheran family.

But Matt wasn't there. And so at the reception, Lulu drank every glass of champagne offered—the first big mistake for Lulu-the-lightweight. The second was to forget to eat more than one of her mother-in-law's mini-meatballs.

Lulu finally lost her battle to hold it together alone in the bathroom when she dissolved into an orgy of self-pity and grief. As she hiccupped through her hundredth sob, Gabrielle opened the door and walked in.

"Oh my God, Lu. Are you okay?" Her sister, a vision of perfection in a shoulder-baring red silk gown, auburn waves cascading perfectly to frame her face, plucked a tissue out of a box on the vanity and handed it to her.

Lulu blew her nose in a series of not-so-elegant honks.

Gabrielle raised her eyebrows as if aggrieved by the noise. As if, Lulu thought, the sound was déclassé or something.

And that was all it took. With alcohol washing away Lulu's inhibitions, her resentment boiled up and rushed out like hot lava.

"Am I okay?" Lulu lifted her hands in a gesture of *what the hell,* the damp tissue clutched in her right hand. "What do you think?"

"I think you're missing Matt a whole lot today and are having a much-needed cry."

Lulu's chest heaved as a fresh stream of tears began. "I'm just missing him today?"

"My God. Of course, not."

"But you really wouldn't know, would you? You haven't exactly been checking in on me, have you?"

"Checking in on you?" Gabrielle took a deep breath. "I've done as much as I could. My life has been a series of—"

"Your life? My life stopped short six months ago," Lulu shouted. "It stopped dead. And since then, my sister hasn't been to see me once. Not once!"

"I called," Gabrielle said.

"You called? The way a cousin calls. And a distant cousin, at that. Or the way a high school friend calls. But a sister?"

"I hear you, Lu, but—"

"You hear me? So where have you been? Our family is the size of a walnut. All this time, I had nobody."

Gabrielle strode to the sink, turned the water on full force, and soaked a wad of paper towels under the faucet. "You had nobody? You had a mother and two sons and about five thousand Quattro in-laws around morning, noon, and night."

"My mother? Our mother? Do you think she offered me solace? Or my sons, who were managing their own grief and their own lives? None of them could take the place of my sister."

Gabrielle wrung out the paper towels and handed them to Lulu. "Here, so your eyes don't get swollen."

Lulu threw the towels into the trash. "I don't care if my eyes swell to slits. I needed you. You, Gabi. You."

"You needed me to take care of you? Honestly? Who the hell do you think was taking care of me? Huh? My life imploded, too. You weren't the only one whose marriage ended."

Tears streamed down both their faces now. Lulu's chest tightened as Gabrielle walked over and loomed from her high-heeled advantage.

"Did you give one thought to what I was going through, Lu? The horrible humiliation of learning my whole life was a lie?"

"Your husband left. He didn't die." Lulu crossed her

arms as she warded off the tiny tentacles of guilt winding through her.

"Yes, Cole left. Along with my self-respect. My reputation. My job. Our money. With our friends' money and his backers' money. And then added the cherry of making sure it looked as though I was as much to blame for the entire debacle as he was."

Cole, a major theater producer, hadn't just been accused of fraud and almost landed in jail, but, as Lulu had learned from their mother, he'd been cheating on Gabrielle for years.

"The play didn't just bomb. Our *life* bombed. I'm sorry if there wasn't enough of me left for you." Gabrielle sunk onto a small white stool in the corner.

"But Cole didn't die. He didn't die," Lulu couldn't shout that last word loud enough. *Die* echoed in the small room. "You left me alone when I needed you most."

"And when *I* needed *you* the most. Why didn't you tell me how you were feeling?" Gabrielle asked.

"Why didn't you?"

"You don't get to be the little sister forever, you know." Gabrielle pushed her hair off her face. "At some point, you gotta grow up."

"That's what you are turning this into? Me needing to grow up?" Lulu shouted. "You're gonna stand there and chastise me? Now? Today? You have some nerve."

The bathroom door opened, and with her usual perfect timing, their mother entered. Bette looked from one daughter to the other. "I can hear you both above the music. Whatever is going on in here must stop right now."

Bette reached into her bag, pulled out a small packet, and handed it to Lulu. "Take one and give it to your sister."

"*La Fresh Makeup Remover Wipes.*" Lulu read out loud with some sarcasm. She looked at Gabrielle to share the *oh-my-God-this-is so-our-mother* moment but then, remembering how angry she was, avoided the eye contact. Instead, she took a wipe and threw the packet at Gabrielle.

Gabrielle glanced at the packet and then into the mirror. "I guess my so-called waterproof Chanel mascara lied."

The subway train lurched.

Lights flickered as they entered the tunnel.

Lulu stumbled against the man behind her.

She and Gabrielle hadn't seen each other since the great bathroom battle, not until almost two years later, last month, at their mother's funeral.

Lulu reached out to get a better grip on the pole. As she did, her coat sleeve rode up. On her shirt cuff were two streaks of bright blue dried frosting from the piping she'd written on the coach's basketball: *Welcome to your new life, Mr. Marsh.*

# Chapter Two

## Gabrielle

Bette returned from the beyond each time Gabrielle studied her reflection. There was no escaping genetics.

Curse or blessing?

As she dressed for the lawyer's reading of her mother's will, it seemed as though the woman in the mirror was Bette-from-twenty-five-years-ago. Gabrielle shared most of her mother's features, starting with their dark green eyes—when Lulu was four, she'd called them spinach eyes.

Dabbing on foundation, thinking about Lulu, Gabrielle sighed. She dreaded today. She and her sister had survived their mother's funeral only because Bette had left such detailed instructions—including her burial outfit—with her lawyer. Lulu and Gabrielle had only needed to show up at Frank Campbell's, the brick and white-trimmed building two blocks away from where Bette had lived. Their mother considered it the Bergdorf Goodman of funeral homes;

neither Gabrielle nor Lulu were surprised that Bette had arranged to say her last goodbye there.

The sisters had both sat in the first row but safely separated by Lulu's sons and their partners. They'd kept in that same formation at the gravesite. Also dictated by Bette's instructions, there had been no sitting shiva.

Gabrielle blended a smear of concealer under her eyes and into the corners, which Bette always insisted was critical after age fifty. Done, she uncapped the blackest liner Chanel made and, leaning forward, applied the soft pencil.

Use thin lines to build to the desired thickness, Bette had instructed. Seal with a slick of black eyeshadow. Finish with a light sweep of translucent powder.

Following Bette's cosmetic rules, Gabrielle then applied lipstick, followed by blotting and a dusting with translucent powder.

As she dabbed perfume, not her mother's Chanel No. 5, but Chanel's Coramandel, which Bette had gifted her, Gabrielle ached. She missed her mother. She was realistic about Bette's faults.

Demanding too much of her and often judging her harshly? Yes.

Screwing up plenty when she and Lulu were little? Yes.

But Bette never failed to answer the phone when Gabrielle called and was ever ready to meet for a quick lunch or leisurely dinner—often to offer advice whether asked for or not. Yes, she argued with Gabrielle and often found fault with her, but your mother lives in your blood. Who you are is who she was. And now, part of Gabrielle was gone. Forever. And today would be an even more brutal reminder of that.

She packed away her maudlin thoughts. Too emotional from the time she was a child, Bette always said, teaching Gabrielle to put a lid on her emotions. Careful to avoid her

makeup, Gabrielle slipped a dark tweed dress ov
zipped it up, and then examined herself. The r
ran up the left hip line was a detail that added interest and
cut the dress's severity. She'd chosen today's outfit from her
carefully preserved pre-divorce wardrobe of edgy high-end
fashion and jewelry that she could no longer afford. Today's
dress came from her Isabel Marant phase. Gabrielle was a
theatrical costume designer—or she had been until Cole cut
her career off at the knees. She'd never lost the habit of
seeing every day as a series of scenes and dressing for the
part she'd be playing.

Today she played the grieving daughter. The reading of
her mother's will called for moving down one notch from
funeral wear. Tweed replaced black, and small diamond studs
took the place of pearls. She slipped on high-heeled suede
boots rather than stacked pumps. The weather looked
threatening, so she'd allow herself the luxury of taking a cab
both ways.

Well, at least she and Lulu wouldn't be fighting over
their mother's estate. Bette had made a point to tell both her
daughters that they would inherit equally. When Gabrielle's
father died, his will had caused a family crisis. And Bette had
said she'd never do that to her daughters. Gabrielle couldn't
quite remember what that problem had been, but she
thought it rested on family heirlooms. She'd only been five
years old when her father died—three days past her birthday.

A sense of doom hung over all her birthday celebrations
after that. And then, to make it worse, seven years later, four
days before Gabrielle's birthday, Lulu came along. Sharing
her special day felt unfair when Gabrielle was younger and
annoying as she got older. Sibling rivalry complicated every
birthday, though, oddly, Bette had managed to provide
bright spots without fail. Her mother, whose self-absorption
could sometimes rival Miranda Priestly's in *The Devil Wears*

*Prada*, always rose to the occasion.

Perhaps over-the-top celebrations were Bette's way of avoiding the tragedy marking the day her beloved husband had passed. Each October twenty-third, smack in the middle of her and Lulu's birthdays, Bette would pull off something magical. One year, she'd orchestrated a birthday dinner at Windows on the World restaurant, ensuring that a cake with candles came out at sunset. The memory made 9-11 feel uniquely sadly personal for the sisters.

For Gabrielle's sixteenth birthday—Lulu's ninth—Bette had hosted their friends with front row seats for a matinee of *Cats* on Broadway and then organized an after-party attended by some of the cast. In costume. Arranged through someone Bette had been dating at the moment, of course. So many of her beaus had connections.

Bette was a special-occasion kind of mother—far better at big-bang moments than daily routine child management.

Gabrielle slipped on her wide Elsa Peretti silver cuff. The bracelet always made her feel fierce, and she anticipated she might need the extra support today. Not just because she'd be seeing Lulu, but because, knowing Bette, there would be some kind of fireworks.

# Chapter Three

## Lulu

Lulu arrived at Diana Hayes Esq.'s office as Gabrielle was hanging up her coat. Her urge to hug her sister battled with fear that their feud might rekindle with a single misspoken word. Gabrielle's wary expression suggested that her sister was just as nervous about being together without buffers. Or was she just anxious about what they were about to learn?

"Hey, Gabi." The childhood nickname slipped out. Lulu offered a tentative smile.

"Hey, Lu." Gabrielle returned an equally uncertain smile.

Was Gabrielle looking at her weirdly? Had she noticed the smear of frosting on her sleeve? And so what if she did? An honest day's work for an honest dollar.

Lulu examined her sister—she wasn't the picture of perfection, either. Yes, Gabi wore cutting-edge fashion, and her boots were unscuffed, but she looked drawn. Her hair didn't have its usual sheen. Her skin looked a tad slacker than it had even two weeks ago. Gabrielle was getting older.

Just like Lulu.

Damn, this was depressing. And with that, Ms. Hayes came out to greet them. They'd only met two weeks ago at the hospital the day Bette had died—a gloomy presence unexpected at their mother's bedside.

"Good morning, ladies. Thank you for being prompt." Ms. Hayes' steely expression matched the monochromatic gray tones of her outer office, ash-colored suit, and sharply razored short, silver hair. Only a strand of pink-toned pearls brightened the sea of drab gray, gray, gray. She offered her hand to Gabrielle first.

Of course. The eldest sister. Always treated with more respect. Next, the Gray Lady—as Lulu would now always think of her—turned and offered her the same hand.

"Let's go into my office. Would either of you care for coffee? I can also offer tea."

Gabrielle asked for water. Lulu said she'd have the same.

Once they were seated in a large and well-appointed room, done in more monochromatic gray, and each had a bottle of water—with a glass—Ms. Hayes lifted the file marked *Bette Bradford: Last Will & Testament.*

"Once again, I am so sorry for your loss. Your mother was a fine woman."

Lulu murmured a faint, "*Thank you.*" Gabrielle did the same.

"If neither of you has any outstanding questions, I'll begin. Are you both ready?"

Lulu nodded. Gabrielle said she was.

Ms. Hayes began. "I intend for my daughters—"

"Could you give us copies to read ourselves instead?" Gabrielle interrupted.

"I'm afraid not," Ms. Hayes said. "Your mother requested that the reading proceed this way."

"But she's not here," Gabrielle said. "And I hate people reading at me."

Lulu sent a silent *stop* towards her sister; she just wanted today to go smoothly.

Ms. Hayes picked up a silver pen, wrote a few words on her yellow legal pad, and half-smiled. "Duly noted."

Lulu shook her head slightly at Gabrielle, hoping she'd let the issue go. Gabrielle's responding eye roll signaled that Lulu should stop being such a wimp.

How could they, at what should be the most solemn of occasions, still manage to bring out the worst in each other? Lulu wanted to let go of everything from the past two years just wish it away. Last month, she'd agonized over picking out Gabrielle's birthday card, growing impatient when she read the treacly Hallmark cards filled with sisterly adoration. Where were the cards emblazoned with Emily Dickenson's wisdom: *Sisters are brittle things.*

"If there are no other issues, I'll resume?"

"Certainly," Lulu said.

Gabrielle nodded.

The Gray Lady picked up where she'd left off, reading in her dry, dispassionate tone. "I intend for my daughters, Gabrielle Jeanne Bradford Winslow, and Loire Bonheur Gold Quattro, to preserve and value—"

Hearing her given name, *Loire*, startled Lulu.

"Did Bette think we'd be confused with another Gabrielle and Loire if she didn't use all four parts of our names?" Gabrielle interrupted again.

Ms. Hayes cleared her throat and continued.

Gabrielle reached into her huge Prada bag and pulled out a small notebook and pen.

"No need to take notes. I'll be giving you a copy of the

will," Ms. Hayes said.

"I just think better with paper and pen in my hand," Gabrielle explained.

Lulu watched as her sister sketched an oval, followed by almond shapes, then a triangle, and started shading. In seconds, a likeness of Bette began to appear. Gabrielle, Bette, and Lulu all used doodling to manage anxiety, but Gabrielle was the most accomplished artist.

Ms. Hayes ignored Gabrielle's sketching and began reading from the beginning again. "I intend for my daughters, Gabrielle Jeanne Bradford Winslow and Loire Bonheur Gold Quattro, to preserve and value, as I did, the items in my collection. Everything is carefully wrapped and particularized in a manner meant to bring forth their appreciation and understanding."

"Appreciation of what?" Gabrielle asked.

"Collection of what?" Lulu asked at almost the same time. The only thing her mother might have collected that interested her right now was cash.

*Come on, Mom. Rescue me.*

Lulu twisted the handles of her black canvas tote. Unlike her sister's bag, her worn carryall bore no label, though it was decorated with an image of Ruth Bader Ginsburg's lace collar. Bette had hated the bag. Lulu didn't know why she'd carried it today; she owned other perfectly acceptable handbags. Why did she still need to rebel against her mother by schlepping around frayed fabric with a political message?

The lawyer tapped her pen on the desktop.

"Sorry. Go on," Lulu said.

The Gray Lady continued. "My possessions are to be divided equally between my daughters. The money I leave is also to be equally distributed." Ms. Hayes looked up and spoke directly to them. "Which, after accounting for the funeral and other incidentals, should be in the range of fifty-one thousand dollars."

Lulu heard Gabrielle's sharp intake of breath, which matched her own. Bette had kept her net worth a life-long secret. When Lulu allowed herself moments of hope, she imagined her mother might be worth multiple millions, although knowing how little Bette deprived herself, she could just as easily have much less.

But fifty-one thousand dollars?

Gabrielle and Lulu stared at each other. The lawyer must have misread the figure. Their mother's last husband was no Midas, but he hung out in the upper brackets. Bette had sold their oversized condo when he died and moved to a rental—alluding to wanting to stay liquid and be safe. By that, Lulu assumed Bette had bought treasury bonds and the stuffiest of stocks. Surely, there should be more left.

The lawyer returned to reading. "Said money is only to be distributed after the proper time and attention is given to decisions around my possessions. Rent must be paid on my apartment while Gabrielle and Loire decide how they want to divide or dispose of what is contained therein. They are to check in with my lawyer, Diana Hayes, Esquire, regularly until they have come to an agreed upon plan, which must then be presented to Ms. Hayes, who will be the sole and final arbiter in greenlighting their decision and allowing Gabrielle and Loire to move forward and release the apartment."

Not only were they not getting a penny upfront, but what the heck was this collection? And what kind of twisted path had Bette concocted for them to go on? Together, no less.

"What the hell!" Gabrielle echoed Lulu's innermost thoughts. "She's gone, but she can still dictate to us?"

"She can, and she has." Ms. Hayes plowed ahead. "Your

mother had an excellent deal for her apartment, so this isn't as bad as it might be. I believe friendship with the building's owner determined the rent."

Lulu knew what that meant.

Bette's first husband underwrote her life. The husband in the middle—Lulu's father—had forced Bette back to work. Her charming third husband—whom Bette had married when she was sixty-two and then lost shortly after—had restored her standard of living back to the level of comfort she appreciated. In widowhood, a *male friend* here and there provided additional support. Her daughters never met those friends, but they'd understood what was going on.

"How much is the rent?" Gabrielle asked.

"Twenty-five hundred dollars per month…"

Lulu added, subtracted, and multiplied in her head. Minus the money spent for the funeral, obituary, and other costs incurred by Bette's death—if they settled upon a decision agreeable to the Gray Lady within two months—about eighteen thousand dollars would remain for each sister. And that was if she and Gabrielle could agree that quickly—an unimaginable possibility.

Eighteen thousand dollars wouldn't make a dent in Lulu's overdue mortgage, home equity loans, and her son's never-ending college loan payments.

"And, of course, you need to include the cost of my going over your plans," the lawyer added.

The dent in her mountain of debt became a dimple.

"Was Bette playing a joke?" Gabrielle asked the lawyer.

Lulu slumped in her chair. "If so, it's a cruel one. But given that our mother was hardly a master of comedy when she was alive, I doubt facing death improved her sense of humor. Her will isn't funny; it's a disaster."

Gabrielle sighed and gave a what-can-we-do shrug. "I guess we just have to unearth this collection. Maybe while we're searching, we'll find a pair of Mom's shoes that will fit you." Gabrielle eyed Lulu's scuffed boots.

"Again. Just to be clear, the collection is to remain intact until I approve of how you want to disperse it. Let me get you the keys." Rising, the Gray Lady walked over to the file cabinet in the corner, unlocked it, and rifled through the top drawer.

"What kind of damn collection could she have that warranted practically writing a constitution?" Gabrielle asked. "And kept a secret?"

"And is using to control us," Lulu added.

"From the great beyond." Gabrielle looked up as though Bette might be hovering above.

Lulu never shared Gabrielle's woo-woo spiritual interests. Still, this time she had a point—beginning with how Bette had left instructions barring them from her apartment after her death until the reading of the will today. Everything needed for the funeral—clothes, makeup, hair instruction, and picture choices for the funeral brochure—Bette had left in the lawyer's possession. Lulu had wondered why. Now, maybe they'd find out.

Ms. Hayes turned, holding a padded envelope. Reaching in, she brought out their mother's treasured keychain. Lulu felt a warm surge of recognition upon seeing the iconic golden Chanel bottle shining in the gray-toned office.

The lawyer swung the keychain slightly as she held it aloft. "Remember. All plans must meet with my approval. No borrowing for personal use, and nothing leaves the apartment."

After their final goodbyes, Lulu trudged out of the office—Gabrielle followed, seeming similarly flattened. Neither spoke as they went down the elevator and through the lobby. The November chill hit them the moment they opened the front door.

Gabrielle raised her arm to hail a cab.

"Let's walk. We're only ten blocks from Bette's. We're not made of sugar." Lulu frowned after the words had popped out. In what world did it make sense to be goading her sister now?

"Oh, God. Are you quoting your Flatbush grandmother? Fine. We'll walk," Gabrielle said and hoisted her shoulder bag higher.

"My grandparents might have been provincial, but your father's parents were snobs. So, we're equal," Lulu said.

Except they were never equal. How did one make equals of sisters who'd grown up in virtually opposite families? Any childhood weekend that she and Gabrielle didn't visit Bette's parents in Poughkeepsie, Lulu was in Brooklyn with her father and grandparents, eating Grandma's roast chicken, ice skating in Prospect Park, and bowling at Leader Lanes. Meanwhile, Gabrielle remained in Manhattan, swanning around Bergdorf's with Bette.

"My toes are frozen." Gabrielle pulled her collar tighter.

"This isn't cold," Lulu lied.

Gabrielle extracted her phone from her bag, hit the weather icon, and held the phone just inches from Lulu's face. "Look! Thirty-seven degrees. Only five degrees above freezing. It's cold!"

"If you wore an actual winter coat instead of that—" Lulu started.

"By actual winter coat, you mean a feathered marshmallow that makes you look like the Michelin man about to ski?"

Lulu eyed her sister's expensive-looking coat, her— cashmere, doubtless—scarf, and the fancy boots. Jealousy rose, along with regret. Lulu wanted to offload the feelings clogging her chest. She noticed her sister falling behind, struggling to keep up.

"You could walk better without stilts, you know." Damn, that wasn't what Lulu wanted to say at all.

Gabrielle stopped and put her hands on her hips. "You know why I wanted to take a cab? These are my last pair of decent boots. I didn't want to ruin them."

Shame rushed through Lulu. She didn't own the patent on misery. Gabrielle had lost so much in her divorce—and now, she'd lost Bette. She'd always been closer to their mother than Lulu was. Gabrielle had never had kids, never left Manhattan, and never rejected Bergdorf's.

"Sorry," Lulu said.

Gabrielle shrugged. "That's okay."

They stopped at the next corner for the light.

"Why did Bette saddle us with that ridiculous will? What was she thinking?" Gabrielle asked.

"Just more of the Bette show." Lulu blinked against sudden guilty tears. Being Bette's daughter wasn't easy, but she was still her mother. And now, she was gone. "She always had such a commanding presence. Except at the end. She seemed incredibly sad the last time I saw her."

"Well, she was in the hospital," Gabrielle said.

"This was different. As if Bette were looking back…" Lulu tried to find the words to describe their mother's mood in those last days. "As though she longed for something. She seemed bereft. Always staring at your father's picture."

"She thought she and my father did it all perfectly. But screwing up a marriage is hard when your husband dies only four years and five months after saying '*I do*.'"

Lulu hugged herself through her puffy coat. Matt's death had provided Lulu with more understanding of Bette's life-long mourning, though she'd trade her insight for her former ignorance. She missed her husband so much that the enormity of wanting him frightened her. The day Matt died, her world had dimmed to a hazy gray, and everything good stopped.

Two and a half years later, Lulu still waited to spot a single bit of color.

"Bette talked about seeing Oliver again—it was the only thing that made her smile," Lulu said. "But about other things, she seemed as if... I'm not sure. Maybe she had regrets."

"Was your father like that before he died?" Gabrielle asked.

Lulu laughed. "Not him. Even his bad decisions satisfied him."

"I envy people like that." Gabrielle wrapped her scarf tighter as the wind picked up. "Sometimes, I wonder what it's like to be satisfied with who you are and your accomplishments. What a miracle for your father."

Lulu turned and stared. Gabrielle's appearance would lead anyone to believe she lived every moment in the comfort of confidence. Though not quite as beautiful as Bette, Gabrielle resembled her to an extraordinary degree: tall and leggy with a model's stride, high cheekbones, and slanted, olive-green eyes that promised rumpled sheets. Bette and Gabrielle were knockouts who attracted male attention like magnets.

Lulu didn't, though the difference didn't bring self-pity. Lulu recognized her qualities and deficits. Glossy deep brown hair was the only asset she shared with her mother and sister. Other than that, while her mother and sister smoldered, Lulu only sparkled, even on her best days. The rest of the time, she counted on cheery and wholesome, grateful that, despite working in a bakery and not walking into a gym since college, her clothing size stayed the same.

Bette and Gabrielle's undercurrent of dissatisfaction frustrated her. What a waste of glamour and beauty. Most of the female world spent their lives chasing what God had gifted her mother and sister.

"You should never be anything but thrilled with yourself," Lulu said.

Gabrielle appeared taken aback by Lulu's praise. "Thanks. I'll spare you an enumeration of my regrets. So that's what you think Bette was feeling? Regret?"

"Learning Sanskrit would be easier than deciphering our mother." Lulu stuck her hands deep into her pockets. "Let's hope this mystery collection—whatever it might be—holds a few clues."

# Chapter Four

## Lulu

Lulu stopped at the corner for the next red light.

Gabrielle glanced to the left. "There's no traffic, c'mon; I can't wait in this cold."

Lulu fell into younger-sister mode and blindly followed her sister's jaywalking.

Gabrielle stepped up to the curb. "I never noticed any so-called collection. For the life of me, I can't think of what it is. Was it something right out in the open that I missed?"

"If you did, so did I," Lulu said.

"Maybe it's something odd and unexpected—like snow globes from every country in the world."

Lulu laughed. "Maybe we'll find a trunk filled with first-edition Wonder Woman comics. Or twenty boxes of Victorian postcards."

"That's such a random and weird idea. I kind of love it. Now I'll be disappointed by anything else." Gabrielle gave

Lulu one of those approving grins that Lulu used to wait for when they were together. Feeling this warmth after so long, she never wanted to lose it again.

"I keep thinking about those last days at the hospital," Lulu said. "She never hinted about a damn collection."

"She didn't say anything to me, either."

Lulu shook her head. "I kept trying to find ways to make her smile, like reading gossipy bits from *Vogue*. Maybe I didn't try hard enough," Lulu said.

"At least you tried. I didn't have any idea what to do," Gabrielle said.

It was true; Lulu had tried repeatedly. Trying to please Bette had been Lulu's hobby since kindergarten. In her first effort to consciously collect one of her smiles, Lulu had memorized her mother's favorite Sarah Vaughan song, *Come Rain or Come Shine*. Bette listened to the album so often that spots of Vaughan's iridescent halter top had worn away.

Once Lulu deemed her memorization suitable, she sat her mother in the living room and performed for her, swaying as she sang. Bette's lips turned up as she listened, even as her eyes shimmered. Seeing her mother's reaction, Lulu became ever more energetic as she belted out the song.

Years later, she'd learned that she'd been serenading Bette with her and Oliver's song.

"Those last days, did she ever ask you for anything?" Gabrielle asked.

"She asked me to hold her hand a few times."

"I think I'm jealous."

"She only did that at the very end." Lulu wanted to mitigate Gabrielle's pain. Once a pleaser, always a pleaser. "One night, she asked me to tell her what I thought she'd done right. As a mother. Be glad you didn't get that."

"Oh, God, Lu. What did you say?"

"I could only think of the wrong things she did. I want

to die thinking about it. What a horrible moment. Finally, I choked out that she always made sure we were well-dressed."

"You didn't!" Gabrielle laughed.

Lulu joined her in the intimate sick humor that only sisters could share. "I felt like shit after I said it. So, I added that I admired the way she kept her apartment immaculate."

"So, we were well-dressed, and she was a clean freak."

"Gabrielle. Please. Don't make me feel worse. I froze. I'd do anything for a do-over."

"Worst Bette; best Bette. Don't think! Just say," Gabrielle said.

How long since they played the familiar game that Gabrielle introduced when Lulu was in junior high? As instructed, Lulu blurted out the first memories that came to mind. "Best: The first time Bette saw Nicholas. My baby! He was only three days old. I thought my life was over. Hell, I was only eighteen years old. Can you imagine? Bette came into the bedroom—we were still living with Matt's parents—and found me crying.

"She took Nicholas, and she held him so naturally, as though she knew what she was doing—which amazed me. I never forgot what she said. 'You never fall in love harder than when you see your baby for the first time. Realizing their life depends on you is terrifying.' She was right."

"She said that?" Gabrielle said. "Wow. She fell in love with me? Why do I find that a surprise?"

"Bette didn't exactly ooze emotions."

Gabrielle nodded. "Quick worst?"

"Oh, God! When she took me shopping for a wedding dress. I wanted something flowing and comfortable. Something suitable for a three-months-pregnant bride. I came out of the dressing room in a cotton dress, inset with lace bands on the long sleeves and embroidered with flowers. I probably looked like I flew in from the Swiss Alps, but I thought I encompassed Mother Earth. I loved it. Bette took one look, handed me her credit card, shook her head, and walked out without a word."

They arrived at Bette's building before Gabrielle could share her best/worst. The pre-war building might not be as elegant as those lining Fifth Avenue, but it carried the coveted 10021 zip code that Bette had worshipped. Bette and Oliver had begun their marriage living in that rarefied section of the Upper East Side, in an apartment she described as only a bit less sumptuous than Windsor Castle. Bette held on as long as possible after Oliver died, but her money ran out. Her next home was a bleak apartment on Second Avenue, far from the fairyland where she'd been so happy.

Lulu's father had turned out to have less money than Bette thought, but pregnancy had forced their marriage. Divorce soon followed. Lulu attended a mediocre Manhattan public school, while Gabrielle studied at the prestigious and private Dalton, paid for by her father's trust.

"Good afternoon, Miss Gabrielle. Miss Lulu." Bette's elderly liveried doorman doffed his cap and opened the door. Harry's gloves were never really white. His uniform was far less starched than his counterparts guarding the entrances around the corner in the expensive co-ops on Fifth. Bette pretended not to see his shortcomings; a doorman was a doorman, and their mother needed a doorman.

When the elevator opened on the tenth floor, Lulu and Gabrielle walked down the familiar hallway. Bette lived there for the past fifteen years, long enough for Lulu and her sister to build arrival rituals. Lulu always walked ahead and rang the bell, while Gabrielle hung back a bit to freshen up her lipstick and check her hair. If Gabrielle didn't walk in looking *done*, Bette's frown appeared. Their mother didn't even step out of the apartment to get the mail without being *done.*

Bette had long before given up expecting much from Lulu in the appearances department.

Lulu inhaled as she stepped over the apartment's threshold. The scent of Chanel No. 5 lingered in the apartment entry. Smelling the perfume saddened her more than the morning's melancholic event. Bette never wore any other fragrance, and just one whiff brought sharp details of Bette to mind.

The sisters stood in the foyer as if awaiting instructions. Bright noon sun lit the pale cream walls of the living room visible ahead. Louis-something-style chairs flanked a long couch—Bette had drummed style nomenclature into her daughters since infancy, but only Gabrielle had cared to learn it enough for the words to stick. Now, though, Lulu saw the apartment with different eyes. How carefully her mother had taken care of her things. The black and gold upholstery, broken up by vivid red cushions, appeared as plump as the day they had been delivered. But despite its pristine condition, an ineffable air of neglect hung over the apartment.

Gabrielle had turned to study the French, early-twentieth-century posters covering the walls. One advertised Dubonnet, one a theater, and two featured, as Bette had taught them, the famous chanteuse, Mistinguette.

"You think those are valuable?" Lulu asked.

"A bit. If they're originals." Gabrielle moved closer to the lithograph showing the singer's face surrounded by roses.

"Paying-off-college valuable, or going-away-for-a-weekend valuable?"

"If they aren't reproductions, they could be worth anywhere from $1,000 to $5,000 each, depending on the quality and the condition."

"Do you think the posters are the collection?" Lulu asked.

"Four posters do not a collection make. You know my father bought these, Lu. God, I love them. The bold colors. The graphics. They're my childhood framed." She hugged herself as she stared.

Lulu didn't feel like talking about Gabrielle's childhood or Gabrielle's father. She hoped her sister didn't think the posters should be hers because Oliver had purchased them. By those standards, Gabrielle might as well get everything.

"I never expected her to die," Gabrielle said, breaking the melancholic silence. "I miss her. I keep expecting her to walk in."

"Me, too," Lulu said.

Their mother had rarely spoken of her end-of-life planning and then only in very general terms—the opposite of Lulu's mother-in-law. Once Annette hit seventy-five, her mother-in-law would regularly invite her children and their spouses for what Lulu and Matt called the death pre-shows. Matt's mom would spread her few *real* jewels, as she called them, across her spotless satin bedspread and then give them the background of each piece.

"This bracelet is gold. Real gold. Eighteen carats," Annette would emphasize, as though describing the Hope Diamond. "From Italy. None of the junk they sell here. My father bought it for my mother in Florence. This bowl." Annette would pick it up as though handling a newborn. "Murano glass. From Venice. *Never let the children play with this!*"

Perhaps it was Lulu's imagination, but she swore her mother-in-law narrowed her eyes at her in particular, as though left unwarned, Lulu might encourage her sons to use the bowl to play soccer.

With every piece, Matt's mother asked, "Now who

wants this?" Annette held up the same treasures at each viewing, never acknowledging past shows or previous hands raised to claim the bowl, the ropy gold chains, or the pearl earrings. The bedroom spectacles were as regular a part of the Quattro tradition as Sunday lasagna.

Bette never invited her daughters into her bedroom to drag out possessions from hidden recesses and discuss who would inherit. Gabrielle's and Lulu's visits to their mother's apartment were limited to company areas: the kitchen, living and dining room, and the small powder room off the foyer.

Lulu walked the living room's perimeter, laying a light finger first on a shining silver nut bowl and then on a Lalique vase.

After a few moments, Lulu realized she was holding her breath while hunching her shoulders. "I keep thinking of how Mom would warn us away when we got too near her precious stuff. She made me feel like a worm sprinkled with salt."

"I swear she copyrighted the way she could say, '*Girls! Freeze!*'" Gabrielle said.

Lulu held up her hands as though halting the memories. "Today, we're under instructions to poke around. Let's figure out what's here, what we want to do with it, and then present our plan to the Gray Lady."

"The Gray Lady?"

Lulu explained the nickname and made her sister laugh. "Do you think she'd shrivel if we waved some color at her?"

"No doubt."

They inspected tabletops and shelves in the living room, then the kitchen, and finally, the dining room, opening every drawer and cabinet. On the way out, Gabrielle picked up a jeweled and feathered bowl off the table. "This is Jay Strongwater."

All Lulu saw was a gaudy multi-colored bowl resembling

peacock feathers. "And that's meaningful because?"

"Because it's magnificent," Gabrielle said.

"Expensive?"

"Bette probably paid about a thousand dollars for this."

"Seriously?" The piece looked no different from the kind of overwrought design cluttering Annette's house. She only hoped Strongwater pieces held their value on the secondary market.

"But it's not part of a collection," Lulu said.

"No, one piece does not a collection make," Gabrielle said.

"What if all of it is the collection?" Lulu asked.

"As far as I can tell, even all added up, it's not worthy of what she suggested in the will." Gabrielle looked around, baffled. "Nice things, sure, but nothing rates the attention Bette wanted us to give it. Nothing matches the words"— she affected the lawyer's voice—"*carefully wrapped and particularized in a manner meant to bring forth their appreciation and understanding.*"

"There's still her bedroom." Lulu pointed to the hallway.

"Sure," Gabrielle said. "But what could be there? Bette lost her serious jewelry."

Lulu nodded. Once upon a time, Bette had owned a king's ransom of gold, gemstone, and diamond jewelry. All gifts from Oliver. All stolen during a rash of inside robberies in the Second Avenue building.

As the sisters walked down the short hall and approached the bedroom, Lulu said, "I don't think I went in her bedroom very often. Now that I think of it, maybe never in all the time that Bette lived here. How weird is that?"

"Very weird. And now that you mention it, I never went in either. Bette wasn't exactly the cuddle-on-the-bed-and-watch-old-movies type."

"But you'd think we'd have gone in there occasionally," Lulu insisted. "That's only normal. What was she hiding? The dead bodies of her old beaus? A chest of handcuffs and feather boas?"

"Ugh. Don't put those images in my head. Privacy. That's what Bette wanted. It was her comfort zone. She never liked us in her bedroom when we lived on Second Avenue, either, remember? Not at six, not at sixteen," Gabrielle said.

They opened the bedroom door, almost tiptoeing as they entered. At first glance, all Lulu noticed was the repetitive monochromatic color scheme. As soon as Lulu had been able to choose her décor at her Binghamton University dorm room, bright explosions of color became her mainstay.

"Does it strike you that this room is tiny?" Gabrielle asked. "Master bedrooms are never this small in pre-war buildings. The whole configuration is odd."

The two sisters stood for another moment, inspecting the space. The paint and wall-to-wall carpet were cream-colored, just like the rest of the apartment. Only the living room's vibrant red accents were missing. Ivory surrounded them. Not practical, but lush. Lushly boring.

Lulu wondered if her mother had ever worn shoes in this room.

A queen-sized bed, covered with a rich cream and gold bedspread, took up too much of the available space. Opposite, a delicate gold and black velvet chair was tucked beneath a vanity table topped by a large, round mirror.

Lulu almost laughed as she compared it to her shabby not-so-chic bedroom at home. Her piles of books. The worn but precious wedding ring patchwork quilt made by Matt's aunts. One of Matt's sweaters that Lulu clung to, hanging over the back of the chair by the desk.

"Well, let's get started." Lulu entered the en suite bathroom outfitted with fluffy black and cream-colored towels. Didn't Bette ever yearn for something bright? She went straight to her mother's medicine cabinet. The top shelf held typical sundries but all in identical black-capped bottles and jars. "They match. Every single one."

Gabrielle joined her. "Chanel. All of them. Serum. Moisturizer. Foundation. Toner. She never bought any other brand."

Lulu opened a drawer, uncovering a portioned lipstick storage unit. "There must be every single lipstick color Chanel has ever made. I knew she bought a lot of cosmetics, but this is crazy."

"You know, this color..." Gabrielle plucked a tube, uncapped it, and twisted the black plastic until a muted red emerged. "Would look great on you." She moved towards Lulu, who swatted the lipstick away.

"I hate the feel of lipstick."

"Of course, you do."

"What does that mean?"

"Nothing." Gabrielle returned the lipstick to the drawer. "Bette probably changed her mind about how to dispose of her so-called collection and did something else with whatever it was. "

"Like selling it to get more lipstick," Lulu said.

"Let's finish up and get out of here. Go get something to eat," Gabrielle said as she stepped out of the bathroom.

How long had it been since she and Gabrielle had shared a meal? Even before the great battle, their lives had diverged. "Why don't we splurge on as much lobster and wine and something chocolate that fifty-one thousand dollars minus burial costs can buy?" Lulu followed her sister back into the bedroom.

Gabrielle had stopped and was just standing by the

window, looking around. "This room is just too small," she said. "And the proportion is out of sync with the other rooms in the apartment."

"Let's not get all caught up in the failings of some 1940-era architect. Think lobster. Chocolate. Wine."

"You're right." Gabrielle walked toward the closet. "We're almost done."

"Maybe Bette was losing it?" Lulu lifted the cover of a small china box on the vanity, praying to see a diamond wink. Instead, she found a small tortoise hair chip. "Could dementia have been starting? Maybe she became delusional and thought the lipstick collection in the bathroom was worth something and—"

Gabrielle opened the closet doors. There was a beat. And then her voice rang out with a new urgency. "Lulu! Come here."

Lulu put down the clip, turned, and joined Gabrielle.

"Holy mother of God," she whispered, all talk of mental capacity and lipstick abandoned.

# Chapter Five

## Gabrielle

Gabrielle froze, unable to move beyond the closet entrance. Nobody beyond the wealthiest possessed walk-ins this large or magnificently appointed—certainly not in Manhattan, where residents coveted every square foot.

Automatically triggered lights spread a warm glow over an astonishing array of what must undoubtedly be Bette's mysterious collection. Gabrielle and her sister might as well have discovered the Alhambra.

Without realizing it, Gabrielle reached for Lulu's hand, unaware she was reprising her childhood role and led her sister inside as though entering the Emerald City. "I guess we found the other half of the bedroom."

"What the hell?" Lulu asked.

Gabrielle let go of her sister's hand and held prayerful fingers to her lips. "Dear God. I think we found the hidden mother lode of Chanel."

Lulu crossed her arms and hugged herself. "Did you have any idea?"

"That our mother wore Chanel or that she hid an entire private boutique in her closet?"

Masses of suits, dresses, and jackets hung in one area, blouses in another, and finally, a smaller section devoted to pants, all coded by color, and then fabric within the colors.

The closet spoke to acquisitive compulsion and extreme tidiness. Multiple shelves for handbags, racks for rows and rows of shoes, and built-in drawers surrounded them.

Mesmerized, Gabrielle stepped forward, opened the top drawer, and gasped. Black suede dividers separated masses of earrings and brooches into small squares, bracelets and bangles glinted from their wells, and necklaces coiled like gleaming snakes in perfect nests.

"Is all that real? I thought she lost—?" Lulu said.

"It's costume—but Chanel costume. An entirely separate category." Gabrielle inspected a black lacquer cuff with the CC logo drawn in pearls. Piece by glittering piece she went, touching a dark green stone in a cocktail ring, squinting at a dangling pair of chandelier earrings, and running a finger over a variety of bangle bracelets.

"The only thing that's eighteen-carat in here is this." Gabrielle held up her father's watch: a wafer-thin Vacheron Constantin. Bette never wore any other timepiece.

"If only half of this were real." Lulu wore a dreamy expression.

"Wake up, Lulu. Everything here is real—real Chanel. This stuff is expensive," Gabrielle said. "Incredibly expensive. You don't have a clue."

Lulu frowned. "Right. I only know brands carried at T.J. Maxx."

"I only meant that you'd never dream of spending this kind of money on so-called costume jewelry. Each of these necklaces goes for at least two thousand dollars."

Gabrielle wondered if her mother had hidden any fine Chanel jewelry in the recesses. Chances were slim, considering the prices, but Chanel's foray into luxury jewelry in the early nineties had fascinated Bette. She'd dragged Gabrielle to the 57th Street Chanel shop within the first few days the collection appeared. Every piece held the history of Coco's designs from decades earlier. Her mother displayed naked longing as she stared at one particular bracelet. The shooting star design made of diamonds and platinum looked exquisite on Bette; the price had been as stratospheric as the celestial design. Despite the cost, her mother had lingered long enough to make Gabrielle think she was going to splurge, but her mother had left empty-handed.

"How much are the earrings worth?" Lulu asked, holding up a pair of golden hoops embossed with the same quilting that Chanel bags were famous for.

"I'm not positive, but they usually start at around five hundred dollars."

"What about this pin?" She pointed to a black lacquer brooch in the shape of a camellia, Coco Chanel's favorite flower.

"I'm not a catalog, Lu. Everything here is expensive. Anything that was runway is lots more."

"Runway?"

"Did you grow up with our mother?"

"I tuned her out half the time," Lulu said. "Especially when she went on and on about fashion."

Gabrielle struggled for patience against her sister's victim stance. "Certain pieces are made just for the runway shows. Being less available makes them more expensive."

"Ah," Lulu said. "The built-in demand game. No different from what Beanie Babies once did, right?"

Gabrielle glowered at Lulu's reverse snobbism and then

went back to her examination of the fantastic collection. "There must be fifty handbags or more. And every one of them Chanel."

"How much are *they* worth?" Lulu asked.

Of course, Gabrielle wondered about the value of the closet's contents, too, but Lulu seemed laser-focused on the money and nothing else. Her sister shared her artistic bent—why wasn't she curious about Bette's passion or appreciative of any of the pieces?

"I haven't looked lately, but they probably start at around twenty-five hundred dollars and go up from there."

"Up?" Lulu's eyes widened.

Gabrielle reached for a classic, quilted, black calfskin bag with the ubiquitous gold and leather chain. She touched the gold double CC hiding the clasp. "This one is basic but still worth plenty."

"How plenty?"

"New, it would be around five thousand dollars. Vintage? In perfect shape like this? It looks almost unused. Half of that?" Gabrielle slid out a smaller shining ruby-colored bag. "This one is made of lizard. The value is much higher."

"How much higher?"

Gabrielle shrugged. "There's more to this than cash equivalence. We have a treasure chest here."

"We have insanity," Lulu said. "Do you know what all this translates into for the boys' college loan payments?"

"Sis, aren't the kids a hundred years past college?" Her oldest nephew, Nicholas, had closed in on thirty, ·which made his brother, Seth, twenty-seven. She loved both of them, but sometimes Lulu doted on them as though they were still boys. And saints. But she heard what Lulu would say next if Gabrielle gave her opinion: *If you had children, you'd understand.*

She'd give a Chanel bag never to hear that phrase again.

"You have no idea what people spend for college, do you?" Lulu pursed her lips, making her resemble her Brooklyn grandmother. The one Gabrielle, thankfully, didn't share with her sister. Bette had called the woman *that selfish crone* for a reason. "Matt and I took out parent loans that I'll be paying off until I'm dead. But I'm not complaining. Those are the things you do for your kids."

Please, not another recitation of the hardships of parenting. Gabrielle took a calming breath and turned her attention to a stack of scarves.

Lulu examined the red lizard bag. "My daughter in law would call this a construct of extravagance."

Gabrielle bit her lip. Hard. Bridget, Nicholas' wife—Lulu's daughter-in-law—traveled the road between being admirably dedicated to all things environmental and being a self-righteous pain.

"Aha!" Gabrielle opened a black, gold, and white silk square. "Diversification. Behold, a Hermès scarf!"

Lulu laughed. "Bette expanded, did she?"

After counting a dozen Hermès scarves, Gabrielle reached for a cashmere Chanel stole, black, edged in cream, and finished with a band of familiar interlocking Cs. She wrapped it around her neck, where the feather-soft material settled, caressing her.

"How did we not know?" Lulu slumped on the floor. "I saw her wearing some of this stuff, but she was just Bette. Dressed the same as always. I don't understand the scope or the depth of this obsession." She spread her arms wide, trying to encompass the enormity. "Was she losing her mind?"

"I knew she favored Chanel—she virtually never wore anything else when we went out. But—" Gabrielle stopped. She could find no explanation that made sense. "But a fixation like this? I'm baffled, too. I never—"

"You went shopping with her," Lulu interrupted. Attitude seeped into the benign-seeming words. "You and Bette had that special consumer connection, yes? How could you not notice anything?"

"Bette would have loved having you ask her for fashion advice or been more open to trying—"

Lulu's eyebrows shot up. Gabrielle stopped, knowing all too well how much Lulu resented Bette harping on her fashion choices. A dressed-up Lulu, their mother swore, resembled an eccentric bohemian who shopped in thrift stores.

*Look at your curious little outfit! Who else would think of pairing a cardigan with a farm dress as dinner attire?* Bette would ask, embarrassing Lulu. Their mother had no bandwidth for those who didn't exhibit a certain level of taste—which meant *her* taste.

Gabrielle didn't wear Chanel, but Bette approved the avant-garde fashion she favored. *"After all,"* her mother had said, *"you're young. You can be experimental."* When Gabrielle had still been able to afford it, and the store had still been there, she'd been a Barney's habitué, and Flying Solo, downtown, when she wanted to discover new designers. Though, as Bette's daughter, she'd always kept her soft spot for Bergdorf's.

Their mother never appreciated how Lulu, though she might deny it, actually had inherited Bette's sense of style—she just showed it in her way. Lulu's look typically included Levi jeans and Gap T-shirts mixed with vintage scarves and belts, put together with an eye for outrageous color. While in high school, her sister had dyed white men's T-shirts until the deep indigo or citrine blinded you.

Gabrielle used to appreciate Lulu's flair for putting together pleasing outfits. Like today—Lulu looked cool, despite the tote bag affectation, pairing chunky boots, navy jeans, and an amethyst mohair sweater. The choices fit her small, trim build.

Gabrielle couldn't remember the last time she'd complimented Lulu on one of her ensembles. Or when Lulu had mentioned Gabrielle's outfits, except today to make fun of her excessively high-heeled boots and wearing a coat that didn't insulate Gabrielle like a sleeping bag. Certainly, it had been before the wedding bathroom fight, but how long before?

Lulu shrugged. "Regardless of what Bette would have appreciated from me, the fact is, you're the one who went shopping with her. You didn't see anything getting out of hand?"

"Truly, I didn't. Our shopping days always began at Bergdorf's restaurant for lunch. Then we'd check out our favorite designers and look at the sales. Of course, we included Chanel. Bette's preoccupation wasn't a secret. The salespeople knew her by name and treated her like a queen. But I chalked that up to how often she visited, not how much she spent. Occasionally, she'd get something, but only sometimes. At least, in front of me."

"Perhaps you didn't pay attention to what she was spending because you were so busy spending yourself?"

"You're going there now?" Gabrielle crossed her arms. "I was an evil consumer while you saved the planet?"

"I'm just trying to understand how our mother threw away a small fortune on clothes and shoes and bags and fake jewelry, and you didn't pick up on it."

"It's my fault? Seriously? How often did we go out all dressed up? She and I had dinner twice a month or so, and yes, she wore Chanel, but I didn't inspect her to see if things were new or not. Was I supposed to remind her to start saving to protect our inheritance? How often did you see

Bette, other than at family dinners?"

"Probably once a month for lunch."

"Where?"

"Usually at Nectar, for her precious tuna salad and iced tea. She wouldn't exactly put on a suit and heels to go to a coffee shop. You were the one who saw her dressed up; you should have paid more attention."

"Jesus. Chanel is classic. The clothes don't shout at you the way Moschino or Gucci can. She was probably wearing Chanel at Nectar. You wouldn't have known. And I wouldn't have been aware of a new piece the way you—"

"Spare me." Lulu turned from Gabrielle as she pushed hangers along the rod. "Look at how many suits are here. Fifteen? Twenty? More? Dare I ask?"

"Yes, we're standing in the reason Bette only left us fifty-one thousand dollars."

"Eighteen thousand after we pay her bills," Lulu said. "I need wine."

"Perfect idea," Gabrielle agreed. "Get a sense of how many shoes she 'collected' while I get a bottle."

Reeling from their discovery more than she'd let on, Gabrielle headed to the kitchen where her mother had kept a decent wine selection. She chose a full-bodied Malbec, uncorked it, and then carefully pulled two crystal goblets from the cabinet.

There was nothing extraneous in her mother's apartment. Other than the closet, there was no excess. Sure, she owned lovely fine china, but she didn't have three sets. How could she have been so self-indulgent with that crazy wardrobe?

Anyone who knew Bette knew she adored Coco Chanel to distraction, viewing Chanel as the uber-heroine of her life—even choosing her children's names from Chanel's given name of Gabrielle and the Loire Valley where Coco was born.

Their mother fancied herself connected to the French designer in some mystical way. Bette had also been born to a family at the edges of respectability, though nowhere near as destitute. Gabrielle Chanel, who had been put in an orphanage by her father, grew up to become the reigning queen of fashion, changing how women dressed for all time. Chanel liberated female style, killing the custom of constricting corsets and putting women into freeing jersey pieces that flowed around the body.

*Blah, blah, blah*, her sister would say.

Bette had recited all this lore since Gabrielle's childhood. Teenage Lulu accused Chanel of being a Nazi, screaming across the dinner table so loudly that Bette rose from her seat, stood, and towered over her daughter, lecturing Lulu for the next hour. She described what Paris was like under occupation, insisting that Chanel had only consorted with the enemy and taken a German lover to rescue her beloved nephew from a prisoner of war camp.

As recently as a few years ago, the topic remained a source of sourness. To put an end to the argument, Gabrielle had spent some time researching the issue. As Snopes put it, World War II wasn't the best period for Chanel to have a love story with a German, even one English by his mother, who Chanel knew before the war. While the evidence appeared to skew strongly in favor of Chanel at least doing some information gathering for the National Socialists, nothing had ever been officially confirmed.

So, was there anything wrong with Bette admiring Chanel? Gabrielle adored Edith Head and had fashioned her career after hers. The difference was that she never squandered hundreds of thousands of dollars, collecting Head's drawings or original designs.

Gabrielle could only guess the depth of Lulu's reaction

to the gobs of Chanel. Her sister refused to use her given name of Loire, holding on instead to the childhood nickname her father had given her.

After fortifying herself by drinking half a glass of wine in the kitchen, Gabrielle returned to the fashion closet with the bottle of wine, a glass for her sister, and her own, refilled.

"What should we toast?" Lulu asked.

Gabrielle thought. "To the wire monkey mother."

In high school, Gabrielle had read about Harry Harlow's studies with Rhesus monkeys. Facing maternal deprivation, baby monkeys would hug, find comfort, and become attached to a faux monkey mother made of terrycloth-covered wire. Even when the scientist removed the fabric, the monkeys clung to the pure wire mamas.

While Bette didn't lack all maternal devotion, the sisters used their pet name for her during her coldest and most demanding moments.

Lulu winced and then tipped her glass. "To the wire monkey mother."

They sipped and then sipped again.

Lulu drained her glass a bit too quickly in Gabrielle's view. She raised her eyebrows, signaling her sister to slow down.

"I'm not interested in judgments today." Lulu ostentatiously poured more.

Gabrielle raised her hands to ward off Lulu's displeasure. "I didn't say a word."

"You gave me the famous Bette Bradford eyebrow," Lulu said.

"I didn't." She had.

"You're always looking for ways to accuse me of something."

"You do the eyebrow thing, too," Gabrielle shot back and then shifted the subject. "You know, Bette would be ready to kill us right about now."

"Why?"

"We're drinking red wine, sitting on her cream-colored carpet, surrounded by her exquisite clothes. Listen. Do you hear her shrieking at us from up above?"

"I bet she didn't speak above a whisper in this closet. She'd be afraid of bruising the suits. Disturbing the bracelets."

"Upsetting the handbags. Depressing the scarves," Gabrielle said. "Wait. Why would Bette be talking in the closet?"

"Communing. People sing to their plants. Bette could have prayed to her suits." Lulu sipped. "I have a bizarre urge to spill some of this wine."

"You wouldn't."

"We can't sell the carpet, right?" Lulu waggled her eyebrows. "I didn't see it on the balance sheet."

"Stop, Lulu! This closet is pristine—don't ruin it. Bette loved this space. You can't."

Lulu stuck her finger in the goblet, dipped it in, pulled it out, and held it up. A fat drop of blood-red wine slowly made its way down her finger.

# Chapter Six

## Gabrielle

Gabrielle watched, mesmerized, as the droplet traveled in slow motion. Just before it fell, she scooped her hand under Lulu's finger and captured it.

"Not now. Not today. I know. Bette could be difficult. And distant. But, not today, Lu." Gabrielle had hardly cried at the funeral and not at all during the will reading. But now, hot tears fell onto the Chanel stole still draped around her neck.

"I'm sorry." Lulu rubbed a soft circle on Gabrielle's back.

"It's okay." Gabrielle's dark hair mingled with Lulu's as she leaned against her. The comfort felt so good after such a long absence. Nothing had been resolved; their fight hadn't magically disappeared, but they were alone in this together, and that made a difference. Not a large one. The iceberg hadn't melted, but the very top layer of permafrost had softened. For that, Gabrielle gave thanks.

After a moment, Gabrielle unwound the scarf from her neck, inspecting it for tear stains. She already missed the feel of the soft fabric.

"What are we doing to do with all this, Gabi?" Lulu gestured vaguely towards the closet.

"Right now, I only have one idea—I'm going to be Cinderella tonight. I'm forcing myself to attend a benefit at the museum, and Bette's going to be my fairy godmother..." She stood, a tiny bit unsteady from drinking on an empty stomach, and turned toward the shelves of bags.

"I thought you retired from the museum's board," Lulu said.

"Retired? Ha! They bum-rushed me out, using fancy words that came down to *people's minds go straight to Cole and his lawsuits and failures when they see you*. Anyway, board membership requires mega contributions. Every year. Hardly something I can do on my Quills & Feathers paycheck."

Before her divorce, the specialty bookstore catering to costume design and art had been one of the places Gabrielle went for inspiration when faced with challenging costume designs. Now, she worked there.

Everything seemed to always pivot back to B.D. and A.D. *Before her divorce* and *after*.

After majoring in fashion at college, Gabrielle had become a costume designer for an off-off-Broadway theater on Bleeker Street, shining enough to get called out in *Village Voice* reviews.

She first met Cole when he was brought in to be the director in residence. *Variety* had called him *"a talent to watch."* Gabrielle watched all right—and became smitten with the brilliant director, eventually falling so deeply in love that she finally understood Bette's life-long attachment to Oliver.

Suddenly, she believed in soul-mate love, in every romantic song ever written, and in the idea that Aphrodite smiled on them. Gabrielle kept the flame roaring for almost two decades even when Cole's bad choices had blown their world apart with the biggest flop on Broadway since Paul Simon's *The Capeman*.

Cole and Gabrielle had lost their Greenwich Village brownstone, their cottage on Fire Island, and then liquidated their holdings to pay their creditors. Still, she'd stood by her man. One mistake, no matter how big, was not enough to shatter her faith.

Nancy Dunlop accomplished that early one March morning.

After the debacle, Gabrielle and Cole moved into her post-college, one-bedroom condo, the place she'd held on to all those years as an income property. Gabrielle performed cartwheels to keep her husband's spirits up, insisting that starting over was possible. Off-off Broadway would welcome Cole back with big, sloppy kisses. He'd find a new play and fresh investors.

Nothing she said made a difference. He drank, blamed others, and wallowed until the intercom buzzed that Saturday morning.

Cole answered it and then, without saying a word, walked to the hall closet, pulled out an already-packed suitcase, and left.

Gabrielle ran to the window and watched with horror as Cole exited the building, stepped into Nancy Dunlop's arms, and then disappeared into her idling limo.

She shattered.

Humpty Dumpty had nothing on her.

At least, she'd had her work. But then the theater world turned its back on Gabrielle. Cole and Nancy's whisper campaign—*you know Gabrielle was the one who pushed that terrible play, right?*—ensured she couldn't get work as a costume designer, either.

Only one person would hire her: Thea, the owner of Quills & Feathers. And for a meager salary at that. But since she owned her apartment, Gabrielle could live on what Thea paid her if she practiced abstemiousness. Never her strong suit.

At his lowest point, when everything else was gone, Cole had almost strong-armed her into selling her investment condo. Making him happy had always been her default, but she wasn't sure she trusted his instincts, given his depression. So, Gabrielle had gone to her mother for advice.

Bette had brought her to Sant Ambrocus to lift her spirits and ordered cappuccinos and a slice of their pink Princess cake—to share, of course because no matter what, you always watched calories.

"Hold on to the apartment and your IRA as though it were your very breath," Bette had lectured.

"But I love him." Gabrielle shredded a napkin until Bette placed a hand over hers.

"No man should ask a woman to remove her oxygen mask as the plane goes down. You have to make sure that if you have nothing else in this world, you will always have a roof over your head. Promise me you won't sell." Her mother locked eyes with Gabrielle. "Promise."

Gabrielle promised. Thank God. But now, standing in the closet of Bette's rental apartment, she wondered why her mother hadn't followed the same advice.

Lulu sorted through a pile of leather gloves. After pulling out a cherry-colored pair, she tried them on. "Now these I like. Surely, we can take a pair of gloves for ourselves, yes?"

Gabrielle studied her sister's hands. "Nice. Looks good on you. Where'd you buy your last pair?"

"Um. Marshalls?"

"How much did they cost?"

"Who remembers. Maybe $19.99?"

"Those you have on? Bette probably paid around eight hundred for them. And they look new. Do you see a tag?"

Lulu pulled the glove off, peeked inside, and then pulled it off. "No tag. God, I want these. So, if you got fired from the museum, why are you attending their gala tonight?"

"My friends, you know them—Daria and her husband—bought a table. She convinced me that going and holding my head up high would be good for me and remind people of what I accomplished." She wandered to the racks of clothes. "Now, help me figure out what I should wear."

Lulu put the gloves back into their compartment as though tucking in a baby. "You're not actually considering wearing something from here, are you?"

Gabrielle stumbled from one glowing possible outfit to another. "I haven't bought a new piece of clothing or an accessory in two and a half years. So, yes. I am."

"You can't. You heard Diana Hayes, Esquire." Lulu emphasized the *Esquire* and then mimicked the lawyer's voice. *"Before you decide on anything, even what you take for your personal use, you must present it to me for approval."*

"Guess what?" Gabrielle pulled on a midnight-hued jacket, hand-embroidered with minute pearl beads and lined in silk. The piece fit as though sewn right on her body. "Going to the Gray Lady for permission isn't going to happen. 'Cause she won't care how fabulous this will look over a black silk camisole, my YSL black silk pants, and…"

Gabrielle circled the closet, considering, inspecting, and enjoying every moment of wine-driven freedom until, after much inspection, she plucked a silver evening bag off the shelf. "And I shall carry this little number with it. Perfection, right?"

"You look like a model. Stunning." Lulu smiled with

genuine admiration. Gabrielle could hug her sister for the shot in the arm.

With a hand on her hip, Gabrielle struck a *Vogue* pose. "This feels wonderful. You know, Bette never stopped asking why I never wore Chanel."

Lulu sat, legs crossed, looking up at Gabrielle. "What did you say?"

"That it felt almost too classic. A bit dull. But I lied."

"You didn't want to compete with Bette?" Lulu asked.

"No. No, not that." Gabrielle frowned. "Bette didn't want me to compete with her, and I knew it. She wanted us to shine, but never more than her. Radiance was Bette's department."

"Sad, but true," Lulu said. "I hate to be the one to say this, but you can't wear those things. You really can't take them out of here—"

"Then don't be the one to say it, baby sister. What's the Gray Lady going to do? Sue us? Bette isn't watching from above, waiting to scream, '*Freeze!*' Tonight, I'm going to be the radiant one."

Fifteen minutes later, as Gabrielle locked the front door, a voice called out to them.

"Gabrielle!! Lulu!"

Gabrielle turned around and saw their mother's neighbor, Imogene. The opposite of Bette, she exuded the artsy-grandma vibes of the kind of women who spent Thursdays leading school kids on tours of the Tenement Museum. Oddly enough, though, she'd been a good friend of Bette's.

Gabrielle raised her shopping bag filled with Bette's donations for the evening in greeting. "Hi, Imogene."

Lulu ran down the hall and threw her arms around the woman.

"What are you two doing here?" Imogene shook her

head in sympathy. "Are you cleaning out the apartment? Do you need help? When Morty died, every part of losing him was terrible, but cleaning out his closets was a whole new level of terrible."

Gabrielle and Lulu locked eyes and began giggling.

Lulu hurried to explain. "We had some wine. Too much. And it's all—so many emotions. I know you know." Now she teared up.

Imogene patted Lulu's back, giving Gabrielle a sad smile. "There's no right way to manage death. I'm here to help if you need it. Just ring the bell the next time you come over. Going through Bette's things with you would be my pleasure. I'm sure there will be all kinds of surprises—some good and some not so good."

"You have no idea," Gabrielle said.

"Well, don't forget, I'm here if you need me. Any time." Imogene kissed them both goodbye and headed down the hall in the opposite direction. "I know Bette would want that."

Gabrielle prayed that she looked more radiant than terrified as she entered the museum's grand rotunda. She loved this space. Elegant classic columns, marble floors, and enormous vases of seasonal flowers or greenery—tonight's were white-bleached branches—welcomed her. She felt exhilarated to be back and desolate that this was no longer her domain. Fighting the onslaught of feelings, she searched the crowd for Daria and Martin.

Not seeing them, she ventured deeper into the room. She'd never attended a function here without Cole. *No, no, no*, she warned herself—no skipping down memory lane now.

As surreptitiously as possible, Gabrielle adjusted her jacket to ensure the fabric hung perfectly. Tempted as she'd been, thank goodness she'd not called Lulu and confessed how much the piece could fetch. She'd googled and found the piece on a vintage site selling for $7,000.

Tomorrow would be soon enough for confessions.

The chandelier earrings she'd secretly slipped out of Bette's drawer turned out to be a rare pair from the eighties, selling for $2,600. The embellished strappy-heeled sandals Gabrielle wore sold retail for over $900. If anything, borrowing the never-worn shoes brought some guilt. Could they still call them pristine after a night out? The moment she got home, she'd clean the soles.

What fresh hell was this? Did Cinderella worry about using Windex on her glass slippers?

In the grand hall, waiters in black tie drifted by, carrying trays of champagne and canapés so exquisitely crafted that their flavor almost didn't matter. Anyway, three-quarters of the women in the room wouldn't eat a thing.

As bubbles of cocktail conversation floated, Gabrielle's experienced eyes appraised the crowd, estimating that two hundred and fifty plus of New York's elite attended. A few people gave her what appeared to be genuine smiles of recognition. Her hands shook as she took a proffered flute of champagne. She could do this. She had to do this. Every step meant getting closer to freeing herself of the past. Bette used those very words when she'd encouraged her to accept this invitation three months ago.

Now, as people started to fuss over her, she experienced a tentative optimism. Perhaps she didn't have to wear a cloak of invisibility for the rest of her life.

*Where have you been?*

*Let's get in touch!*
*Lunch! Dinner!*

Prurient interest might be behind their air kisses, but she still felt a bit the prodigal daughter.

When dinner was served, Gabrielle followed the crowd inside and found Daria's table. As she sat, she heard a murmur go through the room. Twisting in her seat, she looked around. For a moment, nothing registered.

And then she saw him.

Her ex-husband strode across the room with his trademark all's-right-in-the-world grin, smiling at all as if he were the master of ceremonies and only now, with him here, could the festivities begin.

Stomachs did drop.

Sweat did break out.

And throats did close.

Gabrielle took in the woman hanging on Cole's arm. Nancy wore an elegant sheath of floating white silk with a single strand of pearls as her only embellishment. Gabrielle shrank back in her chair, feeling like an overdressed girl wearing her mother's costume.

Daria leaned over Martin and took Gabrielle's arm. "Don't. Nobody here is on his side. Don't let them ruin your night."

Gabrielle nodded. She stared, riveted, as Cole's eyes met hers. He winked.

Winked?

The fucker winked?

She clutched her wine glass, frozen. Cole took Nancy's hand and then indicated Gabrielle's presence with a tip of his head.

They headed toward her, big smiles pasted on their detestable faces. Nancy led. Her x-ray body, topped by a filler-inflated face, resembled a female Tootsie Roll, teetering on stick legs.

"Gabrielle!" Nancy leaned in and performed an Olympic-speed-worthy kiss-kiss.

Gabrielle tamped down the raging desire to nip Nancy hard enough to let the air out of her pumped-up cheeks.

Cole approached more cautiously, giving Gabrielle's shoulder a light squeeze. He must have sensed biting in the wind. "Gabi. How are you? I was so sorry to hear about your mother. Had she been ill?"

"Did you get our flowers?" Nancy's sympathetic expression sickened Gabrielle. Maybe slapping her would be better than biting.

"No," Gabrielle lied. She ignored Cole's question, just as he'd ignored societal expectations of not putting his dick in other women.

At least Cole had the decency to look uncomfortable as Nancy smiled and nodded as though Gabrielle had just effusively thanked her.

"Please give my condolences to Lulu," Cole said.

"About Bette? Or her husband?"

Hating someone you once loved took a powerfully awful kind of energy.

For the second time that day, welling tears surprised Gabrielle. Weeping would not do. Bette's apparition delivered a lecture through clenched, ghostly teeth. *Don't let him see your pain. Don't let anyone see his effect on you. Pull yourself together.*

"Excuse me." She nodded at Cole, stood, and walked away from the table, leaving her ex-husband and his despicable wife standing in her wake.

As she crossed the room, Gabrielle unclasped the silver handbag and reached inside for a tissue, forgetting she held a borrowed bag. No packet of tissues waited in the zippered compartment, but something else did. Whatever it was could wait.

She entered the ladies' room. Once safely inside a stall, Gabrielle dabbed a square of toilet paper at her eyes and soaked up her tears. That bastard deserved not one more piece of her. She'd rented Cole an unholy amount of space in her head for far too long.

Despite remembering the pain and humiliation he'd heaped on her, the cruel way he'd wrenched her from her life, she missed him. Shards of pain almost doubled her over. She missed belonging to someone she loved. She missed how they'd own any room they entered. How amid his admiring crowds, at galas like this, or after openings at wrap parties, Cole would slip an arm around her waist and then with the slightest pressure, let her know they belonged to each other.

Until they didn't.

Leaving the stall, Gabrielle stared at herself in the mirror.

What would Bette tell her? She tried to conjure her mother's ghost.

Nothing came.

Repairing her makeup didn't interest her; regaining her party energy required a miracle she couldn't invoke. Leaving was the only option. She'd text apologies to Daria once ensconced in the back seat of a taxi.

She fumbled in the bag for her phone, feeling that same unfamiliar edge of rigid paper she'd found before. Gabrielle pulled out a stiff unsealed envelope. Opening it, she drew out a correspondence card.

A single line flowed over the heavy cream paper, inscribed in Bette's decisive but elegant cursive. Gabrielle shivered as she read the words. At that moment, she couldn't help but believe that Bette had put it there for her.

*If you are sad, add more lipstick and attack.—Coco Chanel*

# Chapter Seven

## Lulu

The next day, an early morning phone call jarred Lulu from the first decent night's sleep she'd experienced in ages. Courtesy of Nyquil, but nevertheless, she'd slept.

As always, Gabrielle skipped the niceties. "Meet me at Bette's, right now. "

"What's wrong?"

"Nothing's wrong. But something important happened."

Lulu glanced at the clock. "At seven in the morning?" Groggy morning fog and a pasty mouth reminded her why she avoided using sleeping aids.

"No. Last night. Be grateful I didn't call you at midnight. Look, I don't want to tell you on the phone. Why are you sleeping anyway? I thought you were already at work. Don't you keep baker's hours?"

"I don't work on Tuesdays."

"Great. Then you can come right over to Bette's. Hurry. She's sending us advice," Gabrielle said.

"Gabi, I don't know how to break this to you but brace yourself. She's gone."

"Funny. Listen, our mother is sending us messages from the beyond."

"Explain." Lulu stumbled as she headed toward the bathroom. "Fast."

"This requires eyes-on attention, not a phone call. How soon can you get here?"

"Coffee. Shower. After those, I'll come."

"You know how people always say *take your time*? Well, don't." Gabrielle disconnected.

Ghosts didn't exist, but if they perchance did, of course, her sister would be the one to get Bette's messages. Even from the great beyond, she'd prefer Gabi.

Lulu stepped into the clawfoot tub and lifted her face to the pounding water from the showerhead Matt had installed. As she rubbed in her favorite rosemary-and-mint-scented shampoo, she reminded herself that jealousy had to stop somewhere. Wouldn't death be the perfect marker to choose the path of finally growing up?

After toweling off, Lulu headed into the kitchen. As always, the prospect of making coffee disheartened her. Matt had woken her with a mug of coffee every day of their marriage. The production—grinding and weighing beans, pouring water as if a volatile chemical reaction might result if the measurements were off the slightest bit, and the flourish with which he placed the cup on her nightstand—had been his morning dance.

And Lulu had loved every step.

Now, she used a Keurig, despite being ashamed that each used K-cup pod brought the planet closer to destruction. Her son, Seth, had gifted her with the machine soon after Matt's funeral. He realized that using Matt's complicated brewing methodology would be emotionally tricky—not to mention that the twelve steps would drive her crazy.

No matter how many advice books she read, or grief groups she joined, Lulu couldn't move past her husband's passing. Two and a half years after being struck down by the heart attack doctors called a widow maker, she still waited for his return. Anger rushed in at odd moments each day. How dare Matt abandon her? How dare he, a healthy, fit man in his forties, jogging daily in Prospect Park, succumb to an old man's disease?

Death was so fucking permanent.

Lulu prayed for those miracle mornings when she woke blankly cheerful, forgetting for the moment Matt was gone—when happiness swirled until the truth hit, leaving her to spend the entire day chasing its flicker of joy.

Lulu missed being loved. She missed the ways she and Matt had completed each other. Her talents were creative. His skills lay in the realm of the analytical—he handled spreadsheets; she invented cake recipes. He measured twice and cut once. Lulu eyed ingredients, feeling her way much of the time, even within the chemistry of baking.

Never in a thousand lifetimes would Matt have let their debts crawl up, ignored and uncounted as she had, blaming it on her grief. If he watched Lulu from above, he must be screaming every time she threw an estimated payment at this company, that mortgage, or some lender, praying the amount was sufficient to cover another month.

*You need to know what you owe. You need to know if Bette's estate can help. Trust me; it's time to face the truth.* Did Matt whisper from the same beyond from where Bette sent messages to Gabrielle?

Lulu squared her shoulders, grabbed her coffee, and

walked to her office. Gabi could wait a few extra minutes.

Lulu sat at the desk and looked at the pile of bills, now thankful for the lingering Nyquil fog that offered a cushion against the truth she was about to face.

After shuffling the papers into a pile, Lulu grabbed a pen, gripping the cheap Bic so tightly it broke, spreading ink over the top page. She rushed to keep the spreading blot from covering the numbers.

What would Matt tell her if he were there?

*Stop bullshitting.*

*What is, is.*

*Hiding from reality doesn't make it go away.*

She reached for a pencil and then put it down. No erasing! She grabbed a Sharpie and pulled out a pad of lined paper.

Going back and forth from bill to list, from bill to list, she wrote without stopping.

*Second Mortgage:*

**Owed: $10,400**

*Three months behind.*

*Foreclosure notices start at four months.*

*College payments:*

**Owed: $35,000**

*Five months behind for each son.*

*Credit card payments:*

**Owed: 3 cards w/ total balance of $40,000.**

*Making only minimum payments.*

Holding her breath, she tallied the numbers. Without even adding in her smaller bills, Lulu was within touching distance of owing the impossible sum of $90,000. She stared at the paper.

Ninety thousand dollars.

Grieving Matt, she'd ignored the bills for too long. Without Matt's salary for the last two and a half years, she'd gotten so far behind that catching up now seemed impossible. If she cut back on absolutely everything and took on some extra hours in the bakery, she could eke out enough cash to keep the foreclosure at bay for how long? Maybe one more month?

A text came through from Gabrielle.

*What are you doing? Whatever it is, stop—come now. You need to see what I found.*

The commuters edging into the subway car at Cortelyou Road looked like Manhattan refugees. Noses pressed to their phones, they didn't notice their computer bags banging against her legs. Aftershave and perfume overwhelmed the overheated car.

Brooklyn changed more each year.

When she and Matt moved into the house that his parents sold them for next to nothing, the neighborhood hadn't sported the now ubiquitous brunch and organic coffee spots. When the gentrification wave came, Matt snarled while Lulu shrugged. They'd been lucky. Newcomers hadn't overwhelmed their community on the outer edge of Ditmas Park the way they'd made Williamsburg a Greenwich Village/Soho mashup. But they had enough newcomers to bring fresh money into the bakery.

Lulu had convinced Matt and the rest of the Quattro family to renovate the bakery and update their offerings. She'd reached into her art background and designed what became sought-after cakes, thrilling both competitive brides and helicopter moms. Quattros' still provided Italian cookies and birthday, bar mitzvah, and confirmation cakes to the regulars, but she'd added trendy cannoli drizzled with espresso-chocolate lacing and hip hamantaschen that expanded the poppy seed/prune filling to include salted caramel. Lulu added gluten-free options before her in-laws had ever heard the word *gluten.*

Quattros' became a destination bakery. Her in-laws, Annette and Mattias, impressed by the renovation, turned the day-to-day running of the bakery over to the next generation while remaining the power behind the throne.

After Matt died, everything Lulu had found creatively challenging and satisfying stopped providing even a spark of joy. She'd married the bakery along with Matt. Now Quattros' only reminded her of her husband. She dreaded the smells of sugary sweetness and cloying chocolate. She found fault with every person in Matt's family, most of whom she worked in far too close proximity. Only Drea, who'd married a Quattro but chose medicine over baking, escaped Lulu's exasperation.

For all its success, the renovation had required an infusion of cash. The brothers and their wives shouldered equal shares, but now Lulu paid her and Matt's share alone, adding to her pile of debt.

Closing her eyes, Lulu let the rocking train send her into a semi-oblivion of marriage memories. She'd taken their habits of love for granted until they disappeared, like how Matt punctuated every goodbye kiss by running a quick finger over her wedding ring. "Just checking you're still mine," he'd say, wearing the same sweet grin all the Quattro boys sported.

They'd had a lovely life.

A worthy life.

Built on real friendship and caring.

And loans.

They'd borrowed without a second thought, with the

sureness of a couple confident of their guaranteed successful future. Ah, the arrogance of being alive.

Juggling a Trader Joe's cloth bag, her handbag, and two hot coffees, Lulu rang the bell of their mother's apartment. Before the chimes stopped, Gabrielle opened the door.

"You need to make me a copy of the key," Lulu said.

"Good morning to you, too."

"Why did I have to get here so early?" Lulu handed Gabrielle one of the cardboard cups, shrugged off her coat, and dropped it onto an upholstered chair.

"Closet?" Gabrielle pointed from Lulu's coat to the hall closet.

Lulu hung up her coat. That the older-younger-sister dynamic remained so far into adulthood was a topic she'd reserve for therapy. If she ever decided to see a shrink—something her daughter-in-law pushed all too often, saying it was time Lulu think about *freshening the house of Matt's presence.*

Nobody understood that Lulu didn't want to rid herself of Matt—she craved keeping him as close as possible. If she could, she'd drink in huge draughts of him with her less-than-perfect morning coffee.

At least her sons weren't suggesting she change. Seth and Nicholas were simply grateful that she no longer spent her days crying.

Lulu held out a bag with the mini babkas she'd taken out of her freezer. "I thought you might want some soul food."

They grinned. Though Bette acted as though she was to-the-Wasp-manor-born, the truthful answer checked in the space marked *religion* would be Jewish.

Upon marrying Gabrielle's very non-Jewish father, Bette had left kugel, menorahs, and the Catskills for icy martinis, summering in Nantucket, and twinkling Christmas trees. During her very brief marriage to Lulu's Jewish father, she'd allowed an occasional bagel back into her life. But upon her third marriage, she returned to her faux Protestant roots and remained firmly in place.

Lulu and Gabrielle loved to tease their mother by toting in what they called soul food—everything from Zabar's chicken soup to knishes from Yonah Schimmel's. They all had a particular soft spot for babkas.

After arranging a pastry for each of them, Lulu brought the plates to the living room and plunked them onto the coffee table. "Please don't tell me we have to eat in the kitchen."

Gabrielle shrugged and broke off a piece of crumbly cake. "Fine. You'll be the one she haunts."

"Not if you're also eating. See? I tricked you." Lulu smiled, sinking into the camaraderie until something glittering on the side table caught her eye. "What's that? We promised to go through Mom's stuff together. Only together. I should have made you pinky-swear."

"Are we twelve?"

"Are you? You couldn't wait?"

"I didn't go into the closet. Remember? These are the things I wore last night. I didn't want to go back into the closet without you."

Lulu looked past the bag and jacket to see other things. "Earrings? Shoes? We weren't going to take anything from the closet without telling each other. How am I supposed to trust you?"

"Jesus, Lulu. We're talking about a pair of earrings."

"And shoes. And how much are they worth?" Lulu

asked.

"I don't know."

"You're such a liar."

"I'm not lying," Gabrielle said.

Lulu picked up the gold earrings studded with what she assumed were rhinestones, but who the hell knew? Held aloft, they glittered as they swung. The double CC logo— already becoming tedious—nestled between flowery stars. She placed them gently back on the white handkerchief, where her sister had laid them.

"You never think about me." Lulu took a bite of the babka, chewed, and then took a long swallow of coffee. "And you are lying."

"I'm not lying."

As Gabrielle spoke, Lulu peered at her sister.

"Why are you staring at me?" Gabrielle asked.

Lulu took her sister's hand and led her to the hall mirror. "Look at yourself while you repeat what you said."

Gabrielle obliged.

"See how your lips quiver? They do that every single time you lie. It's your tell."

# Chapter Eight

## Lulu

Damn. Lulu had crossed the line.

Declaring Gabrielle a liar would only make her sister want to lie more. She knew because she did the very same thing. Lying had always been the best way to avoid Bette's wrath.

Ignoring Lulu's accusation, Gabrielle rose and headed for their mother's bedroom. Defying her sister's orders, Lulu grabbed the coffees and pastries and followed. Gabrielle went into the bathroom. The click of the lock sounded like a punishment.

Lulu placed the plates on her mother's bedroom vanity with as much noise as possible.

Finally, Gabrielle emerged, clutching three tubes of Chanel lipstick. "I'm taking these. Plan to call the Gray Lady on me?"

"Not if you show me the color you thought would look

good on me." Lulu hoped the request would get them past the tension she'd induced. She'd handled seeing the borrowed finery horribly.

Gabrielle gave a weak smile. "I do know—the earrings and shoes are worth over $3500, and I was desperate to show off. Jesus, am I just as bad as Bette?"

"No." Lulu pushed the coffee cups to a safer spot. "Bette never admitted to her faults."

Gabrielle threw herself onto the bed. Lulu followed.

"I didn't want to dive into a discussion about how many things I could or couldn't borrow," Gabrielle said. "All I cared about was getting to that dinner and looking good."

"So, how was it?"

"Awful. Wait a sec." Gabrielle left the bedroom and returned a moment later with the clothes and bag she'd worn the previous night and laid them out on the far side of the bed. "The night turned out horrible and humiliating. Guess who showed up?"

Lulu listened as Gabrielle told the story of her evening, pointing to the outfit for dramatic flourishes.

"And so, at that point, my choice was to leave or have a public breakdown. Imagine Nancy and me in a hair-pulling fight. Nice, right?" She stretched over and grabbed the silver pocketbook. "I opened the bag to get my phone to text Daria and tell her that I was leaving. That's when I found this." Gabrielle reached in, drew out a cream-colored card, and handed it to Lulu.

"*If you are sad, add more lipstick and attack. Coco Chanel,*" Lulu read aloud. "Bette left herself a note in her bag?"

"No, I don't think it was to herself."

"Then what?" Lulu asked.

"I'm not sure."

"Well, it can't have been from Coco Chanel to Mom."

"C'mon, Lulu. Open your mind. I think it was from

Mom to us. To me. Right when I was falling apart. It felt like she was telling me to get a hold of myself. Not to let Cole control me."

"You read all that into a message about lipstick?" Lulu shrugged. "You think next that she'll tell us how to turn all her stuff back into the fortune she spent on it?"

"Lulu, don't you see how incredible this is?"

"I think Mom was writing someone a note, didn't finish it, stuffed it into her bag, and forgot about it. Then you found it and read a whole lot into it."

"I think it was much more than that."

"Okay." Lulu decided not to argue. If Gabrielle needed to believe her mother had sent the message, she'd let her. She stood. Crumbs littered the spread. If Gabi was right, and Bette was watching from above, she must be insane with anger at their carelessness. "You clean off the bed. I'll take the dishes to the kitchen. And then we'll head into the closet and commune with Mom's spirit."

"Don't make this into a joke," Gabrielle warned.

Lulu ignored her and left with the plates. Gabrielle was already in the closet when she returned, sitting on a small stool, holding a black leather purse. Lulu plopped on the floor beside her, crossing her legs as though in kindergarten.

"You've always been the flexible one."

"Only with my body," Lulu said. "My head's stuck in first gear."

Gabrielle opened the bag in her lap, inspecting the stitched logo's intricacy decorating the interior flap. She reached into the pocket and checked all its compartments but came up with nothing. "Empty," she said. "Maybe you're right, and Mom was just reminding herself to wear lipstick."

Lulu took the bag from her sister. "You didn't check here." Lulu pointed to an unobtrusive skinny zipper on the top of the inside flap. As she pulled, she listened to the tiny teeth purr as they opened. "What is this weird space? I can't even get in three fingers."

"That's for money. So you don't have to open your purse all the way when you—" Gabrielle stopped speaking and pointed to the edge of a cream-colored card identical to the one she'd found the night before. "Look what you found!"

Lulu's pulse pounded as she pulled out the card and saw her mother's handwriting. She read the words aloud twice: "*Sin can be forgiven, but stupid is forever. —Coco Chanel.*"

"See, Bette knows I took the stuff last night. That I broke the rules," Gabrielle whispered.

"You think Bette's ghost wrote this from Heaven and snuck it in the bag this morning, so you'd find it now? You think she's sitting up there watching what we're doing and magically sending us messages to suit the occasion?"

"Fine," Gabrielle said. "You explain it."

Lulu shrugged. "Let's look in another bag."

Gabrielle stared at the shelf of bags. "We need to be careful and think this through. Who knows what it means?"

"I don't think it means as much as you want to believe it does."

"Maybe, maybe not. But we need to be careful and keep everything in order until we understand better."

"So, we take out one thing at a time? Inspect it?" Lulu asked. "And then put it back?"

"Yes. And we can write every item down, so in the process, we'll also wind up with a master list," Gabrielle said.

Lulu nodded. "Of course. You're excellent with lists."

"What does that mean?" Gabrielle kept staring at the words on the card.

Lulu held her hands up, palms out. "Nothing. You've always been best at organizing. You're right; we should itemize it all." She started laughing. "Will you listen to us?

Still trying to be Bette's good girls."

"I suppose we'll be trying forever. I'll get some paper and a pen," Gabrielle said.

"Why don't we use one of Bette's special journals?" Lulu lifted her eyebrows and made a mischievous face.

"Without asking, though. I'm sure as hell not calling the lawyer about our mother's stationery. The Gray Lady would probably call it a collection."

"Just call us Bonnie and Clyde. Go get one."

Moments later, Gabrielle returned, carrying a pristine blank journal covered in a deep red pebbled leather.

"This isn't simply a pretty journal, you know," Gabrielle said.

"Gabi, I might have slipped down several classes by marrying into the Quattro family, moving to an outer borough, and becoming a baker, according to you and Bette, but I haven't forgotten about our mother's talismanic items. The journal is Smythson. Bette's idea of stationery perfection. British, handcrafted, and expensive." Lulu took the notebook and inspected the sumptuous leather and deep ruby color—but even without knowing what it cost, she doubted it was worth what Bette had paid. "How much?"

"You have to understand," Gabrielle said. "She—"

"God. Stop pimping for the journal! How much?"

"About $300. But remember, Bette always hit Smythson's once-a-year sale to stock up on her signature gifts."

A wave of jealousy hit Lulu. Her mother had never gifted her with one of the notebooks. "How did you say that without laughing? Her signature gifts? How many are there?"

Gabrielle raised her eyebrows as she stroked the journal. "Enough that we can make them our signature gifts for a while."

Lulu grimaced. "Yeah. Annette and Mattias will love

them for Christmas. My in-laws appreciate nothing as much as a well-made leather journal from England. Okay, we have paper; we have a pen. Let's begin. How should we pick?"

Gabrielle looked around with reverence. "The closet will tell us."

Lulu studied her sister, praying she was joking. Gabrielle's streak of magical thinking never failed to mystify her.

"Well, the closet is telling me to go methodically, left to right, top to bottom." Lulu waved at the array—the range dizzied her.

"Boring." Gabrielle floated from dresses to bags to shoes as though she wanted to alight everywhere. "Let's see which item Bette uses next to speak to us."

"Seeing the return of your tarot-card side is quite the thrill." Lulu remembered the brief period of Gabrielle's life pre-college when she became obsessed with astrology, crystals, reincarnation, and everything alternatively spiritual. "You choose. The force is with you."

Gabrielle looked from left to right, examining the contents. She tried a jacket pocket. Nothing. The inside of a pair of boots. No note. She ran her hands through a pile of handkerchiefs.

"Maybe they're only in the bags," Gabrielle said.

"Why would that be?" Lulu asked.

"I don't know, but let's explore." Gabrielle reached to the top shelf and brought down a small clutch.

She handed it to Lulu, who turned it over and then ran a finger over the crystal-embellished leather. "Sparkly," Lulu said. "A princess bag for a little girl."

"Hardly," Gabrielle said.

"So, are you going to open it?"

"Not yet. We should itemize each thing before we look," Gabrielle picked up her iPad, typed in some information, and scrolled through pages of evening bags until she found the matching bag with its description. "I'll read; you make notes," she told Lulu. *"From the Pre-Fall 2017 Collection. Métiers d'Art Runway. Pewter metallic crystal-embellished leather Chanel evening clutch with silver-tone hardware, drop-in chain-link and leather shoulder strap, tonal satin lining, and push-lock closure featuring CC accent at top. Condition: Very Good. Light scuffs at hardware; minor wear at interior lining. Price: $2,700."*

Gabrielle inspected the purse from all sides. "And this isn't even a rare bag. Wait till we find one of those."

"No more borrowing for you," Lulu said.

"Pinky-swear promise. Now, for the moment we've been waiting for." Gabrielle opened the bag with a theatrical flourish.

Lulu saw it before her sister drew it out.

Gabrielle slit the envelope, pulled out the card, and began reading. *"I don't care what you think of me. I don't think of you at all.—Coco Chanel."* Gabrielle shivered.

"You okay, Gabi?"

"Bette absolutely chose this one for me. Last night, I came face-to-face with the power Cole still held over me. My empty future. If I adopt this attitude towards him, I'll be free. It's true, Lu, Bette's reaching out to us through these quotes."

Recognizing her sister's fragile side, her deep desire—or need—to believe frightened Lulu. Cole's crimes of the heart had been far more devastating than his other sins. She finally understood.

She wished she could think of the right words to offer comfort, but while she was still coming up with something to say, Gabrielle spoke. "Now, you pick."

Lulu looked around. Though she'd never admit it, she hoped a bag would call her. The last quote so entirely matched Gabrielle that Lulu longed for her own bit of Bette-crafted wisdom.

Lulu touched a beaded navy satin, ran a light finger over a red quilted bag, and then perfection caught her eye.

Bronze, small, shimmering, and decorated with an eight-sided jet starburst. Lulu wanted this bag. No, she coveted it. And was ashamed by how much. She drew it out with care.

"Let's look it up before we open it."

Gabrielle searched online until she found its twin. After clearing her throat, she read the description. "*Authentic Chanel Old Medium Crystal Boy Bag Metallic Bronze Goatskin with Ruthenium Hardware 2016. This shimmering compact bag has all the glitz and glamour you could dream of, one of the most beautiful boy bags Chanel has ever made. Extremely rare and impossible to find on the market. Gorgeous metallic bronze gave a lovely shine to the leather and embossed Swarovski crystal glows from every single angle.* Lulu, the price is nine thousand dollars."

Lulu put the pen down. She drew in her breath. Picking up the bag with the utmost care, she unclasped it. Inside, leaning against the bronze satin lining, rested another card inscribed with Bette's perfect penmanship.

*You start by wanting money. Then you get swept away by the love of work—Coco Chanel*

# Chapter Nine

## Gabrielle

"You get money and loving work; I get wear lipstick and ex-husband references. Great."

"It makes perfect sense." Lulu stared at the card. "Bette thought you could be an artist and get by on your good looks. Me? I wasn't any kind of stunner—not even extra-pretty—so she figured I needed to make money. Remember how she suggested I take business administration courses? During my senior year, she left catalogs for Baruch College and brochures for technical schools around the house."

"Like what? Auto repair?"

"Once."

"Seriously?" Gabrielle asked.

"See? You bought that. That proves you knew what Bette thought of me. You were willing to believe she thought I'd make a good mechanic."

Gabrielle had believed Lulu. How awful was that? And

how complicated was their mother? "What are we going to do with all this? I feel as though Bette had some insane expectation, some dream for this collection, but what? I'm clueless."

"Why couldn't we have a goddamned normal mother who just left us her damn stuff without restrictions or a nursemaid to make sure we follow orders?" Lulu flopped down on the carpeted floor and put her feet up against one of the built-in dressers.

"Good to see you're handling this with such grace. Bette would be so proud," Gabrielle said. "Let's keep this inventory thing going."

"You realize going through everything in this stupid closet is going to take forever."

"I know, but..." Gabrielle walked straight to the box at her eye level. Under the lid lay a red messenger bag, the logo slightly raised on the flap. Inside, a thick piece of leather divided the bag into two.

She didn't wait for Lulu. While her sister was looking up the bag, Gabrielle inspected it. The back section held the anticipated envelope.

"Look." She held it up.

"Read it," Lulu said.

"*I told myself that the dead are not really dead, as long as people think about them.—Coco Chanel.*"

Gabrielle's stomach lurched. Coco's words smashed through to her heart. And then her coping mechanism, her habit of cataloging life, kicked into high gear. "There's too much inventory in here for the journal. And we don't just need lists. We need pictures of every quote and the item that held it. We need to track it all. We need albums. Good ones. Maybe Smythson albums. Let's budget some money to record the Bette project."

"Whoa! We can't spend money on fancy photo albums.

Especially when Bette left some for us."

"What are you talking about?"

"Look." Lulu pointed to the top shelf where there were four Chanel hatboxes and, at the far end, a stack of oversized leather-bound books. "Photo albums. We can use those. Save our meager funds for what might be ahead."

"Did you ever notice those before?" Gabrielle asked.

Lulu rolled her eyes. "I've never been in here before."

"I mean since the other day or earlier today?"

"No."

"Don't you think it's coincidental that as soon as I mention albums, those appear?"

"Sure, Gabi. Bette's moving albums around as part of her master plan."

"There's more to the world than what we see on this plane of reality," Gabrielle said.

"That's exactly and precisely the fact behind the fiction of psychic phenomena." Lulu sat up. "We both probably saw them, but they didn't register on a conscious level until you mentioned albums."

"Did you know that Bette kept albums?"

"Sadly, but not supernaturally, no." Lulu retrieved the stepstool. "I wish I had known because—"

Gabrielle held up her hand, interrupting. "Don't."

"Don't what?"

"Don't tell me some story about how Matt's parents went through every family album with all of you every Thanksgiving."

"You think you know me so well," Lulu said. "That is not what I was going to say."

"Then what?"

"It was Christmas. They go through the family albums every Christmas."

Gabrielle's phone alarm sounded. "Damn."

"What is it?" Lulu asked.

"Work. I set it to remind me when I have to leave. Thea's at a doctor's appointment today; I have to open the store."

"It's my day off. I can spend some time sorting through the closet." Lulu ran a hand over the rack of clothes with a possessive touch.

"No. We need to do everything together," Gabrielle insisted.

"Don't you trust me?"

Gabrielle pondered the question. What did she imagine Lulu would do? Run out and hold a street sale? Give away pieces to her many sisters-in-law?

"At this point? I don't trust either of us."

A half-hour later, Gabrielle fit her key into the bookshop door. The moment it swung open, the papery odor of books softened by a lavender scent greeted her. Thea kept small bowls of scented glass rocks stashed throughout the store to provide the calming flowery fragrance. Her devotion to all nurturance was apparent everywhere in the shop she owned.

Quills & Feathers, a specialty bookstore in a city where almost every interest ensured a matching shop, focused on the arts—from painting and sculpture to jewelry, fashion, and theater arts. Books on perfume—which Gabrielle considered an art—had been her addition. Besides the curated book selection, Thea devoted a small section to fountain pens, inks, and journals, a carry-over from her late husband's influence.

Thea also had a tradition of offering complimentary tea

and cookies to shoppers and staff, the staff currently a team of one. Gabrielle had replaced the three elderly booksellers who'd retired over the past few years. She shuddered, imagining herself in their position in twenty years, living on Social Security and doddering in for cookies twice a week.

Of course, that scenario contained a gaping hole. Thea, who was in her early eighties, wouldn't be baking cookies anywhere in twenty years. Just one more worry to push away. For now, Gabrielle was grateful for a place to work. During her tenure, she'd reinvigorated the store, bringing in new customers, which had helped with the cash flow. She'd instituted a monthly book club and partnered with local florists, offering coffee table books to sell with their flower arrangements, making for unusual offerings.

Gabrielle's creative efforts helped her put off her dreaded future career decisions. As long as she lived in the lap of frugality, she could postpone figuring out the next chapter for a while. Maybe her life didn't provide passion. Or joy. Probably not even contentment. But she was okay, and okay would have to do for now. Her divorce had unmoored her more than she'd imagined, and she'd just begun coming to terms with enforced singleness when Bette died.

She shook away thoughts of just how much she did not want to lean into being *just okay* by picking up the pile of envelopes, catalogs, and other mail lying by the front entrance.

As usual, Thea had left teetering mountains of books needing shelving on almost every surface in the store. Gabrielle put her coffee on the only empty spot on a tea table and added the mail to one of the book towers.

"Quite a mess, eh?" a man said.

Gabrielle jumped. She spun around towards the front door, positive she'd locked it.

Nobody stood there.

"Over here."

By now, the voice sounded slightly familiar. Gabrielle turned and saw Thea's son, Nigel, standing in the entrance to the back room.

"How did you get in?" she asked, more annoyed than nervous now that she knew who it was.

Nigel's condescending laugh grated on her. "I came through my mother's apartment. So, I arrived through the back staircase."

"Is Thea okay?" Gabrielle asked, suddenly worried for her employer and the woman who'd become such a dear friend in the last two years.

"My mother's fine. She's at her checkup."

"You almost gave me a heart attack, Nigel. Why didn't you come in the front?"

"I tried. A few minutes ago. According to Mother, the shop opens at half-past eleven. Seems you arrived late."

Gabrielle glanced at the clock. Noon.

Nigel stuck his hands into the pockets of his chinos, leaning back slightly as his eyes traveled down Gabrielle's body. His resemblance to his mother lay in his thin, graying reddish hair and short stature, but where Thea possessed a tiny bird-like appearance, Nigel's fleshiness strained his shirt and trousers. His neck overhung his collar.

"Can I help you with something?" Gabrielle's instant dislike of the man the first few times they'd met continued to hold up.

"Yes, I thought with Mother busy at her appointment, we'd have a chance to chat."

"I thought you were taking her." If Gabrielle had known that Thea was visiting the cardiologist alone, she'd have insisted on accompanying her. Their relationship had evolved to the point where Gabrielle worried about Thea's health habits, and Thea lectured Gabrielle about her choices in men.

"My wife is with her."

The idea of that woman—Pamela—being with Thea during the medical visit discomfited Gabrielle. Thea's atrial flutter required careful monitoring, as did her tendency to downplay symptoms. All Pamela monitored was the growing value of the Quills & Feathers building that continued to increase as the Greenwich Village neighborhood grew in real estate importance.

Gabrielle crossed her arms and waited for Nigel to speak. Making things easier for him wasn't on her current to-do list. As he stood, discernibly wanting Gabrielle to ask what he wanted, he began moving from one foot to the other.

Lifting an armload of books to shelve, Gabrielle turned her back on him and walked toward the front of the store. When the sound of shuffling envelopes began, she whirled around.

"Those are addressed to your mother." Gabrielle put the books down and got to Nigel in a few quick strides. Without hesitation, she reached over and snatched the mail from his hands.

"How dare you?" he asked.

"I'm in charge here when Thea's out."

"This is my mother's store." He clipped each word in an imitation of an upper-class to-the-manor-born accent, despite being raised in Queens.

"I need to ready the shop for opening. Tell me what you want, Nigel."

He telegraphed his attempt to regain equilibrium with a deep breath, replaced his hands in his pockets, and set his lips in a pinched line that suggested he was not trustworthy. Finally, he spoke.

"Pamela and I are worried about Mother."

Gabrielle gave the most noncommittal of nods.

"Honestly, we don't think she's up to running a bookshop any longer. Even in the manner in which—"

"Whoa." Gabrielle lifted a hand to ward off Nigel's words. "First, your mother is a fully competent person. Talking to you about her business or anything else is wholly inappropriate."

"But—"

"Second," she continued, speaking over him, "your mother is my dear friend. I'm not going to help you undermine her."

"Now you just wait a minute, Gabi—"

"My name is Gabrielle."

"Whatever the hell your name is, listen up." Pure street New York replaced Nigel's upper-crust pronunciation. "My mother is losing her grip. Pamela and I are not about to let things fall apart. Not on our watch. We thought you might help us and help yourself in the process. We don't want to see you lose your income overnight."

Pamela, years younger than Nigel, had only been his wife for about ten minutes. Gabrielle didn't know what bothered her more—his avarice or his underestimation of Gabrielle's loyalty.

"Listen carefully," she said. "The sole reason I'm not going to tell your mother about this conversation is that I can't bear to break her heart. But consider this your warning. You try to cheat your mother out of the peace she has here, and you'll be taking on me, my sister, and an army of lawyers."

Gabrielle had no idea what she was talking about or why she'd included Lulu in the threat. The one thing she was sure of without a doubt: no matter what, she would take care of Thea.

# Chapter Ten

## Gabrielle

Late that afternoon, Gabrielle and Lulu met back at Bette's apartment. Armed with crystal glasses filled with their mother's best Bordeaux, they sat side by side at the dining room table with a stack of albums, one already opened.

Gabrielle pointed to a baby picture of their mother with their grandparents. "Beautiful, even then. Bette couldn't have been more than a year old."

Lulu leaned close. "They're staring at her as though the Messiah just arrived."

"Nobody was more adored than Bette. Can a child be over-adored?"

"Imagine if we'd had even a tenth of the attention Bette got."

"I can't believe we never saw these albums," Gabrielle said as she kept staring at the photo taken in the living room of their grandparents' place on DuBois Avenue in

Poughkeepsie. They had owned that house with its ground-floor tailoring shop for over fifty years. Grandpa had the talent to copy any design, and he'd taught Gabrielle to sketch dresses, make patterns, and sew, using her Barbie dolls as models. Among her friends, only Gabrielle's Barbies wore Diane von Furstenberg wrap dresses.

In Poughkeepsie, she learned about fabric. Her grandfather watched her choose the superior marbled velvet over a cotton velvet, nodding approval as he chewed on an unlit cigar.

If she picked something he didn't think worthy, he'd instruct her on the why. When she chose a cheap satin, he shook his head. *Crush it in your hand. Feel the nap; learn from the fibers. See how it creases and stays that way? You don't want fabric like that. Schmattas never hold up.*

If Grandma were in earshot, she'd always add her opinion. *Like choosing a man. You want one that gets better and more comfortable with age. Not one that pills and feels rough.*

*Which one am I?* Grandpa would ask.

*Australian Merino. Damask from Syria. Gabardine from Italy.* Grandma's answer would change each time.

*And you are mulberry silk.* Grandpa's response always remained the same. *Mulberry silk is stronger than steel fibers of the same diameter, but the fabric combines strength with beauty. Always look for both, Gabi.*

What material described Cole? Gabrielle had believed she'd married cashmere from the Gobi Desert, but the man who left her had turned out to be a lying, cheating piece of polyester.

Gabrielle closed the album's final page.

"Let's get some work done," Lulu said.

"Not yet. Let's look at one more."

Lulu sighed hard. "I can't stay too late; I have that engagement party."

"With the size of Matt's family, I'm amazed you ever have an evening free. And who has an engagement party on a Tuesday night?"

"Quattro family functions come so fast and furious, they have to stick the lesser ones—like engagement parties—on weeknights. Why am I even going, for God's sake? All they do is look at me with sad eyes, feeling sorry for the widow."

"Let's do just a few more photos. Maybe there's a secret message for you about that in one of these books." Gabrielle flipped open the next album.

Pages filled with tear sheets from fashion magazines showing Chanel outfits and accessories alternated with Polaroids of what appeared to be all of Bette's Chanel outfits and items with captions.

"Bette put everything in here," Gabrielle said, astonished. She turned another page. "When she bought it. Where. Comments on the provenance. We're in such luck."

"Luck?" Lulu asked. "How?"

"We can make this our inventory book—she's done half the work for us. Mom could have been an incredible curator."

"*Mom* could have been about ten thousand things other than what she was." Lulu reached over and tried to close the album. "So, we have what we need. All done."

Gabrielle held the album open and pointed to another tear-sheet. "This looks like the '50s when Chanel returned to—"

"If you make me look at one more Chanel anything, I'm going through Bette's medicine cabinet. What did Coco take? Uppers? Downers? Morphine? Whatever it was, Bette would have them in her honor. I'm sure I'll find something to save me."

"Okay, okay. Closing it now." Gabrielle's chest

tightened. The time her mother devoted to Chanel bordered on mania, and seeing how many hours she'd obsessed over it suddenly depressed her. Why had this all mattered to Bette so much?

Lulu touched Gabrielle's shoulder. "Hey. Are you okay? Are we doing something wrong?"

Gabrielle shook her head. "I haven't a clue what's right or wrong anymore. I just can't figure this all out. Can we look at one more? For some clues? Is that okay?"

"One more." Lulu passed her sister an album.

Gabrielle opened it and saw her birth announcement. Soft pink satin ribbon laced through the outer edge of the thick card stock. Hand-done calligraphy spelled out Gabrielle's vital statistics: name, date, weight, and height, all illustrated by a fairy tale baby sleeping in her cradle.

Gabrielle traced the drawing. "Do you think Bette drew this?"

Lulu bent toward the picture. "I guess."

Gabrielle ignored her sister's begrudging tone—she recognized Lulu's jealousy. Turning the page, she stopped on a picture of Bette and Oliver gazing at each other, with a pint-sized Gabrielle staring up at both.

"Look how much love they held for each other. What about me? Do I seem sad?" Gabrielle tilted her head, trying to get a read on her four-year-old mood. "Left out?"

"You look content." Lulu squinted at the photo. "Extraordinarily neat and clean. Beloved. And adorable."

"Everyone's adorable at four."

"Perhaps, but you're completely burnished," Lulu said. "And I'm invisible."

"How could pictures of you exist when I was a baby? You weren't even born for another three years."

Anxious now to find a photo featuring her sister, Gabrielle rushed through the following until she finally came to an image that included Lulu.

Perfect, pinafore-dressed seven-year-old Gabrielle held her baby sister, who wore a soiled pink onesie, food smeared on her face.

"Jesus. Look at me. I was a baby urchin," Lulu said.

"What do you mean? You're so cute! You're only what, five months, and you have all that hair?"

"Urchin hair," Lulu said. "Mom always said I resembled a little urchin. She said that even before I walked, I looked like a baby hobo."

"A baby hobo! What the hell does that mean?"

"You can see it right here." Lulu tapped the ludicrously long infant hair sticking up five different ways. "And my clothes! They're stained and rumpled."

"You're a baby!"

"You were never rumpled. At least not in any pictures. Mom wouldn't allow anyone to immortalize you like that." Lulu turned the page, pointed, and then gave her sister a look. "How about this one then? In Poughkeepsie for my birthday."

There was a big, pink-frosted cake. Gabrielle—a sophisticated nine-year-old in a white dress with smocking across the front, lace anklet socks, and shiny patent leather Mary Janes—sat prim and poised next to their mother. In contrast, Lulu, in a matching but messy, food-smeared dress, sat on her grandmother's lap, Grandma laughing as Lulu plunged her hand into the cake, grabbing at the oversized plastic number two stuck in the frosting. Bette's pained expression masqueraded as a smile.

"Yeah. You're right. You were a little urchin," Gabrielle said.

"And you were always the perfectly wrapped Bergdorf child." Lulu slammed the album shut and took a sip of wine.

Gabrielle considered her options before reacting. Lulu's

anger sparked Gabrielle-embers that could hit and flare at any moment—she had no desire to go up in flames.

"I have an idea," she said. "Remember how Mom let us play dress-up with her clothes and shoes?"

"Mom never let us do that," Lulu said.

"Exactly. Follow me into the forbidden land." When they entered the closet, Gabrielle held her arms far apart to encompass the entire collection. "The time has come!"

Lulu held back for a moment until Gabrielle thrust her forward and then watched her push the hangers along the pole until a black velvet jacket caught her fancy.

As her sister slipped on the jacket, Gabrielle pulled on a long silver sweater. "Now, shoes!" she called out as if they were in a race to see who could put together an outfit fastest. She turned to check on Lulu as her sister plucked a pair of black ballet flats and tights. Lulu's feet were a half size smaller than Gabrielle's and Bette's, so the shoes were too large, while the jacket was the tiniest bit tight across her shoulders.

"Okay, so they're a little loose," Lulu said. "I'm not going for a hike. Who cares?"

Gabrielle's phone buzzed. When she saw *Diana Hayes Esq.,* she hit *decline.* The Gray Lady was not going to spoil their fun.

She slipped into a pair of gold high heels that fit as though handcrafted for her and then opened a jewelry drawer. "Now for the decorations. Pearls! Tons and tons. I must wear rows and rows of them. For you, I declare gold."

"I bow to your superior fashion sense." Lulu bent from the waist with a flourish.

Gabrielle, wearing only a long sweater and heels, draped herself in ropes of Chanel necklaces. When she caught a glimpse of herself in the mirror, she twirled. "Behold the world's most expensive hooker."

"How about me? What do I look like?" Lulu cocked her head at the image of herself wearing only the blazer, tights, and a dozen golden chains.

"Like Judy Garland giving a Christmas show." Gabrielle put four Bakelite bracelets on one wrist and then pinned a giant, white enamel camellia brooch to her sweater; Lulu slipped on a ring with a similar camellia in black. Each snapped on a pair of gold hoops.

Examining themselves in the mirror, they fell over laughing.

"More wine!" Lulu stood and lifted her hair into a chignon.

Gabrielle retrieved their unfinished Bordeaux.

Lulu held up her glass to Gabrielle's. "To Mom's closet."

Gabrielle echoed the toast and then declared, "Let's try on more!"

The two stripped off the clothes and began again until exhausted. They sprawled across Bette's bed in one final outfit.

"Mom would kill us."

"Maybe she'd be laughing."

Lulu cocked her head and caught sight of her black leather boots. She ran her finger over the CCs stitched on the side in a beigey-pink thread. "God, these are perfect."

"You think so? They make you look like a cowgirl."

"Too bad," Lulu said. "I love these boots, and I'm going to wear them forever. Nothing else will ever touch these legs."

"Okay, Annie Oakley." Gabrielle held out her left leg, clad in black, mid-thigh suede, the front bisected by an eye-catching zipper. Next, she lifted her other, vamped up in over-the-thigh red snakeskin with a four-inch-plus stiletto. "Look and learn, Lu. Behold. A boot, Lu. Not a shit-kicker."

"At least I won't trip and break my legs."

Gabrielle took turns lifting one leg and then the other like a can-can dancer. "Which one's better?"

"Why choose? Wear them as a mixed pair. Start a new trend," Lulu answered. "Hey, Gabi. Pretend you're sober. Find the perfect outfit for me. You got to wear Bette to your gala; tonight's my turn. Pick out something for me to wear to this engagement party. Something splashy. Something that shouts that Lulu isn't dead yet."

# Chapter Eleven

## Lulu

Lulu stared at her reflection in amazement. "I don't even look like me."

The high-heeled black boots, red silk blouse, and black pencil skirt transformed her. She turned to see herself from the back and then faced forward again. Her lips, outlined in a matching shade of Chanel red, brightened her face just like Gabrielle had said it would.

Not that she was ready to admit it.

Despite being Bette's, the boots were almost her size, but Lulu hadn't worn heels this high since Nicholas's wedding. Her feet would kill her by the end of the night, but she didn't care. She'd sit.

Gabrielle approached, holding out a black alligator bag, slipping it over Lulu's shoulder. "Perfect." She stepped back, cocked her head, and inspected her work. "You look like a million bucks, which isn't far off. Want to guess how much that entire ensemble is worth?"

"No. And don't tell me; let me just enjoy everything. Besides all these prices that you keep quoting, who is going to pay that?" Lulu asked. "Where are we going to sell this stuff? Goodwill?"

Gabrielle sat up and stared at Lulu as though she were a Martian. "Goodwill? Have you understood what I've been saying? The resale value of Bette's collection is incredible."

"Resale value? The pocketbooks, the jewelry, okay. I almost understand that. But skirts? Sweaters? Shoes? How much can you get for secondhand clothes?"

"Secondhand? You're not wearing day-old bread. Try precious vintage." Gabrielle sat Lulu back on the bed. "Look at the soles of those boots—pristine. They'd probably go for at least a thousand."

It was starting to sink in that maybe if they could sell this collection fast enough, she could save her house and pay off all her loans. She started getting undressed, pulling off her boots. "Forget it. I'm not wearing any of this. It's all too expensive."

Gabrielle raised her hands. "Calm down. I had my turn at being Cinderella. Wear it and enjoy it. You look lovely."

Lulu leaned in towards the mirror and admired her reflection again. How long since she'd taken this sort of care getting dressed? When was the last time she'd worn more than a fast swipe of lip gloss? "Did you learn how to put all this together from Bette?"

"Perhaps you've forgotten the years I spent working in the theater?"

"But Bette pushed you. Gave you a head start."

Gabrielle shrugged. "You ran off and got married before she could push you anywhere." And then, as if her sister could read her mind, she added, "Stop playing the victim."

Lulu began to answer and then stopped. "Sure. If you stop being the arbitrator of all things worthy."

"We've played our parts equally well." Gabrielle began straightening up the bathroom, cleaning the splotches of makeup dotting the sink and counter. "Look at this mess. Two drunks must have snuck in and done this."

Lulu accepted the peace offering to end the argument and smiled at her sister's weak joke. "Here. I'll help."

"Don't." Gabrielle held up two hands to ward her off. "You don't want to get anything on those clothes. Leave it to me. Are you going straight to the party?"

She checked her watch. Six-thirty. Her old Timex with the giant face, perfect for the bakery, appeared ridiculous against the black resin and rhinestone Chanel bangle. Gabrielle said it was worth $1800. The cost of the bracelet could cover the price of thirty Timex watches. How could anyone spend so much on one tiny circle made of resin and crystal?

And yet, it looked so damn pretty.

"It's an early party—so, yes, I'll go straight there."

"Tuck the pearls under your coat. Oh, and keep the purse there also," Gabrielle said.

"Because every subway thief knows the price of old pocketbooks?"

"When it's Chanel? I can't imagine any New York criminal stupid enough *not* to know that logo."

Lulu arranged her original arrival clothes in a neat pile on a bench in the closet. She folded and then laid her jeans on top of her old, scuffed boots and then placed her stretched-out sweater over both items. Then she tucked the Chanel pearls under her neckline and pulled the sleeves over the bangle. Finally, she switched her wallet and other purse ephemera into Bette's bag.

Lastly, Lulu took her hair from the topknot she'd made while making up her face. Waves tumbled out, full from being pulled upward. For the first time in a long time, Lulu smiled at her reflection. Lipstick, eye shadow, a double coat of mascara, and lots of eyeliner—plus her version of big hair—vanquished the old widow.

"Why are you here?" Gabrielle's voice floated in from the living room.

Who was her sister talking to? Lulu walked out of the bathroom and into the bedroom.

"Because you didn't answer the phone."

Lulu didn't recognize the woman's voice.

"But how did you get in?" Gabrielle sounded miffed.

"Did I forget to tell you that I have a key? Your mother spelled out my access in the will. After three calls, I decided I'd better come over and see if anything was wrong."

"What could be wrong?" Gabrielle's voice rose. "Hey! Where are you going?"

"Just making sure everything is in order."

"Why wouldn't things be in order? Bluntly speaking, this seems way out of line, you bursting in like this—"

Gabrielle's words got louder until the visitor walked into the bedroom and looked at Lulu standing by the bed.

With her hands firmly planted on her hips, Diana Hayes Esquire examined her up and down, taking in Lulu's outfit and then eyeing the mess in the closet. "Was there something about the will's instructions that were difficult to understand?"

Lulu held her hands up as though the Gray Lady were arresting her. "You caught me. I was modeling for Gabrielle."

Her sister, who'd come to stand by her side, nodded in agreement. "How can we come up with a plan if we can't get a hands-on feel for this stuff?"

"Wearing it and simply inspecting are two different things," Lulu added.

The lawyer sighed as though facing two children. "You do know this place smells like a winery, right? Take the clothes off. Put everything back." She pointed to the purse over Lulu's arm. "Are you aware of the worth of that particular bag? Used, it might fetch twenty thousand. And that one you're using to play dress-up is brand new."

Gabrielle brought forth her haughtiest attitude. "I am familiar with the prices."

"Well, so am I. I went through every item in this closet with your mother." She stared at the two sisters like an angry hall monitor. "Take everything off, Lulu. Put it all back. Your mother didn't leave this all to you to play dress-up. She wanted you to understand what it meant to her. And what it can mean to you. Otherwise, I could have simply given you a list of the contents of her closet. Concentrate. Both of you. Show some respect."

The Gray Lady left Lulu to change in privacy. Gabrielle stayed behind long enough to share a WTF look with her before following the lawyer to the living room. Lulu unzipped the skirt and stepped out of it. Who did that woman think she was, lecturing them on Bette? They'd never heard of her before their mother's death. And she was going to teach them about respect?

Once again wearing her crappy old clothes, she looked at herself in the mirror and sighed. She felt like Cinderella at midnight. She glanced over at the boots she'd taken off—her very own version of glass slippers.

Lulu rushed down Seventh Avenue towards Da Nonna Rosa Restaurant. After stopping at home to change, she was now forty-five minutes late. Her head pounded. There was something about what Diana Hayes had said that Lulu couldn't decipher. She'd spoken as though she were so much more than Bette's lawyer. What had she meant about Bette wanting them to understand what the collection meant to her and what it could mean to them? All the closet had revealed so far was Bette's indulgence and selfishness.

At the moment, it all felt like a burden. And one that could wait until tomorrow. Lulu had a party to attend. She pasted on a happy face and walked inside.

Tons of Quattros, Quattros' spouses, plus-ones, and Quattros' friends filled the private room above the main restaurant. Food stations lined the far wall; linen-covered tables encircled the perimeter. Oak floors gleamed in the dimmed lights.

Large gold letters hanging over a large mirror spelled out *Happy Engagement, Kitty & Donnie.*

Lulu searched the room until she spotted her sons and their beloveds at a table in the back. After smoothing her ancient black knit dress over her hips, Lulu headed toward them. How long since she'd worn this outfit? For so many years, it had been her go-to. Before knowing what hung in her mother's closet, she'd been proud of the Ralph Lauren dress bought on sale at Macy's years ago. Matt had adored the way the wrap-style jersey hugged her.

"Wow!" A sweet whistle always followed. He never forgot to compliment her when she dressed up.

Now, her arms felt cold, and her old black pumps wobbly as she walked toward her sons.

Seth, her baby, waved. He so resembled Matt that sometimes she gasped when she saw him. Like now. Standing arm in arm with his husband, Gus, huge grins across both their faces, they greeted her.

When Seth and Gus eloped last year, she'd worried they were too young. Not being able to witness the ceremony had shattered her. Gradually, both concerns faded when she learned they'd married in secret because Seth feared she would have insisted on paying for the affair. If they put their worries about Lulu above their love of huge parties, they were old enough for commitment.

She hugged them both, having to stand on tiptoes to reach Gus's cheek for a kiss. Next, Nicholas and his wife, Bridget, came in for an embrace. Where Seth possessed all the Quattro features—the almost-black hair, the deep brown eyes, and the tendency toward five o'clock shadow by three in the afternoon—her older son was a blend of Lulu's parents. His spinach-green eyes matched Bette's and Gabrielle's, and he had the curling light brown hair she remembered from her father.

"You're looking gorgeous, Mom," Nicholas said.

"Yes! And with all the work you've been doing," Bridget said. "You must be exhausted going through all that stuff."

Silently, Lulu thanked Gabrielle for the makeover. At least the Gray Lady hadn't insisted she take off the Chanel makeup her sister had applied.

"Are there treasures upon treasures everywhere?" Seth tugged her down to sit with them. "Tell us everything!"

"Did your mother actually have an altar to Chanel?" Gus asked.

"What?" Lulu used a toothpick to spear a mozzarella ball on a basil leaf from the platter in the middle of the table.

"That's what Aunt Gabrielle said," Seth said. "I went to see her at the bookshop."

"She didn't mean it literally," Bridget said.

"Oh my God, Bridge. We know," Gus said, lifting his eyebrows at her. "I was speaking figuratively."

"But were you?" Bridget made a face at him.

Her daughter-in-law and son-in-law had a weird competitive thing going on as they vied to be number one in her affections.

Both fair-haired Bridget with her first-generation Irish

roots, and dark-skinned Gus, a child of Queens by way of Haiti and Guyana—had absorbed enough Quattro traits to hold their own with any crowd of Italians, Jews, or Italian-Jews. And she loved them both for it.

More family pressed in, praising Lulu's outfit as though they had never seen her in a dress before. News had traveled fast; Bette's collection seemed on everyone's mind.

*"So, what did you find?"*

*"Are you going to be rich?"*

*"Someone said your mother was related to Coco Chanel!"*

Eventually, Lulu made her way from the table and headed over to congratulate the bride-to-be and her fiancé. She felt the eyes of Matt's multitude of male cousins as she walked past, and even though she knew it was wrong, the admiration brought a forgotten pride. Maybe Coco Chanel was right, and lipstick did make a difference. Swaying, Lulu used the heels for all their purpose.

She kissed her niece on both cheeks. "Kitty! You look stunning. Love agrees with you."

Annette, Lulu's mother-in-law, sitting at the couple's table, nodded like a queen. "Who doesn't need love?" And then, as though remembering Matt, she put a hand on her heart. "Or memories of love, eh? Oh, Lulu, you look so beautiful yourself. Matt treasured you in that dress! I remember. How nice that you wore it tonight. He'd be so proud."

Now ashamed of her plan to arrive swathed in Chanel like a big show-off, she leaned forward and hugged Annette with extra enthusiasm. When she finished, Annette took both her hands. "My sweet girl, how are you? How awful to lose your darling mother. And now you and your sister going through all her stuff under the eyes of that awful lawyer!"

Did anyone in the family not get word of Bette's will? Matt's family had its own phone tree, with the bakery as its heart.

Her hands still caught in Annette's, Lulu nodded; suddenly so tired from the day of confronting memories, drinking too much wine, and trying on clothes, she wanted her bed more than breath itself. "The work is putting a strain on both of us."

Annette looked down, letting go of one of Lulu's hands while holding the other with both hers. "What is this?"

Lulu followed her mother-in-law's glance and smiled. While the Gray Lady had been so busy worrying over the million-dollar alligator bag, the beautiful bangle had escaped her eye. The bracelet had remained hidden under the long, baggy sleeves of Lulu's shapeless sweater in the apartment.

"This was my mother's. Gorgeous, huh?"

Annette squinted at the bracelet with a sour look. "Eh. So, I guess everything isn't the real deal. Sweetheart, this is plastic. Your mother had costume jewelry, too, huh? Bring me anything left over." She pointed towards a gaggle of girls, Annette's grandchildren, and great-nieces. "The girls, they love playing dress-up."

Lulu opened and then closed her mouth.

"How is your sister holding up?" Annette asked.

"Gabrielle sends her regrets. She would have loved to come, but work has her beat." When Lulu had shared the party invite, Gabi had almost seemed tempted for a moment, though she'd ultimately passed.

"So, Lulu. Everyone's talking about the big collection. Worth a fortune, I hear. Promise me you're not going to sell it and leave us. It would kill Matt to think you'd do that. You're family. We need you." Annette leaned forward and whispered loving words that chilled Lulu's heart as though Annette had cursed her. "What you bring to the bakery— nobody else has that magic touch. You're our lucky star, sweetheart."

# Chapter Twelve

## Lulu

Wincing, hungover in a way she hadn't experienced since college, Lulu lifted the mug away from the Keurig machine, poured in milk, and then, after a moment's consideration, added sugar. Typically, she drank it without, but she hoped the sweetness would soothe her rocky stomach while the caffeine did its job.

Plus, the sugar would double for breakfast.

And probably lunch.

Mug in hand, stopping for a sip every few steps, she headed back to the bedroom. The mess on the floor suggested that Lulu had come home from the party and invented a fun new game called *let's toss all the clothes into a pile.*

First, she spied the previous day's jeans and wool sweater. Pulling them out, she searched around for her shoes. After a moment of kicking away at the heap, the pressure in her head knocked her to her knees. Like a blind woman, she felt around in the jumble.

Finally, she found them. Sitting back, she put on the left shoe and then the right. Getting on first one knee and then the other as if she'd suddenly hit her late eighties, she rose slowly.

She took a step.

Something cracked under her foot.

What fresh hell now? A forgotten mug? A rejected high heel?

She bent down as slowly as she'd risen. She picked up her Ralph Lauren dress. Beneath it she found a pair of limp black tights. Underneath them, glinting, were the shattered pieces of the stolen Chanel bracelet.

Late for work, Lulu tried to rush down Cortelyou Road, but her queasiness slowed her. Ambling was the best she could manage while traveling from her house to the bakery. The previous night's wine wasn't all that was making her sick. Her guilt over the bracelet shards burning a hole in her bag added to her discomfort.

The familiar scent of the bakery hit Lulu the moment she opened the door: sugary, yeasty, and laden with hints of cinnamon and vanilla. Her stomach rebelled. She reached into her pocket and popped another of the ginger candies she'd grabbed from her kitchen, hoping they'd calm her nausea.

The bakery's fragrance and the taste of the ginger took her back a million years. While pregnant with Seth, her nausea never stopped, and she'd eaten every form of ginger known to bakers, hungover drunks, and Thai restaurants. In the process, she'd had an idea for a way to bring in money. Perfumes to sell in the shop: small crystal flacons in the shape of a cake with *Quattro* written in cursive. Inside would be a unique fragrance: a bakery-scented perfume. After weeks of sketching the bottle, she'd experimented, using essential oils, almond or jojoba oil, and pure alcohol. During evenings when Matt worked late, Lulu tinkered, formulating two solid combinations.

For a week, she dabbed them on in rotation, waiting for Matt to compliment her efforts, positive she'd hit on the idea to forge her path to becoming the CEO of a new Caswell-Massy. What could be sexier than the sweet, spicy scent of rum and caramel? Who wouldn't love ginger, orange, and vanilla?

Matt. That's who.

On night eight of the fragrance gyrations, he turned to her in bed and said, "What the hell are you wearing these days? At first, I figured the smell from work was embedded in your hair, but you just took a shower. Are you using cake batter for face cream? Is it a pregnancy thing? The smell is filling the entire apartment. I feel as though I'm still at work."

She'd snuggled up close, stroking his warm skin. "You like? I made it."

"You made it?" He sniffed the crook of her neck. "You mean you made a cake?"

"No. I invented a perfume based on the bakery's scents. We can make them in bottles shaped like a cake. We can start by selling them at Quattros' and then—"

"Is that even legal? Where would you make it? How would we pay for the ingredients? The bottles? Who is going to get the approvals and do the paperwork and all that stuff?" Matt tipped his head in the manner that said he'd moved into analytical mode. "Not to rain on your idea, babe, but I don't think it's easy to sell homemade perfume. And, honestly? After working in the bakery all day, cake-scented perfume is the last thing I want to smell. Please. Can you go back to that flowery one you used to wear?"

Blaming Matt for her short-lived perfume career seemed unfair, especially now, with him gone. Sure, she'd been disappointed, but he'd virtually grown up in the bakery. Why on God's Earth would he have wanted to smell the place on her? Working at Quattros' hadn't been his dream any more than hers. Matt had headed for college with the expectation of earning a pre-law degree. Lulu planned to study art and become a painter who synthesized various art forms to create a new style, like her hero, Chagall. Plan B? Commercial art.

She and Matt had met rom-com cute on move-in day at Stony Brook College amid jams of people. Most students arrived surrounded by a few family members—in Matt's case, his entire family came. His parents, brothers, grandparents, and ninety-one-year-old great-grandmother formed a chain of Quattros, leading up the steps in the co-ed dorm. Everyone carried something, including Great-Grandma, who cradled a bakery box in her still-strong arms.

Lulu, accompanied by nobody, passed them as she struggled up the stairs with a preposterously overloaded laundry basket. Embarrassed by her lone state, she averted her gaze, trying not to meet anyone's eyes.

Three steps to reaching the landing, she tripped. Clothes, bedding, and towels spilled down the stairs in a storm of fabric.

"Stop!" Matt's mother held out her arm as though blocking a series of bombs about to detonate. "Get those things off the steps before everyone trips."

Lulu froze, hearing the woman's tone. Tears threatened. Just as she was about to give in to full-out sobbing, Matt swooped in to save her and then wound up distracting her with his perfectly squared shoulders and rock-star-floppy, almost-black hair.

"Ma. Stop." Matt picked up the scattered bits of Lulu's life and repacked them in her basket. When he discovered that she was moving into the dorm alone—while he'd arrived with enough troops for a set of triplets—Matt appointed himself and his youngest brother as Lulu's helpers.

"Don't you need to supervise what your family is doing with all your stuff?" she asked after he'd given her an hour of his complete attention.

"Supervise?" His grin revealed a chipped front tooth. Football, she'd later learned.

"You know, make sure they know what they're doing?" Lulu wished she'd worn a nicer shirt. Much nicer.

"Letting my mother direct this whole operation and my father carrying it out? I'm giving them a present. The grandmas will fold every T-shirt, Dad will arrange the furniture with a better flow, and Mom will make the bed military-style, fill every drawer, and line up my books in alphabetical order."

Having that sort of trust and belief in his family made Matt and the Quattro clan seem like visitors from another world—a better one. Matt told her later that he couldn't believe he'd bumped into a woman who rocked faded old jeans and a Fruit of the Loom white T-shirt while casually carrying her life in her arms without help. He loved what he called her lack of making a production.

The Quattros could make any life moment into a major production.

After growing up in the quiet, female-centric Second Avenue apartment with a mother who valued solitude, and a sister who escaped at every chance, she reveled in the

Quattros' energy.

By the time Lulu got pregnant at the end of their freshman year, Lulu and Matt knew they would be together for life and bowed to the inevitable. They left college and married, notwithstanding Bette's horror, and allowed Matt's family to absorb them.

While they waited for the baby, Matt went back to work at Quattros'—thinking it a temporary move. Lulu joined him.

Temporary had lasted forever. Now, all these years later, he was gone, and she remained at the bakery. On the days when grief didn't overwhelm her, the store bored her.

As Lulu made her way through Quattros' front room, she was pleased to see that all the tables were full. During the renovation, she'd come up with the idea of installing a seating area. She'd given it 1930s retro décor, which was nostalgic but bright and fun, with curved counters and walls painted ice-cream colors. Her final touch had been covering the walls with blown-up photographs from when Matt's great-grandparents first opened the bakery.

"Hey, Lu." Matt's brother Leo raised a hand in greeting from behind the counter; Lulu waved back.

A short, stocky version of Matt, Leo managed the business with two of his five brothers. *Four*, Lulu corrected herself. She'd be doing that forever, she thought: forgetting for a split second and then remembering with a fresh stab of pain.

Lulu swung open the door to the back room where she baked—her little kingdom.

"Good morning," Leo's wife chirped.

Victoria's voice came in two settings: chirp or cry. Was it possible that she had an undiagnosed mental disorder? Probably, but the family had absorbed Victoria anyway and assigned her a role like everyone else. Matt's mother,

Annette, had handed them out. If you wanted to remain a happy Quattro, you accepted what you got without argument.

Victoria *The Fragile One* became Lulu's assistant.

Matt *The Rock* was expected to weather anything they threw at him.

Her mother-in-law had pigeonholed Lulu swiftly. A month after the wedding, Annette had deemed her newest daughter-in-law *The Responsible One*.

Lulu put on her reading glasses and studied the baking schedule pinned to the bulletin board. Behind her, Victoria straightened boxes, waited for instructions, and snuck peeks at Lulu. The whipped-dog routine drove Lulu to thoughts of calling Drea for lunch. No one could trash one sister-in-law like two other sisters-in-law.

But according to today's schedule, there'd be no break for lunch or anything else. At least, Lulu thought, being that busy might keep her from obsessing over the broken Chanel bracelet. The price of which represented about a week's salary.

She turned to Victoria. "Okay, we have two cakes to start first; then we need to make ten dozen cookies for the Halstead bridal shower."

They fell into their routine. Lulu pulled out bowls while Victoria assembled ingredients. Every cake started with some basic combo of the same flour, sugar, salt, eggs, butter, and baking powder, followed by chocolate or fruits and jams.

"First, we'll tackle the Leaning Tower of Pisa," Lulu called out.

She hated making that cake; getting the exact angle for the *lean* wracked her nerves. Why anyone wanted a crooked monument to celebrate their wedding was beyond her, but Annette insisted on keeping it on the list among Lulu's wildflower, enchanted forest, and castle cakes.

"The neighborhood families love it," Annette maintained each time Lulu tried to remove it from the rotation.

"I guess I'm ready." Victoria placed a gentle hand on her nonexistent stomach. "I'm so bloated. I just feel awful. It's that time of the month. Leo thought I should have stayed home. You know. The cramps. But I couldn't do that to you."

Translation: *Please send me home.*

"Did you take some ibuprofen?"

"You know those pills nauseate me." Victoria's mouth turned down as she sat on the stool and brought her knees up to her chest. "But don't worry. I'll be okay."

Lulu knew Victoria was waiting to be excused, but she'd be damned if she gave her sister-in-law another day off. Lulu was the one who was nauseated for real, and she wasn't complaining. She turned the recipe book toward Victoria. "Measure out the dry ingredients, and I'll begin creaming the butter. Did you take it out to soften?"

Victoria clapped her hand to her mouth. "Oh, no!"

*Of course*, Lulu thought, *what was I thinking? How could I expect Victoria to remember the everyday fundamentals when it was* that time of the month?

An overwhelming heaviness came over her. Matt hadn't just left her lonely—he'd abandoned her to indentured servitude. Her mortgages and loans loomed with no solution in sight now that she'd learned that Bette hadn't died a millionaire. If Lulu lost her house, she'd have to move to the tiny upstairs apartment above the bakery where she and Matt had lived when they first married. At which point, her entire life would revolve around Quattros'. Then, before she knew it, her sons would have children, and she'd be a grandma, rocking babies with one arm while still stirring cake batter with the other.

"Oh..."

Lulu turned to the small moan coming from behind her. Victoria almost crumpled as she measured flour from the bin.

"Sorry. I'll be okay." Victoria took slow, small steps back to the table as though about to faint.

Lulu fought against her instinct to send Victoria home yet again, which conflicted with her deep desire to shake her. Last week it had been an oncoming cold. The previous week, depression had consumed her.

"Make a cup of tea if you need," Lulu said.

Victoria gave a weak nod. The woman personified useless and irresponsible. What had her sister-in-law done after Matt died? She came down with pneumonia, forcing Lulu back to work just days following the funeral, twining fondant flowers and buttercream vines through a haze of Xanax and tears. Leo had commandeered two older nephews to help out, but supervising them had been yet one more job to handle.

Leo stuck his head into the kitchen. "It's getting crazy in the front. Can Victoria sit at the register?"

"Oh, thank you, honey! Sitting will help me so much." She turned and made a babyish *please* face. "Is it okay, Lu?"

"Sure, it's okay," Leo answered. "Lulu's a pillar."

Lulu sighed as Victoria forgot how sick she was supposed to be and practically skipped out to the front room. As she creamed the butter, Lulu wondered how many more Leaning Towers she'd bake before looking up to see eighty-five candles on her birthday cake. She imagined her life rolling by in a never-ending line of pies, cakes, and cookies.

Was she doomed to give her soul to Quattros' forever because of Bette's busy credit card? How much could the Chanel collection bring if they sold everything at once on one of those sites Gabrielle kept referencing? Why the hell hadn't Bette had the collection appraised, told them what it was worth, and left them a suggestion of what to do with it?

She cracked an egg extra hard.

Over her sister's shoulder, Lulu had seen screen after screen of secondhand Chanel. Gabrielle called it *estate* or *vintage*, but really, wasn't it just secondhand? The prices were astonishing and probably inflated. Even if they were, they should offload all this crap while there was still a market. Everyone knew how tastes changed.

Depression seeped in as Lulu leveled off two cups of sugar. Why had so much of her mother's world been wrapped up in tweed, leather, braided trim, and those damned gold buttons?

As she poured out a spoonful of vanilla extract, she nodded. Yes, selling fast was the only option. Take the collection to one of those vintage stores or online places. Would the Gray Lady approve? Why not? Nothing in Bette's stupid will had said they couldn't just sell it.

Lulu switched off the mixer and stared down into the silky cake batter. How much of a cut would a vintage store take? Too much of the profits that giving them the collection wouldn't be worth it? What if they held a sale themselves? A benefit, a ball, or an auction—one of those events to which Gabrielle's crowd always flocked.

Except if they parted with it too quickly, would they ever learn what the closet meant to Bette?

Far more than she'd admit, Lulu wanted the answer to the last question more than any of the others.

# Chapter Thirteen

## Gabrielle

Once upon a time, Gabrielle had felt anticipation when she walked to work, but then she'd been designing electrifyingly modern costumes for one of Cole's new plays. Now, she shelved books.

As she turned off 6th Avenue onto 10th Street, she gave herself the usual pep talk: *You're lucky to have this job. Thea is the best boss possible, and you have an adequate salary.*

But paying for cable bills, going out for dinner occasionally with a friend, and using the subway as often as possible didn't energize or even engage her.

Gratitude was no substitute for excitement.

Nothing captivated her anymore. She'd been divorced for more than two years, and she still missed Cole. Even more, she missed her life with Cole. But, as she had to remind herself every day, he hadn't been who she thought he was, and their life had been a lie.

She knew she spent too much time looking backward for clues. But the man never gave her one hint that he was displeased with anything in their relationship or life. He'd never flagged in the bedroom—during the years he'd had his secret mistress, he'd been extra amorous—which she finally understood. During her spate of obsessively studying affairs, she'd read how the thrill of getting away with extracurricular activity could increase a spouse's libido.

But what did it matter now? She should have spent the hours and hours she'd wasted trying to understand the end of her marriage lifting weights. Or reading. Or learning to speak Italian. Or feeding pigeons. Or anything.

Cole wasn't a monster. He was a flawed man, who saw his universe as a play that was his to direct. Whether at work or home, his entire life—and therefore, hers—had been a construct. Gabrielle played a character on Cole's stage. And at a certain point, she'd been recast. And now, it was up to her to find a new part.

Shaking off her melancholy, she opened the door to Quills & Feathers and stepped into the store with forced brightness.

"Morning!" she called out as she shrugged out of her coat.

"Hello, dear." Thea stood by the front desk beside a pile of cartons, boxcutter in hand.

As Gabrielle watched with horror, her elderly boss sliced the first box open.

"Please! Let me do that." Gabrielle raced over and grabbed the Exacto knife. "I swear to God, Thea, I'm hiding that knife. No matter how many times we talk about it, the minute I turn my back, you're at it again. My heart can't take it. Hand it over."

Thea sighed, having no ground on which to argue, and reluctantly gave Gabrielle the tool. The last time Thea had slit open a carton, she'd nicked off a piece of her thumb and bled over Saint-Exupéry's *Vol de Nuit*—illustrated with engravings by Josso and worth $1800. Despite appearing to be made of iron, even at eighty-three, arthritis which swelled Thea's knuckles to gigantic proportions made her clumsy.

An hour and only one browsing customer later, Gabrielle had unpacked all the boxes and shelved their contents. Daria had once asked her if the worst part of landing at Quills & Feathers was her loss of status. Other friends assumed that living a more modest lifestyle gave her the most trouble. Of course, both those things made for misery. But moment to moment, day to day, Gabrielle's actual trial was stultifying hours of boredom.

In her obituary, they'd list monotony as the cause of death.

"Where do you want to put this?" Gabrielle held up a folio of lithographs of Matisse's stained-glass windows in *La Chapelle du Rosaire*. She knew the perfect place to shelve it, but Thea got testy when Gabrielle didn't consult her.

The shop owner raised her eyes from the plate of cookies she arranged—precisely at ten, as always—to perfection. Thumbprint butter cookies dotted with raspberry or apricot jam were available at one every afternoon; raisin or ginger scones appeared at four. A pot of tea and a pitcher of ice water replete with floating lemon slices accompanied the treats.

Thea believed these offerings burnished the store's reputation as a beacon of civility in Manhattan. Whether or not the treats brought in business didn't seem to be the point. Enjoying the company of other white-haired women in their eighties who delighted in nibbling treats pleased Thea as much as any sale.

"You decide," Thea said. "I can't make every little decision."

The answer, so unlike Thea, startled Gabrielle into silence.

Lately, Thea's mood steadily dimmed as the day progressed. First snapping and then sighing, Thea acted like an octogenarian moody teenager ruled by hormones. Perhaps when Gabrielle got home, she'd research the emotional stages of the ninth decade of life.

And maybe afterward, she'd get three cats and then start knitting an afghan. Take up cross-stitching samplers. Start a bullet journal dedicated to the upcoming programs she wanted to watch on Channel 13.

Or she should say screw all the above and go to the Four Seasons' Ty Bar, have a dirty martini, and pick out a different kind of treat.

"Thea, are you okay?" she finally asked.

"Sorry," Thea said. "I've been unkind of late."

"You could never be unkind." Gabrielle placed the folio in an open cabinet next to Salvador Dali's *Alice in Wonderland.* "But you do seem out of sorts. Is it that doctor's visit you had? Are you okay?"

Thea brushed Gabrielle's question away with an impatient gesture. "That was nothing. The doctor told me he should be as healthy. It's my son who talks about me as though I'm on death's door and considers my cholesterol medicine is akin to chemotherapy. He's what I'm worried about, and it's making me snippy. I apologize."

Gabrielle wondered if this had something to do with Nigel's sneaky visit a few days ago. "Is there anything I can do? Talk to him, maybe?" She put down her work and sat at the small table where Thea arranged cookies—strawberry jam today.

Thea sighed. "You are a dear. I don't think so, but you might as well know. Nigel and his wife have become quite intrusive recently. They think I'm getting too old to keep running the shop and are nagging me to sell the building. They're treating me as though I'm feeble."

Gabrielle wasn't surprised. Nigel had said as much to her the other day. She needed to start watching out for Thea more, including keeping track of Nigel's and Pamela's visits.

"Sorry to say this about your son and his wife, but they're crazy. You're a dynamo. God. Why else would I have to wrest the Exacto knife from your hands day after day?"

"Nigel is my only child. He's all I have," Thea said sadly and then let out a deep sigh.

"That's not true." Gabrielle snapped a thumbprint cookie in half. "Do you know how many times I come in and almost say, '*Good morning, Mom?*' Because, really, after working here for almost two years, you feel like a mother to me."

Thea rose, came over to Gabrielle, and enveloped her in a powdery, violet-scented hug. "That breaks my heart and warms it all at the same time. I'm honored and grateful."

At six-fifteen that evening, Gabrielle entered Ty, the upscale watering hole tucked inside the Four Seasons Hotel on East 57th Street. Sidling up to the marble bar, she took a seat on one of the luxurious leather stools and examined the dimly lit room while waiting for the bartender.

The Ty Bar drew her the same way cigarettes had once called. Even as every drag appeased her screaming need for the nicotine back then, she'd felt filthy.

When the bartender arrived, she ordered a dirty martini. "Very dirty." She smiled at the irony. Or was there any?

He nodded and left her to peruse the crowd. As was

typical for most weeknights by six p.m., the Ty man, a particular type—for better or worse, *her* type—had begun filling up the bar.

*He,* the man she invariably chose over and over, considered himself one of the rulers of the universe. Sharply dressed, he never registered Ty's high prices, easily affording a round of the barrel-aged Michter's bourbon at sixty dollars a glass or a thirty-dollar Stoli Elite martini. Years of self-importance had swelled his head into believing he possessed God-given rights to search out a beautiful and shapely woman if that was what his mood dictated. Regardless if he was married or otherwise involved.

Gabrielle touched the spot where her wedding ring had once sat. She made the automatic gesture far too often. Sometimes, Gabrielle envied her sister's ability to keep wearing her gold band. Other times, she had an unkind urge to ask when, if ever, Lulu planned to remove it.

Gabrielle's ring, which she and Cole had designed together, now resided in a blue velvet box in her lingerie drawer. Sometimes, on the worst nights, Gabrielle took it out and slipped it on. She'd sit in the dark and run her right thumb over the eternity band's emerald-cut diamonds and remember how Cole had once enjoyed picking up her hand and turning it from side to side to send rainbow reflections onto the wall.

"Our love is all those colors, Gabrielle," he'd say. "Intense, beautiful, magical."

And then, alone in her tiny apartment, she'd remember the rest of his bullshit and shove the ring back into the drawer.

Bette had repeatedly suggested she sell the ring, exchange it, or have it redesigned. Maybe one day, she'd figure out why she held on to it. Not now, though. Now, she had something else to do.

While the men looked her over, Gabrielle directed her gaze back at them. After a lifetime in the theater, she had an uncanny ability to sort the nasty, self-absorbed men from the self-absorbed but safe and almost considerate ones. She could tell with a glance who was disappointed by her age versus those unafraid of an age-appropriate assignation.

Gabrielle skipped anyone wearing a wedding ring or sporting a white band of flesh, signifying a wedding ring hidden in a pocket. Man-shopping brought on enough self-loathing as it was. She'd never choose to do to any other woman what Nancy had done to her.

As she took delicate sips of the dirty martini the bartender had set before her, Gabrielle examined that evening's choices with practiced eyes. After narrowing it down, she watched for clues among the two she'd selected.

Was he alone?

She didn't like interacting with a crowd.

Did he seem at ease?

Gabrielle wasn't trying out for the role of a nursemaid or therapist.

Was he scanning the room too ardently?

She wanted a man who she thought would appreciate the company but didn't consider her desperate for it.

Mr. Right-for-the-Night sat at the end of the bar. Not so old that he needed to prove himself with a woman who was too young for him. Not so young that he'd consider his presence a gift.

Another good sign was that he wasn't attempting to hide his thinning hair, indicating healthy self-esteem.

She further evaluated him: tortoiseshell glasses, broad shoulders, and just enough paunch to shore up her self-assurance—plus, no wedding band.

Gabrielle needed a night off from living inside her head, and this guy seemed like he'd fit the bill.

She sent him vibes. And waited.

Gabrielle had shared her skill at romantic telekinesis only with Daria—her sister-in-law and most judgment-free friend—who'd been fascinated by Gabrielle's ability to draw a man's attention to her via such subtlety. Daria had even insisted on coming with her one night, sitting a few stools away and observing. She'd walked away, duly impressed. Only Daria knew that, post-Cole, Gabrielle had slept with more men than in her entire life previously. Daria never chastised, though she never failed to chant: *"Condoms, condoms, condoms."*

In return, Gabrielle sympathetically nodded each time Daria admitted how severely she hated spending time with her stepchildren. Since her husband's girls had hit adolescence, Daria fantasized about divorcing Martin simply so she could have every other weekend free from his snotty daughters.

While Gabrielle waited for Mr. Maybe Right to decide if he would respond to her silent invitation, she studied her phone as though dozens of messages demanded her attention. When she finally looked up from her imaginary business, the man smiled, clearly waiting to catch her eye. Over the next few minutes, they performed more wordless rituals of bar mating: she gave him a Mona Lisa half-smile, then went back to scrutinizing her phone. He held her gaze with a glance that said: *I'm interested, but only in a respectful way.*

The mutual attraction sparked a fire inside Gabrielle. Even though she assumed the encounter would end the way most of them did—with her alone, regretful, and in need of a shower—she didn't allow reality to temper her lust. She craved the escape.

Gabrielle walked into her apartment with Mr. Right-for-the-Night. Their kiss just inside the doorway was an adequate if not a stomach-dropping thrill. Moments of regret didn't bubble until the all-too-familiar conversation began.

"Beautiful apartment." He looked around as though seeking something specific upon which to remark. She put money that he'd choose either the antique rug or the art hanging over the couch. The large blow-up of a vintage black and white photo of Broadway's theater district lit up at night generally got the most attention.

Joseph Truscott, III had emphasized the *third* during their formal introduction, an affectation that had at first annoyed and then reassured her. Reassured because it seemed unlikely that a man planning to assault her would add that fillip of a descriptive—annoyed, as it suggested stuffiness.

Stuffy turned her off.

She bet on the rug.

"That rug must have been in your family for generations," he said.

The item had indeed lived many decades in the family—but the family had been Cole's.

"Yes," she said. "It's an antique Feraghan Sarouk. Probably woven in the mid-1800s. Mother was generous. Anything I admired, she gave me." Gabrielle swept her arm in an inclusive arc. "My grandmother had a story about every piece and—"

She stopped, unwilling to continue the fairy tale. She'd acquired almost every item in a drag-out battle with Cole. Gabrielle didn't even want most of them anymore. The abundance crowding her small apartment represented piece after piece of punitive damage. She wasn't proud of her greediness. If she had money to spare, she'd redecorate with clean-sweeping mid-century modern, streamlining the space and herself.

"Drink?" she asked.

"Yes. Brandy?"

She turned to the antique gold and glass French bar cart, which Cole had bought at an auction. She pulled a pair of Baccarat balloon glasses forward, picked up the matching carafe, and poured. The crystal had been a wedding gift from Bette. Gabrielle's marriage may have died, but the accouterments of the union still surrounded her.

She handed Joseph, III his drink and walked toward the couch.

"Should we sit?" she asked.

Following a step behind, he ran an inquisitive hand down her back. "You're stunning."

There had been a time when her looks required little aid. One post-college boyfriend had asked if she modeled. "*Sleek, lean, large eyes, great bones,*" he'd whispered after asking. "*You could be on any magazine cover.*"

Now, she relied on shelves of creams and serums and a closet of well-cut clothes. Once-chiseled cheekbones now needed artful shading. Once-full lips lately required lining to define their shape. She'd added oils to the skin that no longer glowed on its own and chose colors that flattered her touched-up hair. She designed herself the way she'd once created costumes, so compliments meant a lot. Probably too much, so she didn't respond. The very last thing she wanted was to appear needy.

Joseph the third removed his jacket, carefully placing it on the back of an occasional chair. Gabrielle noticed the label. Ralph Lauren Purple. Top of the line, but a safe choice. He loosened his tie as he walked back toward her. Hermès. She recognized the pattern. She felt as though she were about to bed Saks Men's Department.

"What do you do for a living?" he asked as he sat beside her.

She tried to think of a career insignificant enough to check any further conversation. Then, she almost laughed. Her actual job was perfect.

"I work in a bookstore."

Her instincts were right. Joseph's only response was to pick up his brandy. She followed suit, wondering how long it would take this one to make his move. She wished she weren't so jaded, but she'd done this too many times already. The mutual uncovering of careers, family, and hopes had become a monotonous prelude to the first act.

As he replaced the glass on the coffee table, Gabrielle noticed his Cartier gold wristwatch, which came with at least a $20,000 price tag. Joseph the third was both wealthy and appropriate, as Bette would say. Why that mattered, Gabrielle didn't know. Her sole goal was sex. But even so, she allowed the net worth of her one-night stands to measure her value. She was, after all, her mother's daughter.

# Chapter Fourteen

## Gabrielle

"How come Bette only gave you a membership to this place?" Lulu asked.

Gabrielle shook her head in disbelief. "Buying someone who lives and works in Brooklyn a membership to a library on 79th Street in Manhattan would be only slightly less than insane," she whispered.

They shouldn't be talking at all. The New York Society Library's reading room required silence. They'd come here to research the articles their mother had torn from magazines and saved in her albums. Gabrielle wanted to find their missing dates for the inventory; the library had decades of fashion magazines bound and shelved in the stacks. She'd taken advantage of their treasure trove to do research here many times during her years designing costumes.

After two hours, they were thankfully almost done with their work and more than finished with each other. Gabrielle had hoped the wood-paneled library's crackling fireplace and big, comfortable, leather armchairs would induce a sisterly calm, but Lulu had arrived in a mood that hadn't abated.

Lulu shrugged. "Whether or not I'd use it isn't the point."

"Then what is?"

"Bette saw you as deserving of this rarefied place, but not me."

"Oh, Lulu. You know that's not true. She gave you a gift certificate to that spa near you for the same amount. She was nothing if not fair."

"To the penny maybe, but not with her opinions of us. This library proves she thought you were the more intellectual and cultured one."

Gabrielle ached to respond honestly to Lulu's self-pitying words but instead rolled her eyes.

"Don't do that," Lulu said.

"What?"

"Dismiss how I feel."

"I'm not."

"Okay, if that's true, then I have an idea I want to talk to you about," Lulu said.

"We're not supposed to talk in here. Can't it wait until we're finished here and back at Mom's?"

"No, I don't want to wait. Besides, we're the only ones here."

Lulu had a point.

"I came up with this idea last night," her sister said. "And I can't stop thinking about it."

Gabrielle waited, hoping it wouldn't be something she'd have to veto. Her sister had some pretty crazy ideas. *Creative ideas,* Gabrielle corrected herself. She had to be more generous and not fall into the Bette trap of being so judgmental. She should appreciate that Lulu was wildly inventive because if they were ever going to get their relationship back on track, Gabrielle had to be more respectful and open-minded.

"I think we should liquidate the closet by having a fundraiser. We can pick a charity and give them a percentage of the takings, but the rest will be for us. Do something important with what Bette left us while being fair to ourselves at the same time."

"How cute. Mother Theresa in Chanel." Gabrielle's snark slipped out. But she couldn't help it. It was an appalling idea. "Lulu, this is Bette's legacy. Not something to relegate to a stoop sale."

Lulu glared. "Nice to see you're not being dismissive."

Gabrielle slammed closed the massive volume of 1950s *Vogue* magazines, letting a cloud of dust billow up.

A gentleman in his seventies entered, giving the sisters a harsh glare that shushed them straightaway.

"Let's go," Gabrielle hissed. She seethed as she stacked the piles of bound magazines they'd retrieved.

Gabrielle was frustrated. She'd hoped today's excursion to the library would reveal Bette had some Chanel pieces important enough to offer them for sale to some of the more prestigious costume institutes. Meanwhile, her sister had been thinking about peddling them—and to Gabrielle's old friends, no less. That's all she wanted to do. Invite her old crowd to see how pathetic her life had become, working in a bookstore, and auctioning off her mother's wardrobe.

They left the library in silence, walked down the marble steps, and out into the street. Gabrielle wrapped her scarf tighter and gingerly stepped over a pile of gray slush.

"Can we at least consider my idea?" Lulu asked.

"Sure. Consider the stoop sale considered; my vote is no."

"Come on, I'm not talking about anything close to a

stoop sale, and you know it. I'm talking about a lovely event to benefit a good cause. Call it *Chanel for Charity*. We could raise money for say a battered woman's shelter in the city. You can get your friends to come. You were always going to fundraisers with them. Surely it wasn't just for fun. You all must have loved doing good, too."

Lulu's idea struck Gabrielle as an assault on so many levels. "Those kinds of events—luncheons, galas, shows—require months and months to organize. An entire year. We could never get anyone to come to a last-minute, glorified tag sale. Plus, I'm not in touch with those women anymore. Except for Daria, they all decided they had no use for me once scandal tarnished me. More importantly, I think Mom wanted us to develop something inspired for her collection. Something meaningful."

"What's more meaningful than helping women who've been assaulted and raped?" Lulu crossed her arms. "What do *you* think Mom would consider meaningful enough?"

"How about you learning not to be so goddamned holier than thou every second? I'd vote yes on that idea."

"Get over yourself. You are not the only person who matters. Or have you forgotten that yet again?"

Gabrielle didn't respond, not wanting to say something she'd regret. She had *not* forgotten Lulu when Matt had died. She'd done as much as she had been capable of at the time. Meanwhile, Lulu had her whole perfect family to surround her with love and pity. Gabrielle had had no one to help her weather her storm of loss.

"You know, buying vintage is very green these days," Lulu said, not at all reading her audience. "The planet is choking on junk," she continued as though Gabrielle were rapt with attention. "We'd make that the cause and be climate change warriors. And if you need it to be fancy, I'll bake the fanciest cupcakes you've ever seen."

"Right. That's what society fundraisers are—church basement socials with upmarket versions of Hostess Cupcakes. I have a better idea, Lu. Why don't we simply distribute the Chanel to the homeless tonight?"

"Oh, of course! A much better idea." Lulu matched her sister's sarcastic tone. "Shall I run that by the Gray Lady? Want me to call her right now?"

"You've never been even a quarter as funny as you think. I'm not going to change my mind about any kind of fundraiser. Drop it."


Lulu and Gabrielle entered Bette's lobby, barely talking as they stomped ice from their boots before entering the elevator. They had just reached their mother's front door when they heard a voice.

"Girls! Gabrielle! Lulu!"

Gabrielle turned around to see Imogene, Bette's friend. The last thing she wanted was to be polite and social right now. She raised her gloved hand in greeting. "Hey there."

Before she could stop her sister, Lulu ran down the hall and threw her arms around the woman. Gabrielle watched them embrace. Lulu probably hadn't met the woman more than a few times, but she could connect to people in a way that neither Gabrielle nor Bette shared. She must have inherited it from her father.

Not for the first time, Gabrielle felt a pang of jealousy. She'd lost her father when she was five. He'd never been there to teach, help, shelter, or love her as she grew up. Lulu's father had always been there for her; her sister benefited from having him in her life in a way that Gabrielle had never experienced.

Leaving her sister chatting with Imogene, Gabrielle walked inside Bette's apartment. She stood in the foyer, taking off her coat and praying Lulu wouldn't drag the neighbor back with her. Gabrielle had never been good at small talk at the best of times, and these were anything but the best.

Dealing with Bette's legacy had become depressing as well as confusing. They'd only faced the task for a bit over a week, but she woke each morning feeling the weight of the job as though it had been dragging on forever. Gabrielle sat on the bench to pull off her boots, and sure enough, Lulu and Imogene came through the door arm in arm.

They weren't guest-prepared. Dust gathered on the whatnot table. Coffee cups and plates sat in the sink from the last time she and Lulu had been here. Wine glasses, too. In her entire life, Bette hadn't left out a single unwashed dish. Gabrielle couldn't conjure her mother leaving as much as a sweater flung over a chair back or an unfolded newspaper.

"Sorry for the mess," Gabrielle blurted.

Imogene glanced around. "Looks perfect to me. In ten minutes, this place would be ready to receive the Queen of England."

"Come. Sit." Lulu led Imogene into the living room.

Gabrielle rushed ahead to pick up the empty bottle of wine and rumpled napkins they'd left on the coffee table during their previous visit. "Bette would have another coronary if she saw her apartment like this."

"Sweetheart, if you are going to try to live up to Bette's housekeeping standards, give yourself a big red F. Don't drive yourself crazy. I never did." Imogene came over and wrapped her arms around Gabrielle, not an easy task as Imogene barely hit five feet tall.

"We're already going kind of crazy because of how impossible Bette is making things," Lulu said.

"Just how does a dead woman manage that particular

miracle?" Imogene asked as she sat on the couch.

Gabrielle bit down on her impatience. She wanted to finish here, go home to her living room, pour a glass of wine, and lose herself in a fat novel while Miles Davis played in the background.

Work today had been brutal. First, hours of boredom, then a visit from Eleanor Lampert, a theater director for whom she'd once designed. Eleanor, who'd arrived looking like mutton dressed as lamb, actually laughed aloud when she spotted Gabrielle.

"Darling," she'd crowed. "I'd wondered where you disappeared. Never did I think I'd find you working as a shopgirl. Well, it agrees with you. You look adorable."

Gabrielle had wondered what sin she'd committed in a former life to earn such exuberant *schadenfreude*. Perhaps hitting the now-gone trifecta—great job, beautiful apartment, beloved husband—had required more humbleness than she'd exhibited.

"I've been right here in plain sight the entire time," Gabrielle had answered. "I'm surprised no one mentioned it."

Of course, Eleanor knew she'd find Gabrielle at the shop. The truth shone as clearly as the Juvederm plumping the woman's face. Gabrielle's slide down the pyramid of Manhattan's pecking order had been such juicy gossip.

"Can I get us some tea?" Lulu suggested.

Her sister seemed a little too excited to have Imogene there, Gabrielle thought. Probably because, with a guest present, the sisters couldn't keep up the bickering they'd begun at the library.

"How about something stronger?" Gabrielle suggested. If she couldn't have a glass of wine at home, she might as well have one here.

"Yes!" Imogene glanced at the liquor cabinet. "I would

very much not mind a bit of Belle de Brillet in honor of Bette. Your mother and I shared a glass after dinner at least twice a week. She loved the stuff."

Lulu gathered snifters. "Belle de Brillet?"

"Nectar of the gods. May I?" Imogene nodded to the well-stocked bar cart.

"Make yourself at home," Lulu offered.

Imogene reached for the bottle without needing to search, an abstract rendering of a glass pear filled with a golden liquid. "Let me serve you, girls—you both look worn out. Gorgeous, of course, but a bit ragged."

"That was my mother's favorite?" How did Gabrielle not know this? She turned to Lulu. "Did you know?"

"I don't even know what it is."

"It's pear liqueur," Gabrielle said. "French."

Imogene shook her head with a bit of sadness. "Daughters never know their mothers in full."

Imogene poured a small amount into each of the three glasses she'd taken off the cart's bottom shelf. "Shall we toast Bette?"

Gabrielle and Lulu shared one of those glances that pass between sisters even when angry at each other. Within seconds they'd acknowledged three things:

*1) Whatever they said needed to be one hundred percent positive—this was a friend of Bette's.*

*2) Imogene shouldn't feel forced to toast first.*

*3) The eldest sister should begin.*

"Here's to Bette. Immortal in her impeccability," Gabrielle said.

They clinked glasses, and then Gabrielle took a sip. Sweet and spicy heat filled her mouth.

Now Imogene lifted her glass. "To Bette, my best friend. I—"

"I didn't realize you were her best friend." Gabrielle was

aware they'd been close, but not that close. It must have been an attraction-of-opposites friendship. Whereas Bette's fluid grace gave her the air of a Modigliani, Imogene reminded Gabrielle of a nurturing mother painted by Mary Cassatt.

"Surprises you, right?" Imogene asked.

Gabrielle didn't know what to say.

"Don't be embarrassed. On the surface, we never seemed to have much in common."

Gabrielle knew the woman's history from Bette. Imogene was born into the mores of the Upper West Side: Zabar's bagels and progressive politics. Upon marrying into banking money and the Upper East Side, Imogene had wound up a bit of a fish out of water. Despite her new circumstances and ability to afford couture, she continued to prefer Eileen Fisher over Chanel, donating the difference in price to Emily's List.

Imogene's husband had fallen in love with her when she'd been a kindergarten teacher and never asked her to change—quite the opposite. He begged her to remain the woman he'd chosen. Telling the story, Bette had laughed, saying the man didn't have to worry. Imogene remained more Macy's than Bergdorf's, other than falling in love with expensive massages and the occasional designer coat or bag.

Imogene squeezed Gabrielle's hand. "The rocks in your mother's head fit the holes in mine." She raised her glass again to finish the toast. "To Bette, my best friend. I miss the hell out of you. Here's to your wicked observations, your ability to laugh at yourself, and your founding the SES."

Wicked observations? Sure. But Bette's ability to laugh at herself? And the SES? Gabrielle drank the last of her pear cognac, relaxing under the luxurious fruity embrace. "The SES? What's that?"

"The Style Endures Society," Imogene said.

Gabrielle shook her head, clueless.

"She never told you?" Imogene asked.

"Not a word," Lulu said.

"Well, you both know your mother was fond of Chanel, yes?" A mischievous smile appeared on Imogene's face.

"Fond? That's putting it mildly," Lulu said.

"She used to quote Chanel all the time—" Imogene continued.

"No kidding," Gabrielle interrupted and shot her sister another look.

"One of her favorites was: *'Fashion changes, but style endures.'* We all loved that sentiment."

Lulu refilled their glasses. "Who's we all?" Lulu asked.

"The SES. Like I just said. You really don't know, do you?"

"Mom was a bit of a sphinx," Gabrielle said—proud of her quick thinking. Sphinx seemed a far kinder description than an emotional lockbox.

"Talk loud," Lulu said. "I'll prepare a snack."

"We're a group who met each other about ten years ago." Imogene raised her voice so it carried to the kitchen area. "We were all about retirement age, suddenly at loose ends. It turned out none of us liked competing with the young mothers at the fancy gyms. We'd each had the same idea and wound up taking yoga at the 92nd Street Y. Less Lululemon, more tunics with tights."

"Bette took yoga?" Gabrielle asked in wonder. Yet another unknown Bette aspect.

Lulu came back with an unopened package of Carr's Cheese Crackers. "I didn't know she knew what a Y was."

"The more you discover about Bette, the more you'll be surprised." Imogene reached for her snifter and drank deeply. "Bette could be a bit of a snob—all of us have our little flaws. But your mother was extraordinary in so many ways. She shined like the brightest star. We all looked up to her."

Lulu appeared confused. "For fashion advice?"

Imogene laughed. "Yes, but also for so much more than that. Her wisdom kept some of us afloat during our worst times. Bette encouraged everyone to bring their better angels to whatever problems they struggled with."

"I love hearing that, but I don't recognize the woman you're describing," Gabrielle said, surprised but also a little in awe.

"You might if you look harder and deeper."

"What do you mean?" Lulu asked.

"Bette never achieved her dreams and couldn't bear the thought of you two following in her footsteps. She probably pushed you both too hard. Impossibly hard. And when you didn't quite achieve her insanely unfair expectations, she felt like she'd failed. And that made her angry at herself. And, I suppose, sometimes you girls."

As though a series of movie shots played, Gabrielle saw the many times Bette had seemed so disappointed in her or Lulu. Was it possible that she'd been disappointed in herself? And if that were the case, how sad on all counts. Because she and Lulu had been relatively happy with their lives; they hadn't thought they failed. At least, she didn't think Lulu had. And Gabrielle hadn't until her marriage dissolved.

"We girls in the group weren't mirrors of your mother's past the way you both were."

"What do you mean?" Lulu leaned forward. She looked, Gabrielle thought, as if she were drinking in the reminiscences.

"You, Gabrielle, reminded Bette of losing her beloved Oliver. Lulu, you reminded her of the mistake she made by marrying your father, I'm sorry to say. We were just her friends—it was easier for her to be generous and show us compassion. Though, trust me, at one time or another, we all got sliced by her sharpness."

"What else did she hide from us? The secret room and now the Style Endures Society," Gabrielle said.

"Secret room?" Imogene asked. "What are you talking about?"

"You don't know about the closet?" Lulu rose.

"The closet?"

Gabrielle gestured for Imogene to get up from the chair. "Even you didn't know? Wow. Time for some show and tell."

So, it turned out Bette hadn't only kept secrets from Gabrielle and Lulu: Imogene, they learned, had never stepped foot in the bedroom. Of course, that made sense. Living in the same building, she'd have immediately seen that Bette had cut the room in half.

They led Imogene into Bette's bedroom, where the older woman immediately put her hand to her heart. "What did she do?"

Gabrielle walked to the closet and opened the door. "Behold."

Imogene stood on the threshold of the walk-in as though blinded by the array of black boxes slashed with Chanel's logo, the shelves of bags, and the rows of clothes on silk hangers.

"I knew she was a, um, fan. But this? I never imagined." She turned to Gabrielle. "Can I go in?"

Gabrielle laughed. "I know. Lulu and I felt like we needed to ask permission when we first saw it, too."

"Neither of you had any idea?" Imogene asked.

"The first we heard was when the lawyer who presented Bette's will read the words *her collection*."

Imogene stepped into the middle of the closet and made a slow circle. "Have you gone through it all yet?"

Gabrielle ran a hand over one a row of pocketbooks. "We're inventorying the clothes and shoes fairly quickly, but we're handling the bags more slowly."

"Why?"

"Get ready for another surprise." Gabrielle reached up for a mid-sized black box, opened it, and tipped it toward Imogene. "So, inside all of the bags so far—"

"Oh," their mother's friend interrupted as she pressed her hand to her mouth at the sight of the rare black alligator bag. "This is like finding out Bette owned a unicorn."

"You recognize it?" Lulu asked.

"I may not indulge in high-end Chanel. Well, not often. But Bette and I were big window shoppers. At least, I thought she was just looking. I had no idea. For goodness sake, she'd scrimp on dishwashing liquids, buying the generic brand. 'What does it matter?' she used to say—'I decant.'" Imogene touched the handbag gently as though it were a bubble in danger of bursting. "Only Bette would decant generic detergent into a cut-glass bottle."

Lulu and Gabrielle laughed at the same time.

"She may have passed on a trait or two," Lulu said.

"You girls know what this costs?" Imogene asked.

Gabrielle nodded. "Yes, we've been looking everything up. I saw this bag listed on a resale site for thirty-eight thousand dollars." Gabrielle put one finger on the precious object.

"Which is why we need to hold the fundraiser ASAP. While there's still a market for these things."

Gabrielle glared.

"What fundraiser? What's wrong?" Imogene asked.

"Lulu's ready to put everything on the block. She wants us to hold some sort of yard sale—"

"Not a yard sale—" Lulu argued.

Gabrielle held up her hand to halt Lulu's words. "But

I'm not ready to dispose of the collection so quickly. I think we need more time to take stock of it and understand what this is. What it means."

Lulu scowled. "It means money. How many times do you need to look these things up to know what they're worth?"

Imogene stood and put out her arms like a referee. "Nothing will be solved right now, not by arguing. Take a breath, both of you. Now, Gabrielle, you were starting to say something about what was inside the bags? The reason you're going slowly?"

"Right, that's what I wanted to show you." Gabrielle opened the pocketbook, slipped her hand inside, ran her fingers over the opulent satin lining, and drew out an envelope they'd previously read. Carefully, she lifted the flap, pulled out the notecard, and read.

"*If you were born without wings, do nothing to prevent them from growing.—Coco Chanel.* And it's in Mom's handwriting."

"Ah!" Imogene nodded.

"You knew about the notes?" Lulu crossed her arms over her chest, hugging herself.

Imogene pursed her lips as though deep in thought. She took a beat and then said: "I'm familiar with Bette's love of Coco quotes."

"We've found one in every bag so far. We read one, sometimes two a day," Lulu said.

"Why so few, sweetheart?" Imogene asked.

Lulu shrugged, seemingly unable to answer.

Gabrielle moved next to her sister and made a gentle circle on her back. Lulu didn't mean to be so challenging—her sister was as lost as Gabrielle. She missed Bette, too; she just showed it differently.

"I think…" Gabrielle hadn't tried to articulate it before, but now she knew exactly why they were spacing out the bags. "I think because when we finish finding the notes, then Mom's truly gone."

Beside her, Lulu gave a sigh that sounded that quavered with unshed tears.

"Have you read one yet today?" Imogene asked quietly.

"Not yet," Gabrielle said.

"How many bags do you have left to open?" Imogene asked.

"Dozens," Lulu said.

"The last one was Lulu's. Next one is mine. We take turns."

"Why is that, dear?"

Gabrielle felt embarrassed, telling Imogene about her theory, but she'd gone this far. "The idea sounds crazy, I know, but I think our mother meant each saying for whichever of us opens it. I feel as though Bette is speaking to us. Nuts, right?"

"Oh, but not at all. It's a wonderful concept. I love that you believe that!" Imogene put her hands together and held them to her lips. "Can I witness an unveiling? I miss Bette so much. Nobody talks about being widowed by your best friend. Every day I wait for her to call or go to call her. There should be a name for this loss."

Gabrielle turned and looked over the shelves, willing a box to call her. She'd hated her life today. Hated that she'd spent the previous night cheapening herself with James the third, hated that her old crowd disrespected her for working at Quills & Feathers, and hated that she and Lulu were still bickering. Perhaps a new note would shine a light on a new path.

Gabrielle stretched for the hardest to reach box and pulled it down. Opening it slowly, she revealed a multi-colored concoction.

Imogene peeked over her shoulder. "Look at that damn

bag. Lord knows I never had a hint that your mother bought this."

Trompe l'oeil watercolor swatches that appeared to be hand-painted covered quilted white leather.

"You recognize it?" Lulu asked.

"The Style Endures Society made a bit of a game of discussing important iconic fashion statements. Like this one. The Colorama Flap bag from about six or seven years ago. I especially love the fun bags, and this one is as amusing as they come. And extremely rare."

"How did she manage to buy things like this?" Lulu asked.

"By decanting generic detergent," Imogene said. They all laughed. "Go on, Gabrielle. Let's see what's inside," she urged.

Gabrielle turned the double CC clasp gingerly, lifted the flap, reached inside, dug into the interior pocket, felt for the card, and pulled it out. After reading it twice, she shook her head in disbelief.

The magic had happened again.

"I swear. I had a day today, and while I was searching for a bag, I thought about it. And sure enough, this fits. Bette's ghost is speaking to us. I don't know how, but she is."

Lulu reached for the card and, in a whisper, read the words. "*My life didn't please me, so I created my life.—Coco Chanel.*"

"She's not just speaking to you. She's speaking about herself. Bette was the patron saint of reinvention. What wonderful advice." Imogene swiped at her tears.

"But what do we do with all this? What did she want us to do?"

"Girls, you need some help. I think it's time you met the women of the Style Endures Society."

# Chapter Fifteen

## Lulu

Lulu raced from finishing at the bakery to get to her mother's apartment by six-thirty, already exhausted by the idea of an evening of smiling for her mother's friends. She couldn't believe Imogene had arranged the meeting overnight. More unbelievable was Bette having a group of buddies who'd tagged themselves with a name like a gaggle of thirteen-year-olds. The unknown Bette. How many more facets were there to her mother?

As she rode up on the elevator, Lulu's growling stomach almost led her to break down and open the cookie bag she'd grabbed from the bakery. Producing a snow-themed wedding cake, replete with scenes from *Dr. Zhivago,* had made for a long day. Why would a bride or groom want a homage to romantic infidelity, loneliness, and revolution? Nevertheless, she'd spent hours painting a swirling storm on fondant. Finding the exact ratio of edible silver luster dust, so the snow sparkled against the stark white frosting, had taken much longer than expected.

She semi-dreaded tonight's visit, afraid it would be a futile waste of time. Lulu couldn't understand how the group could help; she hoped Imogene hadn't planned the night to show off that she was the first to know about Bette's hidden treasures.

She sighed. Yet one more roadblock to get through before they became serious. No matter how much Gabi swore that Chanel would never lose its value, Lulu felt they needed to strike while there was still such a robust market for expensive old clothes. Thomas, the brightest of her brothers-in-law, had taken Lulu aside just that morning, warning her the economy was heading for a downturn. He urged her to divest her holdings into the safest possible vehicles.

Lulu didn't have the heart to tell him that the only stock she owned came from what she boiled down from chicken bones. Matt had had many outstanding qualities—but she'd never added financial wizard to that list. Whatever extra they had, went towards the boys' education and extra-curricular activities.

"Just in time to help." Gabrielle let Lulu into Bette's apartment, raised her eyebrows, and gestured towards Imogene in the living room. "We're putting out food. Lots of food."

Lulu hung up her coat and joined her sister and their mother's friend. Seeing the lavish spread arranged on Bette's coffee table, Lulu's mouth watered.

Squares of thinly sliced dark rounds of bread made a ring around a sable and smoked salmon platter. A bowl of frothy cream cheese sat in the center. Another tray held mini new potatoes topped with dollops of crème fraîche and grains of ebony caviar.

"I'm sorry. I didn't bring anything more elaborate than a bag of Italian wedding cookies," Lulu said.

"Since we don't need anything but cookies, you brought the perfect thing. Here, give them to me." Imogene took the bag and began arranging the cookies on a blue buffet plate ringed with gold leaves.

"I don't recognize these dishes, but I love them," Lulu said.

"They're mine; I didn't want to rummage through your mother's shelves," Imogene said. "Okay, I'm lying. I wanted to but knew it would upset me to go through Bette's things."

"Going through Matt's things almost killed me," Lulu said.

"You had to do that alone?" Gabrielle appeared stricken. "I assumed Nicholas and Seth helped."

"They offered, but they were grieving themselves. I wanted to spare them."

"Oh, Lu," Gabrielle said. "I should have been there."

Lulu remembered the rage she'd felt towards Gabrielle during those weeks. In retrospect, maybe her sister had provided a safe place for her anger. Rather than cursing Matt for dying, she'd cursed Gabrielle for abandoning her. Now, for the first time, Lulu tried to put herself in Gabrielle's shoes. What had those early days of her sister's divorce been like for her? Misery shouldn't be a competition.

She touched Gabrielle's shoulder. "What the hell. Neither of us was in any shape to help the other."

"But death—" Gabrielle started.

Lulu looked around at the furniture in their mother's living room. The black lacquer screen behind the bar, the ivory coasters, an intricate silver figurine; every piece carried Bette's DNA just like her and Gabrielle.

Lulu nodded. "Yeah. Death. But there's more than one kind of death, isn't there?"

"Absolutely," Gabrielle said. "Thank you, sis."

Lulu felt tears threatening and needed a distraction. She didn't want to cry right before everyone showed up. "Let's get the glasses," she said.

The two of them went into the kitchen. Gabrielle opened the cabinet, and they both stared at the sea of crystal stemware and barware—a fortune in breakables.

"Is what we leave behind the ultimate sum of who we are?" Lulu couldn't help it and began crying. "Damn it. Now I'll look even crummier than when I walked in."

"Wait here," Gabrielle said and left, returning in thirty seconds, holding one of Bette's ivory handkerchief edged in lace. "Here. Keep it. We don't have to tell the Gray Lady everything."

Lulu shuddered, thinking about the broken bracelet in her bag. "No, but I do need to tell you that—"

Just then, Imogene walked into the kitchen, interrupting Lulu's confession and taking note of the tears and the handkerchief.

"None of this is ever easy. I know." She put an arm around Lulu. "And it's never what you expect that throws you for a loop."

Lulu leaned her head on Imogene's shoulder. "When I went through Matt's things, it was a file filled with LSAT practice tests hidden in Quattros' accounting drawer. I guess he thought I'd never stumble on them there. He must have taken a dozen of those tests over the years. And I never even guessed he wanted to go back to school."

"Was law his plan before you got pregnant?" Imogene asked.

"Yes."

"But Matt only had…what? Two years of college? How could he have gone to law school?" Gabrielle asked.

"He hid all sorts of information in that drawer.

Apparently, you can become a lawyer in four states without going to law school. All you need to do is pass the admission test and then apprentice with a lawyer. He never let on that he still wanted it so bad." Lulu let out a sob.

Imogene hugged her closer.

"Enough of this." Lulu straightened up. "What kind of hostesses are we? Bette would be horrified. We have guests coming, and the glasses aren't even out." She used the handkerchief once more and then folded it up and shoved it in her jeans' pocket. She'd keep the fragile piece of cloth no matter what the rules were about taking possessions out of the apartment.

Over the next ten minutes, Imogene's and Bette's three friends arrived one by one, each carrying large totes, which they placed, as per Imogene's instructions, in the foyer.

"What's in the bags?" Lulu asked.

"Patience. All will be revealed. Don't you love a little mystery? Your mother certainly did." Imogene gestured to the group of women, inviting them to come closer. "Okay, ladies, let's get this show started."

Everyone took seats in the living room, the newcomers perched on the long couch.

Ruby Simms sat furthest to the right. She was a series of circles from the fiery corkscrew curls that must have earned her name to her apple cheeks. A loose paisley tunic and black palazzo pants did nothing to hide more roundness. Double C logos were stitched on the tip of her silver ballet flats. Not long ago, Lulu would have been blind to their provenance; now, she recognized them instantly.

Next came Yvette Lenox, the epitome of cutting-edge chic with her razor-cut bright platinum hair and manicured blood-red nails. A black spandex-tight dress wrapped her whippet of a body like a bandage.

Francesca Wright looked ostentatious with stacks of glittering rings on most of her fingers, armfuls of gold bangle bracelets, and big diamond-studded hoop earrings. In Lulu's Gap-driven fashion opinion, Francesca's patterned dress—a combination of leopard, tiger, and zebra prints—and repeated Gucci signatures went overboard for a woman of her age.

But what was her age?

Imogene had told them the Style Endures Society women ranged from sixty-two to eighty-three; Ruby looked like she might be around seventy-five. But Lulu couldn't figure out how old the other two women were. Injectables and other work made so many of Manhattan's wealthy age-indeterminate.

Reminding herself that she was a co-hostess, Lulu picked up the bottle of Sancerre from the coffee table and held it toward Francesca.

"Would you like some wine?" she asked, careful not to use the word *more*, as in "*would you like more wine?*" Bette had taught her that nicety of upper-crust language. Asking someone if they want *more* infers that they've already had some, perhaps too much.

"Yes, please." Francesca held up her glass. Even if limited by surgery, her smile held warmth, and Lulu felt shame as the woman's kindness washed over her. She'd slotted Francesca as a type, one for which she didn't have much use—based on appearance.

Now, all signs pointed to Lulu having been magnificently wrong.

"When's show and tell?" Ruby leaned, holding a cheese-topped cracker away from her as she nibbled, ensuring the crumbles tumbled to the carpet rather than on her clothes.

Lulu imagined Bette itching to sic her Roomba on the

dirt before it got ground in.

"First, we finish eating. No food enters the bedroom," Imogene ordered. "In the meantime, Gabrielle, why don't you tell everyone about the dilemma you and your sister face?"

Gabrielle sat straighter in the armchair. "Well, it seems my mother left my sister and me an extraordinary legacy. A remarkable collection. In her will, Bette charged us with coming up with a plan of what to do with her worldly goods."

"What's the problem with that?" Ruby asked.

"Our plan has to show that we understand the meaning behind the legacy. And only then will the executor, Bette's lawyer, approve it."

"And we're lost," Lulu added.

"My sister's right. We're clueless about how the collection—this legacy—came to be without us knowing anything about it. And we don't understand what it means. So, Imogene thought if we showed you all our mother's collection, you'd possibly help us figure it out."

"That sounds like our Bette." Ruby sighed and shook her head. "A flair for the dramatic, even at the end. I certainly do miss her."

Yvette nodded. "So do I. One thing's for sure. Your mother never did things less than one hundred percent."

"I feel like we're getting Bette back for a few glorious moments." Francesca smiled sadly. "Tell us about this collection."

Imogene stood and held up her hands to stop the conversation. "Telling will ruin the surprise. Brush off your clothes, girls, and wipe your mouths. Bette's ghost will not be happy if she discovers you sullied her treasures."

Ruby excused herself to duck into the bathroom. Yvette and Francesca squeezed sanitizer on their hands.

Lulu came close to laughing. Bette's ability to intimidate persisted even without her corporeal presence.

When they finally trooped into the bedroom, Yvette was the first to notice its size. "This room is tiny." She turned in a circle, seeming disappointed.

"Yes, and here's why." Imogene nodded toward Lulu, who opened the closet door, followed by Gabrielle swooping her arm to invite them into the walk-in.

*En masse*, they stepped forward.

For a few moments, they all stood in awed silence.

"Dear Lord," Ruby said after a few minutes. "Is it wrong to be jealous of a friend who's gone?"

"My closet is as large," Francesca said. "But it has never been this impeccable."

"Impeccable was Bette's middle name," Yvette said. "Yours could be slapdash—and I only mean that in the most admiring way."

Ruby gave Yvette a warning glance. "She means because you're so imaginative, Franny."

"Fine. I'll use my imagination and take it as a compliment. Can we touch?" Francesca asked Gabrielle.

"Be our guests," she said.

"But don't get anything get out of place," Imogene warned.

The women approached the shelves and racks like explorers stumbling on a paradise.

"Look at this." Francesca held out a cashmere wool cape with a large Byzantine jeweled button and studied the fabric. "My right arm for it."

"That would never work on you," Yvette said. "You're not as tall as Bette."

"I'd have it altered." Francesca pulled the cape away from the pole.

To Lulu's relief, Imogene took the black silk hanger out

of Francesca's hand. "The girls are trying to figure out what to do with all this—they're not hosting a giveaway party."

"Giveaway?" Francesca looked insulted. "I'd pay top dollar for this. It's brand new."

Lulu gave Gabrielle a *see-I-told-you-so* glance.

Gabrielle ignored her.

Francesca peered into the necklines of one dress and then another. "Did you notice the array of sizes? I don't know why she bought things she couldn't wear, but Bette sure has a diverse selection."

Yvette held up a red blouse. "You're right. This would swim on Bette."

"Would you like to see some of the jewelry? Bags? Belts?" Gabrielle offered.

"No," Ruby said.

"No?" Imogene asked.

"No. We don't want to see *some* of anything. We want to see each and every piece."

"Open the drawers, girls," Imogene said. "Knock their eyes out."

The women's reactions ranged from gasps to shrieks as Lulu and Gabrielle brought out bags and opened accessory drawers. They held their breath in awe when seeing a heavy gold chain coin belt from the 1970s—and clapped at the bizarre, super-glossy white patent leather bag with crystal and faux pearls that had so confused Lulu and Gabrielle. The *Lait de Coco* pocketbook debuted in the 2014 supermarket-themed autumn/winter runway show. Lulu couldn't imagine who'd leave their house with a glittery milk carton slung over their shoulder. Bette might have owned it, but no way she'd ever worn it.

"And now for part two." Imogene gave Lulu and Gabrielle a dramatic nod. Lulu stepped up. Today it was her turn to unearth a quote. She studied the array of pocketbooks and then chose a burgundy quilted flap bag.

"Oh, Bette loved that one," Francesca said.

"It was her staple," said Imogene.

"As it should be," said Yvette. "You can never go wrong with a basic. And that color! Just perfect."

"Girls, hush, watch," Imogene instructed. "Bette left a secret legacy within her secret legacy."

"Ah." Ruby nodded.

"Ah?" Lulu asked.

"As I said before," Ruby said, "Bette had a flair for the dramatic."

Lulu opened the bag and reached inside. For a moment, she thought it was empty and felt a wave of disappointment. She looked at Imogene, who pointed to a second inside flap. Lulu unzipped the compartment she hadn't know about and touched the edge of the envelope. With a flourish worthy of her mother, she withdrew a cream-colored notecard and, in a voice that got shakier as she read, recited, *"A girl should be two things: who and what she wants.—Coco Chanel."*

"We've been discovering them in all the bags. And they always seem entirely appropriate for whichever one of us finds it. Oddly prescient," Gabrielle said.

"Use the word you mean." Imogene spread her hands in a wide arc. "Magical. The messages are words from beyond."

"Can I see that?" Yvette asked.

Lulu handed it over solemnly. The other women crowded around as if it was the rarest of a rare treasure.

"How wonderful that she left you messages. How very Bette." Ruby's appraisal of Bette's action sounded oddly unsurprised—more proof that their mother's friends knew her better than her daughters.

"So it appears," said Gabrielle.

"And different messages for each of you specifically?" Yvette asked.

"It sounds crazy, right? But yes, the quotes do seem to fit the one of us who opens the envelope," Gabrielle said.

"Like magic." Francesca nodded and exchanged a glance with Yvette.

Gabrielle ran her fingers through a long strand of pearls that one of the ladies had left on the island top. "The veils between worlds may be more porous than we know."

"In other words, my sister thinks our ghost mom is mystically guiding us." Lulu had wrestled with herself to sound non-Judge Judy but lost that particular battle.

"What do *you* think Bette was doing?" Ruby asked her.

Lulu held up her palms in a gesture of confusion. "I don't think Bette meant the sayings for either of us. Maybe Mom just liked to keep Chanel's pearls of wisdom at hand." Lulu hugged herself. She might sound blasé, but she longed to wrap one of her mother's warm shawls around her at that very moment. One that still carried the scent of Bette's ubiquitous Chanel No.5.

"Magic takes a hell of a lot of forms," Imogene said, "just like love. Bette didn't scream about it, but trust me, you two owned her heart. If anyone could come back from the grave to help you get on with your lives, it would be your indomitable mother."

Ruby put out her hand and patted first Gabrielle and then Lulu's arm. "She spoke of you both with so much love. So very often."

"You know," said Francesca, who had returned to examining the shelves, "what surprises me is how many of these clothes and accessories aren't Bette's style."

"I was thinking the same thing!" Ruby picked up the gold coin and chain belt and examined it. "This wasn't just someone expanding her wardrobe."

"Exactly what I was thinking," Yvette said. "Rather it's a curation of some of the very best of Chanel that—"

"Almost as though she were creating a museum," Francesca interrupted as she pointed to a white sleeveless boucle dress decorated with black braiding. "Isn't this runway?"

"Yes," said Yvette, who seemed the most Chanel-educated. "And so is this." She pointed to a black coat dress with white chiffon ruffled sleeves.

Gabrielle touched the corner of the dress with reverence. "I haven't been able to check out everything yet. I knew there was some runway, but not as much as you're pointing out. How did she get it all? She certainly wasn't jetting off to Paris every season."

"The Chanel boutique on 57th Street has an exclusive sale twice a year that includes runway." Yvette ran fingertips over a black tweed jacket with gold threads shining through the weave. "Bette never missed one. I went with her a few times. But even so, I had no idea she was erecting a shrine to her Coco."

"Bette always showed up in lovely clothes. Different from my taste, of course." Francesca gestured to her dazzle of prints. "But these..." She pointed to a grouping of three glittery metallic gowns. "They aren't anything I can imagine her wearing."

Lulu looked at the closet with her new eyes, trying on the idea of a Bette as an art collector rather than an out-of-control consumer—imagining her mother loved her daughters so much she would come back from the dead.

"Okay, girls, back to the living room. It's our turn now," Imogene said.

"Your turn at what?" Gabrielle asked.

"Playing fairy godmothers," Imogene said. "You girls need us. And to tell you the truth, we all miss Bette so much that we need you."

# Chapter Sixteen

## Lulu

Once everyone was again seated in the living room, Imogene clapped her hands like the kindergarten teacher she'd once been. "Okay, ladies. Our turn."

Yvette brushed off the bottom of an impeccable black nylon tote and placed it on her lap. "I'll start."

Imogene nodded. "What did you bring, and why? I'm guessing it's not that new Prada."

Yvette laughed. "No." As though conjuring magic, she pulled a white and lavender silk shawl out of the bag. "This was my grandmother's. And this—" She unfolded the fabric and pulled out a small box.

Lulu leaned forward.

Yvette opened the tiny leather box and revealed the ring nestled inside. Three brilliant diamonds set into a gold band shone. "It's Fabergé. From the 1880s. My great-grandfather gave it to my great-grandmother on their third wedding anniversary. He was an architect in Russia—until the pogroms destroyed their lives. After the Cossacks slaughtered two of their four sons, they had no choice but to leave. If they hadn't, who knows what would have happened to them? My mother might not have been born. I might not exist.

"Once in New York, he took the only work he could find—sharpening knives on Delancey Street. They'd brought almost nothing from their homeland except the ring that my great-grandmother had sewed into a skirt the moment the raids began. Once they were here, she offered to sell it so he could go to school and return to his profession, but he refused." Yvette shivered and then brought the ring to her lips. "He insisted they hold on to the ring—in case the worst happened. He never believed America was exempt from what had occurred in Russia. He never knew when he might have to buy the lives of one of his children."

Lulu held her hand to her chest, moved by Yvette's story.

"Francesca?" Imogene nodded at her friend. "Your turn."

"Imogene told us the two of you were baffled by the idea of Bette's possessions and thought if we brought some of ours and told you what they mean to us, it might shed some light. So, this is my treasure." Francesca reached into her Metropolitan Museum shopping bag and brought out a cloth pouch with something bulky inside.

"Your Birkin," Yvette said in a slightly hushed tone as befitting an object of great reverence. "I wondered if you were going to bring it."

Out from the felt came a shocking pink ostrich skin purse. Francesca petted the bag as if it were a kitten in her lap. "I rarely use it. I can't bear the idea of anything happening to it." She placed the Birkin on the table, gazing at it lovingly.

"And the story?" Imogene prompted.

"Splurging was difficult for me—I grew up with a single mom who worked as an ER nurse—but my husband loved to treat me. Teddy bought this for me to wear to my daughter's graduation from medical school; he thought I deserved to celebrate as much as she did. He was always like that, my Teddy. But he was sick at the time. Very. May he rest in peace. He never made it to graduation. But carrying the bag made me feel as if he was there, watching over us still."

They went around the room, Imogene next, and then finally, Ruby, showing valued possessions and sharing memories.

Forty-five minutes later, Lulu slowly closed the door after saying goodbye to the SES ladies. Imogene had stayed behind to help the girls clean up.

"Those stories," Lulu said.

"You're such strong women," Gabrielle said to Imogene. "Carrying so much inside."

Lulu thought of her mother-in-law's frequent tours of her glass cabinet, telling stories about these wine glasses and those candlesticks. Lulu got impatient with the repetition, but now she realized that Annette worked to pass on some of what made the Quattros their particular family.

"Handbags, jewelry, and even shoes can have a history. Each can be a meaningful treasure," Lulu said. "But how do you tie all these stories to a collection like Bette's?" Lulu asked. "None of these things were passed down. They're not heirlooms with history. She bought them."

And spent almost every last dollar she possessed buying them. The thought caused an unpleasant shiver of resentment, despite Lulu's desire to understand.

"Perhaps Bette was trying to write a history to pass on

to us," Gabrielle said.

Lulu looked from her sister to Imogene. "Do you think that's what she was doing?"

"That's for the two of you to decide, not me. I'm just here to help," the older woman said.

After they sent Imogene home and were finishing up straightening the apartment, Gabrielle's phone rang.

"It's the Gray Lady." Gabrielle made a face and then answered the call. "Hello?" She listened for a moment. "Hold on, let me ask her." Gabrielle pressed mute and turned to Lulu. "Are you free at ten o'clock tomorrow morning?"

"What's that about?" Lulu asked after her sister said they'd be there and then had hung up.

"She said that she was checking in to discuss—with a heavy emphasis on the word discuss—our progress."

"We're being called to the principal's office for being tardy?" Lulu's stomach lurched at the thought of the broken bracelet.

"Seems that way."

"What do you think she wants?" Lulu asked. "What, what, what?"

"The lawyer? I just told you."

"No. Bette." Lulu picked up the plates and took them into the kitchen. As touched as she'd been by her mother's friends, she couldn't connect their stories to Bette's things. With extreme care, Lulu placed the delicate dishes into the sink. She still hadn't gotten up the nerve to tell Gabrielle about sneaking out with and then smashing the Chanel bangle. How was she going to explain?

She could go with a straightforward confession: *Remember that bracelet I wanted to wear to the engagement party? I got drunk and broke it.*

Or she could employ the show and tell method: slip the

broken wrapped bits of bracelet from her bag and spread them before her sister along with a whispered: *Guess what I did?*

Or there was always the pathetic little sister routine: *I am so ashamed. And such a stupid klutz.* Then she could show Gabrielle and begin crying.

Except crying would make her seem manipulative; show and tell would make her look sneaky, and admitting to being drunk would suggest she was stupid and weak. No matter how she did it, she'd be giving Gabrielle all the power.

Lulu took a matching brush and dustpan into the living room to clean up the crumbs left by the women where Gabrielle gathered the used napkins.

"I was thinking. Maybe Imogene planned today so we'd look at Bette differently. As a person. Not concentrate on her failures as a mother," Gabrielle said.

"Do you think that's possible for us?" Lulu asked.

"I don't know. You're a mother. Do you, can you ever see your children as adult people, totally separate from being your children?"

Lulu slumped down on a chair, holding on to the brush she'd been using. Would she ever be able to observe Nicholas and Seth as separate beings other than her children?

"No," she admitted. "They'll never stop being my babies. And, yes, I know how stupid that sounds, but it will always be my job to protect and shield them from harm."

"You make motherhood sound like a forever unfinished job."

"More like constant fear mixed with prayer. And a need to be on guard. There's no relaxing." Lulu shook her head. "I'm probably talking trash. Ever since Matt died, I'm on the lookout."

Gabrielle sat beside her. "For more tragedy?"

Lulu nodded. "Maybe losing someone to death is like losing your virginity." Lulu stretched and retrieved her purse from where it lay next to the hassock. "Once you experience it, there's no going back. Before that, you know on an intellectual level that people can and will disappear. But intellectual means shit. Once someone dies, there's no more denial. You realize death is just terrifying. No matter how many times you reach for them, they're gone. And you can't find out to where."

"I guess it's easier for people who believe in Heaven." Gabrielle glanced upward. "If you are positive that you'll meet again, perhaps hope gets you through the hardest days."

"What a conversation, huh?" Lulu reached into the purse. "Maybe it will put my admission into perspective."

"What are you admitting?" Her sister watched as Lulu withdrew a wad of paper towels.

"I'm just sick over this. I. Um. Remember the Gray Lady showing up just before I was about to sashay out with Mom's clothes?"

"Remember? You were swearing as I've never heard you."

"Yeah, well, I'm not exactly proud of that. And here's something I'm even less proud of. I snuck this out. Don't ask why—I can only attribute it to my incredibly low tolerance for alcohol." Lulu's fingers shook as she unwrapped the resin and crystal remains. "Chalk this up to sheer clumsiness. And more alcohol. Do you think someone can fix it?" She bit her bottom lip.

Gabrielle picked up the fragments and examined them. "Nope. No jeweler could repair this—at least not back to making it saleable. You're now the not-proud owner of a broken Chanel bracelet. I suggest turning it into a piece of art."

"Oh, no." Lulu stared at her sister. "Are you serious?"

"No. But I am seriously concerned about your reaction here. Are you anxious that I'm going to—what—punish you for this?"

Without meeting Gabrielle's eyes, she nodded.

"Oh, Lulu, don't you know I love you more than I care about a damn piece of jewelry? Stop torturing yourself."

"But what do we tell the Gray Lady tomorrow?" Lulu felt the beginnings of relief, but she was still worried.

"Just don't bring it up."

"What if she has a list? Or photos of every item? I don't believe Bette would have given her all that power without making sure she knew the closet's exact contents."

"Don't you remember the first tenet of true sisterhood?"

Lulu shook her head, not sure of Gabrielle's message.

"When faced with a common enemy, lie, lie, and then lie some more. You never told Bette when I broke the lamp, right?"

Lulu laughed, remembering how they'd once *fixed* a black ceramic lamp that Gabrielle had knocked off a table. Without access to glue, they'd built it back together like Humpty Dumpty and gave it the widest possible berth. When, as was inevitable, Bette brushed against it, the lamp fell to pieces.

When Bette asked what had happened, they shrugged and pled complete innocence.

And, quite literally, till the day Bette died, the sisters had kept the secret. At least once a year, Bette would shake her head and bring up the great unsettled lamp question.

But Lulu never ratted.

Now it would be Gabrielle's turn.

Diana Hayes glanced at her watch. "It's ten-thirty. We scheduled this meeting for ten. I can't wait any longer."

Lulu tried not to show how upset she was. Family sticks together, right? Where the hell was Gabrielle? She needed her support here and now.

"Subway problems, most likely."

"You managed to get here on time. From Brooklyn." The lawyer's face remained impassive.

"True, but it's —" Lulu stopped. It was what? Where was Gabrielle? "Let me try her." Lulu pulled out her phone and texted.

*Where the hell are u? I've been waiting at the Gray Lady's office for half an hour?????*

Moments later, her sister wrote back.

*OMG!!! Sorry!!!!! I forgot!!! Say I got called into work early. Nothing you can't handle, right?*

Lulu looked up from her phone at the lawyer, whose crossed arms indicated deep disapproval of Gabrielle's tardiness. "My sister sends her deepest apologies. Her boss—she's elderly—needed her help. Sounded serious. You know, Gabrielle is far more than just an employee to her."

A momentary smile rippled across Diana's lips, an expression saying, *I don't believe you, but I'll play pretend.* For the first time, the lawyer's mantle of iciness fell. "I suppose we should go ahead then." She opened a file and turned a few pages. "It's been two weeks since you and your sister got keys to the apartment and the collection—what can you report?"

Lulu thought of answering honestly: *We think Mom is sending us messages from beyond. We're fighting over barely formed ideas. I'm broke and want to sell everything ASAP—on the street if necessary. Gabrielle loves every piece of clothing and each accessory and probably wants to keep them all encased in crystal.*

Lulu crossed her legs. "We're still doing an inventory."

"That seems to be taking a goodly amount of time. Surely, you have some ideas to report."

"We both have full-time jobs, Ms. Hayes."

"Please. Call me Diana." The lawyer's face softened. "I know this must be very hard on you both. I'm not trying to pressure you—just get an idea. Every week is costing you and your sister precious capital. Before she passed, your mother shared your recent widowhood with me." The sympathy lacing the lawyer's words surprised Lulu. "Going through her things must be difficult coming so soon after your husband's demise. Not to mention that this is an unusual inheritance."

Lulu laughed. "That's an understatement."

"What were you expecting?"

"I guess I expected money. That sounds crass, I'm sure—but that's what I imagined. I never thought my mother would spend her fortune on clothes. And pocketbooks. And fake jewelry. Shocked doesn't begin to cover how I feel."

Diana took off her glasses and leaned forward. "The temptation to get rid of it all must be strong."

"Get rid of it?"

"Yes. To sell it en masse."

"Is that what you think we should do?" Lulu felt a tremor of excitement. If the Gray Lady agreed with her, maybe she could convince Gabrielle after all.

"No, not at all. I don't think that's what your mother intended. I'm just trying to get a sense of what you and your sister are thinking. I want to be helpful, but I can't lead you. Bette didn't want that."

"So you know what she wanted?"

"I have an idea."

"Why can't you tell us? Wouldn't it be easier to follow her wishes if we knew what they were?"

"In this case, the answer lies in the journey as much as the destination. And Bette wanted you to take that journey."

# Chapter Seventeen

## Gabrielle

Gabrielle disconnected from Lulu, feeling guilty but relieved. She needed a break. Worrying about the closet, her life, and her future was exhausting. The Gray Lady wanted answers, but all she and Lulu could offer were more questions.

Lingering on the streets of Greenwich Village on her way to and from work always relaxed her. This morning was no different. The neighborhood, first settled in the early 1700s, bore little resemblance to the rest of the city. Breathing in the Village felt more comfortable. The sky seemed closer. Here, buildings rarely rose more than four stories. Trees lined the streets, window boxes were plentiful, and well-tended seasonal plantings decorated brownstone entrances. Now, with the holidays approaching, multitudes of evergreen wreaths and garlands cheered doors and windows.

Changing her route from the West 4th Street subway station to Quills & Feathers was one way Gabrielle offset her job's tedium. At least once a week, like today, she detoured past the FDNY Squad Company 18, stopping in front of the bright red building framed with gold and black to pay respects to the *Line of Duty* bronze plaques memorializing the squad's fallen. Like many New Yorkers who'd lived through 9/11, her gratitude to the NYFD remained constant.

From there, she detoured a block north to peer in the windows of the most fanciful florist she'd ever seen. The owners created fairy tale scenes, combining antique dolls, dollhouses, and tiny furnishings with curious flowers and plants as well as books borrowed from Thea's shop.

As she rounded the corner and headed towards Quills and Feathers, the Terrier Lady waved as Gabrielle passed. The older woman walked her sweet but yappy trio of Maltese at least a half dozen times a day. Thea stocked dog biscuits at the shop, ensuring the Terrier Lady would stop in every day at three for a cup of tea, a treat for the dogs, and a restorative chat.

Gabrielle typically noted every neighborhood change as she walked, but today she relived the previous evening. Watching Bette's friends show off their treasures and share why they mattered so much might not have explained Bette's collection, but they'd sparked Gabrielle's imagination.

Learning the story behind Ruby's treasured watch struck Gabrielle hard. As a barely paid resident at Bellevue Hospital, Ruby's husband had worked one-hundred-hour weeks while she'd refolded endless piles of scarves as a Macy's salesgirl six days a week. One year to the day after he finished his residency, he gave Ruby two surprises. First, the amazingly timeless Cartier Tank watch, which he purchased on credit and hope. In Ruby's story, her husband—who had zero fashion sense—based his purchase on reading that Jackie Kennedy—Ruby's idea of perfection—wore that particular watch.

Ruby treasured the other gift, a letter of love and promise, even more. She had unfolded the softened paper with trembling fingers and then read her husband's words aloud to the group.

*"She is more precious than rubies: and all the things thou canst desire are not to be compared unto her."*

*There's little in this world more precious than you, my love. You sacrificed much so I could reach my dream. Usually, the following sentence would be, I can't begin to repay you—but in fact, I can and will start today. And I will never stop.*

*Now you must find your truest dream. Chase it knowing I will invest myself in helping you make it come true.*

*Unless both of us are happy, neither of us will flourish.*

*With my constant and never-ending love,*

*David*

That fall, Ruby had returned to college and eventually became a sought-after budget analyst—not Gabrielle's idea of a dream job, but one that had brought Ruby great joy and success.

Ruby's husband's words replayed in a loop. Once, Gabrielle had believed she'd found her truest dream, too. With Cole's support and financial help, she'd created one of the most respected costume institutes in the country. She'd been fulfilled and satisfied. She'd loved her life, her husband, and her job.

Now, she envied Lulu and Bette their widowhood. Death seemed preferable to a husband deciding you were no longer deserving of his love.

Gabrielle climbed up the three steps to the shop and then stopped short. The sign in the door read *Closed.* Unless Thea had a doctor's appointment, she always came downstairs well before Gabrielle arrived, lovingly putting things in order before turning the sign to *Open.*

Thea hadn't said anything about being out this morning. Had she just forgotten to tell Gabrielle, or was something wrong?

With shaking hands, Gabrielle pulled out her keys and unlocked the door. Inside, the shop smelled stale. That was unusual also, as Thea's first ritual of the morning was refreshing her lavender-scented rocks.

Half-finished cups of tea from the previous night sat on the tables. Haphazard piles of books remained on the counters from the afternoon before. Chairs had been left randomly askew. The scene warned of trouble.

Where was Thea?

Just as panic set in, Gabrielle heard Thea's tired, almost-whispered, *"Hello."* There in the shadows, she sat in her usual spot with a cup of tea. Uneaten biscotti and ginger cookies were scattered on Thea's most disliked plate: a murky green and orange ceramic horror. When Gabrielle had once asked why she kept it, Thea said even ugly dishes deserved a chance. She *took turns* with her stack of crockery—occasionally cheating when special guests arrived, sneaking the ugly plate to the bottom of the pile.

Thea's outfit today was yet another harbinger of trouble. She wore an oatmeal-colored cardigan over a bland beige dress without a spark of jewelry to alleviate the monotony.

Thea's clothes and accessories always gave away her mood. On happy days, she favored purples, greens, and blues with gold or silver finery. When she was ornery, she wore washed-out grays or stark black, letting Gabrielle knew to tread lightly and avoid controversy. Any shade from ecru to tan indicated depression.

That morning's beige so drained all life from Thea's naturally rosy cheeks that without even taking off her coat, Gabrielle sat down opposite the older woman.

"What's wrong?" Gabrielle popped off the lid from the paper cup of coffee she'd brought with her.

Thea sighed and shrugged.

Without asking permission, Gabrielle broke off a piece of the biscotti, a move that generally brought a scolding. Today, Thea just pushed the plate towards Gabrielle. "You might as well eat them all."

"How about some coffee in place of that sludge?" Gabrielle pointed to the cold-looking black tea. "I can share."

"This so-called sludge is a proper builder's tea. Strong. Which is what I greatly need right now."

The tea looked more evil than proper.

"Why? What's wrong, Thea?"

"I can't say." The older woman buried her head in her hands, which clutched a lace-edged handkerchief. A faded cream-colored sad piece of cloth. "I'm afraid if I do, it will come true."

Fear gripped Gabrielle. She had never seen Thea appear so disconsolate.

"Are you ill?"

Thea shook her head.

"Is someone in the family ill?"

Thea shook her head again.

"What is it then?"

"Nigel..." Thea started to speak but stopped herself. She brought the handkerchief to her mouth to hold back a sob.

"Bad news about Nigel? Pamela?"

"Yes, and no."

Gabrielle took both of Thea's hands in her own. "Whatever's bothering you, not telling me won't change a thing. Let me help."

Thea squeezed and then let go of Gabrielle's hands. She

sipped her tea and sighed deeply. "I might as well. After all, this crisis will affect both of us; I'll try to get it out all at once. Nigel and Pamela came to visit last night and took me out to dinner."

That was a bad start. Those two rarely went out of their way for Thea—taking her out for dinner was their equivalent of flying her to Hawaii for a luxury weekend. Gabrielle nodded as she broke off another piece of cookie and then left it on the plate when she realized she had no appetite.

"They laid down the law. Can they do that?" Thea pulled her cardigan close and answered her own question. "Of course, they can. They can make any demands they want."

Gabrielle didn't try to rush Thea and ask what *law* the woman meant—"*bad news can always wait*" had been her Poughkeepsie grandmother's favorite saying. Funny how the wisdom of elders fell into place like a once-ignored jigsaw puzzle as the years passed.

"Spit it out," Thea demanded of herself. She sat up straighter. "They think I'm getting too old to run this place—"

"We talked about that. You know it's ridiculous! Besides, I'm here. I can do anything you need me to."

Thea held up a hand to quiet Gabrielle. "They're insisting I sell it all. The building. Quills & Feathers. My apartment. Everything. Pamela wants to bring over a friend who's a top real estate agent. They said this so-called plan would ensure I have enough money to be taken care of."

"Taken care of? You're fine, for goodness sake. What in the world are they thinking?" Stupid question. Gabrielle knew what they were thinking. The building might be pencil-thin, but it was a brownstone with a finished basement and a good-sized shop. Stairs led up to an offbeat but endearing two-bedroom apartment. Eighteen hundred square feet might not equal extravagant in many cities, but the place was worth a fortune in this desirable Manhattan location.

"But certainly, Nigel knows they'll get it all when…" Gabrielle struggled to find polite euphemisms. "When the time comes, they can sell the property and have all the money they or you will need."

"I said the same thing!" A bit of Thea's pep reappeared. "But they insisted that now is the time. *'What if you get suddenly sick? Where will you be?'*" Thea said in a pretty good Nigel impersonation. *"'You can't sell on a dime,'"* Thea imitated Pamela's nasal tone perfectly. "Blah, blah, blah. Pamela couldn't stop reminding me all my money is tied up here." Thea gestured around the shop. "All of it, she kept saying. *'And in an emergency—'"*

"Don't they have enough money to cover an emergency?" Gabrielle asked.

"Frankly, after this conversation, I don't think my son or his wife would part with one red cent for me. Pamela informed me that if I can't cover my own emergencies, they'll leave me to the kindness of strangers."

"Nigel let her say that?" Gabrielle couldn't hide her shock.

"Well, he didn't contradict her."

"I will never let that happen. I promise you," Gabrielle said.

Thea reached for her hand. "I know I can trust you with my life. But, my dear, you had to come to me for a job. And under difficult circumstances, shall we say. If there is an emergency, it will require ready cash. Something I'm sadly but fairly certain that you lack."

The words sliced into Gabrielle's heart. Thea had been one of the first—and few—people who had helped when Cole left her. She would protect Thea no matter what she had to do, just as the older woman had done for her.

After work, still troubled by Thea's confession, Gabrielle, desperate for comfort and quiet, headed uptown to the Met.

Gabrielle walked up the granite hill of steps towards the entrance. The Metropolitan Museum of Art had been her safe space since third grade. Other children pumped on the swings at the nearby 84th Street playground; Gabrielle sheltered at the museum. Bette had considered the Met, with its plentiful uniformed guards, an ideal babysitter for her child. As an adult, Gabrielle found it hard to imagine merely dropping off a child at a museum, but her mother's decision had inspired Gabrielle's life.

Within three months, Gabrielle had learned the name of every guard on duty in the European painting department, her favorite section. It never occurred to her not to feel safe with them watching over her as she sat on the floor, drawing copies of the elaborate clothing worn by the women in the paintings.

In fifth grade, she'd discovered and practically lived at the Met's Costume Institute. In tenth grade, she got a summer job interning with one of its department's curators, returning the following summer and the one after that.

What a long time ago that had been, when the whole world appeared wide-open and waiting for her.

Now, Gabrielle sat on a bench in front of her most beloved painting: *Madame X* by John Singer Sargent. From Gabrielle's first sighting, the woman captivated Gabrielle; she'd chosen to write about her for an art history paper in the tenth grade.

When Sargent had first shown the portrait of Madame

Pierre Gautreau at the Paris Salon in 1884, the public had been shocked and outraged that he'd painted the young socialite with one of her dress straps slipping down her shoulder. Stung, the artist kept the painting hidden in his studio for more than thirty years, eventually repainting the strap so that it sat properly and appeased society's mores.

Gabrielle thought about the notorious American expatriate, Virginie Amélie Avegno Gautreau, who had possessed such a daring style. When it was unheard of for women of her stature to even model, she'd posed in a revealing costume. Despite the practice being scandalous practice for the era, she dyed her hair and eyebrows and wore lavender-colored face and body powder that gave her an otherworldly glow. The woman had lived the way she wanted, hampered by no one, despite being hounded by gossip.

As a girl, Gabrielle had seen Madame Gautreau as a tragic but heroic creature, born in the wrong era. Now she realized the American woman had taken charge of her life. Freed herself from rules and expectations—something Gabrielle had not done at all.

Every day since her divorce Gabrielle had indulged her worst fears and obsessed over how far she still might fall. She'd imagine winding up as an elderly saleswoman at Bergdorf's, having to drape former friends in Valentino and Dior. Gabrielle pictured herself toting heavy beaded evening gowns, five or six at a time, to a waiting doyen. As she'd approached the dressing room, she'd hear her old acquaintance faux whispering on the phone, thrilled to share the news of Gabrielle's fall down society's ladder.

*You can't imagine who's waiting on me!*

While the dressing room scene might be a fantasy, the truth was that Cole and Nancy had circulated ugly rumors about Gabrielle that were so hurtful, she'd felt she had no choice but to hide out at Quills & Feathers.

Just as she had when she was a teenager, Gabrielle now looked to the painting for answers. But Madame X—who felt like a family member after all their shared hours—wasn't impressed by Gabrielle's pity party.

*Stop. Simply stop. You can powder your skin pale lavender; you can pose for a painter—you can do anything except this: no more wallowing in defeatism. Take charge of your destiny and stop looking back.*

Gabrielle stood and smiled at her old friend, silently thanking her for the pep talk. Walking out into the darkening evening, she decided she would solemnize her new attitude by dining at Bette's favorite restaurant, just two blocks away on Madison Avenue.

Stepping inside Sant Ambroeus, Gabrielle felt instantly at home as the maître d' greeted her warmly. He'd always looked out for her mother, and now he was looking after her. Gabrielle asked after his family as he escorted her inside to Bette's favorite corner table.

Being here without her mother felt both familiar and strange. Bette had loved the eatery for its delicious Milanese food but also because she said the room's signature peachy-pink hue flattered women of a certain age so much that years fell away.

A waiter arrived with a tumbler of water, a bread tray, and a little pot of creamy butter.

"A cocktail?" he asked.

Gabrielle smiled, remembering Bette declaring Sant Ambroeus's house rosé the best in the city. She ordered a glass and told the waiter she wanted to hold off looking at the menu for the moment.

She pulled a pencil and notebook from her bag and began writing, only stopping to thank the waiter and then to take intermittent sips of the wine. It was indeed the best rosé in New York. By the time her glass was empty, she had filled four pages.

*Moving Forward Ideas*

*1. Sell all the Chanel and invest money in an annuity to give me more security.*

    * *I'll still have to be careful, but at least I'll never have to work in Bergdorf's in old age.*

*2. Sell all the Chanel, invest in Botox and personal trainers; meet a rich man and marry.*

    * *Requires me admitting I am an idiot.*

*3. Work on resume and try to get a job as a costume designer.*

    * *Requires fighting Nancy's blackballing. Could probably do it, but wouldn't it be better/smarter to move forward?*

What was the right thing to do? Her mother had to have had something in mind for the collection, for Gabrielle and Lulu. These elaborate rules and conditions, the notes in the bags, it couldn't all be a lark.

She closed her eyes and invited Bette's spirit to inspire her. And as the waiter appeared a moment later with a second glass of her mother's favorite pale blush wine, so did the idea.

The following morning, Gabrielle arrived at Quattros' fifteen minutes after the shop opened. Matt's brother, waiting on the before-work crowd, tipped his head toward the swinging door. "She's in there."

A blast of hot sugary air hit Gabrielle as she stepped into the kitchen. Lulu stood over an enormous bowl, sifting flour.

She looked up with an expression of surprise as she took in her sister. "Gabrielle? What are you doing here? Are you okay?"

"I have an idea."

"And you've given up using electronic devices?"

"It's an in-person idea. Do you want to hear it or not?"

"Yes, but don't expect me to stop what I'm doing. I've got to get out a massive batch of bridal shower brownies—each one stenciled with powdered sugar bunnies. Don't ask."

"Keep working then. Just listen."

As Lulu measured sugar, Gabrielle explained in one long run-on, mixed-up sentence—stopping when she saw a frown crease her sister's forehead.

"What's wrong?" Gabrielle asked.

"A store? Are you crazy? What are you thinking?" Lulu asked.

"Not just a store. A perfect store. A breathtaking store. A gem."

Lulu broke egg after egg into the bowl. "After working in a *store* for what seems like a hundred years, I can guarantee you there is no such thing as a perfect store. Certainly not a, what did you say? Breathtaking one? A perfect place to shop? Maybe. A perfect place to work? Give me a break."

"Can you just listen? Be even a little open-minded?" Gabrielle asked.

"Like you were with my fundraiser idea?"

"Point taken. But please let me explain. We have jewels from the past and present in our possession, and—wait. That could be the name!"

"Jewels of the Past and Present? That sounds like the name of a semi-boring museum exhibit." Lulu went back to mixing the heavy-looking batter with a silicone spatula.

The effort appeared exhausting. Gabrielle couldn't imagine working here. She crossed another one of her "emergency if I am ever starving" jobs off her list.

"Hear me out," Gabrielle said.

"No. Forget it." Lulu poured vanilla extract into the bowl and then resumed stirring. "Have you gone nuts? Why would I want to open a thrift shop like two old church ladies in Poughkeepsie?"

"Not a thrift shop, Lu." Gabrielle concentrated on staying calm. "An upscale vintage store. You heard Bette's friends telling us about their treasures, right? Everything we own comes with a history: the boots we wore when we met our husbands. The bracelet we got from a man we loved—and then threw in the Hudson River when he betrayed us. Possessions tell the stories of our lives."

"And how does that translate into opening a thrift store?"

"*Again.* Not a damn thrift store! Jesus. Now you're just trying to annoy me."

Lulu gave her sister the grin she'd perfected at the age of six. "Yup."

"Please. For ten minutes, take this seriously. We were fascinated when the ladies told us their stories. We can do that with Bette's collection. Vintage has history, Lulu, and resale has become a huge thing. Repurposing can be part of saving the planet—you were the first one to point that out to me. And ever since you did, I keep seeing articles about shopping green. Even in the freaking *New York Times,* for heaven's sake. We'll take vintage as upscale as it can go when we open Jewels of the Past."

"Jewels of the Past? That's the *second* most boring museum exhibit ever." Lulu reached for a measuring cup of dark cocoa powder and sprinkled it over the batter, drawing back as a puff rose and dusted her nose. She brushed it off.

And then, like the sun coming out, Lulu's face lit up.

"What?" Gabrielle asked.

"The name of the damn store…"

"Yes?"

"Coco Street. Not that I'm considering this stupid idea. And it is stupid. How the hell do you think we could afford real estate in Manhattan? But Coco Street would be the perfect name."

*Coco Street.* The name resonated so profoundly that Gabrielle ran over and hugged her sister. *"Coco Street!* Perfect, perfect, perfect. Can't you picture it?"

"I'm seeing the rumpled, smelly thrift shop where our grandmother took us to drop off used clothes. Mothballs and body odor. I gave you a good name because if I had to listen to you come up with another jewel name, I'd scream." Lulu ladled chocolate batter into five baking tins. "Mothballs and BO. That's what we should name it. And even if I were to consider it, how in the world could we afford it?"

"Us? We can't. But if Thea goes along with it, which I bet she will because what her son is proposing is will kill her, then—"

"Thea? How is she involved in—"

"Can you just listen for a minute?"

# Chapter Eighteen

## Gabrielle

Despite huffing and rolling her eyes, Lulu did listen as Gabrielle laid out her plan for taking over Quills & Feathers. "We'll rent-to-own, with the promise that Thea will have a job at *Coco Street* forever, even if we have to roll her around in a wheelchair. We'll care for her like she's our mother."

"Better, I hope," Lulu said. "But why does she need us to care for her? What about her son?"

Gabrielle explained as Lulu smoothed the batter in the pans, nodding in a way that left Gabrielle clueless about whether her sister was actually paying attention or just humoring her.

"The minute the two of them sell her building, they'll stick her in the cheapest assisted living place they can find, so deep in Jersey we'll never find her. Without her store—a place to go every day—Thea will curl up and die. At the same time, Nigel is her only son. If she cuts all ties to him, she'll be miserable. My plan solves everything."

"How do you suppose we work this out? Rent-to-buy? Is that a thing?" Lulu asked.

"Yes. All we need to do is get a lawyer to help, and I know one who owes me. Big time. Jack Hunter-Holmes."

Lulu put down her spatula and retied her apron, which had looked perfectly fine to Gabrielle. She instantly recognized her sister's habit of showing her agitation through fidgeting.

"You're moving a little fast, Gabi."

"Not according to the Gray Lady. If we move any slower, we'll wind up paying Mom's rent from our own non-existent funds."

Carrying the hope of getting Thea's blessings to explore the idea, Lulu's sort of willingness to listen, and her own shaky optimism, Gabrielle set up an appointment with her lawyer friend for the following Tuesday morning.

She and Lulu met in the lobby of the Art Deco Fuller building on Madison Avenue and 57th Street. As they walked across the marble floor to the elevator bank, Lulu craned her neck to admire the ceiling's ornamental décor.

"Whoever this Jack is, he has a snazzy setup," Lulu said as they stepped into a similarly decorated elevator. "Why does he owe you?"

"Despite being *our* close friend and practically a brother to me, the jerk agreed to represent Cole during the divorce."

"And you got screwed. So why are we here?"

"We're here because we can't afford a lawyer of his stature except as a favor. And the fact is that in the end, Jack didn't screw me. He came up with a very equitable settlement, but when Nancy saw the papers, she went wild and convinced Cole to dump Jack. Then she hired the biggest bastard in town."

"So you and Jack both got screwed."

"Yup. Jack apologized, repeatedly, for not explaining that he'd taken the case believing it would be better for me if he were Cole's lawyer and could ensure I got what I deserved. But he could have told me that instead of letting me think he'd betrayed me. Helping us now will be his chance to make it up to me finally. Plus, knowing Thea, things will be more comfortable for her if our lawyer comes with a cup of kindness. And that's Jack."

On the fortieth floor, Gabrielle led the way. As they walked down the hall, she glanced at Lulu. They were visiting a lawyer to ask for help. Surely, her sister owned something other than jeans, right? Gabrielle smoothed down the aubergine crepe dress she wore and kept her comment to herself. She needed Lulu on her side if Coco Street was going to happen.

They reached the door with *Hunter-Holmes, Remy, & Bullard Attorneys at Law* spelled out in gold lettering.

"Hunter-Holmes?" Lulu asked.

"He's one of the original Jack-has-two-mommies kids," Gabrielle said as they went inside.

Moments after giving their names to the receptionist, they were ushered down another hall and into Jack's office.

The lawyer stood as the sisters entered, coming around to the front of his desk.

"What a pleasure to see you, Gabrielle." He hugged her as though they were still the best of friends.

She held back her sarcasm and smiled; they needed him. "You too, Jack."

"It's been too long," he said.

"Yes, but here I am now." She held her arms wide. "Looking for a favor."

Lulu put out her hand unenthusiastically. "I'm Lulu."

"Of course, I remember. We met you at your sister's wedding—"

"What a view," Gabrielle interrupted. She didn't want Jack to realize he'd brought up the inappropriate subject of her nuptials and become embarrassed.

After he offered refreshments, they settled around the large walnut table in the corner.

"So, how can I help?" Jack asked.

Gabrielle pulled Quill & Feather's blueprints from her tote, laid them out, and launched into her plan. She described everything from their weird inheritance to the square footage of Thea's building, including the problem with Nigel and Pamela. When she got to the subject of rent-to-own, Jack interrupted.

"You're talking about subdividing the building?"

"Yes. Lulu and I will rent to buy the store, while Thea will retain all ownership of the basement and her apartment."

"Can you work within the confines of the space the shop offers?" he asked as he examined the marked-up blueprint. "You don't need the basement?"

"No. We'll have the back room for storage."

Lulu leaned in, appearing skeptical. "Are you sure? Don't you use the basement now?"

"I'm sure. Besides, if we need that space, Thea won't mind," Gabrielle said with a whiff of exasperation.

"You two are on the same page, yes?" Jack looked from Gabrielle to Lulu. "No judgment, but surprises are a lawyer's worst friend."

Lulu shook her head. "Our pages are chapters apart. I have cold feet—despite being chained to a hot oven most of the day."

"Matt didn't chain you to Quattros'," Gabrielle said.

Lulu appeared unsure of whether to take umbrage or laugh. "I loved a man who was deeply embedded in his family business," she said to Jack by way of explanation.

"Past tense?" Jack glanced at her ring finger.

Lulu twirled her thin gold wedding band. "My husband died two years ago. Suddenly."

"I'm so sorry for your loss." He put his hand on Lulu's.

Gabrielle noted the touch.

"Your husband was a lucky man," Jack said to Lulu.

Gabrielle sure would love to know how Jack had arrived at that observation.

Lulu beamed. "That might be the nicest condolence I've ever received."

Gabrielle saw her sister take in the lawyer's mop of silver-black hair and Paul Bunyan-in-a-suit appeal.

"My mothers taught me to always acknowledge true love."

Gabrielle almost gagged but hid her reaction. Could Jack be flirting with Lulu? She recalled his vitals: age, marital status, children. She remembered his being accompanied by both his mothers, one on each side, to Cole's last play—at least the last production Gabrielle had attended. Right. One marriage. Divorced. No kids.

Over the next half-hour, Jack asked more questions, gave advice, and helped Gabrielle and Lulu develop a fair and practical plan to present to Thea.

When they said goodbye, it seemed to Gabrielle that Jack held on to Lulu's hand a shade too long, and her sister made no effort to disengage.

"Well, he seemed very nice," Lulu said as the two sisters rode down the elevator.

"Nice enough to convince you we can do this?"

"Nice enough to have me listening." Lulu pulled on a pair of wooly mittens. "I still have no clue how we can afford the time it's going to take to get all this done. We both need our salaries to live, for goodness sake."

Gabrielle took a deep breath. Admitting when Lulu was right never fit into her comfort zone. "Of course. I know that. I can manage while you keep working—I have some savings." Savings that were supposed to keep her from eating cat food at ninety. "I'll carry more of the load until we can both jump in."

"Do you think something like Coco Street is really possible?" Lulu asked

Gabrielle held the door open for her sister, and then they both walked outside into the chill.

"Possible? Yes. Hard? Very." Wind muffled Gabrielle's words. "On the other hand, stasis could kill us both.

At two, over apricot thumbprint cookies and tea, Gabrielle laid out the specifics of the Jack-approved proposal to Thea.

"Yes!" Thea gave the first genuine smile that Gabrielle had seen in too long.

"Wait a week before you say yes." She feared Thea's agreement came too readily. She didn't want the woman signing on from fear or desperation.

"When it's right, you know it's right—especially at my age." Thea crossed her arms and stuck by her decision as though offered a life raft.

"At least bring in your lawyer," Gabrielle insisted.

"I will, but he'll see this is the solution to my problem. Nigel and Pamela call every day to ask if I've decided to agree to sell. I guess it goes to prove that no matter how good a mother you try to be, nurture can't overcome nature when your child inherits your husband's greed gene. I don't know how I chose someone as awful as Nigel's father and then someone as good as my next husband." She put her hand on Gabrielle's arm. "But thank God I found the right one the second time around. Love is the worst place to make the same mistake twice."

Gabrielle nodded at the wisdom but still felt the need to be sure that Thea was making the wise decision. "Remember. Nigel is your only child. Your only family."

Thea shook her head in disagreement. "No. Family is more than giving birth. You know how you can fall in love with a man and know it's forever? The same magic can happen with a friend."

"But if this causes you to lose Nigel—"

Thea interrupted. "The last thing I want to do is lose Nigel, but the truth is he's no longer the son I've known.

"He's always been a bit stuffy and vulnerable to suggestion, but since marrying that woman, he's changed. Before her, he used to take me to brunch every Sunday. Without fail. He loved to surprise me; we'd discover a different place every week—and of course, being New York, we could have gone on for years finding new restaurants. Now? I'm lucky if he and Pamela bring a few measly brownies when I cook dinner for them." She hesitated, shook her head, and then continued in a lower voice. "I haven't mentioned this—I guess I was embarrassed—but he's pressured me into some other awful things since she came along,"

The bell over the door sounded. Both women looked up, but it was only the UPS delivery man. As he put a new shipment of books on the desk, Thea wrapped two cookies in a napkin and held them out. "Your favorites today, Ken."

He grinned. As a much-loved fixture of the neighborhood, he brought daily joy along with packages. "What would I do without my favorite girl?" He took the proffered sweets, saluted, winked, and finished one of the cookies before reaching the door.

"That's what I mean. Happiness doesn't just come from those you are related to by blood," Thea said.

"What awful things were you talking about, Thea? What did Nigel talk you into?" Gabrielle asked, returning to the conversation they were having before the delivery.

"You remember my cottage on Squam Lake?" Thea asked. "The one I said you could borrow any time?"

"In New Hampshire?"

"Yes. So beautiful. Gerald and I bought it when we got married—a getaway where my husband could fish, and I could paint. Even if I was mediocre at best, I loved to capture the colors of the sunset over that lake. Nigel pressured me to sell it last year. So Pamela could invest the money in her business."

"What business?" Gabrielle asked.

Thea shrugged. "Supposedly, the woman is an interior designer, but I've never seen a hint of her work."

"Does she have an office?"

"She works—so she says—at home."

"Does she even have a website?"

"Just a placeholder. I looked."

Gabrielle couldn't bear to see the sadness on Thea's face. "I'm so sorry you sold the cottage."

"And that's not all. Next, Nigel insisted I give Pamela some of my good jewelry. To prove that I'd accepted her into the family. '*Where are you going to wear it?*' he asked me. '*I never see any of it on you.*'"

"That's not true." These stories made Gabrielle so angry that she wouldn't be surprised if steam came from her ears.

"You wear a different piece almost every day."

"I know." Thea picked up her cup with an unsteady hand. "But he pressured me so much, I finally relented." And then she gave a mischievous grin. "But just a little."

"What did you give her?"

"Junky pieces—just enough of them to satisfy Nigel. A gold-plated daisy pin that I said was the most sentimental piece I owned—which, of course, was baloney. And a few rummage sale necklaces I claimed were my great-grandmother's. Wait till that woman has them appraised. And she will. Oh, yes, she will."

Thea and Gabrielle laughed together as they pictured Pamela getting that news. But then the levity passed, and the look of anguish reappeared on Thea's face.

"I miss who my son used to be...but I have to accept that he's made his choice. He's abiding by Pamela's wishes now, and mine be damned."

By Friday, the deal between Thea, Lulu, and Gabrielle had been agreed to in principle and now awaited all the various lawyers' approvals—Thea's, Jack's, and most of all, their mother's lawyer, who was currently considering their proposition.

That evening, before going to Bette's apartment, the sisters stopped in to see Imogene and share their nascent idea. Somehow, she'd become the bookend to the Gray Lady. As their mother's closest friend, Imogene's approval mattered as much to them as their mother's lawyer.

"So, obviously," Gabrielle said, "this is still the earliest stage of development. Though, we want to move fast. And, of course, keep the name Lulu came up with—Coco Street."

"Your mother would love that!" Imogene toasted them with one of the cheese puffs she'd served.

"Nothing's written in stone yet," Lulu said. "We don't know for sure if this will even work."

"I'm sure you have a million details yet to figure out." A pensive expression came over Imogene's face. And then it turned into a smile. "But I'm certain the girls of Style Endures are going to want to help."

Imogene called in the troops. By ten am Saturday morning, the apartment looked like a bazaar.

Imogene had instructed Ruby, Yvette, and Francesca to bring the bags, shoes, clothes, and jewelry they wanted *displayed* at Coco Street—a more genteel descriptor than *sold*—and they'd get fifty percent of the price they fetched. The women had arrived with items galore.

On the side, Imogene told Lulu and Gabrielle that none of the women would ever ask for a penny.

"If we don't open the store, what will we do with all your stuff?" Lulu asked.

"You'll have to sell the collection somehow, yes? We're just adding to the pile. Something we want to do for our Bette's daughters." She'd patted each of their hands in turn. "Let us mother you both a bit."

While they worked cataloging Bette's closet and the new offerings, Gabrielle came up with another idea. Each woman could write the history behind her items, including what they meant to her.

"We'll make them our window displays. Including some

special things not for sale," she said. "For instance, Ruby, for our opening, I'd love to feature your gorgeous watch—with a picture of Jackie Kennedy wearing it and the letter your husband wrote."

Ruby clutched her hands together. "What a wonderful idea, dear."

"We shouldn't get too carried away; remember, all we have so far is an imaginary store," Lulu said as she dragged a rack of suits to the living room. "Let's not plan imaginary displays yet."

Gabrielle caught Imogene's eye and raised her brow. Imogene smiled back and mouthed, "*Don't worry.*"

By six o'clock, they had two-thirds of Bette's collection all cataloged in Gabrielle's neat hand on the pages of a Smythson journal.

Ruby declared it was time for a nosh, and the women collapsed on the couch in front of a platter of bagels and cream cheese.

Francesca lifted a poppy seed bagel and almost sang out, "To our Bette!"

Gabrielle, Lulu, and the other women of the Style Endures Society lifted their bagels in response. "To Bette!"

"Look at all this." Yvette spread her arms, including the stacks of cashmere, silk, leather, and wool in her gesture. "It's the perfect way to honor Bette, who loved fashion and understood what the art truly represents."

Lulu, who sat on the rug, pulled her knees to her chest. "What does it represent?"

"I'm going to have to answer that in a roundabout way," Yvette said.

Francesca laughed. "You mean long-winded?"

Yvette shot a look at Francesca in the way only close friends could. "When we all got together for dinners—and lunches, and coffees—we often got philosophical. We talked about politics, war, climate change—"

"Climate change?" Lulu clapped her hand over her mouth. "Sorry. Just. Bette and climate change?"

"Try not to fall into stereotyping, dear," Imogene said.

"Anyway, to continue." Yvette took a sip of tea and then cleared her throat. "We also talked about the politics of fashion. For instance, flappers are remembered for their short skirts and bobbed hair, but what did those choices represent? They were a direct result of women fighting for their freedom—to go to work, to get the right to vote. Of marching in suffrage parades and standing up to the old guard. The changes in fashions during the 1920s weren't whims. They were emblematic of women's determination to revolutionize the status quo."

"Bette once asked what our *fashion beliefs* were. She ordered us—and you know how Bette could order—to find our favorite quote on what fashion represents," Ruby said. "I'll never forget mine. In the words of Iris Apfel: *'Fashion you can buy, but style you possess. The key to style is learning who you are, which takes years. There's no how-to road map to style. It's about self-expression and, above all, attitude.'*"

"I love that. Do you all remember yours?" Gabrielle asked.

"Of course," Yvette said. "We all took some basic calligraphy—at the Y—so we could ink them up and frame them. Mine came from Miuccia Prada. *'What you wear is how you present yourself to the world, especially today, when human contacts are so quick. Fashion is instant language.'*"

"For me, it's a Michelle Obama quote," Imogene said.

"Your hero." Ruby squeezed her friend's hand.

Imogene took a deep breath and recited. *"'If I can have any impact, I want women to feel good about themselves and have fun with fashion.'"*

"That should be the Coco Street motto," Lulu said. "If

we do it, of course."

"You'll do it. I have faith," Ruby said.

"I only hope Bette's lawyer feels the same way," Gabrielle said. "She doesn't seem the fashion-forward type."

"Don't judge, dear." Imogene leaned back against the couch. "I have a very prescient feeling that she'll love Coco Street."

"How could she not?" Francesca asked. "Besides, fashion isn't defined by any one person. In the words of Yves Saint Laurent, *'We must never confuse elegance with snobbery.'*"

"Do you remember Bette's quote?" Gabrielle laced her fingers, waiting for her mother's choice of wisdom.

"I thought she would pick a Chanel aphorism, but instead, she chose something from the photographer Bill Cunningham. Bette worshipped that man," Imogene said. *"'Fashion is the armor to survive the reality of everyday life.'"*

For a moment, everyone was quiet. Imogene sniffed. Francesca dabbed at a tear.

"Enough chatting. It's time for organizing." Ruby broke the silence. She handed the Smythson to Gabrielle. "Start writing."

By seven p.m., the six of them had an actionable strategy for moving forward with Coco Street.

### To-Do List

* Establish store's sale price w/Thea and how monthly rent will apply towards the sale
* Officially close Quills & Feathers
* Set a budget to redecorate Coco Street
* Create logo/ create signage
*Shop for furnishings
* Using the master list of Bette's items, correlate bags

and quotes
  * Figure out how to pay ourselves???
  *Figure out how to get more merchandise once Bette's items are sold
  * Decide on parameters for accepting outside merchandise
  * Develop tea-time menu

**Differentiating Coco Street from other vintage shops**

  *Events: Style classes, Fashion shows, Fashion Icon & Language of Jewelry Lectures
  *Tea parties featuring experts on matters of age, health, wellness, and love
  *Weekly presentations on vintage and current fashion by designers

Lulu ran a finger over the long list written in Gabrielle's flowing cursive. "I know I'll regret saying this, but this does sound like fun. In a very relative sense of the word."

"So, you're in?" Imogene asked.

"Let's just say I'm not *not* in."

"Now, all we need is to get the Gray Lady on board," Gabrielle said.

On Monday morning Quills & Feathers crackled with new energy as Gabrielle took Thea through the Coco Street To Do list until the doorbell jingled.

They looked up in tandem, startled when Nigel stormed

in, Pamela by his side.

"How dare you, Mother? I've heard from your lawyer. Working with this woman"—he pointed to Gabrielle—" might be the worst idea I've ever heard in my entire life. Father would be ashamed of you for even considering this damn project."

Gabrielle shivered at the vitriol Nigel hurled at his mother. The couple could only have received the letter from Jack Hunter-Holmes—now also acting as Thea's lawyer—an hour or so earlier. They clearly hadn't really considered it with any serious intent.

"Language! And don't raise your voice," Thea said. "The truth is it's your behavior that would mortify your father."

Gabrielle knew the *father* to whom they referred was Nigel's stepfather, who'd raised him. The only father he'd known.

"My behavior? I think he'd want me to call in a doctor and test your competence."

Thea stood, strode over to her son, and shook a finger at him. Her face had turned so red that Gabrielle feared for her blood pressure.

"You know as well as I do that the man who raised you would have moved Heaven and Earth to see me enjoying the sunset of my life. He would be doing everything to ensure that you and your greedy wife didn't try to cheat me out of that."

Nigel moved over to Pamela, who stood by the cash register. The ridiculous symbolism was far too on the nose.

"Don't you dare insult my wife." He put his arm around Pamela.

"Don't *you* dare try and steal my life," Thea countered.

"Nigel, stop yelling. Mother, try to hear what we're saying." Pamela used a syrupy-sweet voice and put her hands out, palms up, as though proving there was nothing up her sleeves. "Mother, we have only your best interests in mind. Poor Nigel stays up night after night worrying about you."

"Ha! Seems to me that this worry only began a month ago. Before that, cobwebs could have grown on the phone before either of you called. If Nigel is worried, it's only about how to get my money."

Nigel crossed his hands over his heart. "How can you say that, Mother?"

"You've lived above your means since you married this woman," Thea said. "What's your plan? Get your inheritance early so you can start spending early? Forget it. You'll get what I give you when I'm good and ready. Everything here came from work your father and I put into this place. We bought a shell, and then he replastered every wall, laid every plank on the floor. This place sheltered us, and it will go on sheltering me and those I love until the day I die."

"I thought I was the one you loved," Nigel said.

Thea's face softened. "Of course, I love you. But I love my life, too. And I love Gabrielle. Her idea will take care of all of us."

With that, Thea, showing she was anything but a doddering old lady, began to enumerate.

"We're going to legally separate the upper living quarters from the storefront with a rent-to-own agreement, complete with a hundred-year lease. The apartment will be put into a trust, with me and you, Nigel, as co-trustees. My right to live there will be guaranteed into perpetuity."

Jack had argued that Thea should be the sole trustee, with Nigel as the benefactor becoming trustee upon her death, but Thea couldn't go that far. "Blood is blood," she'd said.

Now, Nigel stared at his mother with disbelief. "How can you do this to me?"

"How can you not understand how fair I'm being?" Thea appeared genuinely hurt.

Gabrielle took her friend's trembling hand. "Nigel," she said, "your mother is well within her rights to do as she wishes with her building. She's taken your worries about her future into account. Now it's your turn to take her needs and desires into account."

"This is none of your concern," Pamela said to Gabrielle, speaking for Nigel. "Consider this fair warning: Go ahead with this and you'll pay for it."

# Chapter Nineteen

## Lulu

Lulu grated potatoes with a vengeance, shredding anxiety along with the russets.

"Damn," she swore as she caught her knuckle.

It never failed—every damn Hanukah.

"Grated skin isn't particularly tasty," Matt would tease as he bandaged her finger. "Is spicing the potato pancakes with your blood a Jewish thing? Maybe connected to the blood of the lamb, blood on the door?"

"That's Passover. Couldn't it be a Catholic thing?" Lulu would tease back. "Honoring your traditions—like the Holy Communion? The blood and body?"

Lulu blinked three times, pretending onions had brought the tears, not memories of Matt. Mocking their religious, cultural, and family differences and pretending to have mixed-marriage arguments had been one of their favorite games.

Their contradictions strengthened their connections. Instead of focusing on each other's worst qualities, they made their faults into lovable foibles.

"Guess how many times Daddy measured and re-measured the flour while making carrot cakes today?" she'd ask her sons.

"Better than your blasphemous method of throwing in ingredients by feel," Matt would counter.

How did anyone ever recover from love?

"Alexa, play Cyndi Lauper," Lulu called out.

*Shuffling songs by Cyndi Lauper* came Alexa's robotic answer.

Lulu tried to shake off her melancholy by dancing to *Girls Just Wanna Have Fun*, though she should be playing the *Cabaret* soundtrack. Joel Grey singing "Money, Money, Money" would better fit her current situation.

Thankfully, Lulu had been able to talk the bank manager into letting her pay only the current mortgage payments while catching up on the past amounts owed this week. At the end of six months, she'd have to give them a balloon payment—a solution that would only succeed if she found the needed cash.

Her mortgage was just a part of the problem. Since she only paid the minimum amount allowed each month, the interest on her credit cards continued rising, and she'd run out of places to zero-balance transfer.

Then there was her deteriorating house screaming for attention. Paint peeled, faucets leaked, the dishwasher scarcely made it through a cycle without clanging as though begging for life support, and the porch floor buckled more with every rain.

Even if she wanted to sell her home, she'd have to fix it up to get anywhere near top dollar. And that would take more money she didn't have. Granted, given New York's real estate values, she could sell it as is, but then what she would get after paying off two mortgages would barely net enough to pay off her other creditors and buy a teeny tiny condo.

And she didn't want to live in a teeny tiny condo.

She loved her mess of a house.

Before Matt died, she'd loved her mess of a life.

Lulu always thought she was entirely different from Bette, but maybe not? Both married young, both learned to rely on their beloved husbands, and both ended up unsuited for carrying on without them.

Divesting Bette's whole collection as fast as possible in one fell swoop would have been her best chance to recover. Letting Gabrielle talk her into Coco Street had probably been a colossal mistake.

Yet, her sister's arguments sounded enticing.

*We'll make so much more money in the long run!*

*You'll be working in a shop you own! Coco Street will belong to us, not your in-laws!*

*We can come up with new ideas and explore our passions! Wedding cakes will no longer be your destiny.*

But Lulu couldn't afford to explore her passions and indulge her creativity. Maybe she and Gabrielle could divide the collection. Her sister could open the store, and Lulu could sell her half to the highest bidder. Would that satisfy the Gray Lady?

Except. Except. Except Lulu had fallen in love with the idea of Coco Street.

"Mom?"

She looked up, startled by Seth's sudden appearance. Children never got used to ringing doorbells in houses where they once lived. His husband, Gus, stood behind him.

"Guess why we arrived here early?" Her son-in-law seemed hardly able to contain the answer.

"I'm going to be a grandmother?" She went on tiptoes to kiss Gus on the cheek and then hugged her son tightly.

"Not yet," Gus said.

"But you're talking about it?" Lulu brought her hands to her chest, though not in pleasure. When you married and got pregnant at eighteen, you could too quickly become a grandmother at forty-eight. She was so not ready for that.

"Calm down, Mom. And you." Seth pointed at Gus. "Stop."

"But we do talk about it, honey."

Seth rolled his eyes. "Every couple in the world talks about it."

"But *we* were talking about it last night." Gus washed up at the sink.

"We talked about what race our babies should be," Seth said. "Not about finding a surrogate tomorrow. I promise, Mom—it's all a distant *someday*."

Lulu squinted, glancing from Gus to Seth—examining the radiant deep brown and golden olive complexions. "Perhaps Gus's parents should come over so we can explore color charts?"

"You missed your calling, Mom. You should have been a comedian."

"Perhaps if I hadn't married a bakery along with your father, I'd have wound up another Sarah Silverman."

"Does this mean I married a bakery, too?" Gus asked.

"Yes. And at some point, you'll have to do your tour," Seth said. "It's our family's equivalent of being drafted into the army."

"True," Lulu said. "But didn't that Quattros' paycheck support your many high school needs?"

"Yes: many clothes; many electronics." Seth picked up a spatula next to the bowl filled with grated potatoes. "Shouldn't you put a lemon in that? To keep it from turning gray?"

Before she could answer, Gus snatched the spatula. "Your Quattros' tour wasn't long enough. You put lemon on *apples* to keep the brown away. Potatoes get covered with water to keep them from turning color. But not these! The last thing you want with grated potatoes for latkes is water. One of the most important steps is squeezing all the water out."

"One night reading Joan Nathan, and now you've become the world's leading expert on Jewish cuisine?" Seth put his hands up in the air.

Gus pointedly ignored him and turned to Lulu. "We came over early to help and give you a break. So, let me take care of this. Seth is correct about one thing. I've been reading up on Jewish cooking, including potato pancakes, and I intend to use some of that knowledge now."

Lulu opened her mouth to ask what Gus planned and then stopped. He could put in saffron mixed with chocolate and chili if she could get out of the kitchen. She hated frying and never enjoyed the tedious task of flipping latkes.

Kids always thought mothers were more attached to cooking than they were.

She untied her apron and removed it with pleasure. "Don't forget to heat the oven to two hundred degrees. To keep the latkes hot but not dry them out."

Hours later, Lulu, her sons, their spouses, and Gabrielle were all helping put the food on the table. Lulu brought out the brisket, Gabrielle the string beans. Nicholas filled the wine glasses while his wife, Bridget, watched with a frown. She held two bowls: one filled with apple sauce, the other, sour cream—latke toppings to please all tastes.

"Aren't you supposed to wait and fill the glasses while we eat?" Bridget asked.

"You're thinking of Passover, my sweet. Latkes mean Hanukah." Nicholas laughed as he patted her arm. "Don't worry. You'll get it."

"It's not funny." Bridget almost slammed the bowls on the table. "I'm working hard to educate myself. And I know this is Hanukah dinner. I also know there's plenty more to the holiday than potato pancakes."

Seth and Gus exchanged eye rolls, including Lulu in the moment. Making fun of Bridget's determination to master Judaism had become a new family hobby.

"Everything is delicious," Gabrielle said a little while later, reaching for the tongs to get another crispy latke. "I can't stop eating these. These are the best potato pancakes you've ever made."

"No. Those are actually the best latkes I never made. Gus was the chef. And you're right. These are the best ones yet."

"Sometimes you need a little something from the Caribbean and South America to spice things up," Seth said.

Gus groaned. "Can you hide your inner cornball at least a little bit, hon?" He turned to Lulu. "Maybe there's some Jewish in my roots, after all. Don't forget. A sizeable portion of the Jews escaping the Nazis went to South America."

"As did many Nazis," Bridget said. "I wonder what kind of marriages resulted from those diasporas." Bridget twisted her outrageously thick hair into a bun and fastened it with a pen from her bag. Lulu admired so much about her daughter-in-law, but the young woman's continual fussing with her mounds of hair at the table brought out Lulu's inner Bette. Lulu caught Gabrielle's eye as they shared judgmental thoughts via sisterly brain waves.

"So, you're saying that maybe I'm not Jewish, after all—that I have secret Nazi roots?" Gus removed his rectangular glasses and faux glared at Bridget.

"That's a weird thought," Gabrielle said. "Either way. Especially if the Nazi in question was in hiding and then concealed his background from his wife. Who turned out to be Jewish."

Lulu cut a piece of brisket with her fork. It was that tender if she did say so herself. Roasting the meat way past when you considered it done—that was the secret she'd learned from her grandmother, who'd been the one to teach her to cook. Bette had turned up her nose at the recipe—probably because it sounded like it came out of a Poughkeepsie Hadassah cookbook rather than passed down from generation to generation: ketchup, brown sugar, onions, and one secret ingredient: apricot leather.

"Why couldn't the German hiding their past be a she?" Bridget asked.

"Are you trying for feminist equality for female Nazis?" Seth asked.

"How did you end up naming your sons so differently?" Gus asked Lulu. "Seth and Nicholas? One for your family's side and one for your husband's?"

Lulu basked in the swirling cross-conversations. She reached for the wine, determined to keep all worries at bay for this one night. "Yes. I thought everyone would be happy. Of course, Bette hated both names. She was already furious with me for leaving college, marrying down—as she saw it—and then naming you"—she smiled at Nicholas—"for *some saint*. Bette had hoped for a good solid WASP name."

"And how about Seth?" Bridget asked.

"We named him for my father's father. Bette hated it." Wine loosened Lulu's tongue. Like Matt always said, she was a cheap date.

"I bet," Nicholas said. "Bette despised acknowledging Grandpa. She always gave me the impression you were born by immaculate conception."

Seth turned to Gus. "Grandpa was the husband Bette wished had gotten away even earlier."

"Yeah, before I was born." Lulu laughed to show she was kidding, though a slightly inebriated woman often spoke a sober woman's truth.

"What a sad thing to believe," Bridget said.

Lulu didn't linger over her daughter-in-law's observation lest it turn her into a maudlin mess. Instead, she reached for another potato pancake. "Okay, Gus. What's the magic ingredient?"

"Between Joan Nathan, *The New York Times* food section," Seth said, "and *the Joy of Cooking,* he read every potato pancake recipe known to mankind."

"There's no magic ingredient—just a non-ingredient. I didn't use any flour. Only the tiniest bit of matzo meal to hold the pancakes together. *Un peau.* Not a big deal," Gus said.

"No big deal? After reading every recipe created by every Jewish person in the world, he tried out three of them." Seth reached over and squeezed Gus's shoulders. "My husband is a kitchen genius."

Or very anxious to be loved. Lulu knew the paradigm of wanting to be accepted in a new family.

"Can I be your sous chef next time?" Bridget said. "Or yours, Lulu? I'm tired of crunching numbers."

"Thank God one of us is good at it," Nicholas said.

"You have no idea how much I love seeing you all here." Without warning, Lulu lost the war she'd fought all day and burst into tears.

Seth left his seat and crouched before her. "What's

wrong, Mom? Are you okay? Is something the matter?"

Nicholas joined Seth on Lulu's other side. "Are you sick?"

Lulu heard the panic in both their voices. Between sobs, she worked to reassure them. "Not sick. Well, maybe I'm worried sick. I just don't know how I'll do it all."

"Do what all?" Nicholas asked.

"What's *it?*" Seth added.

"Work two jobs. Plus..." She locked her lips, aware of how close the wine had brought her to spilling her debt secrets.

"Two jobs?" Seth asked.

"Plus? Mom?" Nicholas asked.

"Plus...not worry Annette and Mattias."

"Annette and Mattias? What is this even about? What two jobs?" Seth insisted.

Gabrielle leaned toward Lulu. "You need to trust me. I promise I'm going to make this work."

"Make what work?" Nicholas asked.

"You haven't told them?" Gabrielle asked.

Lulu shook her head. "I didn't want to say anything until I was sure."

"Sure of what?" her sister asked.

"Whether I want it and can manage it all." Lulu took a deep breath. "Sure of the lawyer's approval and—"

"Actually," Gabrielle interrupted Lulu. "I was waiting for the right time to tell you. I invited the Gray Lady to the store today and took her through everything."

"You what!? Without asking me?"

"Consider me merely performing an exploratory expedition. I told you I'd take on the heavier load for a bit." Gabrielle topped off her and Lulu's wine glass. "I even brought some catalogs from Sotheby's to show her how big a market vintage bags and accessories have become. I served her tea and cookies, and she met some of the neighborhood regulars. Well, turns out that Diana isn't as hard-nosed as she acts. She became warm as apple pie sitting with the ladies who told her how much they loved coming over for tea every afternoon. When I told her we wanted to continue Thea's traditions, I swear, the Gray Lady positively beamed. And then she gave us her approval."

"What are you talking about?" Nicholas asked.

"Lulu," Gabrielle said, "tell your family."

"Okay. Who knows whether it's the best idea or not—and we can still back out. We can still just sell everything," Lulu said, mostly to her sister.

"If you don't slow down, both of you, and tell us what is going on, we're going to imagine the worst," Seth admonished.

And so, Lulu and Gabrielle explained about Coco Street, what they were hoping they could pull off, and how Lulu had no idea if she could take on the project while still putting in her regular hours at the bakery.

"We're here for you. Let's make a plan," Bridget said as Gus nodded.

Lulu could almost see her son and daughter-in-law rolling up their sleeves.

"Yes," said Seth.

"We can help," Nicholas agreed.

The following day, Gus and Bridget sat with Lulu at a Quattros' wrought iron table, sipping coffee, devouring fresh bear claws, and coming up with ways to help with the bakery.

Gus and Bridget would rearrange their work schedules so they could be at the bakery by four. The software development company where he worked and the accounting firm where she worked were flexible about hours.

They would clean and prep, and, eventually, and only under Lulu's supervision, and always following her written instructions, begin to bake. Perhaps they thought crafting cakes would fast-track them to becoming one hundred percent Quattro-certified. The clan had tentatively approved the idea of them coming on board. Annette and Matthias had wanted the next generation to enter since the first grandchild was born—the brothers and their wives were grateful that Lulu wasn't wholly walking away.

Meanwhile, Seth and Nicholas would focus on renovating and redecorating Quills & Feathers and turning it into Coco Street.

Done with the cookies and the plan, Lulu led her daughter and son-in-law to the back room. They'd seen the kitchen previously—as part of their introduction to the family—but this wasn't a tour. Today was orientation day for the eager trainees.

Gus caressed the giant stainless steel mixing bowl. "Last night, I read all about the tricks of scaling up. If you're game, the first thing I want to try is my grandmother's Haitian cake, also known as *Gateau Au Beurre*." He held his fingers to his mouth, made a smacking sound, and then sent the kiss toward Lulu. "It is like no rum cake you've ever tasted. When I—"

"I was researching too!" Bridget gave Gus a light punch on the arm. "Regional old-fashioned recipes favorites are hot. Wait until you taste my granny's special, also filled with alcohol. Great minds and all, though my cake will outdo yours. Gran's Irish Whiskey and Stout Chocolate Cake. One adds—"

"Before you two out-booze each other, you'll be learning only *my* recipes and the Quattros' standards." Lulu saw them sag a bit. "And then, after you have our basics perfected, you begin baby steps to making your mark."

Standing between them, Gus threw one arm around Lulu's back and the other around Bridget's and shoulder-hugged them both. "All cultures joined together. Before we're finished, Quattros' will be the top destination bakery in all of New York City."

# Chapter Twenty

## Lulu

Lulu smiled as she turned onto Coney Island Avenue towards George's Restaurant, looking forward to her sister-in-law's company and the soothing food. Months had somehow passed since they'd had their once-weekly brunch. In the past few weeks, Lulu worked longer and harder than at any other time.

She'd never been happier.

Seven days a week, she raced from Brooklyn to Greenwich Village, switching from mixing batter and frosting cakes to patching walls, scrubbing hidden corners, and stripping wooden cornices in what would soon become Coco Street. The ragged crew joining her, and Gabrielle had solidified into a tight clan. Seth and Nicholas worked alongside Imogene, Ruby, and Jack-With-Two-Last-Names—who'd surprised her when he'd volunteered to help. Occasionally Gabrielle's friend Liam—an electrician and set designer—showed up, as well. He'd been on Cole's stage crew from the beginning. Working together for over twenty years, she knew he shared her aesthetic and anger towards Cole, who'd stiffed him for months of back pay when he declared bankruptcy.

As everyone threw themselves into Gabrielle's vision of combining fashion with recycling and reclamation, Coco Street became more and more of a reality. Lulu's balloon mortgage payment still loomed, but she convinced herself that May was far away.

Meanwhile, though Bridget helped enormously, Gus raced toward becoming an accomplished baker at record speed, inculcating Lulu's experience and recipes faster than Lulu had ever learned under Annette. He was a natural. Of course, Gus wasn't juggling morning sickness, followed by a screaming hungry infant.

When Lulu had left Quattros' just minutes ago, her son-in-law had been immersed in building his Valentine's Wedding Extravaganza—the first cake Gus had designed and executed alone. His sketch illustrated a seven-layer red velvet cake covered with bright white buttercream frosting, decorated with ruby hearts, and sprinkled with edible gold flakes. As she gave Gus a goodbye hug, she smiled at the streak of red fondant on his chin and flour dusting his hair, the embellishments turning his handsome carved features into a whimsical portrait.

Gus and Bridget were the first grandchildren to join the business, and their presence had sent Annette and Mattias over the moon. Her in-laws had always dreamed of seeing their legacy pass on to the next generation. They now hoped that when their seventeen other grandchildren—ranging in age from six to twenty-nine—saw how content Bridget, and especially Gus, were at the bakery, more would follow suit.

Though Annette and Mattias's joy should only delight

Lulu, hints of creeping jealousy shocked her.

Lulu opened the door of George's Restaurant and saw Drea already seated.

Even now, during the Christmas crush, Drea occasionally ditched her stethoscope for an apron and pitched in—apparently, sprinkling sugar crystals over giant gingerbread snowmen could be fun when it wasn't a permanent sentence. So, confessing to Drea would come easy. She understood the pull of the Quattros.

After the two women had ordered lunch and gotten the small talk out of the way, Lulu revealed her green-eyed feelings.

"I'm a small, horrid person. How can I be jealous of how well they're treating my son-in-law?" Lulu took a bite of her favorite tuna melt. "I should kiss the ground he walks on instead of wondering why they treat him like the ghost of Julia Child."

"They've always been a little afraid of you. Gus simply makes them happy." Drea groaned in pleasure as she spooned up rice pudding.

"Me? That's the first I ever heard."

"Seriously?" Drea asked.

"Seriously." Lulu took a sip of coffee and shook her head. "Afraid of me? I've been terrified of them since the day we met."

"Okay. Then it's mutual."

"But why?"

"At first, they were scared that you'd convince Matt to leave the bakery. They'd always counted on him to replace Mattias as the brains of the operation. Only after they realized Matt was staying and you joined the business did they relax a bit. And they constantly talked about loving your artistic touches."

Lulu swallowed a forkful of coleslaw. "Touches? I redid

the whole damn place."

Drea shrugged. "They saw the changes as additions, not revisions. When Matt died, they became afraid again—but this time, afraid that you'd leave. Gus offers security you don't: respect for the old, plus even more new ideas and endless energy without an air of frustration or dissatisfaction."

"Are you saying I give off an air of frustration—"

Drea held up a hand to keep Lulu from finishing. "I think what's really behind their love affair is this: Annette and Mattias believe Gus will join Quattros'. Maybe even pull in Seth." Drea scraped the very last of the pudding from the bowl.

"And here I'd been concerned they'd never truly accept their marriage." Lulu leaned back on the high-backed leather stool. She studied the wall with its framed photos of the generations who'd managed George's. Every time she came here with her in-laws, they'd point out how much the place hadn't changed.

*Except*, they'd always say with a finger raised in the air, *except for the stools! We used to twirl on the old chrome ones. And those had no backs!*

As though twirling on backless stools had been the equivalent of living through blizzards and sandstorms.

"Are you kidding?" Drea gestured to the waiter for a coffee refill. "They consider Gus the epitome of cool." At this, Drea grinned. "And they expect that coolness will transfer to Quattros', which will then grow exponentially into their dream—a chain of cool Quattros' throughout the city."

Lulu almost choked as she laughed. "No wonder Gus loves them so much. They share the same grand plan."

"Don't laugh," Drea said. "Thomas thinks that Gus's idea of adding multi-cultural baked goods is, in fact, brilliant.

My husband has joined the Gus-can-be-a miracle-man bandwagon."

"I'll say that when Gus gets Victoria to show up in both mind and body more than once a week. The woman doesn't earn half her salary."

"As one sister-in-law to another, here's my advice. Don't be the bad cop—Leo worships her fragile ass. Sic Bridget on her."

"Oh! That's the best idea I've heard in my entire life." Lulu felt better just thinking of her daughter-in-law handling Victoria's hypochondria.

After lunch, Lulu returned to Quattros' to help Gus get ready for the final bakes. Victoria sat out front nursing a cup of tea and yet another set of vague pains. For once, it didn't bother Lulu. She just kept thinking, *Bridget's problem, Bridget's problem.*

At four, Lulu packed a box of cookies and headed to the city. As requested, she texted Nicholas right before reaching the Coco Street stop.

*Do you need me to pick anything up?*

*All set,* he texted back. *See you soon.*

Lulu saw a crowd gathering outside the store as she walked down 10th Street. Upon getting closer, she recognized her sons and Gabrielle, along with Imogene, Thea, and Ruby. Once within hearing distance, she gave full voice to her growing anxiety. "Did a pipe burst or something?"

"Everything's fine," Imogene said. "We were waiting for you. Look up!"

A green tarp covered the Quills & Feathers sign. Nicholas tugged at the rope holding up the sheeting with a grand gesture and pulled it down, revealing a shiny new sign. "Behold!"

Glossy ruby letters, in the same font used by Chanel, spelled out *Coco Street.* A black quilted purse hung from the capital *C*, glossy gold buttons replaced the *Os*, and a gleaming pearl necklace draped through the *S*.

Beneath the store's name was their favorite Chanel quote—which also adorned their business cards and stationery. *"Fashion Fades / Style Endures."* The words honoring their mother and her icon had become their motto.

"Oh, Nicholas!" Lulu's smile widened with business and maternal pride. "It's perfect."

"Gabrielle, Seth, and I designed it together. We wanted to surprise you," he said.

She hugged her sons and sister, pushing away thoughts about why they didn't include her in designing the logo.

*Grace*, she reminded herself. *Have some damn grace.*

After admiring the sign for a few minutes more, the group entered Coco Street-in-progress. Nicholas took Lulu's shopping bag, sniffing the box of chocolate chip cookies. Gus's newest version somehow came out a miracle combination of cakey and fudgy, while crispy-edged, and had immediately become everyone's favorite.

Gabrielle snatched the bag from him. "Another hour of work before dinner."

Butcher paper covered the windows, giving the interior a snug, haven-like atmosphere. Ruby, Imogene, Thea, and Gabrielle picked up paintbrushes, putty knives, and cleaning cloths and got to work. Seth and Nicholas attacked the newly built shelves with sandpaper.

Lulu heard the door open and turned from admiring the smooth wood emerging through her sons' work.

"Sorry to be late," Jack said as he walked in. "Client emergency."

Seeing him, Lulu smiled. Jack caught Lulu's eyes, beamed back, and gave her a thumbs-up.

When he'd first volunteered to help, she'd found herself oddly excited when he showed up. In jeans and a well-worn sweater, Jack seemed significantly different from the suited-up lawyer. Handyman style had always appealed to Lulu more than Brooks Brothers.

After another half-hour, Gus and Bridget arrived with bags full of food.

"The sign is perfect. Nobody will be able to ignore it when they pass by. Next, you guys can tackle Quattros'. We could use a rebranding."

"Great idea." Bridget applauded as Lulu's sons groaned.

"Nicholas and I have done everything possible to escape that bakery. Our grandparents put us to work the day we were tall enough to reach the register, right?" Seth said. "And even you are not pulling me back in."

"Did I say you had to work there?" Gus asked. "I'm having the best time of my life."

Seth held an imaginary gun to his temple. "Mom, I'm beginning to understand what you went through when you married Dad."

Lulu wisely kept her mouth shut as she covered the paint-spattered, scratched worktable with a plastic cloth. Gabrielle added Thea's collection of mismatched plates as the older woman arranged heavy silverware, which she'd brought down from her apartment.

"It's good luck to eat with fine silver," Thea said, just as she did every time she laid out the forks, knives, and spoons. "We must live like the success we want to achieve."

Jack turned down the lights, radiating pride in the dimmers he'd helped Liam install.

Seth placed a worn linen napkin at each place setting as Gus arranged white cartons from the Golden Wok Chinese restaurant.

Lulu stuck serving spoons in each white box, grateful that Thea didn't have a remembered tradition of transferring the food from cartons to fragile crystal bowls.

When all were seated, Ruby asked who would say grace. She'd begun the tradition explaining she was so thankful to become a part of the Coco Street family, and she wanted to acknowledge that.

The first time Ruby showed up in work clothes, ready to perform all assigned tasks, she'd held up her bejeweled fingers and promised, "I'm pretty handy. You'll be surprised."

The woman undersold herself. Whether it was painting, sanding, or any other mechanical job, she proved herself worthy of a role on HGTV. She arrived daily via a car service, alighting from the black Town Car holding a bright red tool kit.

Lulu had wondered if Bergdorf's sold designer handywoman bags.

When no one volunteered to say the prayer fast enough for her taste, Ruby did the honors. She cleared her throat, waited for all to hold hands, and then closed her eyes. "We give thanks for the delicious food, the loving company, and the gift of purpose."

With that, they tore in. The scent of fresh paint and varnish mixed with mouth-watering smells of spareribs, beef with broccoli, chicken lo mein, shrimp in lobster sauce, spring rolls, and kung pao chicken.

"Can I start with a chocolate chip cookie?" Nicholas asked.

Seth rolled his eyes. "Are you asking your wife or your mother?"

"I'm asking your husband, the baker." Nicholas reached over towards the Quattros' box tied with red and white string, but Gus caught his hand before he got it.

"Sorry, bro," Gus said. "Spice before the sweet. That's how the palate works."

"A few weeks at Quattros', and you're the expert?" Nicholas asked.

"In fact," Seth said. "Gus is always the expert. On everything."

"Why does that not sound like a compliment?" Gus piled rice on his plate and then topped it with broccoli and beef in a garlic scented dark sauce. "Aren't you supposed to be on my side till death do us part?"

"I am, but being married to a saint wears on a hungry soul." Seth took the Quattros' box from Gus and handed it to his brother. "Help yourself."

"Nicholas, you should have protein first." Bridget twisted and then re-twisted her hair into a fresh bun. "Do we tease too much in this family? Are we covering up for something?"

Lulu reminded herself to buy stronger hairnets for the bakery. Steel mesh, perhaps. "Teasing is love. I learned that after marrying Matt. A family with six brothers? I didn't have a chance."

"Six brothers? What a blessing for their parents." Ruby scooped up a generous portion of lo mein. "We tried for years, but parenthood eluded us. We were going to adopt but—"

A series of demanding knocks on the front door interrupted. Lulu rose to answer, but Jack gestured for her to sit. "I'll get it."

"Ask who it is before you open the door." Ruby moved her chair closer to Nicholas.

Jack unbolted the door without asking—but only a few

inches. After a few moments of muted conversation, he stepped back, and Nigel and Pamela burst into the shop.

"Christ, not again," Gabrielle muttered to Lulu. "What fresh hell this way comes?"

"Who are they?" Seth asked his aunt, who filled him in as Nigel marched in, face flaming, followed by a scowling Pamela.

"What's going on, Mom?" Nigel asked. "You haven't answered your phone in two days! I expected to find you lying in a heap on the floor."

"And it took you two days to come over?" Thea gripped her fork as though holding a weapon. "You aren't that worried about me. So, what is it? Are you that nervous about my money? I don't have to listen to your ranting anymore. It's all settled. I told you."

"You do have to listen, Mother." Pamela placed her hands on her hips, her purple-tipped long fingers claws against a dark red coat.

"No, I don't, and certainly not to you, Pamela. And not to my son right now, either." Thea's voice rose. "I intend to eat my dinner in peace with my friends and would appreciate it if you both left. Write me a letter if you have something to say."

Ruby tipped her head with a puzzled expression. "These are your children? Should we offer them something to eat? Surely, we can work this out."

Nigel ignored Ruby while Pamela sent her a withering glance.

Thea shook her head. "Ruby, I apologize, but these two have worn me to my last nerve."

"You might want to hear this, anyway, Mom," Nigel said. "Remember. I have access to your bank accounts, and I've been checking. What I see is seriously worrying."

A chilled silence fell as Thea visibly shuddered. "You

have what?"

"Don't you remember putting my name on the account last year? Back when you were like most mothers and trusted your son."

"Back when you acted like a normal son? Before you married this—" Thea stopped herself, changed direction, and said, "I gave you that access for emergencies. How dare you use it to spy on me?"

"We consider this an emergency, Mother." Pamela lowered her voice to a concerned, loving tone. "Perhaps you're losing a bit of your, um, judgment."

"Your mother isn't losing anything," Gabrielle said. "She's happy and busy and doing fantastic."

Nigel sent Gabrielle an expression filled with loathing, palpably took a calming breath, and then pasted on a smile. "Mother, we'd like to talk to you." He drew closer. "Alone."

"You can talk here. I have nothing to hide."

"Fine." Pamela pointed at Gabrielle and then Lulu. "These women are in the process of losing, if not stealing, all your money."

"You are talking about my mother and aunt—" Seth said.

Lulu put her hand on his, interrupting him before he could get more embroiled.

"Let us handle this, Seth," Lulu said quietly.

"You don't get to come into my store, my home, and suggest such a thing about my friends," Thea said as she stood, faced her son and Pamela, and matched her daughter-in-law's stance.

"Yes, we do," Nigel said. "Pamela discovered that your account is dwindling more each week. She warned me that these women are fleecing you. Thus, I must step in to perform my fiduciary responsibility."

"It's not dwindling," Thea said. "Nobody is fleecing

anyone. I am investing in my business."

"How can you be so blind? These people are taking advantage of you." Now Nigel stepped forward, forcing Thea back. "These people have not paid rent on the store since this charade began."

He pronounced *charade* as though he were upper-class British.

"Which is how I want this investment handled," Thea said.

Gabrielle rose and went to stand next to Lulu. "There is no ill intent, no hidden agenda. Thea's part of our family," she said.

"Is that how you two got her to agree not to get any rent? Because of so-called *family* ties. Are you going to take care of her if she falls and breaks her hip?" Nigel asked.

Now Ruby stood and joined the group ringing Nigel. "What's wrong with you? This is not how a son or daughter-in-law should treat their mother."

"A son, this son, makes sure these witches don't drain his mother." Nigel pointed at Lulu first and then Gabrielle.

"Hey, buddy. Watch your tone." Nicholas slammed a fist into his palm. "Never talk about my mother and aunt like that."

"I wouldn't have to if they weren't thieves."

"Nigel! That's not true." Thea began to cry. "How can you be so hateful?"

Jack walked over to Nigel and handed him a card. "I'm Jack Hunter-Holmes. The attorney for Coco Street. We can manage the situation very easily if you would just get in touch. I've sent you several letters already—registered. Maybe you overlooked them? I understand your concern, but I can put your mind at ease."

"You are an attorney?" Pamela raked her eyes over his worker's garb. "A lawyer who moonlights as a carpenter?"

Jack smiled. "Do you need one?"

Pamela turned to Nigel. "It's time to tell her."

Lulu thought she saw a mixture of emotions cross Nigel's face for a moment. Sadness, anger, even confusion.

"Nigel," Pamela urged. "If you don't, I will."

"Mother…" Nigel began, "this group of crooks is controlling you. And that includes their lawyer. As you're refusing to listen to reason, we have no choice. We'll be filing for guardianship."

"Expect to hear from *our* lawyer in the morning," Pamela added. Taking Nigel's arm, with a bit of a tug, she turned him around, and then together, the couple walked out, leaving the front door open.

Thea sank back into her chair. "I don't know my son anymore." She began crying anew. "Can you stop him, Jack?"

Jack closed and locked the door. "I'll work harder on that than I've worked for anything in my life."

"But you can't promise?" Thea turned to Gabrielle and Lulu. "Will you help?"

Before they could answer, Nicholas walked over to the older woman and placed a hand on her shoulder. "I promise, Thea, somehow, we will all work to make this right."

Thea gave a shaky smile and put up a hand to hold his.

Lulu was worried. Making promises came easily to the young. The older you got, the more you knew how often shit happened.

*Mann tracht, un gott lacht.* Her Brooklyn grandma had repeated the Yiddish words often enough to scar her with the meaning: *Man plans, God laughs.*

# Chapter Twenty-One

## Gabrielle

Gabrielle walked down the hall toward Jack's office, crossing every finger, praying he'd have an iron-tight plan for staunching the disaster heading their way.

True to his promise, Nigel had initiated a full-on war. He'd begun efforts to have Thea declared incompetent and had served Gabrielle and Lulu with papers accusing them of scamming his mother. He claimed they were taking advantage of what he and Pamela referred to as Thea's "fragile mental state." And he'd started proceedings to break their Coco Street lease for non-payment of rent.

Gabrielle reached her destination and walked into the reception area.

"Can I help you?" asked the woman sitting where Jack's assistant usually sat.

"Is Stephanie out?" Gabrielle asked.

"Just on a break." She smiled. "I'm Meg; can I help?"

"Gabrielle Winslow. My sister and I have an appointment, but I'll just wait for her."

"No problem. Let me know if you need anything."

Gabrielle took a seat and checked her watch. Lulu wasn't late yet; Gabrielle was a few minutes early. And anxious. She picked up last month's Architectural Design magazine and flipped it open to—what else—a Valentine's Day ad for Chanel No. 5. Of course.

Gabrielle gazed up as if Bette hovered above, waiting for her magical abilities to be acknowledged.

Encouraged, she turned the page; maybe she'd find a new idea or two for Coco Street. The store was coming together so well. The last time she'd been so excited was when she'd conceived of the Costume Institute. She wouldn't let Nigel ruin her plans.

Perusing a photo essay on a Malibu home, Gabrielle took note of a bulletin board in the kitchen with recipes stuck under a crisscross of ribbons. She could do the same thing with Chanel ribbons and display pictures of smiling customers trying on Coco Street items. Taking out her notebook, Gabrielle sketched the idea. Then she checked her watch. Lulu was late now. Ten minutes late.

"Do you want me to tell him you're here?" the receptionist asked.

"Let's give it another five minutes. But thanks."

After everyone had finally left the other night, Gabrielle stayed behind. She'd wanted to talk to Thea alone. She'd made soothing cups of chamomile tea and told Thea she was concerned.

"I'm worried," she'd told Thea, "that you might regret your decision to fight Nigel."

Thea had shaken her head in a slow sweeping *no* and smiled sadly. "You're sweet to worry. The only thing I'll regret is not trying to prevent Nigel from marrying Pamela so quickly. I should have made a stronger case for him to slow down. This may sound like a mother's excuse, but I know she's to blame. Nigel's not perfect, but he was never this money-obsessed until she showed up. Never so disrespectful." She'd sighed, wrapped her hands around her cup of tea, and then straightened. "But he's made his choice, as have I."

"Still, I can't bear the idea that you could lose your son! And the store at the same time."

"Nigel will come around. I have to believe that. And Coco Street has been nothing but fun for me. Yes, of course, I've loved the bookshop—and naturally, there's some sadness in closing it—but this? A chance for a new adventure? Sweetheart, that's a hell of a lot better than holding on to the past. You and I both know Quills & Feathers' time was over. Long live Coco Street!"

"Gabrielle? Why are you out here?" Stephanie had returned, the receptionist's cheeks reddened by the cold weather.

"I'm waiting for Lulu."

"Oh, she's already here. She arrived before I went out. Go right in."

Gabrielle walked into Jack's office, shaking her head at not checking.

"Hey, guys!" When she saw them, she felt as though she were interrupting. Lulu, flushed and giddy, was sitting at the table very close to Jack and laughing at whatever corny joke Jack had told. All his jokes were corny. Before Gabrielle's divorce, when she and Jack were such good friends, she'd also laughed at them. But maybe not quite as loudly as Lulu was now.

No question, her sister was in full flirt mode, from the lipstick that Gabrielle had picked out for her from Bette's collection to the wholesome-sexy outfit. No way did Lulu stir batter in what she was now wearing. The pink Oxford shirt, perfectly softened, was tied snugly at her waist with just a hint of a tissue-thin lighter pink T-shirt underneath. And the jeans—almost white with age—doubtless from her college days—hugged just enough to show off curves.

Gabrielle felt old and dreary in her black cashmere turtleneck and wool trousers. What had seemed sophisticated just hours ago now felt sexless.

"I'm so glad you're here. Jack thinks he has a plan," Lulu said. "A brilliant plan."

"What is it?" *Brilliant, I u? Really.*

"Well, I don't know the details; we waited for you," she said. "But I'm sure it's perfect."

And did Jack also invent the moon?

"I do have an idea, but there's a catch." Jack shuffled papers until finding what appeared to be a list. "Nigel and Pamela's suit will have merit in the eyes of the law. Preying on the elderly is a common problem. Thus, paying Thea's back rent is paramount. And as soon as possible. That will derail their strongest argument. You can't be taking advantage of her if you're paying her. Without rent or income from the store, her savings are down considerably. We need to show that you two are contributing. And, as importantly, making sacrifices. Otherwise, it might seem as though you're bleeding Thea dry, leaving her to bear all the consequences on her own. So all you need to do is pay the back rent."

Lulu slumped in her seat.

"How much?" Gabrielle asked.

"Right now, $30,000. And that's with the rent being well below fair-market. How much of it can you each cover?"

Seeing Lulu's expression of despair and Gabrielle's of disappointment, Jack frowned. "Can't you each dip into savings?"

"Savings?" Lulu laughed. "What are savings?"

Gabrielle sighed. Her savings account held $80,000. Most likely, she could risk part of it to start paying off

$30,000, but should she put herself into jeopardy? Not only did she not have a paycheck, but she also lacked children or in-laws for cushioning against disaster. But she did have a separate retirement account.

"What about borrowing against my IRA?" she asked.

"That's not smart, Gabrielle," Lulu said. "You need to keep that sacrosanct. I'll always have the bakery, but without the bookstore, you have no income."

Gabrielle held up a finger, asking them to remain quiet as she thought. Finally, an idea came. "Jack, Lulu and I are putting up ninety-five percent of the store's stock. Almost everything on the shelves comes from Bette's legacy. Can you make that count?"

"And the other five percent is coming from Bette's friends?" Jack confirmed.

"Right."

"Yes, that could be meaningful as long as Thea is going to be your partner. We'd be creating a partnership package with each of you putting in X, Y, and Z. But you'd still eventually need to repay the back rent that accrued before you formed the partnership. If Thea simply forgives the rent, the courts could call it coercion."

"In other words, we should take Thea on as a partner but still come up with a payment plan to repay the back rent?" Gabrielle asked.

"Exactly," Jack said.

"What if she dies?" Gabrielle studied her sister, wondering why she wasn't participating in the conversation.

"I'll write a death codicil into the document where the remaining partners inherit all rights to the store, property, and lease."

"Is this our only answer?" Lulu asked.

"I thought you said it was a brilliant plan." Jack's grin seemed a bit needy.

Lulu shrugged and offered only a lackluster smile.

"If you want to continue building Coco Street, it is the only solution," Jack said. "And there's one additional piece of information to keep in mind—whatever you decide, even if you back out now, you'll still need to pay Thea or her estate the rent you already owe her. So, think about it. Try to come up with a payment plan, even if it's only incremental amounts. A show of faith is better than nothing."

Lulu and Gabrielle barely spoke as they rode uptown to Bette's apartment on the Madison Avenue bus. It wasn't until after they'd disembarked, crossed the street, and were inside the elevator that Lulu broke the silence.

"Maybe it was unrealistic to think we could make this all happen without money from investors. But you had that great business plan which—"

"Which didn't account for Thea's son being a prick," Gabrielle said. "As though he's worried about her. She hasn't been this peppy in years. Or as happy. And he knows it. Look, my IRA is—"

"No. And do not mention it again. I couldn't live with myself if you lost that. There has to be another way. And we will find it." Lulu unlocked the door with the key Gabrielle had made for her, and they entered the no longer pristine apartment. Items brought over from Bette's friends added to the chaos.

"Imagine if Bette saw this mess."

Gabrielle tried to look cheerful. "Perhaps she'd remember what Poughkeepsie Grandma said. '*You can't make an omelet without breaking a few eggs.*'"

"Bette hated her mother's aphorisms."

Gabrielle nodded. "That she did."

"Coffee?" Lulu asked.

"Sure."

Together they walked into the kitchen.

"Lulu," Gabrielle said. "I'm sorry. I feel like I led us down the wrong road."

"No. You haven't." Lulu took coffee cups from the shelf, black glazed china mugs with a thin arc of gold swiped across. She sighed. "You can't blame yourself. Coco Street is more than a good idea. It's an important idea. I saw how important yesterday."

"Yesterday?"

"Yes, I didn't have a chance to tell you. Bridget, wanting us-time, came to the house to take me out to lunch and an exhibit." Lulu put quotation marks around the words *us time.* "You'll never guess what she showed me at the restaurant."

"A time machine to take us back to before I came up with this crazy idea?" Gabrielle measured coffee into the pot.

"We'll look for that later." Lulu took a carton of milk out of the refrigerator. "Unbeknownst to me, my daughter-in-law has been researching our idea and collecting information and articles. There's one called '*You Too Can Play the Handbag Stock Market*' from *The New York Times.* Another called '*The New Generation of Vintage Traders You'll Love*' from *Refinery 29.*'"

Gabrielle worked at tamping down her rising hope.

Lulu reached up for a crystal creamer. "'*Staggering Scale of Waste: Billions of Dollars in Online Clothing Returns Go Straight to Landfills,*'" from a site called *The Mind Unleashed.* Sustainability is a huge issue, Gabrielle. So, your idea? I have to admit, Coco Street can be timely. And terrific. And important."

"Not if we go broke." Gabrielle sat on one of the stools.

"Or we bankrupt Thea."

Lulu took a bag of Pepperidge Farm Brussels Lace Cookies from the cupboard. "Can we let the ideas Jack gave us settle a bit? I need a break from thinking about money for a day. We've talked and worried about nothing else for so long. Let's just go into the closet and take a moment to enjoy Bette's bounty, okay?"

"Now you sound like her. Let's ignore the unpleasant and bury ourselves in her pretty things."

"And you sound like my father. Pushing for the practical." Lulu poured the milk into the fancy glass jug and then held it up. "Maybe Bette was right. Savor beauty. Even at the worst of times."

Gabrielle felt too low to appreciate the little pitcher.

"You know what, Gabi? Forget mugs; let's do this up right. Fiddling while Rome burns, and all that." Lulu opened the cabinet again, pulling out fragile cups and saucers in a delicate iris pattern. "Aren't these the ones Bette saved for afternoon entertaining?"

"Yes, Limoges. Who is this new Lulu? Using good china, talking about beauty? Where's the suddenly depressed Lulu from an hour ago?"

"I'm shaking her off." Lulu arranged cookies on a plate that matched the cups. "I want to tell you the rest of what happened yesterday. And why we need to stick with Coco Street. After Bridget and I had lunch, she dragged me to The Museum of Jewish Heritage. She said she needed to know *that* side of Nicholas better. The Jewish side. She almost shamed me for not having him study for a bar mitzvah."

"Is she pregnant?" Gabrielle tried to imagine extending their family to another generation.

"She drank wine at lunch, so no. I think she's making a plan, though. Bridget is the ultimate manager."

"How does Nicholas feel?"

"About this sudden urge to investigate his roots?" Lulu asked.

"No. About having kids."

"He says sure, he wants them. Speaking in that noncommittal way that men do. I assume they've talked about the timing, but no one has informed me. Anyway, back to yesterday. So, Bridget surprised me with an exhibit on Auschwitz."

"Yikes. That sounds awful. Did she tell you before you got there?"

"Only that we were going to an incredible museum on the Hudson River. And it was on the river. But listen, when your daughter-in-law wants to spend time with you, you go."

Lulu finished putting the tray together and took it out to the living room.

"So how was it?' Gabrielle asked as she joined her sister on the couch.

"I haven't been able to stop thinking about it. Very intense. We were there for four hours."

"That's a long time to be immersed in horror." Gabrielle hated dwelling on the worst parts of the world.

"History and horror. The *before* pictures of the people who were murdered could have been our ancestors. Well, not your father, but Bette, and Grandma, and Grandpa. And my father and his family. And us."

She handed Gabrielle a cup of coffee, poured one for herself, and continued. "The photographs they carried in their suitcases to the concentration camps were heartbreaking. Again, us. Photos of women with dark eyes and thick dark hair. And then, the after. Skeletons."

"I've always been afraid of those exhibits," Gabrielle said. "Cole didn't help. He didn't like reminders of where I came from. He even scoffed at *Fiddler on the Roof.*"

"Who scoffs at *Fiddler*? But forget about him. Listen.

The exhibit was terrifying. The photos and paintings just about killed me. My stomach hurt the entire visit. But something besides the terror stayed with me."

Gabrielle sighed. "What?"

"When the Nazis rounded up the men and women, they told them they would be going to work camps and gave them instructions to pack. Probably to keep them calm with the rifles aimed at them. Those suitcases ended up piled by the train tracks—there were photos of them. Masses of cardboard and leather luggage filled with memories waiting to be pillaged.

"Some of those possessions—the ones not stolen and still in German homes to this day—survived as testimony. Hairbrushes. Toothbrushes. Exactly what you'd imagine people would take. Everyday items. Displayed behind glass. I couldn't take my eyes off them. Sewing utensils. But there were other things, too. Candlesticks, books, a child's china doll. Heartbreaking touchstones. Pieces of their lives. I took a picture." Lulu took out her phone and scrolled through her photos. "Here. Look at this."

Gabrielle leaned over. A ruby-colored, cut glass bowl sat in a spotlight—a dish in which their grandma might have served hard candies. She'd seen similar pieces in antique stores and recognized the style. "That's Bohemian glass. Made in Czechoslovakia."

"All I could think about," Lulu said, "were the women and men who took these little bits of their lives with them, stuffing them in their pockets or their suitcases. These trinkets that we surround ourselves with become us, Gabi. We even carry them into hell. And then those very objects survive us and come out the other side."

Gabrielle sat silently, remembering battling Cole over art deco rugs, George Jensen cutlery, Eames chairs, as though these possessions were her very flesh. As though they would ground and protect her after being exiled from her own life. In a way, they anchored her while she learned to survive the shame of rejection.

Gabrielle drank the last of her coffee, imagining Bette carefully replacing the cup in its saucer. Everything in this apartment was part of her mother's memories. Suddenly, she understood why her mother had held on to everything of Oliver's and always wore his watch.

The sisters logged in more of Bette's things for the next hour, stopping to check and see how the significant online resale sites priced them.

Lulu pulled out a sleeveless shift with a bateau neckline, held it up, and vamped in the closet mirror. The classic black dress seemed made for her petite curves.

"That would look perfect on you. Try it on," Gabrielle urged.

"I'm not inviting trouble again."

Gabrielle swept her hand over the closet. "This is all ours. Forget the rules. We've only played dress-up once. Okay, twice. You just told me in the kitchen that we should focus on beauty. Wouldn't Bette want us to get joy out of all this stuff?"

As Lulu unbuttoned her blouse, Gabrielle rummaged through a drawer in the center island.

"Here." She held out a pair of semi-sheer black tights. "Put these on with the dress. I doubt we'll be selling Bette's unworn hosiery at Coco Street."

Lulu took the offering. "Not unless we want to move from high-end vintage magic to depressing, body odor, thrift shop offerings. Not that anything of Bette's would smell of anything other than Chanel Number 5."

Gabrielle went through the rack of jackets. "Got it! The

perfect complement to that dress." She handed Lulu a tweed jacket with a broad asymmetrical portrait collar. "Try this."

Lulu slipped it on and then showed off, strutting and placing her hands in the pockets.

Gabrielle held a hand to her chin. "The jacket fits you to a T, but not with that dress." She pushed a dozen hangers to one side and kept searching until she found the skirt that fit her vision: black, made of fine crepe wool, and featuring a side slit.

Lulu replaced the dress with the skirt, buttoned the jacket so it worked as all the top she needed, and twirled a few times. She gazed at her reflection with an intensity Gabrielle hadn't seen since they were teens.

"I think I detect a sudden interest in the clothes," Gabrielle said.

"Maybe."

"And why is that?"

"Truth? I have a date," Lulu confessed. "And it's tonight. I'm meeting him in two hours—my first date since Matt died. I'm petrified, sad, excited, and I'm probably going to throw up. I'm a wreck."

Gabrielle almost blurted out *"With Jack?"* but held back.

"With who?" She stared at her sister with narrowed eyes, ready to sniff out lies.

"Someone I met through the family." Lulu shrugged, looking casual. "You can guess how I feel about that."

Gabrielle could guess. The Quattros were already overly involved in every aspect of Lulu's life. Sometimes Gabrielle didn't know how her sister could breathe pressed in by so many relatives. "Going somewhere fancy?"

"I guess. He's been asking for a while, and when I finally said yes, he made a big deal out of it. We're going to some French restaurant called Jean Georges."

Gabrielle whistled.

"That fancy?" Lulu slumped down on the bed and sniffled. "I alternate between being excited and feeling like I'm cheating on Matt."

Lulu reached into the jacket pocket as if going for a tissue, even though it wasn't her jacket. Habit, Gabrielle supposed, as she headed to the bathroom to fetch a Kleenex.

"Gabrielle!" Lulu cried out.

She turned.

Lulu held out an envelope. "Look! It was in the pocket."

Gabrielle went to her sister's side and looked over her shoulder as Lulu read out the words written in Bette's familiar hand. The quote was more protracted than usual, the writing smaller, and the sentences closer together.

*I don't understand how a woman can leave the house without fixing herself up a little - if only out of politeness. And then, you never know, maybe that's the day she has a date with destiny. And it's best to be as pretty as possible for destiny.—Coco Chanel*

The sisters exchanged a glance. The cards never failed. The quote they found always fit the situation as though Bette was watching and sending precisely the right message down to them.

"Bette has spoken." Gabrielle put a hand on each of Lulu's shoulders. "I'm going to make you invulnerable. That's what dressing up is all about."

"Are you sure? I didn't do so well the last time I wore something of Bette's."

"I'm sure." Gabrielle grabbed Bette's black silk robe off the closet door's hook and pushed it into her sister's hand. "I'm going to do your hair, your makeup, and pick out jewelry. The outfit is gorgeous, and you're going to wear it tonight. Mom's stuff will empower you. You'll see."

"What if I break something?"

"Then it will have gone to a good cause, the best of causes. My sister's happiness."

# Chapter Twenty-Two

## Gabrielle

Gabrielle woke before the sun.

Despite her burning curiosity, she resisted calling to quiz her sister. Instead, she settled on the couch with her Coco Street planning notebook—*and yes, dear Gray Lady, I did take another journal from Bette's stash*—and looked through her to-do list.

Up next was finding the perfect shade of paint for the dressing rooms. From colors to light fixtures—every detail was integral to the store's image. As Gabrielle looked over paint chips she'd stuffed in between the pages, an idea rose. What if they wrote out a timeline of Coco Chanel's rise and fall and rise again, hand-lettered and illustrated on the back of those two dressing room doors? Gabrielle started sketching it out. When she got to the 1940s, she debated whether or not to include designer's love affair with the Nazi. She'd downplay it but not hide it. Showing Coco's human side, including her mistakes, illuminated her life and legend.

Gabrielle wondered if Lulu would agree. In the process of turning Quills & Feathers into Coco Street, the sisters battled over almost everything. They'd nearly come to blows over which cache pots would hold the orchids for the window. Lulu fell in love with ecru-colored terra cotta, declaring the pottery reminiscent of cottages in Cornwall, England, a place Lulu had never visited.

Gabrielle fell in love with Herend Rothschild Garden containers, white bone china decorated with green ivy trim and gold feet. Granted, hers were more than twice the cost of Lulu's choice, but they were at least three times lovelier. She'd gone hoarse explaining to Lulu that if they wanted the shop to be an exquisite jewel, they needed to fill it with gems—not cozy doodads.

To which her sister had replied, "Enough! It's not about *exquisite this* and *enchanting that*—let's just admit we're talking about my taste versus yours."

Gabrielle shot back with one of the recent Coco-found-in-a-bag quotes. *An interior is the natural projection of the soul.*

"Yes, but that doesn't mean it always has to be *your* soul," Lulu said.

Anytime they turned to Thea for a vote, she gave the same answer. "You girls make those decisions. I'll stick to choosing the books."

In honor of Quills & Feathers, Coco Street would devote a corner to books: biographies of designers, illustrated fashion coffee table books, jewelry histories, and even novels with similar themes. Thea had already planned a window display around the nonfiction book, *Stoned: Jewelry, Obsession, and How Desire Shapes the World* and paired it with a mint first edition of *The Moonstone,* a 19th-century mystery set around a brilliant but flawed diamond.

When Thea wouldn't help break the decorating dilemmas between her and her sister, Gabrielle had an ally in Liam. But two against one only made Lulu dig in her heels and fight that much more.

The last time Lulu stomped off, saying she was tired of them ganging up on her, Gabrielle complained to Imogene. She and her mother's best friend often ended up alone in the store; some evenings, they spent more time exchanging histories than working.

"She needs to be more appreciative of Liam," Gabrielle had said while she made them cups of chamomile tea. "He's working at a reduced rate—his nod to how badly Cole treated us both—and saving us a fortune."

"He's not here because of your shared misfortune," Imogene replied as she stirred sugar into her mug. "It's so obvious the man's crushing on you. How does everyone except you see it?"

The idea mortified Gabrielle. "He's at least ten years younger than me—"

"Only eight," Imogene interrupted. "I figured it out."

"I've known Liam forever. Don't you think I'd have seen this so-called crushing?"

"I don't think you'd recognize the right man if he plastered Times Square with billboards."

"I know what's good for me," Gabrielle said. "And I know my type."

Imogene shook her head and then finished her tea. "No. You don't. Otherwise, you'd see that kind, funny, and solid outdoes one-night stands with bank balances in suits."

Gabrielle should never have confided in Imogene.

Now, she imagined Liam there in her living room with her. Between his buzz cut thinning hair and boyishly rounded face, she had to admit he was kind of sexy. His earnest grin always did make her smile. And by any measure of the word, Thea was right: eight years wasn't a significant age difference.

Liam was a good man. Except when had she ever gone for one of those? Not to mention mixing business with pleasure was a sure path to problems. Note to self: When it came to Liam, lamps and sconces were all that mattered.

Next up on Gabrielle's extensive to-do list was deciding how and where to display Bette's Chanel quotes.

Calligraphy stenciled on the floor?

Three-dimensional metal letters affixed to the wall?

Typeset and superimposed on black and white fashion photos behind the cash register area?

None of those seemed right. Gabrielle sipped her coffee, remembering finding the first note in the bathroom at the museum gala, and then she knew.

The perfect solution was to use Bette's actual notes—written in her elegant Palmer cursive—floating on white mats in black lacquer frames. That would honor Better in a way she would have loved.

Gabrielle shut the notebook, grabbed her phone, and punched in her sister's number. She wanted to tell Lulu her idea and hear about the date.

After three rings, voicemail greeted her.

"Where are you?" she asked the cloud where messages lived. "Dying to know about last night. Call me." She was itchy to speak with Lulu. First dates post-loss could go so many ways: teary, guilt-ridden, dazzling.

After losing Cole, Gabrielle's first had been none of those. The one-night stand had been so unmemorable she could remember nothing but that he'd been wealthy and successful. If you had knocked on his heart, you'd get back a hollow echo.

Someone just like Imogene had described.

Hunger drove Gabrielle to the kitchen, where she cut an

orange and tried to savor each slice. *Savor each slice*—another of Imogene's aphorisms that Gabrielle was attempting to take to heart.

Knowing Lulu sometimes left her cell phone in her coat and didn't get messages for hours, Gabrielle called the bakery's landline. After two rings, Victoria-the-fragile answered.

"Gabrielle! I'm so excited about your store! In fact"— she lowered her voice—"Coco Street would be a perfect place for me to work. Fashion is my passion!"

Gabrielle rolled her eyes to nobody. "Be sure to tell Lulu. Can I speak with her?"

"She's not here. Want me to send you to Gus? He probably knows where she is. Perfect Gus knows everything, right?"

"He sure does. I'm glad to hear how much you're enjoying working with my nephew!"

"No. I didn't mean that. I mean, not that I didn't mean that—"

Gabrielle put her out of her misery. "Could you give me to Gus?"

The moment Gus said hello, she asked, "How can you stand working with her?"

"Every day, she provides a new story on which Seth and I can feast. I concentrate on the positive."

"Where's Lulu? I'm dying to know how her night went." The moment the words were out, she cursed herself. She doubted her sister had shared her plans with her son-in-law.

"Oh!" Gus sounded surprised. "So, she told you about the date. I didn't know if she would."

"Told me? I dressed her for it."

"Well, I guess if anyone knows Jack's taste, it's you."

"Jack? Our Jack?"

Silence greeted her. The hairs on her arm tingled.

"Um…it's pretty busy here, Gabrielle. You should talk to Lulu."

"Yeah. You bet."

After stomping and fuming long enough to burn off her initial rage, she dialed Jack's office number.

"Hey, Jack. Know where my sister is?"

"Lulu?"

"Only one I have. Unless you know something that I don't—secrets are your specialty, aren't they? You knew about Cole's plan for divorce before I had a clue. And now you're keeping your interest in my sister from me. Anything else I should know?"

"You should talk to Lulu."

"Isn't that what you said when I called you after the messenger delivered the divorce papers? *You should talk to Cole?*"

"I know you may never believe me, but it's true, and I'll keep telling you until it sinks in. Cole convinced me that you knew about the divorce. He swore that you guys decided to handle it by serving papers."

"And you may never have the answer, but I'll keep asking you anyway. Why on earth would I think being sued for divorce would be the proper way to end my marriage?"

"I was conned, same as you."

"No. Not at all like me."

Gabrielle walked to Fifth Avenue and took the bus. Rolling down the broad street, the park to her right, grand pre-war buildings on her left, almost calmed her. The bus took longer, but today she needed longer. Besides, keeping her eye on the slivers of blue sky peeking between buildings beat the subway's overheated underground crowds.

By the time she reached her stop, Gabrielle's pulse had slowed. Lulu had been alone for over two years. Of course, she deserved to find happiness—but Jack? He was *her* friend. And then to lie about it? The little sneak.

Gabrielle opened the door to Coco Street and found at least a dozen boxes stacked on the trestle table.

Liam, slitting the last one open, beamed.

"Perfect timing, Gabi. You're going to be thrilled with these samples." Only Liam and Lulu used that diminutive—the nickname seldom bothered her, but today it made her scowl.

"Morning, Liam." Brisk and businesslike. That would be her mode with everyone from now on. Jack. Lulu. Liam. She nodded at the boxes. "Looks like an entire store of sconces."

"I know how much you like options."

She did but was surprised he'd noticed.

"Oh, I almost forgot. Imogene was here but said she had some errands to run, plus a luncheon. She said to be sure you knew it's unlikely she'll be back."

It was a setup. Imogene was supposed to look at the sconces with her today. Like Thea, she never let up in her efforts to throw Gabrielle and Liam together. They needed to butt out; he wasn't her type.

Too young.

Too nice.

And if she needed proof, Liam walked over to the coffee maker, held up a mug, and nodded, as though their relationship was so close, no words were necessary.

"No coffee for me." She wanted coffee. Badly. "Let's see the lights you picked out."

"Let me finish unpacking this one." He opened the box and pulled out a well-wrapped fixture. Picking it up, he nodded to the back. "I lined up the others. Come look."

Jack and Lulu had made a fool of her. Why lie about their date? Both of them knew lying was her kryptonite.

Nine distinct sconces covered the desk. Liam now added the tenth.

"I think all these will work, but it's a question of which ones you like the best," he said, gesturing to the array.

Gabrielle stepped closer to inspect them, hands clasped behind her back. Not only were Jack and Lulu lying, but they'd made themselves a little club of two, shutting her out.

She pointed to gold candelabras. "Far too glitzy."

"Then let's move right to more subtle; how about this?" Liam gestured to a simple silver can.

"Too plain."

She stopped in front of a frosted flowery shape and pointed. "That one's a dead ringer for a wilted tulip."

"Good thing that we have seven more."

Gabrielle walked down the display Liam had made. She shrugged. "None of them appeal to me."

Liam's smile turned to a thin line. "Can you give me an idea of what you have in mind if none of these are making the cut?"

She shook her head. "I don't know...just not these."

"Why don't I leave them so you can look later. Maybe with a second viewing, something will appeal to you more. I thought there were some winners here." He tipped his head in concern. "You okay?"

"Does there have to be something wrong with me just because I'm not fainting in delight at your sconces?"

He put up his hands. "All good here. No problem. I'll come back for the samples later. I think you need a timeout." Sounding suspiciously patriarchal, he stomped from the room. Not so Mr. Perfect after all, eh, Imogene? Thea?

Gabrielle covered her sweater with a smock, grabbed the radio, a bucket of tools, and went into the bathroom. After putting on the music and turning the volume way up, she attacked the walls with her knife, spackle, and putty. As she worked, she concluded she had the opposite of a magic touch when it came to men and would never see kind-hearted Liam again.

She was still spackling a half-hour later when hearing her name called made her jump. With the radio blaring, she hadn't heard anyone arrive.

"Gabrielle?" Lulu shouted from the doorway.

Instead of pivoting around, Gabrielle turned the volume up even more, ensuring that Aretha would drown out any chance of conversation.

"Gabrielle, can you lower that?"

Ignoring her sister, Gabrielle continued to slap putty on the wall.

"I didn't call because we need to talk in person. I was planning to tell you about Jack; I just didn't want to jinx it."

Gabrielle ignored every stupid word.

Lulu reached out and snapped off the radio. Gabrielle spun around, holding the spackle knife like a weapon. "I dressed you up, did your makeup, fussed like the mother hen we never had, and you lied to me. You said the Quattros fixed you up. Did you and Jack get a good laugh about making a dope of me?"

"Laugh? Don't be crazy. Jack didn't even know I hadn't told you until this morning."

Gabrielle ignored Lulu as her sister's last words registered. "Jinx it? Why would telling me jinx your date? Am I a bad luck symbol? Uh-oh! Watch out for the bad juju Gabrielle gives out! Not like perfect-love Lulu. Lulu-the-delicate flower, who'll fall from one paragon's arms into another!"

"What the hell? Why are you mad at me? I was nervous. I didn't want you to think I was a jerk—and I was afraid maybe you knew something about him that I didn't. Something not good. And, honestly? I wanted to know him without prejudice."

"Without prejudice? So now I'm also the harbinger of doom? And I already told you something *not good* about him."

"He explained that. And why are you screaming at me about something that's making me happy? I haven't even smiled at a man in over two years."

"And we haven't been this close for almost that long. How could you put Jack before me?"

"Before you?" Lulu asked.

"You lied to me. You went behind my back."

"We're not Cole and Nancy, for goodness sake."

"Then don't act like them."

"I'm not. Let it go, Gabi. I want to tell you what a good time we had. I'm flying high, and you're part of it all. I felt like Cinderella dressed by the Chanel Fairy."

Happiness flickered off her sister as though she were a Roman candle.

"Can't we go have lunch?" Lulu asked.

"I have someplace to be. If you want to do something, come with me. There are lights to pick out."

Still fuming, she walked into the back room and looked over the lighting choices on the table. Damn Liam, he'd been right. Now that she was giving them a second perusal, she did like some of them. She pointed to the top two choices.

"These are my picks. Decide which you like best and put a sticky on your favorite." She took her coat from the battered stool where she'd flung it. "Don't forget to lock up when you leave."

The bartender set another dirty martini in front of Gabrielle. "This is from the guy down the end."

Gabrielle peered down the length of the glossy wood bar to evaluate her potential Prince Charming for the night. Steel-gray hair so perfectly groomed, the comb's teeth marks seemed permanent. An Armani suit hung from his broad shoulders. Age-appropriate lines crinkled around his eyes.

Gabrielle's kind of guy

After lifting the glass in a gesture of thanks, she studied her phone, wishing someone would text her. Imogene. Thea. A friend from the old days. Liam. She'd be happy if Lulu texted, even if only to argue. Did no one notice she existed anymore?

She sensed the presence of Crinkle-Eyes and glanced up. Up close, his good looks almost overwhelmed her.

An uber-handsome man liked her.

Ergo, she was beautiful.

Gabrielle-math.

He approached and then held out his hand. "Spenser with an S."

Spencer with an S? An homage to Robert Parker's sensitive he-man character?

"Natasha." Why not? Spenser's name was probably as much a lie as hers.

"So, what brings you here tonight, Natasha?" An ingratiating undertone offset the pleasing resonance of his deep voice.

*Thinking of getting laid, Spenser. You?*

"I'm in New York for a conference," she said. "Teaching teachers how to teach. Kabbalah. I just arrived from Israel last night."

He appeared baffled. "I don't think I've ever understood what Kabbalah means."

She reached into her memory and pulled out some lines from a play Cole once produced. "Imagine Judaic culture overlaid with true mysticism, evolved with the esoteric overlay of the sacred text. And you?"

"Um, I'm in banking. Working late." He raked his eyes over her. "So, Natasha, what does it mean to teach Kabbalah? By the way, don't get insulted, but that's a sexy word."

"Sexy?"

He drew out the syllables in a ridiculous parody of a woman. "Kaa baa laa."

She glanced down at his hand. He hadn't even bothered taking off his ring.

Gabrielle finished the remains of her original dirty martini—actually, it was her second. "Hmm. Why would you think making fun of my work is the path to my heart?"

"I didn't mean—"

Gabrielle picked up the still untouched martini purchased by Spenser and downed that one in a few swallows. "Here are some hints, Spenser-with-an-S. Don't insult a woman's work. Don't wear so much product that your hair looks raked. And take off your damn wedding ring before hitting on someone."

After banging the glass on the bar, she stormed out on unsteady legs.

Screw all the Sir Galahads who wanted to protect her precious sister and the pricks ready to sleep with Gabrielle. Most of all, screw Cole. Lying fucker, living with a woman whose facial skin likely sat in a topknot on top of her head from her scads of facial surgery.

Gabrielle clicked down the sidewalk in her Jimmy Choo

boots. The heels were wearing down. How long would these last remnants of her former life be wearable?

Reaching Park Avenue, she stepped off the curb and held up her hand, hailing a taxi, relieved Lulu wasn't there to remind her that she couldn't afford it.

"West 10th Street, corner of Waverly Place."

For most of the ride, she barely focused. Instead, she sat back, watching the city lights dance. When the cab reached Coco Street, she stumbled up the stairs, and then rummaged endlessly for her key.

After feeling a ridiculous amount of pride from finding and then fitting the key into the lock, she lurched into the store.

Once lights flooded the shop, a wave of pleasure washed through her. Even still in the throes of renovation, the space appeared elegant. Bette would be proud. Gabrielle imagined the room finished. Gleaming glass cabinets and matching countertops with brass edging. A curated selection of chic clothes on black velvet hangers. As she spun around, she pictured women at marble-topped tables enjoying Thea's morning and afternoon tea. Others lounged on window seats, flipping through fashion books.

Coming here instead of going home had been a good idea. Coco Street was a good idea.

*Right, Bette?* she asked the blown-up picture of Bette that leaned against the wall. Bette, wearing black trousers, black ballet flats, a white turtleneck sweater, and a black fitted jacket with its gold CC buttons—pure Bette, except for a single element. Three-year-old Nicholas clutched his grandmother around the leg, holding on with hands covered in cookie batter that had oozed out between his fingers.

Lulu might accuse Gabrielle of being the doppelgänger favorite, but in truth, neither of them measured up to their mother. Even with her designer pants smeared with flour, sugar, and chocolate chips, she radiated magnificence. Compared to Bette, Gabrielle and Lulu would never be anything but fashion orphans.

Gabrielle noticed that the lights shone from the storage space, perhaps forgotten by Ruby. A doll, that woman, but not much in the attention-to-detail department. Congratulating herself for noticing, Gabrielle went to shut them off—staggering, but just a bit.

She'd descended the first of three steps when her spikey heel caught on a divot in the wood. She reached out, but nothing met her hand—the railing had been taken off for painting and not yet put back. She felt her fingers sliding down the slippery, newly painted wall.

She landed and felt a searing pain shoot through her right ankle. Even drunk, she knew she'd snapped a bone.

Gabrielle laughed as a saying floated into her addled brain.

*Pride goeth before a fall.*

A not-from-Chanel quote.

# Chapter Twenty-Three

## Lulu

"Gabrielle?" Lulu shouted softly, not wanting to alarm the neighbors.

"Here," sounded weakly from the back of the store.

Lulu and Jack rushed towards Gabrielle's voice, finding her lying in a heap at the bottom of the short set of stairs leading to the storage area.

Kneeling beside her sister, Lulu took a quick inventory of the damage. Blood smeared her sister's forehead and stained her coat collar. A purple stain around her cheekbone portended the black eye to come. Most frightening, her right foot pointed in a grotesquely wrong direction.

"Don't move." Lulu looked up at Jack. "Should we call an ambulance?"

"No!" Gabrielle reached for Lulu's arm. "No ambulance. Promise."

"Let's make sure." Jack's steady voice seemed to calm

her Gabrielle. "First—do you know where you are?"

"Stuck on stupid."

Lulu smiled. "Okay. You're oriented." She pinched Gabrielle's thigh. "Can you feel that?"

"Ouch. Do you carry pliers in your bag?"

"Does your head hurt? Do you feel nauseous? Is the room spinning?" Jack asked.

"I'm nauseated with myself. I think I broke my ankle. When I tried to stand, I collapsed. That's how I hit my head."

Jack knelt. "Put your arms around my neck. The car's right outside—I even parked illegally for you. Let's get you to the hospital."

After a brief exam, the emergency room doctor sent Gabrielle for x-rays. Now Lulu waited with her sister to see if Gabi needed surgery.

Gabrielle slept fitfully, under the influence of painkillers, lying in a curtained area pretending to provide privacy. Lulu hated the sterile hospital atmosphere—hated the lights so bright they scorched your eyeballs, and the antiseptic smells that overlaid the odor of blood, unwashed bodies, and panic. She imagined steaming piles of germs on every surface—the chrome instruments, the laminated counters, and the blocky furniture. Most of all, she hated the memories that being here had brought up: Sitting with Bette in her last days. Holding Matt's hand as he tried and then failed to hold on to life. Pretending to smile at her father's jokes while he endured endless hours of dialysis.

Only giving birth changed a hospital setting from a

place of anguish to one of surging joy.

Finally, the doctor returned and woke Gabrielle.

"How are you feeling?" he asked.

"Awful."

"Do you have a diagnosis?" Lulu asked.

As the doctor clipped x-rays on the viewer, he shook his head as though he was bearing news that, at best, Gabrielle would just lose her leg. Lulu began to hope that at least her sister would someday walk again.

The doctor clasped his hands behind him and glanced at his patient, completing his imitation of an angel of death.

"Not awful news," he said. "A fracture. A slight one. We call it a stable fracture." He raised the corner of his lip as though he believed he'd cracked a joke. "It's a good thing. It means the bones are lined up—no need to realign anything. No need for surgery. Best practice? We wrap it up and give you a CAM walker."

"A walker? I'll need a walker?" Hysteria laced Gabrielle's words. She turned to Lulu. "I am not using a walker!"

"A CAM walker's just a fancy name for a walking boot." The doctor backed towards the exit. "The nurse will fill you in on best practices when she wraps your foot."

He nodded to the sisters and then, with a small sigh, left and pulled the curtain closed behind him.

"What a jolly fellow," Lulu said.

Gabrielle winced as a cold pack slipped off her ankle. "Sorry for getting hysterical. I was picturing a future of shuffling along with my handbag hanging from an aluminum walker."

Lulu bent to retrieve the blue instant cold pack. "At least it could be one of a zillion Chanels, eh? Now stay still." She laid the ice on top of her sister's swollen and discolored ankle.

"Ouch," Gabrielle said. "Sorry!"

"No need to apologize. Sons, remember? I've been through enough fractures and breaks to be an expert."

"Lu. I do need to apologize. About everything." Gabrielle began ugly crying. "I've been horrible."

Lulu forced herself to listen—she had no patience for wine-induced admissions. Hearing pathetic recriminations always made her want to tell the confessor to STFU. Breast-beating by friends and family brought out Lulu's least admirable parts.

Gabrielle studied her. Like most sisters, she could likely read Lulu's mind simply by observing her expression. "No. I'm not *that* drunk."

"Sorry," Lulu said. "Neither of us is talented when it comes to handling alcohol, right?"

Gabrielle's tears continued rolling. "But this is truth-via-wine, not wine-truth. There's a difference. Can we talk?"

Lulu nodded.

"I can be unforgiving." A fresh round of sobbing began. "We both can."

"But I act bitchier to you than I do to anyone else in the world. I pointed the finger at you, but I was the idiot. You were right. Truth? I was incredibly jealous that Jack wanted you."

A chill washed through Lulu. "Are you interested in him? In Jack? Jesus. I had no idea."

If Gabrielle was interested in Jack, who sat patiently in the waiting room, Lulu gave up. She wanted to scream, but she wouldn't let on how she felt.

Not now. Not just as Lulu built the closeness she'd always yearned to share with her sister.

Not. Now. Just as she began to trust her feelings toward Jack.

Not. Tonight, when he'd acted like a damn superman

and nudged Matt out of the picture, something she'd never believed possible. It might have only been for an hour, but still.

Even as Lulu had been on the phone, trying to make sense of her hysterical sister's words, Jack gathered their coats and then, in what seemed an impossibly short time, drove Lulu from his apartment to Coco Street. He carried Gabrielle to his car, placed her gently in the back seat, and got them to the ER in record time. And he did it all without a single drop of drama.

And now, just when—

"No, Lulu," Gabrielle said. "I don't want Jack—that would be like being attracted to a cousin, though I'd consider my behavior less disgusting if both of us wanted him, and I became insanely jealous that you got him."

"Sounds like a damn soap opera," Lulu muttered. "So, what was it?"

"I've been thinking a lot while we've been here. Trying to figure out why I've been so angry. Finally. Something clicked. Maybe I can thank the painkillers." Gabrielle gestured for a tissue. After Lulu handed it to her, she wiped a stray tear and began shredding the thin paper. "Jack bruised my ego without knowing it. I missed him as my friend," Gabrielle continued. "So much. You have no idea how close we used to be. I'm not stupid. I sensed he liked you—but I thought getting our friendship back on track would be a higher priority for him. Or at least he'd attend to it first. I figured all the helping, being in the store, was about him wanting to make things up to me."

"And then I lied about my date."

Gabrielle wrinkled her face. "Yeah."

"Don't you think it could have been both? Jack showing off for me *and* getting closer to you?"

Gabrielle shrugged.

"How could either of us even figure left from right? We're both struggling with lives turned upside down." Lulu grabbed her own tissue to shred.

"So much loss. So much confusion. So much pressure. Damn Bette for making a terrible situation so much worse." Gabrielle swallowed a sob.

"Best and worst Bette moment," Lulu said. "Best? Once when I came into Manhattan from college, she took me on a shopping spree to any store that I chose—so it was to the Gap."

"Seriously?" Gabrielle cracked up. "And she stayed in the store with you? She didn't just give you money and let you loose?"

"Nope. She came right in and watched me try on acrylic scarves and shitty T-shirts. I swear."

"No groaning? No shaking her head in pity?" Gabrielle asked.

"Well, she did sigh a few times. And gave me that smile of faux-approval when I asked if she liked a pair of acid-washed jeans."

"Acid-washed jeans? Really?"

"I didn't buy them!" Lulu laughed. "I just wanted to see how far I could get her to go. It was my birthday present, so I figured I'd get full value."

"That's quite a best," Gabrielle said. "What was the worst?"

"When Seth was born, my life seemed to fall apart all at once. First, I had that awful bout of mastitis, and post-partum depression hit me hard. And then, Nicholas, who was only three years old, got Reyes disease."

"I remember how awful that was. What did Bette do? I'm afraid to ask."

Lulu took Gabrielle's hand. "I didn't tell you then. I didn't tell anyone. She made me so ashamed of myself. And of her. All that craziness was going on, and then our washing machine broke. We just didn't have the money, and I couldn't deal with two babies without one. So, I caved and called her and asked her to borrow some money. At first, she didn't say anything. The silence horrified me. Then she said, '*I warned you. When you got pregnant, when you got married, and when you moved to Brooklyn, I warned you not to rush into having a second baby. Did you listen? No. You don't listen to me, but you still want my help?*'"

"But she sent you the check, right? Please tell me she sent you the check."

Lulu shook her head. "Matt borrowed the money from one of his brothers—who, trust me, couldn't afford it."

"That's a horrendous story. Worse, it's believable," Gabrielle said. "But why are you telling me now?"

"Because it's my turn for confession, and I wanted to put what I'm going to say in context. Ever since Bette turned away from me that day, I found it unbearable to ask for help. Not just from her. From anyone. I haven't been able to come clean about almost anything without worrying about being smacked down. That's why I didn't tell you the truth."

"About Jack? That was just a sin of omission. A lesser sin than mine."

"I didn't just omit, Gabi. You asked me directly, and I lied—which must be a huge trigger for you after all Cole did. But, no. That's not what I'm talking about." She laced her fingers and stared at the worn wedding ring she never removed. "Here goes. I haven't told you why I've been so back and forth and terrified to jump into Coco Street. Even now, I want to keep lying. But..." Lulu stopped.

"Come on. How bad could this be? Are we talking cheating-on-Matt bad?" Gabrielle asked.

"God! No! Money. And talking about money problems is almost impossible. 'Cause Matt and I made so many

mistakes—at least they feel like mistakes now. At the time—
" Lulu stopped, not wanting to say the words. Naming the problem made it too real. Admitting how deep into debt she'd fallen made it seem like she needed rescue. And that was the last thing she wanted.

"Now you're scaring me." Gabrielle pulled the thin hospital blanket closer around her. "Have you been stealing from Matt's parents?"

Lulu rolled her eyes. "Yes, Gabrielle. That's it. I hacked into Annette and Mattias's bank account and have been slowly draining it since Matt died. I think they're on to me. I want to avoid jail. And that is why I went after Jack. I knew I'd need a lawyer, so I seduced him to get him to help me for free."

Gabrielle tilted her head. "You're teasing, right?"

"You're still a little drunk, aren't you?"

"No. I'm not." Gabrielle raised her hand as if she was in court. "I swear."

She was lying. Lulu knew. Sisters didn't miss the slight slur in the other sister's words.

"It's just that you're making me nervous. I don't have any idea what it is you haven't been telling me."

"Okay. Here goes," Lulu said. "I owe months and months of back mortgage payments to the bank. I cut a deal with them, but they only gave me a short grace period. A balloon payment is coming up. I also owe thousands in credit card debt. Many many thousands. Paying my bills has become a game of who gets paid this month. I haven't wanted to tell you because it makes me seem stupid, and Matt irresponsible. Why didn't we have life insurance? Or more savings?"

"Because you were doing frivolous things like sending your kids to college?"

Lulu breathed a deep sigh of relief at getting to the

truth. "Yes, college. I'm still paying off those parent loans we took."

"What about taking out a second mortgage to cover everything short-term?" Gabrielle sounded surprisingly lucid.

"I'm well past that. We took the second and then the third mortgage to invest in the business. Matt said it was a long-range plan for our future. All the brothers took loans to make the same investment—but he's the one who ended up dead. And they can't help—they're barely able to keep making their own payments. And now I'm about to be homeless. I'll end up living in a studio apartment, baking wedding cakes in an Easy-Bake oven. I'll drop dead clutching a spoon, buttercream in my hair."

"What flavor?" Gabrielle asked. "Hey, you can always live with me. My oven isn't much bigger than an Easy-Bake, but you're welcome to it."

Lulu felt the sting of tears. Gabi's offer was lovely and sincere. She wanted to say something in kind, but what came out stepped away from emotion. "That's a pretty picture, isn't it?" She rummaged in her bag for a pack of tissues. The ones from the box in the hospital room felt like emery boards. "The two of us stuffed into your apartment, trying not to kill each other. One bathroom. One bedroom. And are you calling that postage stamp where you make coffee a kitchen?"

"You know what I can't help but think about?" Gabrielle ignored Lulu's barbed joke. "While you and I struggled so hard for the last couple of years, Bette continued building up her collection. Never offering a hand after Matt died or asking me if I needed any help, either."

Lulu was quiet for a moment. "I never told her what was going on." Sadness and anger roiled and fought.

"Did she ever ask? Like a normal mother whose daughter's husband has just died? Talking about money might be an important conversation to have at some point. Would you ask Seth? Nicholas?"

Lulu nodded. "Why do you think Bette kept buying more and more?"

"To fill some need? To prove something?" Gabrielle asked. "Maybe she was dying from boredom."

Lulu stared at the hospital art on the wall, an abstract portrait of lily pads. "Don't you hate that it's too late to ask her?"

"How would we even have known what to ask? By the way, Mom, why are you throwing all your money into clothes and pocketbooks? Do you care that you are going to leave us with nothing but problems?"

Lulu walked to the window, trying to figure out the question she'd choose, given a second chance. "You know what I'd ask her if I could, Gabi? What in the world did Coco Chanel truly mean to you? You loved her enough to name us after the woman, for goodness sake, even if I only got the river Loire. What were you reaching for, Mom?"

# Chapter Twenty-Four

## Lulu

At midnight, a nurse strapped Gabrielle's ankle, put her in the CAM walker boot, and rattled off home-care instructions, all of which Lulu wrote on the back of a foot-long CVS receipt. Finally, the nurse gave Gabrielle a far-too-fast course on how to walk with crutches. Lulu immediately envisioned her sister tumbling and fracturing her other ankle.

Jack drove both women to his apartment on Central Park West for the night—Gabrielle couldn't be alone, and going to Lulu's would have meant navigating stairs. Staying on Gabrielle's couch, a piece of furniture more attractive than comfortable, wouldn't have provided Lulu anything close to a decent night's sleep.

Twin beds with pale blue linens matching the rest of the blue and gray décor in Jack's guestroom provided a peaceful sanctuary and perfect solution.

"The remote is on the nightstand next to the tissues,"

he said, pointing. "The bathroom is that door. The other one leads to the closet, where there are robes. I'll bring you T-shirts for pajamas. Would you like tea? Something to eat?"

"Too tired to chew or drink," Lulu said.

Gabrielle raised her hand. "Me, too."

Jack nodded, left, and then returned moments later with the ersatz sleepwear. "If you need anything else, let me know. I'll leave you two to get settled."

"Jack," Gabrielle called as he turned to go. He stopped. "You were a lifesaver."

"So, all is forgiven?" he asked.

"For what? If anyone needs forgiving—"

"Okay," Lulu interrupted. "Gabi, stop before the Vicodin brings on more confessions you'll regret in the morning. Say goodnight, Jack."

"Goodnight, Jack," Jack said.

A stab of melancholy hit Lulu as she realized that Jack had the same corny sense of humor as her father and Matt. Was Catskills humor her weak spot?

Jack backed out with a wink and a wave, adding to the long goodbye.

"Alone at last." Gabrielle rolled her eyes as she accepted Lulu's help in getting into one of Jack's T-shirts. "You do know it's my ankle that's broken and not my arms, right?"

"You're a bit wobbly." Lulu pulled a soft gray throw over the comforter. "Snuggle under this. Remember what Bette used to say: a little cashmere never hurt anyone."

"She also said it's just as easy to love a rich man as a poor one. I like that you might be taking her advice at long last."

Lulu tucked her sister in, patting her shoulder gently. "Love isn't a word I'm anywhere ready to use."

"I'm just saying. Jack's a good man. A good man with money. Is that so bad?"

Her sister suggesting that love with a bankbook was a righteous path—especially with the man in question down the hall—necessitated Lulu shutting down the conversation pronto. She placed her forefinger on Gabrielle's lips. "Shh. We don't want to include Jack in this little chat, do we?"

Gabrielle shook her head.

"Okay, then. It's bed then for both of us. I'm beat."

Gabrielle grabbed Lulu's hand. "Thank you." The words came out with a sob.

"For what?" Lulu wanted to cover her ears. Seeing Gabrielle being so weak frightened her. Bette had long ago set up Gabrielle as Lulu's bulwark against all harm.

*Mr. Florimonte's mean dog won't bite you while Gabrielle is with you. Gabrielle will show you how to be brave when you get your flu shot. And most of all, Gabrielle will help keep you safe on the train.*

Between the homeless lying like corpses in pre-renovated Grand Central Station and stories of the electrified third track waiting to shock and kill Lulu, every step of the trip to their Poughkeepsie grandparents' house petrified her. The space between the cars and the platform loomed as a chasm of unmanageable width. Lulu knew if she moved an inch, she'd disappear into its cavernous maw of death.

But always, as the jostling crowd pushed Lulu forward, Gabrielle gripped her under the arms and swung her sister into the subway car, making sure Lulu's short legs landed far enough to prevent any chance of tumbling backward into the fissure.

Lulu still hesitated each time she stepped onto a train.

Her gratitude to Gabrielle was almost a burden, a forever check in her sister's column of who-owed-who-what.

"Thank you," Gabrielle repeated. "Thank you for being there. I didn't have another soul to call. I suppose some friends would have helped, like Daria, but there isn't anyone else who stays and stays."

"Sisters always stay."

"Even when they're angry?"

"Even when they're angry," Lulu promised.

"Even when *you're* angry," Gabrielle sniffed and wiped her cheeks.

Lulu plucked a tissue out of the box next to the bed and handed it to her sister.

"Remember how we used to make fun of you by calling you a little housewife when you played cooking and cleaning? You'd get so mad at us," Gabrielle said.

"I hated it when you did that."

Gabrielle adjusted the pillows Lulu had piled up to elevate her leg. "We were so ignorant. Making fun of you for being different than us."

Bette and Gabrielle had laughed at her, especially when she'd begged for a child-size dust mop and a set of pots and pans. Their shared hilarity humiliated Lulu. Grandma in Poughkeepsie tried to make her feel better by calling her a *balabusta*, as though the Yiddish word for housewife would soothe her.

Instead, Bette and Gabrielle co-opted it and made *baby balabusta* their pet name for Lulu.

"I thought it meant I'd end up like Mrs. Gilman on the second floor when we lived on Second Avenue—"

"Wearing a housecoat all the time? With doilies folded over every chair?" Gabrielle interrupted.

"Watch it. I still have Grandma's doilies," Lulu said.

"But not over your chairs, right?"

"Does under a lamp on my nightstand count?" Lulu kept the lace there as a reminder of the grandmother she still missed.

Gabrielle shook her head. "*Balabusta* isn't a bad word. It means strong. It means you give us sustenance. Being a caretaker isn't an insult."

"But you and Bette meant it that way."

"I'm sorry," Gabrielle said. "And I'm sorry that she isn't here to apologize."

The next day, Jack drove the sisters back to Gabrielle's apartment, where, together with Nicholas and Seth, they rearranged the furniture so she could maneuver on crutches. Watching her sons move chairs and tables, carry laundry baskets filled with books, roll up oriental rugs, and then sling them over their shoulders reminded Lulu of the day she'd met Matt and his family. That same sense of *you-need/we-help* that defined the Quattro brothers then—whether nature or nurture—now imbued her sons.

Matt's memories always hovered, just waiting to spring up and rattle her. She looked over at Jack and feared for this new man in her life. Being measured against a sainted husband couldn't be easy. Lulu knew that all too well—her father never had a chance against Bette's beloved Oliver.

Death glossed over reality; Lulu now painted Matt as a flawless human being who could never have existed. Of course, she remembered a few faults—but they seemed meaningless. Tight? Even a bit cheap? Yup. When Lulu returned from a shopping trip to the city with Drea, armloads of packages filling the entryway, he'd narrow his eyes as though watching her return from Sin City.

His stubbornness had maddened her, too. But at the same time, it was an attribute. No matter what anyone said or did, he protected her and the kids against anything. When Seth came out at fifteen, Matt was the first one he'd told. Not because he feared Lulu's reaction, but because he knew his father would move mountains to protect his son.

"I need to get this out of the way." Seth pointed to the dresser blocking a path to the bathroom. "Mom, help me clear this off, okay?"

Together, they began taking off the dozens of perfume bottles sitting on top of the piece.

Nicholas lifted a side table as though it were paper-mâché. "Where should I put this, Aunt Gabrielle?"

"I have absolutely no idea—wherever it fits?"

"Okay. Once Seth, who must inspect everything you own, finishes putting your one thousand and one perfume bottles in the box, we'll move the dresser and then put this there."

"Just because you have zero intellectual interest doesn't mean I have to rush," Seth said.

"Examining perfume bottles fits the category of intellectual interest?" Nicholas asked.

Seth held up a heavy-looking bottle. "This is Mitsuko from the 1920s. I'm holding sculpture designed by Baccarat. You do know that computers don't create all art, right?"

"And you do know that we're trying to help Aunt Gabrielle rearrange things, not catalog them, right?"

Seth ignored Nicholas, replaced the bottle, and lifted another. He drew out the square stopper from a crystal flagon of Chanel No. 5 and sniffed. "Oh, God," he said. "It's like having Bette walk into the room."

Lulu looked over at her sister and smiled. "Remember how Grandma's scent preceded her into every room, too?"

"Shalimar." Gabrielle closed her eyes as though she were breathing it in. "I have some there. See it, Seth? Fluted glass, almost bat-like, and with a sculpted cobalt stopper?"

"Where is it? I want to smell it!" Lulu said.

Seth found the Shalimar and held it out to her, the slope of the neck resembling a woman's shoulders. She lifted the stopper and inhaled, memories rushing in a shifting barrage. "Ah, yes. Grandma."

Scent deepened memories and sweetened life. When she inhaled her favorite essential oil—a Bulgarian rose she ordered from an Etsy niche perfumer—an ineffable pleasure suffused her. The purity of the bouquet was balm for the soul.

"What should I do with this table and chair?" Nicholas interrupted Lulu's reverie to point to a delicate mirrored vanity and chair. "Looks like a prime candidate to trip you, Aunt Gabrielle."

"Put that in the corner of the living room, I suppose. Out of the way," Gabrielle said.

Jack and Nicholas lifted the vanity and took it out of the bedroom.

"Do you keep those perfumes specifically to remember Grandma and Bette?" Lulu asked.

"Yes. Is that weird? When I want to remember Mom, I open the Chanel. When I want to bring Grandma into the room, I put on a little Shalimar. She saved us so many times. Like you did last night for me."

"Always there for each other. Right?" Lulu said, smiling as she alluded to their makeup session the night before.

"What's going on?" Nicholas asked when he and Jack returned, looking from his emotional mother to his equally emotional aunt.

"Just me talking about how sorry I am that your mother and I were fighting over something as stupid as—"

Lulu opened her eyes wide and sent Gabrielle a warning glance. She noticed Jack had seen it, too.

Jack gave Lulu a nod, suggesting he was giving her and her sons some privacy. "Anyone else starving? I'm going to put together lunch."

"Fighting over what, Mom?" Seth asked.

"Fighting over something so ridiculous it doesn't merit a mention," Gabrielle finished. "Especially now, with Coco Street so close to being finished. I never thought I'd be this happy again. I've loved building something from the bottom up. And unlike the Costume Institute, it's not tainted by Cole."

"Don't get too comfortable, Gabi," Lulu said. "Nigel and his horror of a wife are still out there trying to ruin everything."

"Do you think they can stop us?" Gabrielle asked.

Lulu sank onto the floor, suddenly exhausted. "I don't know, but Jack thinks they can if they get a good enough lawyer. Greedy, evil rats."

Nicholas sat beside her. "Seth and I aren't going to let that happen. We're working on something, and we also want to help with—"

Lulu shook her head and interrupted him. "We appreciate the offer, sweetie, but you have your own lives. You don't need to take this on—you're doing more than enough already."

Seth looked up from the box. "We want to help. We're adults who love you both. What exactly were you fighting about with Aunt Gabrielle, Mom?"

Even if Jack hadn't been in the next room—making telling the boys an impossibility—Lulu didn't want her sons to know that she and Gabrielle been fighting about a man as though they were teenagers. Nor did she want them to think her relationship with Jack had reached a serious stage. Most importantly, Lulu refused to have her kids feel responsible for her. "Sometimes, sisters are just sisters. Like the two of you. Aren't brothers sometimes just brothers?"

"Obnoxiously so." Seth picked up a large bottle of Nina Ricci's L'Air du Temps with its graceful dove stopper and rounded body. "This design knocks me out."

Gabrielle craned her neck from where she sat on the bed. "That's a Bette reject. Too sweet for her—and me, too, in all honesty. I kept it for the bottle alone."

Seth turned it around so the crystal faceting caught the light. "Incredible. I love your collection, Aunt Gabi."

"Perfect," she said. "I'll leave it all to you. But, ugh, please don't ever use the word *collection*."

Seth placed the Nina Ricci into the towel-lined box. "It's going to work out, Aunt Gabi. But for it to work, Mom, you have to stop being Wonder Woman. We're not kids anymore. For the plan to succeed, you need to come up with past rent, right? And given your debt, that can't be easy."

"My debt?" Lulu's stomach fell. She put the pile of books she'd been moving on the floor.

Nick squeezed her shoulder. "Don't worry. You don't have to hide it anymore. We know things are terrible."

"How the heck do you know?"

Seth half-shrugged. "We figured it out."

Lulu gave her sons the look she'd used since they were kids: the thin-lipped suspicious one that forced out all truth. "All I ever said was that carrying two jobs might be too much."

"Hey, if you don't want us to know things, you shouldn't leave your bills and papers on your desktop," Nicholas said.

Lulu whirled around and jammed her hands on her hips. "You were snooping?"

"Not me!" Seth pointed at his brother. "Blame him."

"You went through the things on my desk? You invaded my privacy?"

Nicholas crossed his hands over his chest. "Nobody invaded anything. I was sketching some stuff for the store. I needed a ruler on your desk. You had a pile of bills on top with that stupid bald eagle paperweight—"

"My father gave me that," Lulu said.

Seth shook his head. "Forget the paperweight, Nick."

"Mom, all the bills were right there. With *overdue* stamped all over."

"Baloney. How could you have seen so many without snooping?" Lulu asked. "Only one bill could be on top."

"Cause once I saw *overdue* on the top, I had to keep going, okay? Seth and I, we worry about you."

"I'm handling this. You don't need to worry." Lulu felt as though she might throw up.

"But we do worry, Mom," Nicholas said. "I saw the total you wrote. You don't have to pretend you're doing okay. You're not, and you don't have to handle it alone. We have your back. That's what Dad would want."

"No." Lulu picked up the pile of books. "This isn't your problem. I made this mess. I'll fix it."

"Lu," Gabrielle said in a soft voice. "You really can't do everything yourself."

"I can try." Of every burden, Lulu found the weight of people trying to help the hardest to bear. She stormed out of Gabrielle's bedroom, carrying a pile of books, and ran into Jack. No doubt he'd been listening.

"Hey," he said, catching her before they both tumbled. "Slow down."

"You." She jutted out her chin over her filled hands. "I don't want to hear anything about what you didn't just hear."

"Your logic sounds a bit illogical." Jack put out his arms, inviting her into the circle.

She backed away. "I mean it. I don't want you or anyone else involved in my headaches. I'll figure them out."

Jack's hurt-puppy expression only increased Lulu's anger. Her problems weren't supposed to be grist for their relationship. Having her sons see her as weak was terrible enough, but Jack too?

She shoved the books at him. "I'm leaving. Tell the boys that since they're so anxious to be of service, they can finish rearranging their aunt's apartment without me."

The doorbell rang as Lulu contemplated takeout menus she already knew by heart. She opened the door, not surprised to see her two sons.

"I'm still mad," she said. "Enter at your own risk."

"But we come bearing gifts." Seth held up an overstuffed grocery bag.

Nicholas, his computer carrier slung over his shoulder, wore an expression that imitated Matt at his bossiest. "Give us a break, Mom. We know you're angry. You know we snooped. And all three of us know Dad didn't expect to die, or he'd never have left you in this damn financial jam. Now, you relax while we get the evening ready for all of us."

Seth placed the bag on an entry table and drew out a copy of *People*. "Go. Read. Stay in the living room until we call you."

A half-hour later, by the time her sons summoned Lulu, an article on Jennifer Hudson's dream home and the tantalizing smells from the kitchen had calmed her, but only somewhat.

"Being strong doesn't mean being alone." Nicholas set a bowl filled with tomato soup sprinkled with cheese and croutons in front of her.

"But being alone should mean I get to have a night to myself," Lulu muttered.

"We're not trying to ambush you." Seth placed a platter of perfect grilled cheese sandwiches on the table. Buttery, golden brown, oozing with bubbling cheddar and tomato slices—the food almost induced her forgiveness.

And relief.

"What do you call your behavior?" Lulu couldn't let them off the hook too quickly.

"We call it taking responsibility," Nicholas said.

"Consider how respectful we are. Notice we didn't bring our spouses." Seth leaned toward the soup and tasted it. "Gus outdid himself."

"I'm supposed to be grateful that you realized outnumbering me by four to one would be too much?" Lulu asked.

She was grateful. Bridget's deadly seriousness would have put her straight over the top. Compassion, political awareness, and social responsibility were admirable qualities—but Lulu felt far too fragile to handle her daughter-in-law tonight.

"Though the soup is good," she added.

"Very good," Nicholas said.

"Try the sandwiches. I made them." Seth bit off half of a triangle.

"It's been a long time since I ate grilled cheese cooked in butter. After Dad's heart attack, I've stuck to olive oil. As both of you should," Lulu chided them before closing her eyes in reverence as she bit into the crispy perfection. She followed the bite with a sip of wine and could almost hear Leonard Cohen singing *Hallelujah*.

"First. Seth and I are each taking over our college loans—"

"No," Lulu interrupted before her son could even finish.

"Yes. Enough is enough, Mom. Dad would want us to help, and you know it. It won't solve everything, but we couldn't live with ourselves if we didn't at least do this."

"But it's not your job," Lulu insisted, fighting back the tears.

"Helping isn't a job. It's what family does. What sons do," Nicholas said.

"Don't worry, Mom, we're not making you whole. You still owe a helluva lot." Seth held out a second sandwich.

Lulu laughed through the thickness gathering in her chest. Rising, she went first to Nicholas and then Seth and gave them each a tight hug.

Nicholas cleared his throat. "Come on. Let's examine all the numbers so we can figure out the rest of the mess." He put his spoon down and laced his fingers together, using the same gesture Matt had employed during serious discussions.

"Not tonight. I can't dredge up the energy. Not after spending almost all of last night in the hospital and then reorganizing your aunt's apartment."

"Let us take a crack; we should be able to get pretty far on our own," Seth said.

"And I need any information you can find on Pamela and Nigel." Nicholas walked to the counter and got a pad.

"Anything. Have Gabrielle pump Thea. I've only seen those two twice, but I heard what Thea said about Nigel changing since he's gotten married; I have a few ideas."

"Are you fancying yourself part of the Justice League now?" she asked.

Seth went to the stove for a second helping of soup. "Most certainly. Consider us your superhero sons. Somehow, someway, we're liberating you from those fools."

Usually, being alone in the house with Seth and Nicholas exaggerated the hollow space inside her that Matt had left behind. But right now, for the first time since losing him, she felt him in his sons in a way that simply gave her comfort.

# Chapter Twenty-Five

## Gabrielle

True, Gabrielle had fractured her ankle, but at least the accident had happened in late February and not in January when snow buried the city.

At least she lived in a building with an elevator.

At least she could still afford to take a taxi or an Uber.

And at least Gabrielle's new hobby—practicing positivity—would combat her penchant for reliving every stupid thing she'd ever done, including her alcohol-induced fracture.

She'd begun forcing a new habit of counting down good things—an idea Seth had presented the day the family helped trip-proof her apartment.

After hearing her repeatedly complain about her injury, her nephew had sat down beside her and explained his theory of *at least-ism*.

"It's a great anti-poor-me device, Aunt Gabi," he'd said.

"I do it every morning on the way to work. Whenever you feel sorry for yourself, flip the script. Instead of focusing on something that's wrong or is bothering you, think of something for which you're grateful. When I hate being on the subway at rush hour, I focus on the fact that at least I like my job. Consider it an antidote to negativity and pessimism."

How did she end up with such a damn cheerful nephew? Unless they were eating or drinking, most of the Quattros hovered between stern and dour. Even the do-no-wrong Matt used to sigh a bit too much. And then there was Gabrielle's mother's side. Certainly, nobody accused Dette of being lighthearted. Perhaps Seth inherited his buoyancy from Lulu's father.

Gabrielle surprised herself when she began following Seth's advice—but what the hell. Two years plus of solid moping must have paid her debt to the gods of bitterness.

As she waited for her Uber, she flashed to the last time she'd gone to the Ty Bar. She had no interest in rewinding that tape, but the memory had a mind of its own. Seeing herself in that alcohol-fueled pick-up was, to use the proper word, sobering. Practicing her new self-help exercise, she hit pause and searched for an *at least* to combat the sleeping-around recollections.

Okay. At least during Gabrielle's ankle checkup, she'd stopped at her primary doctor's office and asked for a full panel of tests for every STD in existence.

And at least she'd tested negative for every one of them. Her doctor gave her a clean slate; from here on in, she needed to use it wisely.

That required some changes.

Thea and Imogene were right. Since losing Cole, Gabrielle had flirted with the worst type of men. Taking up bull-taming in her spare time would have been smarter than indulging in those potentially dangerous one-night stands. If she was so hungry for approbation, she should volunteer to rock crack babies or cuddle abandoned puppies.

Five minutes later, when the Uber still hadn't arrived, she raised her arm. Within moments, a speeding taxi screeched to a halt.

At least cabs still stopped for her.

She got into the car in the clumsy way the orthopedic nurse had instructed: bum first, then swing legs in.

Unlearning this shit would be a joy. She planned a near-future *at least*—when, at least, she wouldn't have to slide into cabs like a ninety-year-old with glass bones.

The cab stopped on West Broadway, smack in front of an inviting pale green façade. Gabrielle carefully got out of the car and inhaled the sugar-scented air of Café Ladurée.

Lumbering past cases of pastel-colored macarons in the patisserie section, she headed into the maroon and gilt tearoom.

Thea sat in the corner with a ubiquitous cup of tea and a golden croissant. After shrugging off her jacket, Gabrielle leaned over and kissed her friend's soft cheek, inhaling the comforting violet notes of her equally ubiquitous powder.

Thea reached for her hand and squeezed. "Hello, dear." She smiled.

A grumpy young waiter arrived. Gabrielle reminded herself that at least she wasn't the one carrying trays and then ordered a cappuccino and a chocolate éclair.

"How are you recovering?" Thea asked once the waiter had departed.

"At least I'm getting better every day," Gabrielle said.

"I'm so glad. I hated that you were indisposed. You're such a comfort to me."

"As you are to me. To us." Gabrielle meant it. Thea's axioms, eccentric beliefs, and cozy customs provided the

Coco Street group with a ballast.

Each of them brought something important to the party: Lulu's ability to take everyone's emotional temperature; Imogene's determination to keep them all marching forward; Ruby's unwavering optimism; Seth's artistic talent; Nicholas's down-to-earth wisdom; Gus's wide-ranging curiosity; Bridget's work ethic; Jack's steady hand on the legal issues; and Liam's expertise with every task that required a tool.

And her own skill: adding beauty to everything, everywhere.

At least, she had that.

"I worry that I'm draining you all with all my problems." Thea sipped her tea in a manner that evoked inestimable sadness. "Nigel isn't the man I raised. His greed knows no bounds."

Prickles rose on Gabrielle's neck. "Have he and Pamela done something new?"

Before Thea could answer, the waiter arrived with her order. The pastry looked luscious on the white china plate ringed with a pink and gold design. Gabrielle thanked him and repeated her question to Thea.

"Oh, Gabrielle, it's just so hard." Thea plucked at the large pearls around her neck. "A mother—even if she doesn't approve of what her child is doing—never stops loving him."

Gabrielle thought about Bette, who'd abandoned her daughters at various times, but at least that had made them independent. What if that had even been Bette's goal? What if she'd been trying to imbue them with a sense of independence that she, Bette, didn't have? What if Bette just hadn't realized her methods were cruel?

"I don't want you to worry; we'll figure this out." Gabrielle forced herself to sound optimistic, even as her stomach clenched.

"I'm afraid we don't have much time. Nigel's ramping up his threats. Severely. Now he's threatening to have me tested for competence. I'm sure Pamela is pushing him, but the fact is that he's going along with her. I can't bear the humiliation of having my son dragging me into court to prove I'm daft."

"Tell me how I can help."

"Turn back the clock and make sure he doesn't meet Pamela?" Thea gave a weak laugh. "This is all about money. Do you think if I just pretend that you paid me the past rent, there'd be nothing he could claim?"

"Pretending won't work." Gabrielle considered the idea as she sipped her coffee. "I imagine the court will ask for proof. Certainly, Nigel would demand it."

"I will swear to it. I am, believe it or not, excellent with fabrications."

"Lying will only make things worse. And possibly saddle Lulu and me with legal problems, as well. I'm sure Jack would frown." She tried to make it sound like a joke, but nothing about the situation was funny.

"What if you give me a check, for now, and I cash it, and then once this is all behind us, I give it back?" Thea asked.

"I think that's called fraud." Gabrielle took a bite of the éclair, trying to focus briefly on the small pleasure instead of how Pamela and Nigel were wearing them down.

"How about a sworn statement that I was donating the rent money?" Thea asked.

"Donating it to the store?" Gabrielle moved her achy leg into a more comfortable position. "That would be completely weird and—"

"Not if I'm a partner."

"Even if you are a partner, I think the court would

consider it unfair or some sort of pressure. We're unlikely to be profitable for a long time, and you need to support yourself. We can't have you living on the pittance you get from Social Security. That would just play into Nigel's claim you're not thinking straight."

"There has to be something," Thea said. "I can't choose between losing you and Coco Street versus losing Nigel. Help me, Gabrielle."

At ten minutes to noon, Gabrielle took a seat in a red leather booth at the Brooklyn Diner on West 57th Street and waited for Jack. She opened the menu and read. Only two hours had passed since eating her éclair and half of Thea's croissant.

Who cared?

She imagined Bette raising her eyebrows at the idea of both the diner and Gabrielle falling off the food cliff. But she'd given up men, alcohol, sex, and walking—her only pleasure left was food. Maybe she should go on a daily food tour of Manhattan and then move on to Brooklyn. Her first stop would be to visit that George's Restaurant that Lulu loved so much.

At noon, Jack walked in, on time to the minute, concern darkening his boyish features.

"Okay, what's this about?" He sat opposite Gabrielle. "Why did we need to meet here instead of my office?"

"I couldn't chance Lulu popping in." Gabrielle crushed her napkin into a ball of nerves. When the waiter appeared, she ordered coffee. And then a bagel with lox.

"Just coffee for me," Jack said.

The waiter left.

"Why are you—we—avoiding Lulu?" Jack appeared so concerned, she almost laughed. Since he'd been helping them out, they'd fallen back into their once-natural way with each other, and she felt like she had her friend again. It was absurd Lulu had thought she was interested in him romantically. Sure, he had better-than-decent looks, dry humor, intellect, and strong values. During an emergency, you'd want Jack by your side. But he lacked the edge that didn't matter to Lulu.

Gabrielle always picked the ones with an edge.

The million-dollar question was *why*.

She thought about Cole's sarcasm, how he drew lines in the sand and pushed people until they came around to his way of thinking. If she wanted to pigeonhole him, she'd put him in the king-of-the-world category. Men to whom she was attracted always fit that type, whether their fiefdom was on a stage or a boardroom.

Did these men genuinely appeal to her or squelch her desire to rule her own realm? At some point, not reaching beyond her grasp had become the safer choice.

"Gabrielle? Why are we avoiding Lulu?" Jack asked again.

"We're not avoiding her."

"Fine. Make it hard for me," Jack laughed. "Why are we meeting in a place where we won't run into her?"

Jack's patience astounded Gabrielle. Unlike most men, he didn't fight for the dominant position at any cost. But neither did he just roll over. He played fair. Was that thanks to his two mothers?

"I don't want Lulu to hear what I have to say and try to change my mind." The waiter's arrival with their order provided a moment of rest from the topic. She bit into the warm bagel, taking primal comfort in the crispy and creamy balanced with the salty tang of nova.

"Change your mind about what?" Jack asked.

"I want to pull the plug on Coco Street." Gabrielle took a deep breath.

Jack had been about to sip his water. His hand froze mid-motion. "Stop Coco Street now?"

"Yes. This situation is splitting Thea in two. She's trying so hard to please me and not lose Nigel. But he's her only son, and we've put her in an impossible situation."

"He might be her son, but he's a giant dick. Without Coco Street, she'll wither away in whatever home Nigel and Pamela stick her in." Jack clasped his hands on the tabletop.

Gabrielle pushed her plate away. Jack's straightforward words ruined her appetite. "Not all those places are so bad."

"You and I both know that Pamela will choose the cheapest, blandest place. Thea is an exceptional woman; nobody gears senior living at that level toward exceptional people." Jack huffed out an angry exhalation. "For God's sake, Thea doesn't need assisted living. I'll be damned if I'll help Nigel and Pamela bully her."

Gabrielle put out her hand and touched his wrist. "Isn't there some way we can help her fight them without her losing Nigel? What if we find a first-class tenant for the building and put up all sorts of legal binders so she can stay in her apartment?"

Jack shook his head. "You know that's not what would happen. Now that they have their heads wrapped around guardianship, they won't give up. They're already salivating. Besides, would Thea be happy sitting alone in her apartment without a store to fuss over and people to make tea for?"

"I know. I know." Gabrielle lowered her head into her hands. "But it's not just about Thea. It's a lot about Lulu, too."

"Lulu? How so?"

Gabrielle needed to phrase this judiciously and not break her sister's confidence. "Lulu never wanted Coco Street. I pushed her into it. And now I think it's taking too much of a toll on her. On everyone, really. Seth, Gus, Bridget, Nicholas, Lulu, they're all doing two or three jobs. We just have to shut it down."

"Oh, God. You and your sister are going to kill me." He put his head in his hands, an utterly over-dramatic gesture for her old friend. "Are you making this extra hard on me as punishment for my brief stint as Cole's lawyer?"

Gabrielle laughed. "No. But now, I kind of wish I'd thought of a plan like that. Why would you ask me such a question?"

"Your sister came to see me this morning. She said she'd resolved all her reservations and that no matter what it took, the two of you needed to move full steam ahead with Coco Street. Said she understands how much the store means. To you. To everyone. It's become something way beyond just a business. It's connected the two of you. It's brought your whole family together. She's in love with all the women involved—including Thea. She said if she had to, she'd sell her house—"

"No!" Gabrielle interrupted.

"Don't worry. I won't let that happen. But I have a clear mandate from Lulu. Her exact words were: 'Put on your lawyer hat, Jack, and don't take it off until we've saved Thea and opened Coco Street. We're going to take a stand for every woman bullied by some damn fool.'"

"She said all that?" Gabrielle, astonished, said in a small voice.

"Yes, she ordered me to move—"

"I got it. Full speed ahead."

"So, you see my problem?" Jack asked. "Now you're saying, 'full stop ahead.' Who do I listen to?"

"Are you asking me?"

"No, not for permission. But for your blessing," Jack said.

Gabrielle felt a wave of warmth toward Jack. And her sister. "You've got yourself a woman with demands, don't you?"

"She's finding her fight." He smiled and toasted her with his cup of coffee. "Now, you need to find yours."

# Chapter Twenty-Six

## Gabrielle

Jack leaned into the cab he'd hailed for Gabrielle. "Everything is going to be fine. Thea. Coco Street. You. Lulu. I don't know how I know, but I believe. How about you rent my optimism for today?"

She squeezed his hand in thanks, but as the cab took off, a tsunami of *why*s overwhelmed her at least affirmations.

*Why hadn't she gone to business school?*

*Why had she and Lulu moved ahead with a whim and a prayer?*

*Why hadn't they given a single damn thought to hiring someone to help them with a professional business plan?*

Which led right back to why hadn't she gone to business school?

Gabrielle studied the picture taped on the driver's dashboard—him holding gurgling twin babies in overly ruffled outfits. All three looked thrilled to be in each other's presence.

At least, she and Lulu still had Bette's things. Liquidating them would bring in enough money to make Thea whole and pay off some of Lulu's debt. Gabrielle could swallow her pride and beg for a designing job off-Broadway.

At least, she still had her condo.

At least, Lulu would still have the bakery and a roof over her head.

Sadness overwhelmed Gabrielle. How could she just give up and give in? She leaned forward and tapped on the glass separating her from the driver. "Change of destination. Can you take me to Bergdorf's?" Breathing time. That's what she needed.

"That's pretty much where I picked you up." The driver glanced in the rearview mirror, raised his bushy eyebrows, and scowled. So much for the happy papa.

"57th and Fifth, please." Gabrielle wasn't asking for permission.

"Your dime, lady." He shrugged as he took a left to head to Madison and go back uptown.

"Yes, it is." And at least there was that. Gabrielle still lived on and within her own dime.


Gabrielle hobbled up the sidewalk and through Bergdorf's 57th Street entrance. Clomping around a store probably wasn't what the doctor had in mind when she ordered exercise—but why not? On her last checkup, Gabrielle had noticed a Hermès scarf under the doctor's white coat. Perhaps the fashion plate physician would wholeheartedly approve of this excursion, after all.

Once inside, Gabrielle stood for a moment and breathed in the subtle perfume of luxury. She was back in the fine jewelry department. One of her happy places—or at least it had been when she was married. A long time had passed since she'd visited this glittering mirrored room, with its extraordinary display of pieces from exceptional designers.

Bette had been the one to teach Gabrielle the art of leisurely shopping, admiring, considering, and then, occasionally, buying. Sipping champagne while a salesperson wrapped your purchase became second nature—an experience to be savored, one she'd been missing for far too long.

Tanya, her favorite saleslady, wore a broad smile as she hurried towards Gabrielle. "How lovely to see you."

Gabrielle returned the smile. "And you."

"You've come at the perfect time. We've just received quite a few new selections—but your leg! Can I get a chair for you and bring some things over?"

The woman knew better than to ask why she hadn't seen Gabrielle lately. The Bergdorf staff was well aware that clients didn't visit to focus on life's disappointments but to indulge and enjoy. Or, sometimes, to exact revenge by exploding a husband or lover or father's credit card.

"No, but thanks. I'm supposed to exercise; I'll just wander around."

Gabrielle started her exploration with Featherstone Designs—Deirdre was the queen of colored stones. A flashing peacock blue and green opal pendant immediately caught Gabrielle's eye. Perfectly cut tsavorites, amethysts, and Paraiba tourmalines surrounded the heart-shaped center stone.

Gabrielle sighed. Perhaps this was how Bette experienced a new Chanel bag—this mix of deep acquisitiveness combined with an almost liquid wash of appreciation.

Tanya approached, velvet tray in hand. "Let me show you that piece up close." She reached into the case and pulled out the necklace, the stones casting rainbow reflections everywhere.

"Let see it on." Tanya unclasped the platinum chain, placed it around Gabrielle's neck, closed it, and then stood back.

Gabrielle examined her reflection. Forget being lit from within—the stunning piece arrived with its own fierce blaze. A craven desire to own the necklace clawed. It was time to ask the question—eyeing the tag was considered crass.

"How much?"

Tanya must have checked as she put it on; she didn't hesitate. "Sixteen thousand," she said softly and then added in a more animated voice, "At the risk of sounding pedestrian, it's as if Deirdre made this piece for you."

Flares of oranges and purples flashed among the greens and blues.

Gabrielle wanted it.

She could buy it.

American Express would never limit her desires. She could pay it off over the next twenty years.

Or she could purchase it, wear it for a week or two, and then bring it back.

Or she could hide the necklace away and then declare it lost or stolen. Collect the insurance money. Wait a year or two, then bring it out again.

But why stop at insurance fraud? She'd stroll around the store, letting Tanya show her a plentitude of earrings, bracelets, and brooches—so many that at the end, Gabrielle could walk out wearing the opal, ready to smack her head and demonstrate forgetfulness if Tanya noticed.

Was that what Bette had done? Let desire override all good sense? If Bette's money ran out, would her mother have gone into debt to appease her unfillable crater of need?

Gabrielle stared at herself in the mirror. Buying expensive and insanely gorgeous jewelry on the spur of the moment was no longer part of her life. That existence had ended with her marriage. And even for something this beautiful, Gabrielle wouldn't be tied to a cheating husband again.

With a sigh of regret, she shook her head at Tanya.

"As much as I love it…"

Tanya unclasped the chain.

Gabrielle's neck felt suddenly naked.

At least?

At least, she knew enough not to succumb to a whim, no matter how beautiful it was.

"Did Jack call?" Gabrielle asked as she entered Coco Street.

Lulu sat at a table unpacking boxes, a large cup of coffee at her elbow. "He did."

"And?"

Lulu folded a discarded piece of wrapping into a neat square. "Seems we almost pulled off a sisterly version of *The Gift of the Magi*." She added the paper to a pile of similar ones. They'd reuse them when it was time to bring over the next batch of items from Bette's apartment.

Gabrielle pulled up a chair, reached into one of the cartons, and pulled out the next box. She noted the code: a pink sticky indicated they'd not yet inspected the contents for a note. Weeks before, they'd decided to attend to the tedious task of packing as quickly as possible and not search inside.

Neither of them was yet ready to face finding the last of the quotes.

A yellow sticky meant that the bag or piece of clothing within contained an already indexed note.

No sticky meant they'd examined the item but found nothing.

They'd begun labeling everything in anticipation of hiring a moving company to pack and transport it all in one long day. But as the estate's cash reserves dwindled, Seth, Nicholas, Bridget, Gus, and Liam had volunteered to do the job.

Since only Liam and Bridget owned cars—a battered pickup and a small Prius, respectively—the move from Bette's apartment to Coco Street crept along, one carload at a time.

Gabrielle picked at the sticky, lifting its edge and then pressing it down again. "Lu, we can't keep pretending this is all going to work out. Even if we do open on time, we won't be able to make a profit fast enough to meet your bank deadlines. Doing this is insane."

Lulu stared her dead in the eye. "I have a solution. Don't react until you think about it."

Gabrielle's hand went to her throat as though she expected to find the opal she'd thought about stealing. "What?"

"Promise."

"Okay, I promise."

Lulu took a deep breath and blurted, "I'm going to sell my house."

At the diner, Jack had mentioned that Lulu was considering this, but being forewarned didn't mitigate Gabrielle's reaction. "Are you crazy?"

Lulu held up both hands to quiet her sister. "You promised. So, just listen. I can sell it fast. Maybe not for top dollar, or even high-medium dollar, but more than enough to allow me to pay off all my debts and rent a decent place."

"No, no, no. Your house is your security."

"Not anymore. My family is my security. And perhaps the bakery. But not the house. The place has become my albatross."

"You're lying," Gabrielle said.

"Okay. Maybe I'm exaggerating a little. I don't want to lose it, but I don't want to keep trudging through my days, either. I want to keep this new joy and passion, this fun in my life. I want to keep working with you. And Thea. We needed real change, Gabi. So, if it's our only solution, I'll happily give up the house."

"This all could wind up being a huge mistake." Gabrielle folded a piece of discarded paper until it almost disappeared. "I'm terrified. Aren't you?"

"Yes. But the risk runs either way. Let's make a list," Lulu said. "Pros and cons. We'll give it fifteen minutes and see where we come out."

Gabrielle picked up her phone and set the timer. "Should we each write a list or make one together?"

Lulu stared at her for a long beat. "Together, please."

Gabrielle put the folded wrapping paper aside and then picked up a fresh sheet, laying it flat. "We can use this."

"Not a Smythson?"

Gabrielle smiled ruefully.

Lulu grabbed a Sharpie from their worktable. She drew a line down the middle of the paper, writing *Reasons to Keep Going* on the right. On the left, she wrote *Reasons to Abandon.* "You start. Don't think. Just say."

"Possible bankruptcy," Gabrielle blurted out. "That's on the *Abandon* side."

Lulu made an I'm-not-a-complete-dope *face* and wrote *bankruptcy.*

Gabrielle grabbed the pen and paper. "Okay. You. No thinking."

"If we sell everything flat out, I can pay my debts."

Gabrielle added the words *pay debts* on the *Abandon* side and then handed everything back to Lulu. "Help Thea. That's next."

Lulu held the pen poised. "Which side does that go on?"

"Both, I guess."

"That doesn't make any sense," Lulu said. "Not if we're trying to make a decision."

"But it's true. Helping Thea belongs on both sides, depending on your point of view. The store would help her remain an active, happy person. Abandoning it would allow her to maintain a relationship with her son."

"A good relationship?" Lulu frowned.

"No, maybe not a good one, but a relationship, nonetheless," Gabrielle said. "Thea only has one child, and she doesn't want to lose him."

Lulu wrote *Thea* on both sides and handed the list and the marker back to her sister. "Joy. Put that on the *Keep Going* side."

They went back and forth until the timer dinged.

Gabrielle happened to be holding the paper. She took a quick count. "Ten to ten."

"For real?" Lulu asked.

Gabrielle nodded. "Here, look."

She laid the chart between them.

### Reasons to Abandon
*1. Avoid bankruptcy/ Pay debts*
*2. Help Thea*
*3. Cash in on the vintage market now before it tanks*
*4. Avoid putting family through slow torture*

5. *We have no fucking idea what we're doing*
6. *Place looks great--get out now & help Thea rent it*
7. *Lulu remaining at the bakery better for Matt's family*
8. *Don't throw good money after bad*
9. *We have no money*
10. *Stop the magical stupid thinking*

### Reasons to Keep Going
1. *Help Thea*
2. *Fostering creativity and joy*
3. *Resale is environmentally super-responsible*
4. *Working together*
5. *Future potential: online sales, new products, etc.*
6. *Family loves it*
7. *Making our own family business*
8. *Honoring Bette*
9. *Having a \*good\* reason to wake up*
10. *Building community*

"The abandon side is so negative and sad," Gabrielle said.

"So many of the reasons to keep going are pie-in-the-sky." Lulu crossed her arms and leaned her face on the cradle she'd made.

"We have to decide." Gabrielle pointed at the still-taped boxes ready to be opened. "The point of no return is upon us."

"We don't even know if we can win against Nigel. We can't bank on Jack's hope." Lulu threw her head back and exhaled. "Either way could be wrong or right. Ugh. Let's put it off for a few minutes and unpack some more."

"If we should even be unpacking."

"All the women are bringing their treasures here in two hours. Imogene will kill us if we aren't ready. We can't disappoint them. Even if we only put on a good show for one more night, we have to do it."

Gabrielle studied the box in front of her. "Pink sticky. Maybe there will be a message in this bag."

"Are you thinking what I think you are?" Lulu asked.

Gabrielle nodded. "Let Bette's ghost provide a tie-breaker?"

Lulu raised her arms and looked up. "Okay, Mom—go for it."

Gabrielle lifted the lid, slowly withdrew a purse, and then laughed. "Oh, no. This one. The very meaning of *jolie laide*."

"Fancy words—what do they mean?"

"A woman whose face is attractive despite having ugly features. Just look at it."

Gabrielle held the clutch aloft so they could view it with some perspective. The limited-edition so-called *dollar bill bag* was worth mega-money. The quilted cream leather was embroidered to look like a crass five-dollar bill with an unflattering portrait of Coco in the center and clumsy symbols on either side of her profile.

Judging by the bag's weirdness and its pristine condition, Gabrielle knew Bette had never used it. Had she bought it as some sort of statement?

"Who searched for a quote last?" Gabrielle asked.

"I don't know, but you go," Lulu said.

Holding her breath, Gabrielle twisted the silver clasp, lifted the flap, and reached inside. As her fingers found the envelope, she realized how heartbroken she'd have been if nothing had been there.

"Hurry. Open it." Lulu held up crossed fingers.

After taking a sip of her sister's now-cold coffee, Gabrielle withdrew the card and read the words aloud so they could hear them together.

*"There is no time for cut-and-dried monotony. There is time for work. And time for love. That leaves no other time!—Coco Chanel."*

Gabrielle stared at Bette's writing.

"That's our answer, right?" Lulu asked.

"Yup. Bette's telling us the last thing we want is to live an existence of *cut-and-dried monotony.* If work is more than half of everything, we better make it mean everything we possibly can."

The sound of a key in the door interrupted their philosophical discourse.

"Second load." Seth walked in with a stack of cartons, followed by Liam pushing a hand truck.

"Where do you want it, ladies?" Liam gave the sisters a wide-open country-music smile.

Gabrielle wondered if his grin had always been that enchanting.

At six o'clock, with positive attitudes firmly in place, Gabrielle and Lulu opened the shop to the Style Endures Society. Every one of the women toted shopping bags bearing the names of New York's most exclusive stores.

All of their mother's friends had dressed in Chanel colors for the occasion—gold, cream, black and red—to honor Bette. Yvette's tweed suit hugged her as tightly as Imogene's silky black tunic drifted. A sparkling gold caftan hid but hinted at Ruby's curves in the very best way. Francesca wore a black dress and a white scarf, with the bottom of her stilettos flashing red.

Thea carried in a tray of light snacks. Ever aware of the immaculate stock, the menu didn't include anything messy, just toasted nuts, mini-quiches, and speared fresh mozzarella bites sprinkled with a basil chiffonade. They offered only white wine or seltzer.

Once everyone had an appetizer-filled plate and a full glass, Ruby called them to order. "Okay, ladies, one, two, three—it's showtime. Let's unpack." Excitement laced her words.

Francesca brought out a pair of Hermès navy and gold leather cuffs. Ruby showed off a Vuitton long scarf with a leopard background strategically interwoven with LVs. Yvette's donation was a rock-studded Valentino crossbody bag.

The SES women were the sisters' fairy godmothers, offering up item after item. Finally, Imogene added a pair of Christian Dior back-to-front pearl earrings to the rest of the costume jewelry on the countertop.

"I think that's the last item," Imogene said. "A job well done, ladies."

Yvette raised her glass. "To Gabrielle and Lulu and the success of this exquisite shop."

"Far beyond what Ruby and Imogene described." Francesca gazed at the room. "The shelving alone is a work of art. The spotlights make everything glow."

Ruby beamed. "And look at that cozy corner!"

All eyes turned to the alcove where four gold chairs upholstered in red velvet surrounded a white marble bistro table. A black couch with red pillows faced a low glass coffee table.

"The complimentary tea and scone method worked so well as an incentive to shop at Quills & Feathers. People rarely came in more than twice without buying a little something," Thea said.

Gabrielle worked hard not to react to Thea's exaggerated claim.

"Then you'll need to make sure there are bunches of little somethings near the register." Yvette twisted her wiry body, twirling to take in the entire store. "Impulse items. With a price point of around, hmm, maybe $79? That sounds so much less than one hundred, right?"

The others agreed.

"Ideas for items?" Francesca asked.

All their suggestions were either too expensive or not deemed exceptional enough.

"I have it," Francesca said. "Years ago, Bette mentioned that one of you was tinkering with a perfume formula. Right? She thought it was brilliant. She described it as very creamy, romantic, and classic. Not flowery. Different."

Imogene clapped her hands. "That was Lulu! Wouldn't a signature perfume be a lovely grace note?"

"Let's file that under future-future plans. Far future." Lulu blushed. "Bette told you about it?"

"She was so excited about your idea." Imogene reached for a fluted cup of toasted nuts. "Your mother wasn't the best at sharing her feelings with you girls, was she? Or giving compliments?"

The sisters exchanged a glance.

"I'm probably just as bad with my daughters. They say I can't emote," Francesca said.

"Trust me, Bette thought the world of everything you girls did." Ruby flung her arms out as though taking in the entire universe. "And this? She'd be over the moon."

"I find it hard to imagine Bette bragging about either of us." Gabrielle turned to her sister for agreement, horrified to see tears running down Lulu's cheeks and great heaving sobs wracking her chest.

Imogene threw her arms around her. "Oh, sweetheart. Don't cry. She loved you so much. Your mother would be so proud of you."

Lulu shook her head. "You don't understand. It might not happen. We don't have the back rent to keep Nigel from suing. Or the money to pay our salaries until the shop takes off. Not unless Gabrielle risks her retirement account. That's all she has. Or I sell my house. Otherwise, I'm broke. Coco Street is just a stupid dream."

# Chapter Twenty-Seven

## Lulu

Lulu turned her head. Jack lay beside her on Matt's side of their bed.

She pushed off the heavy comforter inch by inch, not wanting to wake him. The patchwork quilt shouted *traitor*. Matt's mother and aunts had sewn it—slaved over it, as Annette told them repeatedly—to make sure it was ready by their wedding day.

Lulu placed her feet on the floor and eased herself up.

She should have put the quilt away before they went to bed—though that too seemed disloyal, both in the forethought and the hiding. Would Jack notice if it was missing when he visited again?

March had arrived. Quilt-switching was a seasonal move. And why would Jack care what the hell covered her bed?

Living with Matt's ghost wearied Lulu. Finally.

She padded out of her bedroom, went down to the kitchen, and appraised the Keurig. The designed-for-one machine that once seemed like an insult greatly appealed to her this morning. Bridget couldn't be more brilliant. If Lulu had made Jack's coffee using Matt's precious machinery, her husband would have risen from his grave.

Memories of the previous night sharpened as the caffeine hit Lulu's system. Not only had she confessed her financial dilemmas to the women, but she'd also compounded her mistake by sharing her woes with Jack.

He'd held her, calmed her. And then, for the first time, they'd made love. Sleeping with Jack had felt good. Not world-rocking, but not as if she'd cheated on Matt, either.

Well, maybe only a little bit.

Afterward, as they lay in the dark, Jack had offered to lend her the money to pay off her debts. All of them. She'd been stunned—first by his generosity and then because of how much his offer scared her.

Before she could respond, he'd shushed her.

"Promise me you'll sleep on it before you answer."

"You know me that well already?"

"I do. Promise?"

She did. And then she slept—fitfully—with Jack by her side.

Despite the temptation, she couldn't allow Jack to rescue her. If he ended the affair after the spell of sex wore off, he'd be her reluctant banker. If Lulu were the one to break up, she'd owe money to a man who harbored a grudge.

Could Jack handle either of those scenarios? Could she?

Doubtful. Everyone knew money and new love were a terrible combination. Jack's generous offer must have come from passion, not logic because it didn't make a lick of sense. Nobody would be a sadder investment than her. Proven financial disaster; risky romantic proposition; grieving widow still in the throes of loss—who'd bet on her?

An idiot. Was Jack an idiot?

As she finished her single-woman coffee, Lulu tried to come up with ways to turn him down without insulting him. She made a second cup and carried it to the bedroom. Awake and scented with toothpaste, Jack was sitting up in her bed, wearing nothing but an appreciative smile.

"Good morning, is that for me?"

She nodded, handed him the coffee, and then perched on the side of the bed.

"You're a sweet and good man, Jack," she said.

"I can hear a *but.*"

"Yes, but—"

"I was kidding! There's actually a but? Please don't tell me we're having an 'it's not you, it's me' conversation already?" He took a long sip. "Especially after learning you make great coffee."

"Keurig. Very easy to replicate, just buy a machine."

Why would he compliment such an ordinary brew? She found herself sniffing for fault. "No. I'm not breaking up, but I'm not borrowing money, either. It's too soon. Far too soon."

His surprised expression at what seemed so obvious startled her. "But it would make things so much easier for you."

"Jack, I got married at nineteen; before that, my father provided safety and shelter. Every time a bump came, there's been a man to iron them out."

Jack pulled up the quilt. "Nothing wrong with that."

Lulu itched to switch the coverlet for some old Macy's comforter in the closet. Even Nick's old Spiderman blanket would be better. "No, I guess not, but you're the first man I've dated in almost thirty years. I can't complicate that with money. So, while I'd love to accept your generous offer, common sense says: *'No way.'*"

"Common sense isn't always the right choice."

"Maybe not, but don't try and talk me out of my decision. It's backed up with real reasons." She held up her hand and counted as she enumerated. "First, I don't want to be in a one-down position to you. Second, a loan could stand in the way of how I react to you. I don't want monthly payments to get between us—if there is to be an us."

She didn't list the third item—that finally, she felt ready to explore independence without grief. Even if it meant losing her house, she longed for freedom—even the freedom to make a mistake.

"I could make the payment system flexible."

She shook her head. "When Matt and I married, I was pregnant. We loved each other thoroughly, but I couldn't risk fighting things out when things got bad. I needed him. Before I was twenty-two, we had two kids. Standing up to Matt came with too many fear factors. Our entire financial life depended on him, his family, and the family business."

Lulu stopped, aware she was turning her wedding band in circles. She stared at the faithful gold. Had the time come?

"We were lucky. I was lucky. Matt and I never stopped clicking. Reasons to fight didn't come often. But there were things I wanted to try that I never did. Now, before it's too late, I want those chances." She took Jack's hand. "And to figure out what I want from love without the strings of pregnancy. Or money. So, thank you, Jack, for your offer, but I'm turning it down."

"Are you sure you're not turning us down?"

Lulu weighed his words and then her answer. "I would be so very happy to continue enjoying your company. If that's what you want."

In answer, he leaned in and kissed her, first tenderly and then far less so, showing her just how much he did want it.

Lulu and Gabrielle organized the glittering baubles in the front cabinet, trying to keep the display from looking crowded.

"This came from Ruby." Lulu held up a bracelet dripping with diamonds. "Where do you think she wore such a gaudy piece?"

"You don't even know what that is, do you? Not to mention how much that so-called gaudy piece is s worth." Gabrielle took the bracelet, clasped it around her wrist, and then moved her hand, allowing the diamonds to catch the light. "It's part of Stephen Webster's Deco New York collection. Where do you wear it? A Metropolitan Museum fundraiser. A wedding at St. Regis. Hell, if I owned that, I'd wear it to bed just to see it when I woke up." She cleared her throat and began reciting as though reading. "Made of white gold and diamonds, with a detachable tassel, it retails for over one hundred and thirty thousand dollars. I already looked it up."

Lulu touched the ice-white arm candy. "Ruby must have loved Bette."

"And now loves us," Gabrielle added.

"If you have a huge heart and are rich as Mrs. Gottrocks, maybe at a certain point, friendship trumps jewels," Lulu said. "Our insurance policy is in shape, right? Our security system is state of the art, yes?"

Locking up Coco Street at night petrified her. When she turned on the Quattros' alarm, she was protecting flour and butter, not an inventory worth a fortune.

"Yes, your boyfriend arranged both those things."

Gabrielle exhaled. "Thank goodness you're at least letting him do that."

"How often are you going to tell me that I'm stupid for turning down Jack's offer?"

"Until I get over it. Which could be forever." Gabrielle picked up a second bracelet, putting it on her other wrist.

"What's that?" Lulu asked.

"An antique Victorian garnet bangle. Friendship and love notwithstanding, Ruby must have a hell of a collection if she's parting with these beauties. According to Imogene, she's unbelievably loaded—toolbelt notwithstanding. Ruby and her husband invested in real estate all over Manhattan."

"Too bad she never had children," Lulu said.

"Children aren't the measure of a person," Gabrielle said. "Becoming a parent is easy, accidental even; being a good person takes thought and care."

Lulu reached for her sister's hand. "I didn't mean anything by that; I was only thinking about how often Ruby talks about missing motherhood."

Gabrielle made a sour face. "Sometimes, I get tired of being on the defensive, you know?"

Lulu thought of how judgmental she'd been about her sister's life choices, from Gabrielle's childlessness to her three-inch heels. "I'm sorry I've been an idiot about so many things."

"Like refusing Jack's financial aid?" Gabrielle picked up a pair of aquamarine teardrop earrings, held them up to her face, and admired herself in the mirror.

"Even if I let Jack lend me the money—which I won't—we'd still have Nigel and Pamela to deal with. We can't solve that problem with cash."

Gabrielle pointed to the carton of bubble-wrapped packages. Each contained one of Bette's framed notes.

"There's a lot of advice there," Gabrielle said. "Maybe

we should be heeding more of it."

Now it was Lulu's turn to make a sour face. "At the moment, I want dinner more than ghost-mother guidance." Just as she finished speaking, Seth and Nicholas walked in, carrying a pizza box. "What incredible timing my sons have."

"Maybe Bette sent them our way. Thanks, Mom! Pizza is perfect!" Gabrielle looked up at the ceiling and applauded. Ruby's bracelets sparkled. "Question, nephews. Did you get toppings that complement garnets and mega-multiple carats of diamonds?"

"Only truffles could do diamonds justice." Seth set down two boxes. "Sadly, my plebeian brother chose pepperoni."

"Which you ruined by adding broccoli. What kind of monster adds cruciferous vegetables to pepperoni?" Nicholas handed Lulu a stack of paper plates.

"One who plans to live past fifty?" Seth said pointedly.

"You've become unbearable since you've gone on your health kick."

As Seth lowered a brown shopping bag to the table, bottles clinked from within. "I have to do something to fight the waistline expansion brought on by Gus's Quattros' experiments."

"Oh, yeah. A sprinkle of green on top of your pizza is sure to take off those pounds." Nicholas swatted at his brother's midsection.

Lulu held up her hands. "You both sound about fifteen." She reached into the bag and drew out a cold bottle of champagne. "Veuve Cliquot?"

"I earned it." Nicholas took out four plastic cups. "These aren't Thea-approved, but who wants to wash fine crystal?"

Seth took the bottle from his mother and began unwrapping the wire covering the cork top. "Nobody. Mom,

Aunt Gabrielle, grab a glass and prepare to toast."

"To what?" Gabrielle asked.

"I can't promise, but I think we've taken care of a massive problem," Nicholas answered.

"You already did that by taking over your college loans," Lulu said. "And I'll never forget it."

"Okay, but we're not done." Seth popped the cork using the thumb-by-thumb method. *Always careful, my boy,* Lulu thought. "Tonight, we toast beheading the snakes."

"The two of you always did have a penchant for drama. Your father read you too much bedtime Shakespeare. What's going on?" Gabrielle asked.

"Remember I said that I'd look into the Nigel-and-Pamela problem?" Nicholas held out his glass for Seth to fill.

Lulu and Gabrielle nodded.

"Too much about them seemed straight out of some bad B-movie; I had to investigate."

Seth lifted a glass in his brother's direction. "To slaying Nigel and Pamela."

"What? How?" Lulu asked her eldest son. "Legally?"

"Drink first, Mom. Then I'll explain."

"Mmm. That's good," Gabrielle said after a sip. "Now, explain."

"So, you know how Thea said that Nigel wasn't like this before he married Pamela and how distraught she's been over the changes in him?" Nicholas picked up a slice of pizza and took a big bite.

"Yes." Gabrielle hunted in the bag until she came up with napkins. Lulu passed out plates. Her sons might be grown enough to slay dragons for her, but they'd still eat straight from the counter if she let them.

"Her words stuck with me," Nicholas said. "A new wife. Disturbing changes. Plus, Thea is fine—there's not a single reason to try to send her to a home. My rage got out of control."

Seth picked pepperoni off his slice. "He turned into one of the Hardy Boys."

"*We*, not I. Bridget and me. She was just as angry and curious—and you know what happens once she has an idea in her head."

Lulu and Gabrielle exchanged eye rolls.

"Saw that," Nicholas said.

"Sorry, go on, darling."

"My wife proved to be a researching savant. She dug into court records, Ancestry.com, property transfers—you name it—with every free minute she could spare. Facebook. Twitter. Even classmates.com. Some fascinating details emerged about Pamela. Did I mention property transfers?

"Turns out she was married three times before hooking up with Nigel. Every one of those ex-husbands had elderly mothers. Who all owned valuable real estate, to be specific. And in a not-so-strange coincidence, during the time Pamela was married to their sons, all three mothers-in-law were declared incompetent. Continuing the not-so-strange coincidences, Pamela made a pretty penny in each divorce from each of the said husbands."

"Oh, no," Gabrielle gasped. "That's horrible. We have to stop her."

"We're pretty sure we have stopped her," Nicholas said.

"You blackmailed Pamela?" Lulu asked in astonishment.

"Mother!" Nicholas crossed his hands over his chest and raised his eyebrows. "That would be illegal. Bridget and I simply requested that Pamela take a meeting with us earlier this afternoon. Being a cold-blooded snake, she assumed we were also cold-blooded snakes. She thought we wanted to cut a deal. I will admit we let her believe that. Imagine Pamela's surprise when Bridget, in full righteous mode, accused her."

"My God, what happened?" Lulu asked.

"What did she say?" Gabrielle asked at the same time.

"She denied everything at first. Of course. Then we explained how Jack would include our findings to the judge presiding over Thea's competency hearing. And then we asked her if Nigel knew about her past."

"You'd already told Jack what you found?" Gabrielle asked.

"We kind of twisted that particular truth. We didn't want to put Jack in a difficult legal position. We figured it was better if he didn't know until he had to—we're going to wait and see what happens. We gave Pamela twenty-four hours for her and Nigel to contact Thea, give her their blessing to continue with Coco Street, and withdraw their request for guardianship. And if we don't get it, we will tell Jack what we found out."

"I am so proud of you," Lulu said, her voice thick with emotion. "And bless Bridget. That girl will never do me dirty."

Gabrielle tipped her glass towards Nicholas. "Amazing work. I couldn't be prouder."

After clinking her glass, Lulu took a sip of champagne. Gratitude suffused her, but she still had mortgages, credit cards, a job that bored her, and a house falling around her—a place she'd miss despite what she said. Did craving security mean she had to accept mediocrity?

Lulu needed to talk to someone. Not a sibling, someone or someone to whom she had given birth. And certainly not someone who wanted to be her Sir Galahad.

"So, what do you think?" Lulu curled her legs in the flowered chintz armchair in Imogene's living room. Family photos and grandchildren's framed artwork hung in places of honor. A haphazard stack of books was next to the couch; a wilted bouquet dropped rose petals on the coffee table.

"The time has come to stop dithering. I should be one hundred percent sure, right?" Lulu said as she finished her list of worries. "I don't have two dollars set aside for retirement. But if I lose this chance, there might not be another one. Ever. Except if this doesn't work, then what? I have nothing. Nothing! If I'm going to put the brakes on, now's the time. I feel like I'm just compounding mistakes."

"You did what you thought was right." Imogene took a deep breath and looked around. "None of us are without regrets."

"I feel as though I'm trying to staunch an amputation with a Band-Aid. The kids think making Nigel go away will solve everything."

"Are you sure you shouldn't accept Jack's offer to help out financially?"

She shook her head. "I just can't. I have no idea if we'll go from glitter love to real love. Being tied to a man by his money sounds like hell."

"I think you're giving Jack short shrift." Imogene stood and opened the cabbage rose-patterned curtains. "Funny, I close them during the day to keep the sun off the carpet. And then I open them at night for the lovely street view. Look, there's Mrs. Franklin, giving her dog the last walk of the day. The lives of lonely widows, eh?" She turned to face Lulu. "I can lend you the money to cover your debts."

Lulu made prayer hands. "Thank you. But no. I can't take it from you any easier than Jack. I can't be in debt to either of you. I just can't. I think I'll have to talk to Gabrielle about closing before we open. Or just sell the house."

"Is that truly what you want?"

"No. Of course, not." Lulu felt the tears coming. "Everyone is so happy. We've built this magic family. I don't want to break it up. I want to keep it going. And I'm not ready to put my house on the market. I'm so torn."

"Sweetheart! Listen. You took the first steps by coming clean and telling the truth. Your amazing son and daughter-in-law are saving Thea from a fate almost worse than death. Can you hold on, despite the anxiety, for a few more days? Give me a chance to think about all of this, okay?"

# Chapter Twenty-Eight

## Gabrielle

Four days later, Gabrielle and Lulu waited for Thea in the lobby of Ruby's Fifth Avenue apartment. Imogene had invited them to a meeting of the Style Endures Society but refused to explain why.

Restless, Gabrielle paced from the elevator to the front door and back again until Lulu grabbed her arm, saying, "Stop."

Gabrielle shook her off. "I'm nervous."

"Chew gum." Lulu lifted her chin at the doorman. "I think he's considering calling an ambulance from Bellevue."

Just as Gabrielle started to tell her sister exactly where she could go, Thea arrived. She looked better than she had in weeks and started talking before she even reached their side.

"You won't believe what happened! Nigel dropped the suit. He even apologized."

Lulu and Gabrielle exchanged a look and then grinned.

"We're so happy for you." Gabrielle hugged her friend, so grateful that she'd bear no responsibility for rupturing Thea's relationship with her son.

"Happy for all of us, you mean," Thea said. "One oversized problem gone! Two problems, actually. Guess what else happened? Pamela walked out on him. Imagine? She walked out without saying a word. I know it's all connected, but Nigel didn't want to explain, and I was too happy to press him. At least, for now."

Gabrielle and Lulu exchanged a second look just as the elevator arrived.

They all stepped inside.

"Do you know why we're here?" Thea asked as the doors slid shut.

Gabrielle pressed the button for the fifteenth floor. "Not a clue, but Imogene called this a command performance. And she sounded happy—so I have a good feeling."

"Making plans based on feelings, hunches, and quotes can be risky." But Lulu winked and squeezed Gabrielle's hand. "I spoke to Imogene, you know. About my doubts."

"What did she say?"

Before her sister could answer, the elevator opened straight into Ruby's apartment. All the Styles Endures women were there, already sipping wine and nibbling canapés.

After taking off her coat and sharing hugs and air kisses all around, Gabrielle wandered over to the large windows, taking in the expansive view of Central Park. The western sky glowed purple as twilight settled over the city. April breezes blew through the open terrace door, coming close to turning Gabrielle's silk skirt into a parachute.

Ruby cleared her throat. "May I have everyone's attention?"

"You already have it," Francesca said. "We're dying for you to begin."

Gabrielle, Lulu, and Thea settled on the couch; Bette's friends sat across from them on a facing couch. The women nearly bubbled with palpable excitement.

Yvette held up a pad as if it were a trophy. "I shall take notes. This is so exciting, isn't it?"

"Yes, you have us on pins and needles," Thea said. "Or is it waiting on pins and needles?"

Before they could break into a discussion of word usage, Imogene clapped her hands. "Either works. Now, all eyes and ears on Ruby, and all will be clear."

The room fell silent except for the sound of Yvette uncapping her pen, and Francesca's taffeta dress rustling against the couch.

"Gabrielle. Lulu. Thea." Ruby smiled. "We've called ourselves the Style Endures Society informally for years, but now, it's official. So, welcome to the first board meeting of the officially registered SES."

Ruby looked over at Lulu, Gabrielle, and Thea as if waiting for a response.

"Thank you," Gabrielle said uncertainly. "Are you inviting us to join your club?"

"Not exactly. We're asking your permission to affix our newly born non-profit museum to your beautiful Coco Street shop. A museum devoted to style and its meaning within society. Of course, according to the in-kind services of our lawyer, Jack Hunter-Holmes, there's still some red tape—"

Imogene interrupted. "I hope his helping this way is acceptable to you, Lulu."

"I'm clueless." Lulu looked confused. "Helping how and with what?"

"According to Jack, we can qualify as a museum as long as we fit into these parameters. Yvette, do you have Jack's description?" Ruby asked.

Yvette cleared her throat *"A non-profit, permanent institution in society's service and its development, open to the public, which acquires, conserves, researches."*

Because of Gabrielle's work with museums, she was familiar with words and phrases, but she didn't know how it related to them and their shop.

"We'll use the historically important and rare pieces that we planned to give you—some of Bette's, too, if you agree—and feature them in a revolving exhibit to showcase how style endures."

"Well, that sounds perfectly lovely," Thea said. "But—"

"But you want to know how our museum can help, right?" Imogene asked.

Relieved at not having to beg for the explanation, Gabrielle nodded.

"We can all make tax-deductible donations to the museum, which in turn can pay your salaries and expenses until the store is self-sufficient. We'll fund exhibits, lectures, and classes; the museum will become the non-profit arm of Coco Street. We'll be your board of directors and your benefactors. You"—she looked at Gabrielle—"won't need to dip into your retirement fund. And you"—she looked at Lulu—"won't have to sell your house. And you, Thea, don't have to argue with your son ever again."

"This is incredible. Too generous," Gabrielle managed to say, her voice shaking.

"But we're not—is this charity?" Lulu seemed more skeptical than her sister that this was a kosher solution.

Ruby laughed. "Well, they say charity begins at home. And you've become family to us. And we want to keep you as family, forever."

Francesca pursed her lips as she figured out her answer to Lulu's question. "The truth is, all four of us are extraordinarily comfortable. Between us, I couldn't begin to count the hours and dollars we've devoted to charities all over the city. But none of those efforts mean what this one does."

"But you want to know why we are doing this? Because we want Coco Street to work," Ruby said. She nodded at Francesca to continue.

"For centuries, men created the rules. Wielded the power. But no matter how oppressed and repressed women have been, we've used clothes and accessories to express ourselves. We wore white dresses during the suffrage movement, and donned amethyst and peridot rings and brooches to proclaim our independence. We thought nothing of turning a dress inside out and re-sewing it late into the night so our daughters weren't embarrassed to wear hand-me-downs. We refused to give up what made us feel feminine and drew seams on the back of our legs during World War Two when we had to sacrifice silk stockings for the war effort. Fashion isn't frivolous—well, it can be—but it also is our armor."

"We, the women of the Style Endures Society, want to celebrate fashion and its history and its value. At Coco Street," Imogene said.

"That's wonderful," Lulu said. "But I'm a bit perplexed—"

"Not that we don't appreciate what you are doing," Gabrielle interrupted.

"Of course, we do," Lulu agreed. "As Thea said, the museum is a lovely idea. So thoughtful."

Imogene nodded in agreement. "And we could keep doing that kind of charity for years."

Yvette ran her hands along the sofa's damask covering. "But with this museum, we will be creating something that matters to us personally and helping three women we've grown to dearly love. Is it charity? Yes, but every one of us will be getting back even more than we are giving."

Finally, opening day dawned. At three p.m., Lulu and Gabrielle would be hosting an invitation-only reception. But before they could welcome their guests, endless details needed their attention.

"Does the store look too pretentious?" Lulu asked as she straightened a frame.

"No. It looks elegant, Lu. Just like the things we're selling. I know about stage sets, and this one works from the color of the walls to the beveled glass on the mirrors. Trust me. We accomplished exactly what we set out to do."

Two weeks before, they'd fought about that beveled glass so vehemently that anyone listening would have thought one of their lives were at stake. "We need Friedman Brothers mirrors," Gabrielle had insisted. "We need the best. Mirrors are everything in a clothing store. Everything!"

"You think everything is everything. Friedman mirrors! Currey & Company lamps! *Acqua de Parma* handwash! What next? Branded toilet paper?"

"If it were up to you, we'd have soap from Costco and mirrors from Walmart." Gabrielle pointed to Lulu's shoes. "You still think clogs are a fashion statement."

"You try baking on your feet all day wearing Lichtensteins or whatever you call those things you teeter around on."

"Louboutins."

Gabrielle knew her sister was fully aware of the designer's correct name and baiting her, but that was fine.

After years of bickering and resenting each other, teasing was a joy.

"Well, I hope you're enjoying those shoes," Lulu had said. "Because if the store doesn't take off, you might not be able to afford another pair until you're eighty. Do they make them in an orthopedic style?"

"Lu, have you ever heard of cost-per-wear? Buying things that last forever is always the wiser choice."

"We could have at least looked for the mirrors at the flea market. That would have made financial sense *and* been far more environmentally correct."

Gabrielle just shook her head in disbelief. "Still?"

Lulu had grinned and then hugged her sister tight. "Just kidding."

Now, Gabrielle's hands shook as she arranged a tray of rings for the third time. She reminded herself that this was the easy part; only friends and family were coming to the celebration. The real test would be when they opened the doors to the public later that day.

She walked over to where Lulu realigned a display of Thea's antique pens. That's when Gabrielle noticed it. She peered closer to make sure what she was seeing. Or actually, what she *wasn't* seeing.

"When did you take it off?" Gabrielle asked, illustrating her question by tapping the fourth finger on her right hand.

"Good eyes. Last night. I decided I should start this venture on my own."

"How does it feel?"

"Honestly? Scary. Weird. Empty." Lulu blinked back tears.

"Don't think of it as vacant space, but one that's ready for something new." Gabrielle squeezed Lulu's hand. "There's a whole world waiting for us."

Finally, there was nothing left to dust, straighten, fix, or fuss over. Guests would start arriving any moment. Gabrielle saw herself and Lulu reflected in one of their beveled mirrors— Bette would have loved their outfits. Both sisters wore little black dresses borrowed from their mother's collection, accented with Bette accessories: jeweled black resin cuffs for Lulu and the gold chain CC belt for Gabrielle.

What they weren't wearing were Bette's shoes. They'd picked out a few pairs to try on the previous day, but Bridget, who they'd also outfitted, shrieked when she saw them.

"Don't you know that's a *shanda!*" she'd shouted.

Hearing Bridget use the Yiddish word for disgrace surprised them both. So did her admonition.

"Shoes are a *shanda?*" Gabrielle asked.

"You never wear the shoes of a deceased person lest you follow in their footsteps. It's a Jewish custom. I can't believe neither of you—"

"How is it that you know at least ten thousand more things about being Jewish than I do?" Lulu asked. "Are you planning to convert?"

Bridget appeared hurt. "I just want to be part of the family in every way."

Gabrielle hunted through a drawer of some Chanel pieces they hadn't yet put in the store. Finding a leather and gold chain bracelet, she slipped it on Bridget's wrist. "You've always been a part of the family, but this makes it official. Shalom."

At three on the dot, Lulu's sons and their spouses were the very first to arrive and step inside the brand-new shop.

Gabrielle noticed the bracelet shining on Bridget's arm. The door had barely shut when it opened again—within fifteen minutes, Coco Street was crowded to overflowing.

"There are more people here than were at Bette's funeral," Lulu whispered to Gabrielle.

"I might have gone a little overboard with the invites," Gabrielle said. She'd shamelessly dipped into her contacts from her years on the museum board and theater circuit.

"I thought you vetoed that idea when I suggested it." Lulu smoothed the jersey dress that hugged her hips.

"That was when you were proposing a sidewalk sale. Not a chic Greenwich emporium," she said as she glanced around.

In one corner, Thea served tea and coffee from the antique cart Gus had carried down from her apartment. In another corner, Lulu's sister-in-law, Drea, and Imogene sat at the marble tea table, their heads close together as they pored over Bette's photo albums.

"Everyone seems to be enjoying themselves," Gabrielle said.

"They do, and—oh, look." Lulu nodded toward Ruby, steering Annette on a tour of the store.

Gabrielle squeezed Lulu's arm. "See. Matt's parents want you to be happy, honey. We all do. You've mourned long enough."

For a moment, Lulu remained quiet. Gabrielle knew her sister was fighting back tears and wasn't surprised when Lulu went for a joke instead. She pointed at her mother-in-law, now examining a piece of jewelry. "A hundred bucks that Annette's schooling Ruby in the superiority of Italian gold."

"What will you do when she wants us to sell some of her cruise ship baubles?"

Lulu scrunched up her face. "I'll tell her how crushed her granddaughters would be not to have the sacred pieces passed on to them. If that doesn't work, I'll whisper in her ear that eBay gets better prices."

From across the room, Francesca raised a wine glass to the sisters. Lulu threw her a kiss in return.

"She looks like the millions of bucks she has in the bank, doesn't she?" Lulu asked. "Not only younger than seventy-two, but...I don't know. Fresher? Maybe even fresher than last week, right? You think it's Botox?"

"Complemented by whispers of Restylane. Plus, a fairy god-surgeon who waved her magic wand over Francesca's eyes."

The woman's coldly perfect splendor was undeniable, unlike Ruby's beauty, which was warm and welcoming, precisely because of the crinkles around her eyes.

"Do you think Bette had work done?" Lulu whispered.

"I'm not sure, but if she did, I'm sure she used Francesca's doctor."

"Would you have work done?" Lulu asked.

"The idea terrifies me. But. I don't know. Maybe. Would you?"

Lulu touched the lines on her forehead. "I do hate these. But I'd need to find a doc I could pay in Chanel dresses."

"That probably wouldn't be that difficult. File under future conversations," Gabrielle said.

"Gabi. I need to say something."

"Please! No more awful confessions."

"No! This is a good confession. I need to tell you. I was always jealous of you—"

Gabrielle grimaced. "Do we have to process this now?"

"Let me finish. For so long, I thought Bette gave you everything. Lucky Gabrielle. Poor Lulu. Now, I know we both got short-changed in some ways and rewarded in others—I don't want to gauge Bette's love with a measuring cup anymore. So, when we close up the apartment for good, I want you to have those paintings you love. The ones in the living room."

"The posters? We haven't appraised them, Lu. They could be worth serious money."

Lulu threw her arms around Gabrielle. "You know what's valuable? What's worth serious money? You. Us. Your father loved them, and you loved your father."

"I'm—"

Lulu pressed her finger to Gabrielle's lips. "Shh. Why should I care that Bette worshipped him? You lost him when you were five. I had a father my whole life—he might not have been a god to Bette, but he loved me. I want you to have those posters. Now, go start our welcome speech."

Gabrielle embraced her sister. "Love you."

She walked to the center of the room, clapped for everyone's attention, and when they'd quieted, she lifted her wine. "Let's all raise a glass to Bette. An enigma wrapped in Chanel—a woman who built and rebuilt herself with guts and determination. Bette did everything with style—from how she dressed, to how she decorated, to the gifts she gave. Fashion changes, but style endures. Coco Chanel said those words; Bette lived them. This store and museum are born of Bette's appreciation of Coco—a love that my sister and I didn't understand at first."

She gestured towards the Style Endures bronze and glass vitrines. Liam had installed lights that made the cases gleam, illuminating the rare clothes and accessories. Beneath each item was a handwritten card describing the piece and where it fit into fashion's timeline.

"Chanel was born in poverty to unwed parents and raised in an orphanage. Bette's immigrant parents earned their living as tailors. My grandparents escaped anti-Semitism; Chanel famously slept with the enemy during

World War II and lived exiled in Switzerland at the war's end. It almost feels as though this dichotomy represents the many personalities contained within both Coco and our mother.

"Coco Chanel reemerged at seventy—imagine that—to change fashion for a second time. She designed the little black dress, redefined costume jewelry, and established an utterly new handbag style. The Jewish Wertheimer family, who she'd treated so poorly, first outwitted her attempt to wrest back control of her eponymous perfume line, and then financed her renaissance. Who won? I suppose both. To her dying day, Coco Chanel remained a fighter who never stopped celebrating and creating beauty. Just like Bette."

Gabrielle turned and nodded to Lulu, who took up the speech.

"Our mother left us many gifts, but none greater than her dear friends." She stopped to look at each of them. "Imogene, Ruby, Yvette, and Francesca. Like our beloved partner, Thea, you've taken us into your homes and hearts, and, along with Bette, you are why we're here. You helped us understand what our mother knew all along. And what she wanted us to learn. Whether it be diamonds or brass, recipes or comic timing, inheritances are to be treasured. And for that, we'll be eternally grateful," Lulu finished.

She and Gabrielle raised their glasses. "To all of you. And to our mother. To Bette," they said in unison.

"To Bette," the guests echoed back. And a tissue or two fluttered.

A crowd gathered around the sisters after their toast. After it thinned, Bette's lawyer, Diana Hayes, approached them, a rare smile on the Gray Lady's face.

"Thank you for inviting me. What you've built far exceeds what you described. Bette would have loved Coco Street," the lawyer said.

"You think so?" Gabrielle asked.

"I know so. Could we sit down somewhere private?" Diana asked. "I'd like a moment to speak to you both."

Gabrielle led her to the back room, where Liam had created a modest office. Lulu sat behind the desk, Diana took the guest chair, and Gabrielle perched on the desktop.

"I'll jump right in," Diana said. "Your mother and I first met about ten years ago; both of us were volunteering for Emily's List."

*Emily's List?* Gabrielle couldn't have sworn to Bette voting regularly, much less working with a women's political organization.

"Eventually, she asked me to become her lawyer. She needed my help with her shop."

"Her shop?" Gabrielle asked.

"Bette planned on opening a shop. Not a vintage one like this, but a boutique like Inès De La Fressange's in Paris. Are you familiar with her?"

Gabrielle nodded yes; Lulu shook her head no.

Diana smiled at Lulu. "I'd never heard of her either, but Bette educated me in all things fashion-related." The lawyer swept her hands over her plain navy suit. "Though I didn't prove to be her best student."

"De La Fressange resembled Chanel to a scary degree," Gabrielle explained to her sister. "In the eighties, she became Karl Lagerfeld's muse. About fifteen years later, she broke away from him and created a shop—clothes, accessories, and lifestyle items—devoted to her own aesthetic and style. It's a fantastic place."

Gabrielle remembered the trip to Paris when she visited the store with Cole. Maybe it was okay to hold on to the good memories. Wasn't that part of what Coco Street stood for? Recognizing the value of the past and cherishing it even as you move on?

Diana nodded. "Bette wanted to open a similar shop in Manhattan. She wanted it to be about fashion versus fad. To be the epitome of style. If Chanel could reinvent herself at seventy, as you so aptly said in your toast, Bette decided to best her and do it at seventy-seven."

"Just how many secrets did our mother have?" Gabrielle asked.

Diana chuckled. "More than you know. I'm sorry if I came across as a hardass when we all first met. Bette made me promise I wouldn't interfere but let you figure out for yourselves what to do with her inheritance. She wanted you to witness how life can become more interesting as you get older and wiser—if you just honor the magic."

Hearing the word *magic* spill from this stern lawyer's lips thrilled Gabrielle. Clearly, nothing in the world was impossible.

"How far did Bette get with her plans?" Lulu asked. "Is that why she had so many unused things?"

"Yes. She was buying for the shop. That's why you found a variety of sizes and all those limited editions. She was working on a detailed blueprint but didn't want to share it with you both until she was ready to implement it."

"Bette the sphinx," Gabrielle said.

"Your mother's illness surprised her. Shocked her, truthfully. She still felt young." Diana laced her fingers. "She had to abandon her plans, but I'm certain she'd be ecstatic to see Coco Street. I think you've created even more than she could have hoped for."

"I'm not sure how we got here, but I know who led us. Thank you, Gabi," Lulu said.

Gabrielle blinked, then looked down and fussed with her Chanel belt. "We better get back outside to our guests."

"Just one more thing." Diana reached into her bag and drew out two small, black jewelry boxes. Chanel's logo was emblazoned on top. "Bette had me keep these separate from her collection and instructed me to give them to you at the right time."

She turned one over, checked something written on the bottom, handed that one to Lulu and the other to Gabrielle.

Lulu opened hers and looked down at a ring, white gold with stars, studded with tiny diamonds. She let out a slight gasp when she saw a familiar card.

"*To my North Star, Loire,*" she read out loud, "*with love, your mother.*"

Lulu looked at the empty spot on her left hand, hesitated, and then slipped it onto her right ring finger.

"What did she give you, Gabi?"

Gabrielle lifted the lid, revealing a ring in the shape of a bow, also studded with tiny diamonds.

"Read the card," Lulu prompted.

Tears streamed down Gabrielle's cheeks. She shook her head and handed the note to her sister.

"*It has been a gift to love you and be your mother.*"

"Bette said these would be her last birthday presents to you both." Diana leaned over and gave them each a brief but welcome hug. "Now go and enjoy your party. It's what Bette would want."

At four p.m., Lulu and Gabrielle opened Coco Street to the public. Ruby and Gabrielle had sent out press releases to newspapers, fashion VIPs, bloggers, and Instagram influencers—but no one had written about the opening. No matter how many times Lulu and Gabrielle googled, they found nothing.

The trickle of customers wandering in appeared to be curious locals just passing by. Only a few inexpensive items sold, and Gabrielle knew those were pity purchases made by her old acquaintances and Bette's friends.

Fifteen minutes before closing time, a woman in dramatic, bright red glasses touched Gabrielle's shoulder.

"I'm Emma Bernier, fashion writer. Freelance. Could I ask you and your sister a few questions about the goals of the shop and the museum?"

The word *freelance* suggested an Instagram feed with a few hundred followers. But on the other hand, nobody else was clamoring for her attention.

"Sure." Gabrielle dug deep to sound upbeat. "We're ridiculously excited by the potential in recycling high-end designer treasures and showcasing important fashion *objets d'art*. I'll introduce you to Lulu and then our board of directors, who can explain more about the goals of our small museum of extraordinary fashion. We believe that in vintage, fashion has met sustenance."

By six p.m., everyone had left, along with every shred of Gabrielle's and Lulu's optimism. Not a single stranger had made a purchase.

# Chapter Twenty-Nine

## Gabrielle

"I'm turning off the router," Lulu whispered. "You okay with that?"

Gabrielle looked up from her phone. She'd been trying to decide which of the photos she'd taken that morning was Instagram-worthy. The shot of the red Chanel boy bag on a black velvet cushion? Or the one where it hung from a silver hook against the white wall?

"Why would you do that? And why are we whispering?" she whispered back.

"So that guy doesn't hear." Lulu tipped her head toward a fifty-something man wearing khakis and a wrinkled blue plaid shirt, sitting in the corner tapping away on his laptop. He looked out of place yet seemed totally at home as he stopped typing long enough to take a sip of tea and then a bite of a lemon wafer—one of three on his plate.

"I'm tired of supporting this Starbucks ex-pat," Lulu

said.

Gabrielle weighed the chances that he might become a paying customer. Just because his salt-and-pepper hair was too long and his shirt was rumpled didn't mean she should jump to conclusions. After all, not everybody dressed to match their stock portfolio, and the truth was, they couldn't afford to lose a single sale. Coco Street had been open for three weeks, but business wasn't exactly booming—or even brisk. Far from it, in fact. Most days, only the neighborhood regulars stopped in to have morning or afternoon tea and trade gossip with Thea, their wallets firmly tucked away in their purses.

"How long has he been here?"

"Over an hour," Lulu said. "This is the third time this week."

"He must think he died and went to Heaven," Gabrielle said. "The guy's probably writing a manifesto to take over the world while we provide free food and online access."

"So should I turn off the Wi-Fi?"

"No. I need to finish posting the bag-of-the-day." Gabrielle waved her phone, currently open to the Instagram application.

"But he's just sitting there and eating up profits we aren't making."

As if on cue, the man bit into yet another cookie. Beside her, Gabrielle felt Lulu tense and knew her sister was ready to explode.

"I'll handle this." Phone still in hand, Gabrielle walked over to the table and stood, arms folded, by the man's chair.

Eventually, he glanced up. "Yes? Can I help you?"

"Can you help me?" Gabrielle laughed. "Do you know where you are?"

"Do I know where I am?"

"Are we having a repetition contest?" She sat in the

chair opposite him. "I'm Gabrielle. One of the owners."

He stuck out a hand and smiled, revealing even, white teeth where she'd expected a yellowed frown. "Kevin Chamberlain. My dad lives down the street."

She rested her elbows on the table. "So, you know this is a shop, right? For women's clothes and accessories. For profit."

His embarrassed surprise seemed genuine. "Oh, God. Of course. You must think I'm some kind of creep. My sister told me how peaceful your shop is around noon. That's when she shows up to give me a break. I take care of our father—he's got dementia but thinks he's still a physician. Makes for a ton of chaos. Usually, I can work anywhere as long as I have my laptop with me—I'm a graphic artist—but I can't get anything done at his place anymore. Coco Street has been a godsend. I can get more work done in a half-hour here than all day at Dad's. I am so sorry. I didn't think you'd mind me coming during your slow time." He reached into his pocket and pulled out his wallet. "I'm more than happy to pay for the tea and cookies. Please! Take this. I've come in so many times." He held out two twenty-dollar bills.

Gabrielle pushed them away, leaned back, and sighed. "It's okay. It is our slow time. Hell, it's always our slow time." She was about to get up and let him be when what he'd said he did for a living sunk in. "You know, maybe having you here is a godsend for us, too." She held her phone up, screen out, and switched between the two photos of the boy bag. "I need help. For Instagram. Black cushion or white background? Which will get more attention?"

Kevin took the phone and scrolled back and forth between the two shots, offering rapid-fire comments, and then finally took a breath. "Yup, you're in my wheelhouse. I'd love to help. Tell me what your goals are. Image building? Brand recognition? Sales?"

Gabrielle filled him in on their inability to get the word out about the shop and shared some of her ideas. When she mentioned handing out flyers, he held up his hands in horror. "Like one of those electronics stores holding a permanent going-out-of-business sale? God, no. What else are you thinking?"

Kevin declared cookies with the shop's logo and address in icing concept tasty but useless. "I'm your real-life guinea pig. I'd be happy to eat them, but that doesn't mean I'll buy anything. Not that I won't ever buy something," he hastened to add. "I will, and I promise my sister's next birthday present will come from Coco Street!"

"We thought about Facebook ads," Lulu called out from behind the counter. "Do those work?"

"You're not an online business, so that's not cost-efficient." Kevin glanced at his watch. "Stick to Instagram for now. But you need to come up with a strategy to make you stand out. And get followers. Look, I've got to get back to my dad. But I'm going to come up with some ideas for you guys and be back tomorrow."

"Your lapsang souchong and cookies will be waiting," Gabrielle smiled.

The next day, even Kevin failed to show up.

"Do you think we scared him off?" Gabrielle asked.

"Gee, I hope not!" Lulu scowled from where she read *The New York Times*. "I'd hate to think we lost one of our best non-paying customers."

"Hey, he was sweet." Gabrielle sprayed Thea's homemade mixture of vinegar, water, and peppermint essence on the already sparkling glass counter and then wiped it off. "More importantly, he's an expert in areas where we're amateurs. I'm just guessing at what I'm doing on Instagram."

She saw Lulu open her mouth and then shut it. A wise move—they were getting on each other's nerves all the time lately. The pressure of running a less-than-successful shop was taking its toll.

At one-thirty, Kevin walked in carrying his laptop bag.

"I thought we scared you away," Gabrielle said.

"Never. My sister was late." He grinned. "Nice to be missed, though."

"Don't take it personally. We just didn't want today's cookies to go to waste," Lulu said.

"I didn't come empty-handed. There's this." He held out a gold box of chocolates and then opened his computer. "Plus, I have some ideas. I checked out your feed. Right now, you're using only static Instagram posts. If you use stories instead, they'll actively illustrate the history and personal anecdotes behind your items."

Gabrielle was too ashamed to admit she didn't even know the difference between stories and posts. Instead, she said, "I'm not sure I know how to use all those bells and whistles."

"I'll show you. My way of repaying you for your hospitality. Ready for your first tutorial?"

A half-hour later, Kevin was still educating Gabrielle when three of their regulars, sweet women living on Social Security, arrived for their daily tea and biscotti.

"Gabrielle, Lulu, Thea! Today's the day!" one of the ladies called out. "You need to get ready. Hurry."

"Sorry, Kevin—" Gabrielle nodded to the women. "Give me a moment." She felt oddly sorry at having to leave him.

"I have to get back to my dad, anyway. I'll mock up some examples and show you tomorrow, okay?"

"Thank you." Gabrielle smiled with sincere gratitude and watched as he left. For the first time, she began to understand the attraction of a Kevin or a Liam rather than money-market bad boys who saw sex as just another trade. Instead of stalking men at the Ty Bar, maybe she could focus on those she could be friends with first and go from there.

"Don't be a stranger," she threw out as Kevin opened the door.

He turned, gave a thumbs-up, and raked his fingers through his hair.

She could, though, insist on a haircut.

"So, ladies, what do we need to get ready for?" Gabrielle asked the neighborhood grandmas as Thea came out of the back room with a fresh pot of tea.

"You're about to get a crowd," said the one draped in a paisley scarf. Gabrielle couldn't think of her name.

"What makes you think so?" Thea asked.

"We just saw five women with fancy bags heading this way!"

*Alice.* The woman's name popped into Gabrielle's consciousness.

"Fingers crossed." Gabrielle placed three mugs on the table. "But I think I remember you predicting that yesterday, too. And the day before."

On Monday, Alice had confused high school kids on a school trip with shoppers ready to invade Coco Street. On Tuesday, it had been a couple of fashionable nannies with their charges.

"This time is different. I'm one thousand percent sure," Alice insisted.

"I'm not getting my hopes up," Lulu said. "They're probably tourists getting off the subway, who just happen to be headed this way."

Abby, one of the other tea-time ladies, thumped her cane on the floor for emphasis. "No. Alice is right. As I walked by, I absolutely heard one saying, *Coco Street*. And she looked moneyed."

"Well, that does sound hopeful," Thea said with fake enthusiasm as she picked up the sugar bowl and shook it. "Empty."

"You stay, Thea. I'll refill it." Lulu got up just as the bell over the door rang.

Everyone turned toward the sound.

"That's them," Alice murmured. "The ones I saw down the street. They certainly took their time." She sniffed as if they were late for a scheduled meeting.

The group of newcomers, all twenty-somethings, walked in and immediately started chattering as they looked around. Alice had been right. Their Birkin and Prada bags, Louboutin and Gucci shoes, and designer outfits suggested they could afford the very best Coco Street had to offer.

"Welcome." Gabrielle beamed. "Let us know if we can help you."

Before Lulu or Thea could add anything, a forty-ish redhead wearing the expression of a woman on a mission entered. Two minutes later, the bell sounded again. And then, almost immediately, yet again.

In less than twenty minutes, dozens of customers packed Coco Street.

"Welcome!" Thea called out. "Look around. Please, help yourself to biscotti and tea."

"Oh, my God! That's what it said in the article," said a young blonde wearing enormous silver hoop earrings, armfuls of silver bracelets, and a funky geometric Missoni dress. "Do you have any of the ginger-rum muffins?"

"How would this sparkle-bunny in Missoni know about

Gus's muffins?" Gabrielle whispered to Lulu.

"I don't have a clue, but if the word about the baked goods is spreading, at least Quattros' will benefit when we have to close Coco Street."

Gabrielle made a face at her sister before responding to the Missoni-clad woman. "Sorry, it's not muffin day. How *did* you hear about them?"

"From the article," Missoni dress said as if Gabrielle had asked the stupidest question in the world.

Lulu came out from behind the counter. "What article?"

Missoni shook her blonde curls. "Seriously? You don't know? It went online this morning. We were having coffee down the street when we saw it. We hurried right here."

"Online? Where?" Lulu asked.

She dug in her purple Celine bag and pulled out her phone. "I'll show you!" After a few clicks, she held it out to Gabrielle and Lulu. "Look!"

They stood side by side and peered at the small screen.

"Oh, my goodness. It's the Styles section," Gabrielle whispered.

"The what?" Thea asked.

"The Styles section," Lulu repeated. "The damned *New York Times* online Styles section."

"Oh, my stars. Read it aloud!" Thea fanned herself either with excitement or from the heat of the customers crowding the store. Gabrielle made a note to set the thermostat lower.

The assorted patrons picked up on the excitement and gathered around.

"*Top Destination for High-End Vintage: Fashion Meets Sustenance.*" That's the headline." Lulu's voice shook.

"She used my words," Gabrielle said. "She said she was just a freelancer, but she didn't mention that it was freelance for *The New York Times*."

"The subhead reads: *Good for the pocketbook, a necessity for the environment, and a treat for the eyes.*" Lulu stopped, holding back tears.

"Here. Let me." Gabrielle grabbed the phone and began reading. "*Prepare for fashion nirvana, ladies. Sisters Gabrielle Bradford Winslow and Loire Gold Quattro, both named in honor of Coco Chanel, have paid tribute to their mother's legacy by opening Coco Street. The wonderfully curated vintage collection includes Chanel bags, jewelry, belts, scarves, rare and distinctive suits, dresses, and coats. Not to exclude other designers, the store also features coveted pieces from Hermès, Louis Vuitton, Dior, YSL, and Prada.*

"*But offering the highest quality, most-gently-loved—and often never worn—vintage luxury goods isn't enough for the sisters. Twice a day, they serve complimentary (yes, you read that right, complimentary) teas with feast-worthy sweets and savories from Lulu's family bakery— Quattros' in Brooklyn.*" Gabrielle smiled at Lulu. "The family will love that."

"Oh, my God! Gus and Annette will be over the moon." Lulu's son-in-law and mother-in-law had become an improbably inseparable duo.

"*The sisters have filled the shop with chic but comfortable chairs, fashion bibles, and—wait for it—a revolving museum, honoring fashions of the past. Coco Street is a store, a gallery, and a gathering space to honor women, their style, and their friendships—offering sustenance for shoppers' souls and tummies, as well.*

"*Don't miss the touching stories offered on the handwritten labels. From a gem-studded Chanel necklace bought to ease heartbreak to a proud mother's gift of a Vuitton trunk, marking her daughter's debut as a travel writer, Coco Street is far more than the sum of its stunning parts.*"

The steady flow of customers kept up throughout the day. And not just looking but buying, buying, and then buying some more. Women handed over their credit cards, receiving overstuffed black and gold Coco Street cloth shopping bags in return. More than one asked if she could buy an extra tote. Lulu whispered to Gabrielle that they should sell them on their own.

"They cost $4. Let's charge $15."

"Twenty-five," Gabrielle insisted. "Higher prices will make them even more desirable."

At six, once they locked the door, Lulu Gabrielle and Thea collapsed at the tea table. Tired and in shock, they didn't even bother to wipe away the crumbs that remained from the afternoon's teas.

"Finally, we're alone!" Gabrielle said. "I've been going crazy waiting to tell you both. About an hour ago, I got a call and—"

Someone pounding on the door interrupted.

"We're closed," Lulu yelled. When the knocking continued, Lulu went to see who was so insistent and found Imogene and the rest of the Style Endures Society waiting.

"We saw the article. We're here to celebrate!" Imogene lifted a bottle of champagne out of her bag and waved it in the air.

Within a few minutes, Thea had covered the worktable with a linen tablecloth. Yvette put out silverware, Imogene loaded plates with snacks, and Francesca poured wine. Lulu lit the electric candles. Gabrielle looked around and found what she was looking for—an oversized orchid; she carefully moved it from the tea cart to a place of honor in the middle of the feast. Reaching out, she stroked one of the petals and then bowed her head for a moment.

"Would you like to offer grace?" Ruby asked softly.

Gabrielle nodded, took Lulu's hand on her left and Imogene's on her right, and began speaking.

"Bette didn't have much of a green thumb, but she

loved white orchids. I gave her this one when she had her heart attack, and it's never stopped blooming since. It was the first thing I brought into Coco Street once we started to move in. The damn thing has been putting out new flowers, month after month. If you know anything about orchids, you know they rarely bloom for long. But this one never stops. This orchid is magic. Bette's magic. And we're so grateful to be graced by her dream."

"Amen." Ruby touched her hand to her heart.

"Now, show them the surprise," Imogene urged Ruby, who leaned down, grabbed her tote, and with a grand gesture, pulled out a stack of newspapers and handed them out.

"This is tomorrow's *New York Times*. I have a friend there. Now, everyone, ready, set, go—turn to page D1."

"Why are we looking at the Style section—oh my God," Lulu blurted out. "It's the article about us!"

"Is this real?" Gabrielle's hands trembled. "We're in print? In the *New York Times* Style section!"

"I'm so proud we made the real-life newspaper," Imogene said. "I'm personally waiting for a paper resurgence, just like everyone says is happening with vinyl."

Ruby handed Lulu six extra copies. "A few to keep pristine. And one to frame."

Lulu saluted. "Yes, ma'am."

"This is as big a deal as I think it is, right?" Thea asked.

"It's *The New York Times*," Gabrielle said. "After a play, we'd go to Sardi's and wait for hours to get the paper's review and find out if we were alive or dead."

"My daughter said the online article went viral," Imogene said. "I looked, and there are thousands of comments. I read a few. Everyone loves our environmental side—*Chic New Yorkers fighting climate change the stylish way*, they're calling us. Your quotes about reversing our disposable economy, Gabrielle—they're being tweeted like crazy. The media is picking up the article and posting it all over the place."

"Which brings us to my news," Gabrielle said.

All the women turned to face her.

"I haven't even had time to tell Lulu or Thea." Gabrielle, theatrical timing still in her blood, paused a beat for drama. "A booker from *The View* called. They want us on the show."

"*The View!*" Francesca touched her hair as though the camera was already trained on her.

"*The View?*" Lulu repeated in disbelief.

"They loved the angle about the store bringing women together," Gabrielle said. "And when I told them about the Style Endures Society and how you guys, Bette's best friends, saw us through all this, they went nuts."

Imogene reached over and squeezed Gabrielle's hand.

"You better start figuring out which of you will join us on the show." Gabrielle turned to Thea. "I told them about how we're continuing the tea service you started at Quills and Feathers for the neighborhood ladies, and they want you to come on, too."

"I'm going to explode from happiness. Oh, I can't wait to call Nigel. He had a date last night, you know. His first since *she* left! And this one seems almost normal." Thea picked up her copy of the *Times* and held it to her chest. "When I think of how close I came to being stuck in a sterile little room in some senior home… What would I have done?" She shook her head as she struggled to control her emotions.

"We're all so proud of you girls." Imogene tipped her wine glass toward Lulu and Gabrielle.

"You're the ones who made it possible," Gabrielle said.

"All we gave you was a bit of juice," Yvette insisted.

"You brought the work and passion," Ruby added.

Gabrielle nodded to her mother's handwritten quotes, framed and hanging on the wall. "And Bette gave us the inspiration."

"I wonder if we'll ever know what her actual intention was with those quotes," Lulu said.

"You still doubt they were magical messages?" Gabrielle asked her sister.

Imogene and Ruby exchanged glances.

Gabrielle noticed. "What?" she asked.

"You still haven't figured it out?" Imogene asked. "The one last mystery."

"Tell us," Lulu said.

Imogene made her fingers into a steeple. "After her first heart attack, Bette came home from the hospital with a plan. She ordered me to some obscure stationery store on the West Side for a rare ink she adored. *Black, dark as the midnight,* she said."

Francesca smiled as she relived a memory. "She sent me to Tiffany's to pick out notecards and envelopes. She said she trusted my taste."

"She put Ruby and me to work doing the research to find the quotes." Yvette's face fell. "God, I miss her."

"I still don't get it." Lulu turned to Gabrielle. "You?"

"Clueless."

"Your mother," Imogene took a sip of wine, "was never an easy person. Showing emotion made her uncomfortable. That's not news to either of you, I know. The quotes, the cards—Bette wanted to leave them for you so she could stay with you a while longer after she was gone and make sure you understood how she felt."

"Bette always could show better than she could tell," Ruby said.

Gabrielle thought back to the times her mother had

seemed to read her mind. In the eighth grade, when a group of girls had excluded her from their clique, Bette treated Gabrielle to a cutting-edge hairstyle from the top New York City hairstylist. When the drama teacher didn't choose her for a good part in the school play, Bette said nothing, but the next day the sweater featured on the cover of *Seventeen* appeared on Gabrielle's bed. And those were the years when money was scarce.

"We found every word Coco Chanel ever uttered. Bette spent days choosing which ones to write out in her exquisite script—making us check and double-check that every word was accurate. She never told us exactly what she was going to do with the quotes but insisted they'd work like magic." Ruby reached for her wine glass. "That's what she said. Magic."

"She made us promise not to tell you anything until you figured it out for yourselves. She insisted," Francesca said.

"Bette"—Yvette smiled with love—"hid her light. But if you took the time, once you found it, the brightness knocked your eyes out."

Imogene nodded. "No one ever thought of her as Mother of the Year, but she devoted her last months to showing you both the depth of her love, in her way. With mystery. With panache. With enduring style. And she succeeded, didn't she? She made her death a journey of discovery for you two."

"She did," Lulu said. "I didn't appreciate her, but when I needed her, she managed to come through for me."

"Mostly, she did." Gabrielle laughed. "Remember the washing machine? A saint she wasn't."

"But this past year, with both of our lives off the rails, she rescued us, didn't she? With her crazy collections of handbags and shoes—with her insane treasure closet. She brought us this." Lulu spread her arms wide.

Gabrielle remembered how she and Lulu had gone to Bette's apartment after their first meeting with the Gray Lady. They'd walked into their mother's closet like lost children. And how, after playing dress-up, after reliving years of grief and heartbreak, after they started laughing and planning together, they'd walked out of Bette's closet with new lives.

Lulu leaned into Gabrielle, and as if she knew just what Gabrielle was thinking, whispered, "Bette might have left us forever fashion orphans, but she made us sisters again, didn't she?"

Gabrielle shook her head. "No. Bette gave us the push. But we did that, Lu."

"No more part-time, half-sisters?" Lulu asked. "No more *brittle things?*"

"Full-time sisters from here on in." Gabrielle put her arm around Lulu's shoulder. Lulu put her arm around Gabrielle's waist. Her resin bracelet struck Gabrielle's chain-link belt with a lovely chime that made them both smile. They studied the quote they'd framed and hung over the front door.

Their mother's bold cursive stood out in deep onyx ink on cream cardstock, holding Bette's gift of Coco's timeless wisdom.

Words that must have been their mother's deepest wish for them.

Words that were finally coming true.

*To achieve great things, we must first dream—Coco Chanel.*

- THE END –

# Waisted

By Randy Susan Meyers

**In this provocative, wildly entertaining, and compelling novel, seven women enrolled in an extreme weight loss documentary discover self-love and sisterhood as they enact a daring revenge against the exploitative filmmakers.**

Alice and Daphne, both successful working mothers, both accomplished and seemingly steady, harbor the same secret: obsession with their weight overshadows concerns about their children, husbands, work—and everything else of importance in their lives. Scales terrify them.

Daphne, plump in a family of model-thin women, learned at her mother's knee that only slimness earns admiration. Alice, break-up skinny when she met her husband, risks losing her marriage if she keeps gaining weight.

The two women meet at Waisted. Located in a remote Vermont mansion, the program promises fast, dramatic weight loss, and Alice, Daphne, and five other women are desperate enough to leave behind their families for this once-in-a-lifetime opportunity. The catch? They must agree to always be on camera; afterward, the world will see *Waisted: The Documentary*.

The women soon discover that the filmmakers have trapped them in a cruel experiment. With each pound lost, they edge deeper into obsession and instability...until they decide to take matters into their own hands.

A compulsively readable and ultimately poignant examination of body image, family, and friendship, *Waisted* features Randy Susan Meyers's signature "engaging and sharp" (*Publishers Weekly*) prose and is perfect for fans of *Big Little Lies* by Liane Moriarty, *Dietland* by Sarai Walker, *The First Wives Club* by Olivia Goldsmith, and *Hunger* by Roxanne Gay.

# The Last Tiara
By M.J. Rose

A provocative and moving story of a young female architect in post-World War II Manhattan who stumbles upon a hidden treasure and begins a journey to discovering her mother's life during the fall of the Romanovs.

Sophia Moon had always been reticent about her life in Russia and when she dies, suspiciously, on a wintry New York evening, Isobelle despairs that her mother's secrets have died with her. But while renovating the apartment they shared, Isobelle discovers something among her mother's effects — a stunning silver tiara, stripped of its jewels.

Isobelle's research into the tiara's provenance draws her closer to her mother's past — including the story of what became of her father back in Russia, a man she has never known. The facts elude her until she meets a young jeweler who wants to help her but is conflicted by his loyalty to the Midas Society, a covert international organization whose mission is to return lost and stolen antiques, jewels, and artwork to their original owners.

Told in alternating points of view, the stories of the two young women unfurl as each struggles to find their way during two separate wars. In 1915, young Sofiya Petrovitch, favorite of the royal household and best friend of Grand Duchess Olga Nikolaevna, tends to wounded soldiers in a makeshift hospital within the grounds of the Winter Palace in St. Petersburg and finds the love of her life. In 1948 New York, Isobelle Moon works to break through the rampant sexism of the age as one of very few women working in a male-dominated profession and discovers far more about love and family than she ever hoped for.

In the two narratives, the secrets of Sofiya's early life are revealed incrementally, even as Isobelle herself works to solve the mystery of the historic Romanov tiara (which is based on an actual Romanov artifact that is, to this day, still missing) and how it is that her mother came to possess it. The two strands play off each other in finely-tuned counterpoint, building to a series of surprising and deeply satisfying revelations.

# About Randy Susan Meyers

Randy Susan Meyers' bestselling novels of domestic drama are informed by her work tending bar, teaching criminals, and her journeys from bad boy obsessions to loving a good man. Her novels were thrice chosen as "Must Read Books" by the Massachusetts Council of the Book, writing "The clear and distinctive voice of Randy Susan Meyers will have you enraptured and wanting more."

Meyers knows many things saved her—family who warmed her heart, the love of a good man, a circle of extraordinary friends, and the Brooklyn Public Library. She teaches writing at Grub Street in Boston, where she strives to live by the words of Gustav Flaubert: "Be regular and orderly in your life, so that you may be violent and original in your work.

To find out more about her work, visit https://www.randysusanmeyers.com

# About M.J. Rose

*New York Times*, *USAToday*, and *Wall St. Journal* bestseller, M.J. Rose grew up in New York City mostly in the labyrinthine galleries of the Metropolitan Museum, the dark tunnels and lush gardens of Central Park and reading her mother's favorite books before she was allowed. She believes mystery and magic are all around us but we are too often too busy to notice... books that exaggerate mystery and magic draw attention to it and remind us to look for it and revel in it.

Rose's work has appeared in many magazines including *Oprah Magazine* and *The Adventurine* and she has been featured in the *New York Times*, *Newsweek*, *WSJ*, *Time*, *USA Today* and on the *Today Show*, and *NPR* radio.

Rose graduated from Syracuse University, has a commercial in the Museum of Modern Art in NYC and since 2005 has run the first marketing company for authors - Authorbuzz.com. Rose is also the co-founder of 1001DarkNights.com and TheBlueBoxPress.com

The television series PAST LIFE, was based on Rose's novels in the Reincarnationist series.